Deleted

BOOK 2

Return to Alastair

A NOVEL

L. A. KELLY

Revell
Grand Rapids, Michigan

Published by Fleming H. Revell
a division of Baker Publishing Group
P.O. Box 6287, Grand Rapids, MI 49516-6287

Printed in the United States of America

Library of Congress Cataloging-in-Publication Data
Kelly, L. A.
    Return to Alastair : a novel / L. A. Kelly.
        p.   cm.
    ISBN 0-8007-3116-6 (pbk.)
        1. Good and evil—Fiction. 2. Middle Ages—Fiction. I. Title.
PS3611.E4496R48 2006
813′.6—dc22   2005024257

With love to

Anne,
Debby,
Ramona,
Stephen,
Miriam,
Ephraim,
And Roddy (wherever you are).

God bless.

I

Onath

Tahn Dorn jerked awake with a groan. A bird flittered by his open window, and he sat up slowly, thinking it strange to find himself in this room. It was home, of course, but in the hazy light it almost seemed he was still the little boy of his dream, searching desperately for someone on a dismal street. He took a deep breath, and it calmed the thunder in his heart. The nightmare had ended as abruptly as always, with a baby's cry in his ears and an old woman suddenly standing in his path, her long fingers pointing at him and her face twisted by an accusing frown.

He brushed the hair back from his face and shook his head. The dream was recurring almost nightly now. And he still wasn't sure what the place was or even who he was always looking for. But the throbbing hurt wouldn't go away.

He rose and dressed, pushing his mind toward the business of the day. Three new men awaited training. He'd promised to give the children his time for a lesson too. And he'd be checking the wall with the dawnlight, as he always did.

He walked outside to the spring-fed stream that flowed in a half moon around the Trilett estate. It was a chilly autumn morning, but that didn't stop him from dunking his head into the cool depths of the water. He came up shaking his long wavy hair behind him and let its cold wetness trickle down his back. It was a strange habit that had followed him from childhood, and he couldn't quite let go of it. The water had once cooled the burning pain of a terrible memory, and the long hair had helped to cover the scars. Even now when he didn't need it anymore, the habit persisted. Like that dream.

He walked outward to the wall that surrounded the estate and followed it westward. There'd been men at watch in the night, at each of the four corners and the gate. There were always men at watch. But still he checked the perimeter inside and out twice daily. There would never be another slaughter of Benn Trilett's family. The children would never have to fear again. Not so long as he had any power in the matter.

He walked on, thinking of Netta Trilett's soft hand in his. Last night they had strolled together beneath the stars. But he had excused himself from her as he usually did, still feeling uncertain in the face of the lady's affection.

He walked the wall with careful scrutiny and stopped to update his orders for the next guard shift. Then he started toward the big house at the center of the estate.

The call to breakfast came with a clanging bell and the clamor of children. With eight youngsters, the peace here was never very quiet through the day, but it was joyous just the same, and Tahn loved to watch them all. They did everything with excitement, as though the newness of this place would never fade away. He could hear them laughing together as they washed in the pewter basin on the porch. Soon they would be racing in to surround the dining room table. They were so at home. And only a year ago, they had been frightened orphans who didn't even know how to be children.

As he crossed the wide yard, he saw Lady Netta standing on the porch, waiting for him. Not so long ago she had feared him. So much had changed. Now she seemed to trust him with the depth of her heart and expect the same in return.

She looked so regal standing there in the streaming light of the sun. He could imagine her mother standing on that porch, or her grandmother before that, waiting for loved ones to come and eat. *What a wonder it must be to feel so connected, so a part of your own family and past.*

He climbed the steps with a sigh and took her into his arms. This was the only thing he could feel connected to. This lady and the children who were so much a part of him now. He'd brought them together in a cave when all he could think of was their survival. Now they were his heart.

He smiled as he held her and breathed in the scent of her fair perfume. But when she touched his hair and then his cheek, something tensed within him. There'd been another touch, so long ago he could scarcely remember it. He wasn't sure he'd ever remembered it before. A woman had held him once, calming his tears with her gentle hand when he was just a tiny boy. But there was pain in the memory that he didn't understand, and he pulled away, shaken.

"What's wrong, Tahn?" Netta's soft eyes drew him back to her, but a sadness still held him, as though the distant pain had reached out and taken hold.

He didn't try to answer her question. He wasn't sure he could. He was struggling to reclaim the fleeting memory and comprehend the ache it had carried with it. But it was too far away again, in another world.

Netta was so quiet. He held her in his arms again, knowing he should say something to her. She could be so patient, so incredibly kind. But she must be wondering why he was acting so strangely.

"I love you," she finally whispered.

And at that moment, Duncan, barely six and the youngest of the children, came running at them.

"Netta!" the little boy cried. "Netta, please, I have to tell you something!"

Tahn broke away with a nod, and the lady knelt to give the boy her attention. Tahn watched their brief exchange—the whisper, the grin, the loving embrace. So much like a mother Netta was to this child who had never had one.

Tahn started to turn away from them, but Netta reached for his hand as Duncan ran to join the other boys.

"Are you all right?" Netta asked him.

"I'm not sure."

She moved to meet his eyes, but he could offer her no explanation.

"Do you want to talk?" she suggested. "And walk, perhaps?"

He shook his head. "You should stay here. Eat with your father and the rest." He pulled her hand gently to his lips and kissed it. "You are good to me, my lady, not to ridicule me in my foolishness."

"You're not foolish. But I think you are looking past me this morning."

He nodded, wanting to hold her again. But not with his mind so occupied. It had always seemed futile to wonder about his earliest years. But now with one tender memory, questions stirred in him as though the past held a secret demanding his notice. Who was he? *Whose* was he? And what had happened to separate him from that kind hand?

In the dream, he was always searching. Maybe there was someone somewhere who could tell him why. It was a new thought. And not an easy one.

Netta took his hands in hers. He looked into her hazel eyes and thanked God that she could give him her patience. He kissed her forehead softly.

"I don't understand what I'm feeling," he said quietly. "But I think there was someone with me before Samis. Before the hanging in Alastair."

"You mean family?"

"I don't know. A woman. With a soft touch."

"Your mother?" Netta could not conceal a sudden excitement. "Tahn, are you remembering your mother?"

He stared at her for a moment and almost pulled away. He shook his head. "It seems nearly impossible to think I could have had one."

"Oh, Tahn."

Netta hugged him. That he could scarcely imagine a loving hand in childhood made her hurt for him. He'd been bound so long under a brutal master. And before that was Alastair's cruel horror.

"I'm sorry," he told her suddenly.

"Sorry for what?" Netta's heart pounded with a fierce compassion for him. "The devil assaulted you so! Perhaps it is time you knew God's truth. You must have had a mother. Perhaps we could find out about her."

"My lady, I have no one to ask."

"Surely someone would know your name."

He bowed his head. "Many people know my name. But they may think only of my sword."

She started to tell him that the people of Onath thought of much more than that, but she saw his eyes turn quickly toward the gate, and she knew that he was listening now to something more distant.

"A rider has come," he told her.

She sighed. "If they need any of us, the guards will summon."

But he shook his head. "I will go and see. Take your breakfast without me." He started to turn.

"Tahn—"

"I don't need Hildy's fine meal this morning. I need to be alone with this a while if the Lord wills. I'll be at the gate or the southwest corner if I am needed. Don't worry for me. Only forgive me, please, for turning from your company again."

She took his hand with a sigh. "I'll not worry. But don't bear a burden alone, Tahn. We are here for you, should you need us."

"I will always need you, my lady." He bowed to her, painfully aware of the longing in her face. But he could not respond to it. Not yet, with the churning inside him. So he turned and left her standing on the pillared porch alone.

She watched him cross the wide yard, remembering the fiery and tormented Tahn who had walked as though he carried the weight of the world on his shoulders. He'd come so far in such a short time. But there was still a weight on his heart.

God be with him, Netta prayed. *Heal every wound in his spirit and grant him all that he seeks.*

11

2

Alastair

Tiarra Loble pushed around the old broom like she had a quarrel with it. Her long hair fell in dark waves across her back and was dampened with perspiration near her face. Her bare feet stepped swiftly through the dust swirls. The work seemed endless. Every day she had to see to Martica's wants and fetch water from the well for her and for this detestable tavern. Then she had to carry drinks and endure the vile sorts who came to order them. Why sweep? The place would be filthy again in a matter of hours.

She shoved the broom against the wall and left it leaning there, though she knew the tavern master preferred it left out of sight. *Let him yell at me when he gets back,* she thought. *At least he won't be wearing that nauseating grin when he looks my way.*

She glanced out the front door, glad that no one was hurrying yet to bury themselves in their liquor. It left her free for a moment to daydream. She picked up a goblet and studied her hazy reflection. What might she look like in the fine dress of a lady, with jewels to match? Perhaps she should leave this place behind and present herself on Baron Trent's doorstep.

She couldn't do it. She knew she wouldn't. But it was a delicious temptation anyway. Wouldn't Martica throw a fit! The old woman had forbidden her to tell anyone of the kinship. She insisted that Tiarra's mother had wanted her raised common. But how painful it was to be dirt poor and shut out of the world in which her mother once had a part. And with little hope of better work than this loathsome tavern had to offer. It was so unfair!

Martica had made her own work once, creating beautiful paintings on canvas, stone, or leather. She'd been quite a marvel, though it never made her much money. But now she was much too old and sick. And Tiarra, at seventeen, had to provide for them both with no special talent or trade.

She set the glass down. She had nothing really but a fair measure of looks and the stubborn will that so often got her into trouble. Hurry up and marry someone, Martica so often advised. Just find someone willing. Tiarra groaned at the thought.

A horse stopped suddenly outside, and she frowned. Some drunkard had come to break in on the silence. She turned abruptly at the sound of the door, feeling angry already though the evening was young.

"Where's Vale?" the tall young man asked immediately. It was Mikal, the maddening son of an arrogant rich man who lived just down the dirt street.

"He went for two more barrels," Tiarra told him. "He won't let Jak Thornton bring them anymore. He says they're always leaky."

"Should have sent you," Mikal said with a sly smile. "The owner of such a fine business should stay where he can keep his watch over things."

"He'll not be thanking you to tell him how to run his affairs, Mikal Ovny," Tiarra countered. "Go away and look for him again tomorrow."

Mikal laughed. "Shut up and kiss me, Ti! There's no one here to see it."

She jerked the wiping cloth off her shoulder and hurled it at him. "Kiss you? You've promised yourself to Mary Stumping! If you wanted your paws about me, you'd not have sought for yourself some other miss."

Mikal stared at her, his eyes still laughing. "You know it

13

was my father's pleasure to choose Mary for my bride. Don't hold it against me. I've always been your friend."

"You're your own friend! And I've got no stomach for your company tonight. I've got work to do."

"You'll not even ask me where I've been?"

"No." She turned from him and walked toward the back room.

"I'll trade you," he said with a grin. "One of your sweet kisses for news of your brother."

She whirled around, her eyes suddenly aflame with emotion. "Tell me of him, Mikal!"

He laughed again. "Where's my kiss?"

She took one quick step and grabbed for the broom. "Tell me what you know of the villain! Or I'll beat it out of you the way I've seen your mother's cook beat her dog!"

He smiled. "Tiarra, you're a pretty one all angry."

She took a swing at him, but he caught the broom and held it fast. "Ti—"

"Tell me what you know!"

"Will you calm down—"

"No! I am not your plaything. You had your kisses when we were children, and I owe you none now. But you owe me! He's my brother, and it's my right to know what you've learned." She let go of the broom and picked up a bowl from the nearest table.

"Tiarra—"

But he was too late to stop her throw. The heavy bowl hit him square in the chest, and she turned immediately to lift the nearest chair.

"Wait a minute—" He backed up and tripped over the stool behind him. Before he could regain his footing, she shoved at him, and he fell full to the floor with her chair on top of him. From the doorway behind them, several new voices joined in laughter, but Tiarra ignored them.

"Where's Tahn Dorn?" she demanded. "What is he about now? Tell me, Mikal!"

"Yes!" a man at the door echoed. "Tell the wench what

14

she wants before she kills you, man!" A chorus of laughter followed.

Tiarra drew the chair back, aware of the spectacle she'd created. And Mikal sat up slowly.

"He's at Onath. I've just been near there with business for my father. They say he lives within the rich walls of the Trilett estate. He courts the daughter of Lord Trilett as though he were a prince."

She let the chair fall from her hands and backed up from him. For all of Mikal's aggravating ways, he wouldn't lie about this. She knew it of him.

"Do you know more?"

"Only that he's well thought of now in Onath and beyond. That's all."

She turned from him and all the other watching eyes. "Go home, Mikal. Please."

He stood silently for a moment before answering her. "I'll come and see you tomorrow, Ti."

She said nothing. She could only think of the brother she'd chosen to hate because of the things she'd been told, the things he had cost her. Her own flesh and blood—living now like a nobleman! But he was no better than she. Worse, indeed. A killer. That's what everyone said. And most importantly, that's what Martica said.

She could hear Mikal behind her, setting a chair upright. And beyond him, the men at the doorway were now coming in, finding themselves places to sit and enjoy their drinking.

"There's thirsty men about!" someone yelled. "You gonna stand there into the night, girl?"

"Maybe she only pays a heed to the ones who'll let her fell them to the floor," another man offered as Mikal left her in silence.

"I'll fight you, girl," a third man declared. "And it won't be me a-lying beneath, I'll warrant." He walked up behind her and grabbed at her side.

Tiarra spun around and slapped him. Then she kicked the stunned man as hard as she could. There was laughter

15

from the others, but she glared around the room at all of them. "Let another one of you try it!" she challenged. "I've got arm enough for such dogs as you."

But suddenly there was a voice behind her. "You're here to give drink, girl. Not insult my brother's paying customers."

She turned around. Orin Sade. The tavern master's burly kinsman.

"They're here for their drinks, then," she answered him back. "And that would be all."

"Be tellin' the man you're sorry," Sade ordered. "Then get to your work."

Some other evening she might have done what he said. The job was important to her. But she was just too angry to face those laughing eyes.

"He'll be dead before he gets a sorry from me," she fumed. "And you can all fetch your own drinks or dry up like old beans." She stomped to the door and out it, and her toes sank instantly into the mud. *I'll bet my brother has fine boots*, she thought. *With nary a thought for me in this world.*

"Tiarra—"

She turned and saw Mikal standing there, looking at her so strangely. "I told you to go home," she told him, turning away again down the soggy street.

She hurried as quickly as she could, past the dingy houses and shops, wondering what she could tell Martica of why she was home so soon. Suddenly a dirty face peered at her from around a corner, and then she heard the boy's excited whisper. "Hurry—hurry, now—it's Miss Ti!"

Three of them emerged from the little space between the two old houses. They were filthy street children, two boys and a girl, the oldest no more than twelve but far bigger than the others.

"Go on, now!" Tiarra told them. "I haven't gotten my pay. Lord knows when I'll ever see that again. I've no food or nothing. Go on, now!"

The littlest child began to cry, and Tiarra stopped. Every night on her way home, and every time she went out of her house, whether she was in a foul temper or not, the street children approached her. They knew she didn't have much, but she would give them each a morsel of whatever she had.

"Please, Miss Ti," said the girl. "We've not had a bite at all today."

Tiarra looked up at the sky for a moment. She felt like screaming. There was no way she could hope to get much for herself, nor for these hungry little ones who were always underfoot. What it must be like to be Tahn Dorn living in luxury.

She sighed, knowing that she would do without her supper and face Martica's wrath because of these children. But it wasn't their fault. "Follow me," she told them. "I'll see if there might not be meal enough at home for a bit of bread."

"Thank you!" one of the children exclaimed.

But Tiarra had already marched quickly ahead of them so they wouldn't be able to see the tears in her eyes.

3

That night, Netta Trilett made her rounds to each of the children to hear them say their prayers. Temas, the dear little girl. Doogan and Rane, who were so active that no one could keep up. Briant and Tam, who could be so quiet it made her wonder what was going on inside their little heads. Duncan and Stuva, the brothers, who still often slept with their arms intertwined. And Vari, the oldest, who at fourteen fancied himself a man.

She'd been a year now seeing them grow past the fear and want they'd known before. Tahn Dorn had been in her heart that long too. He'd been so good at helping them all adjust. Thankfully, he'd been here through their nightmares and tears. He was often more able to help them than she was, though he'd known even more of the torment than they. Yet he rarely spoke of it with anyone.

When she'd given out her last good-night kiss, she went looking for the quiet young man she'd grown to love. Truly he had terrified her once. He'd whisked her out her window in the dead of night and stolen her away. But it was to save her life, just as he'd saved these children from the cruel future that was planned for them. He would always be priceless to her because of that. And because the love for them, or for any other little one in need, was still so clear in him.

She saw him finally, outside by the pond, his long hair loose against his back. He was staring at the sky and sat so still he seemed almost a feature of the land around him. She knew he was deep in thought, or in prayer, and though she would have welcomed his arms again, she could not disturb the solitude he seemed to crave.

"Give him room," Father Anolle had told her once. "Give him all the time he needs."

She turned back to go to her own bed, praying as she went. *His heart seems so heavy. Dear Lord, help him find his way.*

<hr />

Far away in Alastair, Martica lay coughing in her little room, waiting for Tiarra. "What've you been doing out there?" the old woman asked when the girl finally came in. "You giving our bread to the street rabble again?"

"They're children, ma'am," Tiarra pleaded her case. "Hungrier than we are."

"Not for long, child, if you keep up! Send them away next time. They've got to learn there are other people in this city to beg after."

Tiarra looked past her, the sad thoughts pressing at her heavily. "I'm always surprised that you don't want to help them."

"It's not my obligation," the old woman snapped. "I'm not their Creator nor their kin."

"You took *me* in. And it must have been hard when I was just a baby."

"That was for the love of your mother, God rest her."

"But the little ones of Alastair's streets lack a mother and father just as I did then," Tiarra protested.

"Well, let the church or someone with means help them. I'm not averse to that." Martica drew a deep breath and began to cough again.

Tears blurred Tiarra's sight for a moment. Martica was dying. They never spoke of it, but she knew. The cough was always deeper, its hold growing tighter with every passing day. The old woman could be unpleasant indeed, but it was better to have her than to be all alone.

"Why are you home?" the woman demanded. "Why aren't you working?"

Tiarra sighed. "Vale's brother was there to manage it all."

"Think, child!" Martica scolded. "You should have stayed anyway. Perhaps you'll meet a man well taken by the looks of you, and get you a husband and provider."

"You said once that my mother would have hoped better for me than a tavern drinker."

Martica looked up at her in surprise. "True, child," she said. "But remember that your father was no noble. You can't be thinking too high."

"And what of my brother, ma'am?"

Martica scowled. "What of him? The sorry sort!"

"They say he is with the Triletts now," Tiarra told her. "And courting one of their own."

Martica's coughing started again, suddenly almost choking her. "Such a world!" she sputtered.

"Perhaps they who respect him at Onath don't understand how my mother died, Martica. But just let him come someday to Alastair! Then I will kill him myself!"

Martica shook her head in dismay. "Listen to me, child!" she scolded. "That is not the job of a lady!"

"But I am not a lady, ma'am. You just said I should not be thinking of myself highly."

"Tiarra, child—"

"It's not fair, Martica! I *should* be a lady. But I sit with my feet caked in mud and without a hope for anything good. Yet *he* could marry a lady, ma'am! And live such a good life! Do you think he ever has a care for me in it?"

"Hush, child!" Martica scolded.

But Tiarra only stood and ran out. *Surely my brother knows about me,* she was thinking. *Martica has told me he was old enough. And surely our father's kinsman who took him from this city would have known, too, that Tahn Dorn had a sister. Why has he never come seeking me?*

4

Beneath the cloudy predawn sky, Tahn lay sleeping, his black boots just a few feet from the cold waters of the pond. The wind whisked over him, tossing his long black hair. And the sound in his dream absorbed him completely. A baby crying. Again. He went running down the dirty street toward the sound, searching. But the cry stopped as abruptly as it had started, and he rolled awake with the tension still upon him.

Why, Lord? he prayed. *Why is this happening?* He felt like that little child again, afraid of something unknown. "God, I need to understand. Help me."

He sat up and looked around him. It would be morning soon. The blustery wind had blown in a promise of rain. Clouds now covered the stars he'd watched when he first lay down here last night. It had been good to sleep beneath the heavens again. Good to not let the fine home soften him too much.

But the strange dream had followed him from his bed in the guardhouse to the cool grass. He watched the wind toss the willows on the other side of the water and was glad he'd waked. He'd have been stirred by a soaking if he'd been much longer. He stood, knowing the morning and the rain would be breaking loose together.

He turned and looked at the big house up the hill. Lady Netta would be waking soon. And her generous-hearted father. They would expect him again at breakfast. It was a puzzle to him still, how completely he was accepted here and how completely he'd grown to love them. These children were all safe now, adopted by the noble Trilett patriarch. But somewhere still he could hear that baby crying, longing for someone to answer some unknown need.

He sighed as the dream took his thoughts again. It was always the same. Always the wail of an infant and that same dark street. *But whose is the baby, Lord? What does it mean?* He remembered well the flames of the far worse dreams he'd once had. At least it was only this dream haunting him now.

He looked up at the swirling clouds, trying to piece together the recurring images. That old woman in his dream always stepped from a house different from the rest. It stood out starkly on the gloomy street because it was painted as though some artist had used its walls to practice on. And he suddenly thought he knew the place. So long ago that perhaps he really had run past it with tears coursing down his tiny cheeks. It seemed so real to him. As real as his memory of the unknown woman's soft hand.

Maybe the haunting dream wasn't just a dream.

Tahn felt strangely weak. He reached out to the nearest tree and steadied himself against it, not comprehending why such a distant memory could nearly choke the breath from him. Might he truly have known a mother once, before the burning pain consumed him?

Raindrops met his shoulders, but he stood still for a moment. He'd been looking for the woman with the kind hand, whoever she was. Just before his first clear memories, of the angry crowd and the doomed man they'd surrounded. Tahn closed his eyes for a moment, seeing the big man's feet dangling in midair. The crowd had left the man hanging and turned its wrath on him.

He shook his head. A horrible new life had begun for him that day. But he had no way of knowing the kind of life that had ended.

"Who is the woman, Lord?" he questioned. "Is it her baby?" Seventeen years wasn't so awfully long ago, yet somehow he had little hope that either the woman or the baby could be alive.

The rain continued gently. He sighed and walked toward the shelter of his room. There was nothing he could do about the dream. Not until he could get himself back to that horrible town and try to find someone able to answer his questions.

Pink light was spreading across the eastern sky. The whole estate would be stirring soon, and those blessed children would be filling the place with the music of their voices.

"Tahn!"

He whirled around at the sudden call. It was Vari, the oldest, who was already bigger than Tahn and still growing. The spry youth came trotting across the yard toward him, completely heedless of the wet weather.

"Tahn," he began with a look feigning pain, "I've been thinking it such a long time since I've seen Leah—"

"Only a month."

"Which is sore long," the youth persisted. "Surely you know. I've been thinking it a good time to take a horse and go for a visit. Maybe I could be of help to her father in the harvest. I might learn a thing or two while I'm at it."

It wasn't easy for Tahn to switch his mind to other things just yet, but he smiled at his friend. "You still aim to be a farmer, then?"

"With Leah for my wife someday. And a whole troop of children surrounding us," Vari said with conviction. "You know nothing will change my mind."

Tahn nodded. Vari was grown already in his own mind. And he'd been like that all the time Tahn had known him. "Are you wanting to leave this morning, then? Rain and all?"

"As soon as I can, at least."

"Are you taking any of the little ones?"

"Not this time. The lessons here are valuable to them at the moment."

"And you'd not have your attention divided from your fair miss?"

Vari smiled. "That too."

"Just keep yourself proper with her," Tahn told him as

23

he started again toward the guardhouse. "Remember your youth. Don't stay over a week, and make sure you have Benn's approval."

Vari just stood and watched him for a moment, surprised by his quick answer. "Is something bothering you this morning, Tahn?"

He turned and shook his head. "We're God blessed, and you know it, Vari. I'm fine."

"The baby dream again, wasn't it?"

Tahn stopped and sighed. Vari read him well at such things. "There's no cause for it to bother me so," he said and started to turn away again.

"I think you're plain nervous, Tahn. That's why this is in your head all the time. I think you're looking for the life you deserve, and you ought to go right on and ask for Netta's hand. Could be she's the one to have the baby one day, and you're scared. But this is honey compared to what we've had! We're blessed, just like you said. You know she loves you! And you know Benn is just waiting. He'd sooner give up his name than turn you down, for all he thinks of you."

Tahn shook his head. "I can't."

"Why not? You think it's too soon? We've been here a year."

Tahn ignored the questions. "It's not her baby, Vari. And the street I see is nowhere around here. It's much more dismal than this place."

"You still dream it a lot?"

"Almost every night. But it's a memory, and I'm not sure how to manage it."

Vari's brow furrowed with immediate concern. "A memory? You mean before Samis?"

"Yes."

"I never figured the past would have to matter," the boy admitted. "I know about you, that there's questions if we was to ask 'em. But maybe it's better not to, don't you think? Maybe it's better to enjoy what we got and let everything else go."

Tahn nodded just slightly. Vari's words were sensible

24

enough. But Tahn knew that he spoke them out of worry more than anything else. "How do you let a dream go?" he asked him. "It doesn't let *me* go."

Vari had no answer, and Tahn turned his face to meet the gentle rain with a prayer in his heart. *Lord, why does this hold my mind night after night? You want me to go back there, don't you? To Alastair, to find out what the dream can't tell me.*

It was an unsettling thought. There was no other place Tahn could dread so much. He glanced at Vari. "I think the street was called Vermeel," he said. "But I'm sure the place has changed since I was there."

"You mean Alastair?" Vari caught his breath and put his hand carefully on his friend's shoulder.

Tahn didn't answer the question. "We seem a couple of fools, just standing here in the rain."

"I like rain," Vari said quietly.

"You like everything," Tahn replied. "The world suits your dreams and you always dream happy."

The young man frowned at such words. "It wasn't always that way. We've both changed."

"Thank God for it." Tahn looked over toward the big house. "What a world he's given us! Now we live like princes. When we were but—"

"No," the youth stopped him abruptly. "We were done wrong, Tahn! *You* were done wrong! And it wasn't your fault. So don't be thinking anymore about what we don't deserve. You've got a right to be happy the same as any Trilett or anybody else. And you're just as good as anyone else too."

"Are you going to let me get out of this rain?" Tahn asked, feeling strangely solemn. It was hard to believe what God had done, taking up a band of orphans and giving them a home like this. And himself a man of blood. In truth, he didn't feel deserving. Of Netta's attention, or of anything else.

Together they walked to the guardhouse, to Tahn's generous room at the side of it. Bennamin Trilett had it built on especially for him, and he still felt a little strange every time he entered. He pulled off his soiled shirt and let it drop across the back of his chair. "I need to return to Alastair before long, Vari."

The youth was looking at him in question, his eyes drawn to the scars on Tahn's back as Tahn reached for a clean shirt from a peg on the wall.

"Are you sure?" Vari asked him. "I don't like the sound of it. You've always hated Alastair. And with plenty good reason."

"But there's something about it all that I have to know," he explained. "There must be somebody in that town who can tell me what I was too young to remember."

"Do you mean you think you had family, maybe? A baby brother or sister?"

Tahn sat down. "I need to find out. Samis never told me anything. But you know it wouldn't have mattered to him."

Vari shook his head. "I thought he snatched up street kids who were left alone. Like me."

"He did pay a sum once to take Lorne from his poor family."

"But he wouldn't have bought you burnt as bad as you were, do you think?" As soon as he said the words, Vari's face changed, as though he feared the question was a painful one.

"I don't expect so," Tahn answered him steadily. "There's no telling for certain. I never knew why he took me in that shape at all. Maybe there is someone there who could tell me."

"But Samis was plain evil. That might be something we're better not to know."

"Maybe." He was quiet for just a moment and then looked up at Vari. "What do you think the people of Alastair would do about me coming back to ask about that day? I'd like to know who it was they hanged, and what he was to me."

"You shouldn't have trouble from them after all this time. I'd hope not. How could they hold anything against you? You weren't but four years old."

Tahn looked down at his boots. "It depends on what we did. And I have no idea. But my tender age didn't stop their wrath then. It's a hard town."

"Then I better go with you when you go."

"No. I want you to be available for the little ones here. I don't know how long I'll be." He stood and looked out at the brightening sky. "It's just a gentle rain today, Vari. Go ahead and make your trip if you will. I'll not go until you're safely back."

But the youth shook his head. "I can't just go to see my girl when you're waiting over something like this. I'd feel selfish the whole way! If you think you might have kin someplace, I understand why you'd want to go find out. Even to Alastair."

"If there's family at all, they're probably dead or long gone." Tahn sighed. "I may not find anything."

"You're bound to learn something," Vari affirmed. "Or this dream wouldn't be working on you. God knows. And I can be the one to wait."

Tahn smiled. "You're a good friend to me." He went out again into the gentle rain with the youth following.

"You're going to the spring?" Vari asked.

He nodded. "I'll be soaked to the skin by the time I finish walking the wall. You might as well go back to the house."

"Can I tell them you'll eat with us today?"

"Yes, Vari. I'll need some time with the children before I leave."

Tahn was inside the wall on the north when he heard horses and a voice that sounded familiar. He gave a shrill whistle to alert the guard at the nearest corner and then scaled the wall with the hard-won agility that had earned him reputation among Samis's mercenaries.

As he expected, it was a soldier named Saud, with two others hired and armed by the House of Trent. One of them carried the baron's trefoil insignia and an especially ornate pouch. They were special messengers, that was obvious. But

Tahn could never consider any message from the Trents to be good news.

"The Dorn might be out for your blood, Saud," one of the others was saying. "He'll remember you. Do you suppose they'll break peace before long?"

"Benn Trilett won't break peace. He covets it too much for that." Saud spoke with confidence. He was a big man, coarse and comfortable in command of men. "And who's to say that Dorn is still here?" he continued. "He's got battle in his soul. He couldn't be content with this place for long."

"But a lovely lady can soothe a beast," said the soldier with the pouch. "Perhaps she has fire enough to make him forget his sword."

"Ah, yes, that Netta—" Saud began.

"Be careful what you say," Tahn spoke suddenly.

All three men spun around toward the wall, and Tahn jumped down.

"Dorn!" Saud exclaimed. "You're half ghost! Why do you lurk and spy on us so?"

"I do my job. What is yours today?"

"You can see plainly enough. We've a message for your Lord Trilett. Will you bar us from him as you did the last time?"

"You don't need to see his face for the word to reach his hand. Give me what you bring."

"We haven't even reached the gate!"

"It's not far. You can wait there, and I'll see that you get provisions for your return home."

"The young baron asked that we deliver his happy news in person to Benn Trilett," Saud insisted. "Who is the head here? You or he?"

Tahn was not moved. "I'll ask if he wants to see you."

Saud shook his head. "What could three of us do within these walls? What are you afraid of, Dorn?"

"Your young baron had a ruthless father. He claims he is different, but he has retained you as the head of his men—"

"I'm only the servant of my lord."

28

"You're a murderer!" Tahn countered. "You were with the old baron to take the name of Trilett from the earth. You would have slaughtered Lady Netta. And you would have been happy to see me die with the blame of it! If Lord Trilett asks to have you in, I will give him his pleasure, but without his word, you will never see inside these gates."

Saud stared at him coldly. "There's no war between us."

Tahn stepped in front of their horses. "Give me your message."

"You insult Baron Lionell of Trent!"

"You can explain to him my reasons. Perhaps he would see fit to dismiss you."

The youngest messenger looked up at his captain. "I don't think we'll persuade him."

"Shut up!" Saud shouted.

"Give me your message," Tahn repeated. "Then wait by the gate. I'll come to you if there is an answer. The men will bring customary provision either way."

"You've a cold way with a joyful word," Saud complained. "You'll tarnish your lord's reputation by such rudeness."

"I'm not here for his reputation."

Saud snorted. "Fine. Have the message. Let the Triletts bear the fruit of your conduct till Benn tires of you ruling his gate. Give him Baron Trent's pouch, Hamlin."

The young soldier handed over his message, and Tahn put the pouch over his own shoulder. Then he led them to the gate, where two men were already standing outside, waiting for them.

"Keep them here until I give you word," Tahn told his guardsmen and then went quickly inside.

He ran the distance of the lane toward the great house. Netta was on the porch again, but he barely took time to look at her.

"Where is your father?"

"With Jarel," she told him, her eye on the embroidered pouch. "A message from Lionell Trent?"

"Yes, lady." He couldn't help his frown. Seven Triletts

29

had died because of Trent ambition. And though it had been at the former baron's orders, he did not trust Lionell or his men now.

He hurried inside, to the marble-floored room where Lord Trilett conducted most of his business.

Benn looked up with a smile and saw the official pouch immediately. "Have I guests at the gate?"

"Three soldiers bore the word, sir. They are waiting." He handed Benn his package and glanced for a moment at Jarel, Netta's cousin, who was seated in the nearest chair.

Benn unwrapped and read the roll that had been in the soldier's pouch.

"Is there a problem?" Jarel asked him.

"No." The Trilett patriarch looked up at them. "We are invited to a wedding. Lionell Trent has finally declared a bride."

"You're not going, are you?" Tahn asked immediately.

Benn smiled. "I trust Netta will not choose to go. Your name is excluded from the invitation, though your courtship of her is no secret to the nobles. I know how she feels about that. She'll not be pleased to go without you. And it would be rather a relief to me to have her stay at home."

Tahn shook his head. "Surely you don't entertain the idea of going, my lord, considering what the Trent name has cost you."

"You don't understand the way of nobility, son," Benn maintained. "It is almost a game. Each move has its purpose in how it relates to the rest of the noble houses. I can influence the others by what I do, and God knows the people need that."

"What about you?" Tahn asked Jarel.

"I'm not good at the game anymore," the young man said bitterly. "Nor do I want to play it. Lionell could marry the north sea and I'd have no interest. My brothers should be here to get wives and not be lying in their graves."

Benn nodded. "We don't forget them. But we move on with the responsibilities God has given us."

Tahn studied him for a moment. "They can have a wedding without you, sir."

The Trilett patriarch smiled kindly. "Perhaps they will. I'll not go into the devil's den unless I am bidden of God for a purpose."

Devil's den? Tahn had never heard Benn Trilett speak out quite so harshly. "Has Lionell Trent shown his hand for evil?"

Benn looked over at his nephew, and Jarel suddenly stood. "I have friends," Jarel said simply. "They have told me how he conducts himself."

Jarel's is a different game, Tahn was thinking. *Were it not for the restraint of his uncle and his God, this young Trilett would yet seek vengeance, though the old baron is already dead.* "Will there be a message in return?" Tahn asked.

"Indeed," Benn answered. "Congratulations are in order. And I must send a gift, of course."

Jarel and Tahn both looked at him.

"We do well to cultivate peaceful relationships," Benn told the younger men. "But I respect your cautions." He sat down and took up his quill pen. "With my own hand," he said. "And the Trilett seal. Will you take it to them when I finish, Tahn?"

"Allow me," Jarel told him. "I promised Father Anolle I would come to see him this morning. I'll be on my way to the gate anyway."

Benn nodded. "The sight of a Trilett will do them good. They'll not be able to tell Lionell that we scorned them. But you'll not leave until they are well on their way, Jarel."

"Of course, sir." He leaned back and studied Tahn for a moment, then cleared his throat and caught Tahn's gaze. "So when will we have a wedding around here?"

And Tahn immediately tensed with this sudden change of thought.

"In its good time," Benn answered for him, without even looking up. "I am not averse to patience in such matters."

"Nor to the mysterious Dorn for a son-in-law," Jarel added, smiling at Tahn's discomfort. He crossed his arms

31

and addressed him again. "Her love for you is obvious by now. And your feelings for her have been clear to me from the beginning. Why bother to toy with it? Jump in wholly and tie yourself to us more than you already have!"

Tahn stared at him, not completely sure if he was serious.

"Jarel," Benn scolded. "You make the young man pale. True, he is a part of us, and I love him already like a son, but you can't drive hearts like cattle. Let them find their own way."

Tahn turned to look at Netta's father gratefully. "Thank you, sir."

Benn smiled. "My pleasure." He turned his attention back to the letter he was crafting. "This won't take long, but you may as well breakfast without me. I'll not keep the messengers standing as I eat."

"I'll wait," Tahn told him.

"I think I'll eat in town with the good priest," Jarel told them, watching Tahn again. There was something so deep about Tahn that it was hard for Jarel to imagine having such a creature become the spouse of Benn Trilett's only surviving child. But it would surely happen, and Jarel could almost look forward to the sparks it would create among the nobility in the land. But no matter how far removed Tahn was from noble finery, he was sincere after their safety. And he was sincere in his feelings for Netta. For those things, he had a right to belong.

Benn finished his congratulatory message quickly, wrapped it in fine paper, and tied it carefully with a ribbon. Then he took another paper and wrote out a list. "Jarel, I want you to tell Josef to gather these things to be sent out on a cart in a few days. Lionell and the Lady Elane should be pleased for the gift." He gave his nephew the wrapped message. "This is for the men today. Give them my greeting and make sure they are refreshed."

"Yes, Uncle. And then I need to be going," Jarel said. "I will be back at dinner."

"Don't insult them," Benn added.

"Would I, indeed?" Jarel asked him.

"Pray for them, Jarel, while you are with the priest," Benn instructed. "Pray for Lionell and all his family."

"I hear you," the young man replied. He bowed to his uncle and then left them quickly.

Benn turned to Tahn. "I worry for Jarel sometimes," he admitted. "He does not always understand me."

Tahn nodded. "I could not help him much there."

But Benn smiled. "I think you could help him a great deal. You forgive better than you know. You move on. It is part of your strength."

"I'm blessed of God to have your favor."

"You're blessed of God. That is enough to be said. You needn't return to the gate. Jarel knows wisdom enough for such things. Would you join me at the table now, or have you other business?"

Tahn bowed his head for a moment. "There is another matter I sought to discuss with you, my lord, but at your pleasure."

"Sit down. I'll hear you now."

Tahn sat, watching Benn carefully. He was such a good man. He could be counted on to kindly consider a request. But it seemed such a strange time to make it. "The matter can wait, my lord."

"I don't want to wait," the nobleman said. "Speak your heart to me. I see you by yourself of late, and I know you have a need."

He sighed. "I need to make a journey. And I need money, sir. But I cannot repay you except with my work when I return."

"Every day you work," Benn told him, "and you refuse to receive anything but your upkeep. I owe you much by now. Where are you going?"

"Alastair, sir. I begin to remember a woman. And a baby. I need to know what relationship they are to me."

Benn searched the young man's eyes. There was an earnestness in them, almost a fear. He had often wondered about Tahn's past. He would not refuse him. "The money is for the travel, then?"

"No, my lord. I've traveled many times without money. I would fare well enough. But Alastair is a difficult town. I don't know what might be required to discover what I seek."

"You'll have what you need," Benn assured him. "But consider your safety. Could your past in Alastair still put you in danger? And aren't there men of Samis who are now bandits in that region?"

"You know I shall be watchful, sir."

"Yes, but for the sake of our peace, don't go alone, son."

"I will take Lorne."

Benn nodded solemnly. "When will you leave?"

"As soon as I can be secure of your safety here. Even today, with your permission."

Benn was quiet for a moment. He didn't like the thought of Tahn's absence. And he knew Netta wouldn't like it either. She had taught Benn that this strong soul was often vulnerable, as though the protector himself might need their protection. But God was with him; there could be no doubt of that. Jesus had brought him from a life of blood to one of peace. And the Lord would be with him if any of those still-dark warriors crossed his path.

"I trust the order you have set with our guards," Benn said. "They know what to do. We have no threat at the doors. Do what you must, and godspeed. But remember that you do us no disservice to bear arms in the journey."

5

It was past midday before Tahn was ready for departure.

Benn stood and watched his daughter kiss the quiet soldier. And Temas, the tiny child, reached for the nobleman's hand.

"How long will he be gone?"

"I don't know, child," Benn answered. "But he will be well."

"I would be scared if Samis wasn't dead."

"I know." He knelt beside the girl. "There's no cause for fear now, though."

They watched Tahn and Lorne ride together to the gate. Netta stood apart from the others.

"Are you crying?" nine-year-old Doogan asked her.

"No."

"It's all right to miss him."

Netta smiled. "Thank you." She turned to find all the children looking at her and took a deep breath. "Shall we practice our sums?"

"Do we have to?" Stuva frowned.

"No." She sighed. "Not immediately, I suppose. Go and play a little while, but don't trouble Hildy in the kitchen."

Vari walked solemnly toward the gate. As the rest of the children scattered, Benn turned to his daughter.

"I trust God for Tahn, Netta."

She took his hand. "I can't imagine what it must be like."

"He'll be fine."

"They nearly killed him, Father."

"Do you mean Alastair or the soldiers of Samis?"

She stared at him, suddenly near tears. It was both. And had things changed?

"I'm sorry," Benn told her. "Please don't worry so. You know better than I do the need he has for this."

"I know. But he doesn't even know what he'll face. He may have a hundred enemies we aren't even aware of."

"Or a hundred friends."

But she was not comforted. "Can you imagine anyone deliberately scalding a child? Father, why would they do such a thing? How could they?"

He shook his head. He had heard of such a practice years ago as a mob vengeance against violent criminals. But it would not help to tell her that. Tahn had been helpless in Alastair. A frightened little boy. He pulled her into his arms. "Peace, daughter."

Netta rested her head against her father's shoulder. "Who would have thought the world could be so cruel? For all he's lived through. And all we've lost."

Benn nodded. "He has shared our grief," he said quietly. "Our hearts are tied. Even if you refuse his hand, I would still give him the inheritance of a son, along with all the little ones. I know he would use it well."

Netta stared at her father in surprise.

He smiled. "But you won't refuse him, will you?"

Her eyes grew wide. "Has he talked to you?"

"No. Not yet."

"Oh, Father."

"Jarel is right about the obvious. And I thought you should know my heart. I don't care so much anymore of the old ways. I don't know a single son among the nobles I would want you with. They are all greedy men and wrapped up with themselves."

Outside of Onath, Tahn and Lorne moved quickly. Smoke was pleased to be traveling again. The horse wanted to run, and Tahn let him have his head. Lorne on his red roan was behind, and after a while, Tahn thought it courtesy to slow down and let him catch up.

"Vari was right to say you're well driven today," Lorne said as soon as he was close enough to be heard.

Tahn reined Smoke to a stop. "I've never known such a quest before. How do you think I'll manage it?"

"I couldn't say, not knowing what we'll find."

"What was it like, when you went home again?"

The blond young man patted his horse's neck. "My experience hardly parallels yours."

"I know. I was there to see your face when you realized your father was selling you, even if it was to keep the rest of your family from starving. It must have been strange, going back, despite remembering them so well."

"It *was* strange," Lorne admitted with a sigh. "Frightening. I wasn't sure they'd welcome me. Maybe they would think me a burden, or a shame to them. But you know how they honor me now."

"You've been good to them."

"You've been good to them too. And if we find your family, it will be the same."

Tahn didn't answer. He started Smoke at a walk again and looked deep into the trees ahead.

"Vari was disappointed not to be coming," Lorne told him. "He'll be worrying for you."

"That's just the trouble. He loves me too much to have the sense about him should we encounter any problems."

Lorne frowned. "And you don't think I love you?"

"You'll keep your sense. That's the important thing." He glanced at his companion and then gave Smoke the liberty of some speed again.

There were many miles ahead of them. But Tahn would move through them quickly. He could push himself and his eager horse almost endlessly and was confident enough in Lorne to push him too.

He tossed the young man's words about in his mind as they rode. If he found he had family, what would they think of him? Not that he was a burden. He'd never allow himself to be that. A shame? His heart pounded. That was much more likely. Even just, perhaps. Until he knew Jesus, there hadn't been much about him that anyone could be comfortable with.

But you had your hand on me all along, didn't you, Lord? Tahn prayed. *Even when I was so lost, so angry, you put it in my heart to care about the little ones.*

Tiarra stepped out into the street with a basket under her arm. The last of Martica's painting things. The old woman had told her to go and sell them. She'd always held on to them before, thinking to work when she got well. But this morning she plainly said she'd never use them again. *She knows she's dying. She knows it won't be long.* The knowledge of it cast gloom over an already dreary world.

Tiarra walked rapidly but still hadn't progressed past the third house before children began to make their way to her. Five of them, Tiarra noticed. Maybe even more soon. *Would God that they wouldn't watch for me so!*

"Miss Ti!" a little boy called. "Can you spare bread today?"

"Oh, Jori." She shook her head. She rarely told them no, she so hated to see the despair in their little faces. But in truth, today she had no choice. "I've got nothing."

She watched their faces register disappointment. Two of them began to turn away. "Wait a minute," she told them. "Come here."

They looked at her in question but quickly gathered themselves around her.

"I wish I could give you all a fine meal," she told them. "I wish I had it for myself. But there's not much left. I got Martica medicine just days past and thought to wait till I had pay tomorrow to buy the foodstuffs. But now I don't know if I'll ever see that pay or any other from Vale Sade. And I fear Martica worsens. She will die soon. So I'm about the same as you are now. Just a bit bigger is all."

"Don't be afraid, Miss Ti," one of the children said. "We'll help you."

She smiled. "You would if you could, I know it. But don't you worry. There'll be something. I aim to speak to Mr. Sade. If I've lost my duties, there will be something else."

"Not much work around here," the biggest boy said. "I've tried. But girls can get on with Miss Mara, takin' in men. They always get so bitter and mean, though, when they do that. I'd hate to see that happen to you."

"So would I. And I'd never dare mention it near my mother's grave."

A girl named Jeramathe looked at her quizzically for a moment. "I heard tell a rumor of her once."

Tiarra touched the little head. "Of my mother? Tell me."

"I heard it that she was almost like a lady. With jewels and all. Is it really so?"

Tiarra sighed and looked at all their faces. They had no use for details. It was food they needed. And she would have to help them, whether it did her mother's memory service or not. "Martica always spoke well of her. But I need to hurry on and sell these things so I can buy what Martica ordered me and go find Mr. Sade." She squatted down to the eye level of the youngest. "I know the penalty for stealing. I know my mother never liked a thief. I'd much rather give to you. But we have no choice today. You're far too thin as it is. Follow me to Market Street, and I'll create a ruckus. Each of you grab no more than you can easily hide and be gone as quick as you can."

None of the children said a word. They just looked at her with quiet respect. She'd spoken the truth. She really was one of them.

On her way home later that day, Tiarra's mind was churning over her predicament. Vale Sade had sent her away, angry that she'd left her work unfinished. Martica would be displeased, to say the least. Tiarra had never really managed to suit the old woman. Martica had given up on teaching her to paint. One had to be born with the knack, she'd declared, which obviously wasn't the case for Tiarra. But she

39

didn't seem to be blessed with her mother's gentle finesse, either. All Martica had ever really acknowledged was that she had a temper and a good measure of foolishness to go with it. This would be just one more brick on that cart, and it wouldn't set very well.

But at least she'd managed to sell Martica's things and buy what she wanted without disobeying the command not to share it with the street children today.

Tiarra smiled at the thought of them all in the market, scurrying in different directions with their precious morsels of food. Every one of them had escaped with enough to take away the pains of hunger for a few more hours at least. And none of the vendors could be sure that the children even knew her. Maybe they figured the beggars had just taken advantage of an opportune moment.

She sighed, thinking about tomorrow for herself and for them. What would be next? It made such a tightness in her, as though her insides would burst for the pressure of it. It would have been a pleasure to scream at the world, would it have helped things at all.

She looked up at the spire of the nearby Cathedral of St. Thomas, and the anger rose in her fresh. Why should it be here, within sight of such despair? Why should it stand there so tall and stately as though God cared a mite for the world he'd created?

It was cloudy again and getting dark and cool earlier, now that autumn was upon them. God had made the seasons too, with the bitter punishing cold of winters that not everyone could survive. She shook her head and thought of Martica. Martica had always enjoyed the spring. But it seemed not likely that she would see another one.

Suddenly Tiarra sensed someone watching her. She looked up from her troubled thoughts and saw two young men standing beside the nearest building. They were not dressed well, but not in the rags of street children, either. As soon as they moved, with their eyes still on her, she knew they would approach her, and she knew their intention.

She wanted to fight them; she relished the idea of venting the fury inside her, but she started to run, knowing it was the wiser.

And they gave chase. She stayed easily ahead of them until a third man jumped into her path from a nearby building. She knew she couldn't avoid them all now. She tried. She tried to turn and escape the new assailant's grasping arms, but he caught her by the wrist. She could not pull away. So she twisted into him with all the force she could muster and knocked him off balance. Her bag fell to the dirt as both of them hit the ground. Tiarra used her temporary advantage to strike at him as hard as she could.

The first two men were almost upon them now. She might not be able to get away. They would likely overcome her. But she would make at least one of them suffer plenty for it. Cutthroats. Thieves. Men who would take what they could from a woman. This world was a sorry enough place already without the like of these. She was raging inside, wanting to hurt her attacker as badly as she could, knowing that they had done this before, would probably do it again, to people who could scarcely afford yet another something to endure.

The first two men grasped hold of her, trying to pull her off their friend, but it was no easy job. She fought like a thing possessed.

But one of them struck a blow to her head, and she faltered to one side. And the man who had been beneath her lunged forward and took her by the throat. "I'm gonna kill this one," he sputtered. "The stinkin'—"

But one of the others shoved him. "Let's get her out of the middle of the street first, fool, and lift her skirt."

Tiarra screamed and struck at both of them, knocking one of them into the dirt again. But the third man was suddenly on top of her. She punched at him and screamed again, but he was a strong one and would not fall away easily.

She bit his arm as hard as she could and fought on. She could have bested one of them. Maybe even two. But the three of them were too much. Still, she wouldn't give up,

41

though she found herself with her back to the dirt, staring over at the tall spire of St. Thomas.

Suddenly, there was a shout just down the street, and all three of the men stopped in their tracks. One of them ran immediately. The other two held their ground until the stranger came at them at a dead run. The second man ran with Tiarra's bag in his hand, but the third stayed long enough to meet the stranger with his hard blows.

The black-garbed stranger fought well, and the remaining attacker had no easy time breaking loose enough to run. But the newcomer stopped and looked at Tiarra lying there in the dirt at his feet and gave the assailants no chase. He knelt beside her and gently took her hand. She was untrusting, almost ready to fight him too, until she saw the large cross suspended from his neck. She stared at it in disbelief.

"Are you all right, my lady?" he was asking.

And then she was stunned as much by what he'd called her as by the cross he wore.

"Are you a priest?"

"Not yet. Someday, perhaps. Are you hurt badly, my lady? May I help you to your home?"

She shook her head and sat up, but it set her head to throbbing, and she sat still for a moment before trying to stand.

"I'm sorry for what happened," the stranger continued. "They never had a proper path set before them. Theirs was a terrible teacher."

"You know them?"

He nodded. "They are three of fifteen or so still around Alastair. They set about to steal, but they can scarcely resist viler things when they come upon a lady as fair to the eyes as yourself. It is worse than sad, the state they're in, and what they do to the land hereabout. I am so sorry, lady, for this."

He was a strange one, to talk of it as though it were partly his fault. "Who are you? Are you come from St. Thomas's?"

He smiled. "Yes. My name is Lucas. Can you stand?"

42

She rose to her feet with his careful help. "I've never seen you there," she said.

"It's been four months," he replied. "And I've never seen *you* there."

She scowled. "I haven't been there for three years, and I'm not going back! When your God shows a care for this awful world, I'll come and thank him. And not until then!" She pulled away from him and took a limping step.

"I am sorry about the loss of your bag, my lady. May I help you to your home?"

Tiarra stood in silence for a moment. She hadn't even remembered the bag. But it had held the gain of all Martica had left in this world. She had done right by the old woman, only to lose it, and she would have to face her empty handed.

The tears filled her eyes quickly, and she hated that this stranger would see them.

"Let me help you," he said. "You're hurt."

But she turned away.

"Ti?" Mikal's voice called from somewhere down the street, but she made no attempt to answer. Instead, she moved away with small steps, drying her eyes. For Mikal to see the tears would be even worse than the stranger seeing them.

She could hear him running toward them. But she could get no distance even from Lucas the someday-priest, who seemed to be following her in his concern.

"Wait a minute, Ti." Mikal touched her arm as soon as he was close enough and stopped her determined steps. "I've been looking for you."

She tried to turn away, but he held her and moved to see her face. She would have sizable bruises tomorrow, and she knew that was probably plain already. He stood in tense silence, having come upon the scene too late to know what had happened.

"Who did this?"

"Three of the dark angels who used to haunt the moun-

43

tain," Lucas replied. "The lady is hurt. She should not go on alone."

Mikal looked at her carefully. But Tiarra shook her head. "They stole Martica's bag," she told him. "I'll have to go and tell her."

"Thank you for being here, Reverend sir," Mikal told the stranger. "I know where she lives. I'll help her."

Tiarra looked up at the Reverend Lucas, who still stood so close. "I owe you a thanks," she said. "I am grateful, but I need no more help now, thank you."

Mikal took her arm again, but she pulled away. "Let me carry you, Ti, please," he said.

She turned to him angrily, unable to stop new tears. "No! I'll not be owing you anything. Leave me alone! I know my own way home."

He stared at her, and Tiarra thought she could see anger in his face.

"I'm only trying to help! Can't you see I'm trying to be your friend? Maybe I should have been quicker to tell you about your stupid brother. Maybe you had a right to be angry then. But now? Tiarra—"

"No!" she shouted again. "Don't even talk to me! Vale dismissed me, Mikal. Because I fought at you and left. Why couldn't you just leave me alone?"

He stood in silence, just looking at her. She hated that he was probably seeing the anguish in her eyes. She hated that he had come upon her when she was so weak. Robbed and beaten. Without money, or work, or a father to provide her anything.

By the expression on his face, it seemed he understood. "I'll speak to Vale. Surely if I explain—"

"Go away."

"I'll speak to him," he repeated. "Right now." He turned to the man with the cross beside them. "Please see her home. She'll not have me at the moment."

Tiarra turned away from them both. "I told you I know my own way!"

The man named Lucas followed her anyway. She didn't

44

like it. But she knew she should be grateful. He would be watchful lest her attackers show themselves again, a very real possibility were she walking alone.

As they entered Vermeel Street, Lucas could see here and there a child peering out at the young woman he was trying to escort. But because he was behind her, they would not come near. He knew what it was like. He could remember when he had hidden that way, especially from men, fearful that they would punish him for having to steal in order to live. Alastair was still the same, and it broke his heart.

She stopped in front of the worn little mud-brick house with painted designs peeling away from its outer walls. And he could remember when some of the designs were bright and new. He'd been a little boy then, and the old woman who sat outside painting had scolded him for getting too close.

"I live here," Tiarra was telling him. "Thank you again, sir. I'll be fine."

He was not at all convinced. He could see that her bruises were swelling and gaining color. "You have family near?" he asked, remembering Mikal Ovny saying something about her brother.

"Only Martica inside," she answered him.

He didn't question her, only nodded. "I would like to talk to her and explain what happened, my lady."

She wearily leaned against the wall of the house. "You didn't have to come."

"I know. I only wanted to see you home safely."

Her expression was difficult to read. Certainly not anger or fear, but she was not happy to have been followed, none-theless. "Martica has not been well," she said. "And we can't offer you anything."

"I'd not take anything from you."

She said nothing more. But he could see she was hurt. He stepped forward to help her inside, and she did not resist him.

Lucas looked around the small shelter and noticed first

that there were no chairs. There was precious little of anything. Tiarra made her way past her own mat on the floor to the small doorway in back. And he followed her to the little house's only other room.

When Lucas saw Martica lying on her bedding, he knew it was the same old woman who had painted here some years ago. She looked truly ancient now, and her cough was weak and horrible.

"Who is it with you?" she called out when she saw his shape in the doorway.

"He's from St. Thomas's, Martica. He helped me on my way home tonight."

"Helped you?"

Lucas knelt at the woman's side. "Your daughter was attacked by violent thieves, good lady. They did her harm, and it might have been worse had I not seen them. I would not have her alone—"

"You were robbed?" The old woman directed the question to Tiarra, who sat down and suddenly seemed to be shivering.

"Yes, Martica. I am so sorry—"

"Child! There is no gain from you! I was successful once, in my measure. Before I knew you! God bless your mother, but you carry your father's curse. I lose more and more in the care of you until there's nothing left!"

Shaking, Tiarra pulled herself to her feet again and fled the room. Lucas watched her go and then turned to the old woman and sighed. "She was not at fault. She fought valiantly, lady."

"She's not my daughter."

"But she acts it toward you. Doesn't she?"

"I don't know how she acts. I worry for her. How will she ever survive? I pray for a man who will look only at her face and not see all the trouble brewing inside her."

Lucas shook his head. "It seems to me she would need just the opposite."

Martica looked hard at him. "You come from St. Thomas's, you say?"

46

"Yes." He opened the small bag at his belt. "Permit me to repay your loss, lady. Call it a benevolence of my church." He laid several copper coins in her hand. "It was a terrible thing those men sought against an innocent girl. Give her your patience, my lady. She seemed too brave to be frightened, but I know she is in pain." He stood and bowed his head to her. "God's peace to you."

"Give her my patience?" Martica grumbled. "She's hopeless, that's what she is. Can't keep anything. It's a curse, that's what it is." She started coughing again, and he turned to follow the young woman who had to abide here with such words.

Tiarra sat in the corner in the first room, her head against the wall. He knew she was crying. Without a word, he walked to the hearth, piled kindling, and began a fire. Then he took a cloth that had been on the heavy old table, dropped it into a pail half full of water, and carried both to Tiarra's side.

"You should not be here," she told him.

"It seems almost that you should not be."

She stared up at him for a moment but then turned her head away.

"Forgive me," he said immediately. "I have no right to voice myself so." He knelt beside her and lifted the wet cloth to her face. "How old are you?"

"Seventeen."

"Five years ago, I was that age. And things are very different for me now. Your world, too, will change."

She turned to look at him again. "I think you're wrong, sir. The world doesn't change. We just step from one spot to the next." She took the cloth from his hand. "I can tend to myself. You don't need to stay."

He stood and glanced around. "Have either of you eaten?"

Tiarra looked at him in dismay. He found a bag with a bit of meal in it, and then a single onion. There was no other food. He worked in silence, watching Tiarra, until she leaned down to her mat on the floor. Then he returned to

47

her side to lift the old blanket up to her shoulder and bathe her face again. "You might be more sore tomorrow," he told her. "But it should grow better after that. May I pray for you?"

"I would that you leave me alone," she said in a quiet voice. But he returned to the hearth, where soon she could hear his soft prayers. And before long the aroma of roasted onion and flat bread filled the little house.

6

A full day had passed, but the journey had gone quickly. Tahn knew this terrain. He'd traveled it often as a warrior of Samis, bidden to his dark deeds. Alastair was nestled at the foot of the mountain that had held Samis's walled stronghold. A mountain stream flowed into it and provided water for the thirsty town.

Already the tension of the place stirred in him, and they had not yet reached the border of the city. He had avoided Alastair like a plague before. He had only set foot in it once since Samis had carried him away half dead in the shock of his burns. And that was the night he'd stolen Vari and the children away from Samis, to get them food even as they were hunted.

"Lord God," he prayed aloud, "guide our steps. Help my heart. Lead us to find what we seek."

Lorne looked over at him with understanding. This could not be easy. There were no guarantees for him. He prayed a silent prayer of his own that they find something and not be left with nothing to show for the journey.

Tahn suddenly slowed down and motioned for his friend to stay close. Lorne tensed. Tahn had a sixth sense for trouble, and keen ears as well.

"In the trees ahead," the dark-haired warrior whispered. "I can't say how many."

Lorne started to put his hand on his sword, but Tahn shook his head. "Just follow me." He drove his horse forward, and Lorne followed, wondering why Tahn did not even try to skirt whoever was waiting.

Three riders blocked their path, and Tahn stopped and nodded to the biggest of them. "Burle," he said. "It's been some time since seeing you."

"It's the Dorn!" Another man, still concealed in the trees, had said it, and Lorne couldn't help but smile at the dismay in his voice.

"Come on 'round," the big man named Burle called to someone. Two other men showed themselves. But there were more. A voice continued in the trees to their left.

"What are you doing here, Tahn?" Burle demanded. "We thought you had yourself another haunt by now." He turned to Lorne and shook his head. "I would've expected to find Vari at your side. What's the matter, Lorne—you have no one else to ride with?"

Tahn smiled and gave his horse a fond pat. "I'll give you three minutes, Burle, to clear our path."

The big bandit didn't seem the least bothered by the warning. "Well, that's enough time for a bit of a chat! Have the Triletts thrown you out, man? What do you want up here again? Aren't looking for me, are you?"

"No," Tahn told him casually. "I've got business in Alastair."

Burle laughed. "There's a lot of hot pots on the fire in that town, Tahn. Wouldn't get too close if I were you."

Lorne glanced over at Tahn, but he wasn't fazed by the bandit's cruel taunt. "About two minutes now," Tahn said calmly.

Burle scowled at him. "I hate to disappoint your pompous tail, but I'm not moving for you. The boys and I, we're going to rob you. You've not but one with you, and you know he's no match for none of us."

Tahn's expression did not change. "Lorne was a boy when you saw him last. He's a man now."

"He been with you all this time?" one of the others asked.

"Yes," Tahn told the tall man to his right. "He's been with me."

"There's not but two of them," Burle pointed out again.

"Give us your bags, Tahn, and we'll have no cause to hurt you."

Tahn looked to all the men around him. "See my path clear in another minute, and I'll not hurt any of you."

"Blast you, Tahn!" Burle exclaimed. "I wasn't wanting to do this the hard way!"

"I'd consider your options, then, if I were you."

Lorne could see the anxiety in the men around them. Tahn had been the first man to defy Samis's orders and live through it. He had survived against terrible odds and instilled in all the other warriors a depth of respect for his stamina and skill. He'd been feared, even, and it was still working to his benefit.

"We got no quarrel with them, Burle," a younger man named Judson said. "They've got swords. It'd slow us down to be tending wounded."

Several of the men were already backing up, but Burle hadn't moved. "I reckon we know you can fight, Tahn," he admitted. "We've got you with numbers, but you'd have some blood before we took you down." He shook his head and sighed. "There's no use working so hard for whatever you've got. Jud's right that we've got no quarrel." He turned to his men. "We'll be going to get us some easier meat."

But he turned back to Tahn. "I'm not afraid of you, though. If you give me cause for a quarrel, I'll cut your throat myself, and anyone with you, no matter how charmed they say you are." He started to turn his horse.

"You were boys once!" Tahn suddenly shouted to all the men. "You were hungry and afraid once! Do you really want to live this way, terrorizing the innocent? Don't you remember what it was like? You're strong men now. Why would you be bandits?"

But the men had turned their horses and were riding away. "Remember Samis!" Tahn shouted after them. "You could find an honorable path! Would you rather be hated as he was? And die unmourned?"

Burle's band fled at a gallop. And when they were gone, Lorne turned to Tahn with a satisfied smile. It was a pleasure to see those warrior-bandits back down. Lorne expected Tahn to share his satisfaction, and he was surprised to see him bow his head.

"Why can't they see it, Lorne?" he asked. "They could be free. They could do what you have done, what I have done, in choosing not to hurt anyone anymore. But they let us go because we're strong. Who is to help the weak?"

Lorne looked at him a long time. "You'll meet up with them again. I know you. You'll not let it be this way." He gazed up at the clouds and sighed.

"Do I worry you, Lorne?"

"You didn't. Not until now, sir. But whatever we find in Alastair, there'll be this to face."

They rode on toward the town, stopping to drink and water the horses at the stream. When the first houses came into view, Tahn stopped again.

"What is it?" Lorne asked.

"Someone in this town might know better than I do who I am," Tahn told him with a sigh. "I wonder that I didn't come asking before."

"You couldn't. Some things wait till we're ready. Like the rest of us should have left Samis before we did. But we couldn't. Not till the old man was as good as dead. And this place was just as bad as him to you, I reckon."

Tahn nodded. So clearly he remembered someone rushing through the angry mob to douse him with the contents of their steaming pot. And he'd thought he might spend eternity with his own searing screams.

"The city's quiet this evening," Lorne said slowly.

"Supper time," Tahn replied. "Are you hungry?"

"No."

"Good. Let's go on, then."

In the depths of the little city, Tiarra was feeling better. The strange man from St. Thomas's had stayed all of that night, and in the morning Mikal had come to tell her that Vale Sade had changed his mind. Martica was feeling better too, and had actually gotten up for the first time in weeks.

52

The money Lucas had given her had been enough to replace what was lost and buy more food besides. And now Tiarra was back to work. There would be pay, after all.

But it was never pleasant work, and now it was busy, which made it all the worse. Outside were the sound of horses and the raucous voices of many men. It made Tiarra groan. She hated to see patrons come in already rowdy. They were more likely to grow foul that way. She was glad she worked the day this time and would not have to stay so long into the night.

The coarse voices continued outside for a while, and then six men burst through the door and took up the big table in the corner. She'd seen all but one of them before, and she knew they were trouble. They always had plenty of money. But they were vile and untrustworthy men.

This evening, though, they didn't yell for their drinks with the impatience they usually displayed. Instead, they seemed more intent upon whatever they'd come in discussing.

"What if he stays around for a while?" one of them was saying. "What will we do about it?"

"We'll do nothing if he leaves us alone," said the biggest. "If he doesn't leave us alone, we draw swords."

"It's not like Tahn to give us advantage," another man said. "He'll not let himself get surrounded again if he knows he's got to fight it to the end. He knew we'd move. No doubt of that."

"You heard what he said," Burle answered impatiently. "He's not here to fight us. You act like idiots."

Tiarra managed to get to their table as quickly as she could with six full mugs. The name Tahn had stuck out to her ears like bristlegrass in a barley field.

"Keep 'em full over here, girl," Burle commanded her.

"Yes, sir."

"And when you get a minute," one of the others added, patting his knee, "come and sit right here."

Tiarra turned from them to the next table with an angry heart. These men were selfish, filthy beasts, and she would rather spit on them than sit in their company.

But she was glad they did not bother to talk quietly.

"I think you're wrong about Tahn, Morrey," one of the men was saying. "I can't say that he'd care who had the advantage. He just does what he's about, even when it'll cost him. You saw that last year when he took arrows for that girl we caught."

"The Dorn has a way of surviving, that's for sure," another man added.

Tiarra's stomach knotted. They were talking about her brother. When did they see him? Where?

"I still think we were lied to about Samis," one of them declared. "I think Tahn killed him. You all know Samis wasn't the kind to do himself in."

"Why don't you just ask him about it next time we see him, Kert?" a tall man taunted. "You got backbone for that?"

"Shut up," Burle barked.

"What kind of business you suppose he's got in Alastair?" someone asked.

"I haven't got the slightest care," Burle growled. "And I'm not wanting to hear any more about it, neither. Shut up and let me drink in peace!"

The big man must be their leader, Tiarra decided, because no one wanted him mad. The conversation turned to other things. And the time crawled by slowly for Tiarra, who was now itching to get out of that tavern and run home to warn Martica. Tahn Dorn in Alastair? After seventeen years? What could he want, indeed?

It was long past dark when finally Vale let her go. She burst out the tavern door and almost ran into someone just standing there waiting in the shadows. She jumped back from the man with a cry, but it was Mikal.

"What are you doing here?" she demanded of him.

"I wanted to walk you home. I thought it would ease things for you a mite, considering what happened yesterday. No moon tonight, and you get some rough sorts around here."

"Does your father know you've come?"

"No."

"Well, he wouldn't like it. You know that as well as I do! You're supposed to be developing a fine reputation, Mikal, not carousing about at night."

"Don't you like me anymore, Ti?"

She started walking. "I do and I don't, depending on what you're about at the time."

"Thanks," he said as he followed. "That's better than a straight no."

She glanced at him for a moment without stopping. "I wish you'd tell me just why it matters. Do you suppose Mary Stumping would care at all what I think of you?"

"Well, yes," Mikal declared. "I think she would. In fact, I know she does."

She felt like slapping him. "Tell her I think you're a rat, then! To be out here following me when she's making plans to be your bride! Why do you keep after me, anyway?"

"I like you a lot. I always did." He reached for her arm. "It bothered me what happened. I didn't like seeing you hurt that way."

"Thank you for talking to Vale," she said simply and started to turn away.

But he pulled her closer and touched her cheek. "Don't you think we can still be friends? That doesn't have to change, even when I'm married. Mary doesn't have to know." He leaned his face nearer to hers. "I aim to help you, Ti. I want to protect you."

But she pushed him away. "Who will protect me from *you*? You're still trying to buy my kisses! With protection this time!"

"I can't buy them," he said sadly. "I don't want to insult you again. I just wish you'd see clear to give them up willing."

"You're a dog, do you know that?"

"Aren't you even a little glad I still care about you? Why are you angry?"

"That you don't understand makes you all the more a dog, Mikal! Leave me alone. I'll get home fine."

"But you seemed scared when you came out of the tavern. Did you think I was one of those cutthroats?"

She was quiet a long time. "No," she finally said. "I thought you might be my brother."

"Your brother?"

"He's in Alastair, Mikal. That's what I heard tonight."

"Will he look for you?"

She didn't know how to answer. She wasn't even sure what she wanted the answer to be. She just started walking again.

Mikal followed her. "Tell me about it. Are you true afraid?"

She stopped. "Martica said once that I haven't the sense to be true afraid of anything. And I suppose it's so. But she says he's a murderer, and one of those men said it too. My father was the same way, Mikal. They killed my mother. Stabbed her full of holes and left her lay." She looked up at him. "I don't know why I ever wondered if he'd come seeking me. Why would he ever come back here?"

"Let me take you home."

"I'm not afraid, Mikal. And you're still a dog. What do you suppose your father would say if the neighbors told him you were here with me?"

"I'd have to answer for it. But I'd explain it. That's not hard."

"What if *I* told him?" Tiarra challenged.

"You wouldn't do that."

But Tiarra was fuming. "You'd bed me and Mary both if you could get by with it!"

"Kings have done it, Ti! People do all kinds of things for love. We could be happy. And I meant what I said about protecting you."

Tiarra met his words with an icy glare. "I ought to kill you and my brother both."

He stared at her, stunned. "Maybe you're right," he said. "Maybe I should go on home."

She didn't say anything. She just walked off into the darkness toward Vermeel Street, wondering what Martica would say. The old woman had been her mother's friend. Tiarra might have died an infant had it not been for Martica's willingness to take her in.

It didn't matter about Mikal. As soon as she was out of his sight, she quickened her pace, despite her soreness. The streets seemed especially quiet, as though everyone knew there was something strange afoot.

Then coming around the corner by the potter's home, she saw them. Two horses and their riders in front of Martica's old painted house. And the ancient woman, wonder of wonders, was standing outside with her oil lamp in her hands.

Tiarra's heart pounded. Neither man was very big. One had short light hair. The other had hair of long dark waves like hers.

"Go away!" Martica suddenly shouted. "I have nothing to say to you! Go!"

One of the men said something, but Tiarra could not make it out. Martica was screaming at them again to leave, and the one with the long black locks turned to his horse and mounted without another word. His friend followed, and they were soon riding away, leaving Martica standing alone.

Tiarra ran to her, the tension leaping into her throat.

"Get in the house, child, before they see you," Martica ordered. But she was leaning down weakly, and Tiarra wouldn't go without helping her in first.

"It was Tahn Dorn, wasn't it?" she asked immediately, taking the lamp from Martica's hands.

"Ah, child. You know too much. Don't ask me more."

"Why, Martica? What would they do if they saw me?"

"What do evil men do when they carry off a girl? I couldn't say! But I pray God they don't come back."

"What did they want? What did they say?"

Tiarra set the lamp on the table and helped Martica to lie down again, realizing that she'd hardly heard her cough since that stranger Lucas had been there.

"He probably knows your mother had jewelry. He probably came to claim it for himself."

Tiarra felt suddenly hot inside. "Is that what he said?" She could scarcely believe it, despite all she'd been told about him. Would he really come back here for that? Only for that, after all this time? But she remembered something suddenly, and it made her doubt. "Martica, you told me they took her things and you never saw them again. He would remember that. Why would he think there is more? Why would he come?"

"Child . . ." Martica hesitated. This was all too close now, and she was afraid. She had recognized Tahn Dorn immediately, though it had been so long and he'd been so small. Why would he come, indeed? He was asking about the day of the hanging. He was looking for someone to tell him about it. And she was afraid, lest he discover Tiarra and take her away with him into the life he'd inherited, the lawlessness their mother had loathed. "Child," she repeated, "I didn't tell you true. There were a few pieces they didn't take back then. You didn't see them because they had to be sold as you grew, to provide for you."

Tiarra was looking at her with an unreadable expression.

"I'm sorry. Your mother would have wanted you to have them, but I had no choice."

"*You* sold them, Martica?"

"There were only a few pieces left. That devil your father really did make off with the rest."

"Then my brother's come for nothing."

"Let's hope he realizes that quickly."

Tiarra forced a smile. "You were bold to them. I didn't know you had the strength to be up so long."

"I've been up more today, even while you were out."

Tiarra sat quietly for a long time, and Martica tensed, wondering what the girl was thinking. No one in the neighborhood talked of that shameful, long-ago day. No one wanted to speak of their part in it to the girl who was left behind. Tiarra had only Martica's word for what she knew. And everyone had wanted it that way.

"I would have liked to have seen something that was my mother's," Tiarra finally said.

Martica sighed. "Perhaps there's a way. I sold one piece to Mrs. Ovny, Tiarra. I will go and ask her if she has it still and if she might show it to you."

Mikal's mother had a piece of her mother's jewelry? Tiarra scarcely knew what to think of that knowledge. Perhaps she could reclaim it. Surely she could. The things Martica had said about her mother were precious, like a treasure she could hold inside and draw from when the world made her feel utterly useless. To have something that had been her mother's would be a priceless gift. She leaned and hugged Martica, who suddenly coughed. "Thank you for telling me," she said. "Let us hope my brother does not learn it."

7

Tahn and Lorne found a room for the night and settled down to sleep with few words between them. So far, they'd found no one willing or able to tell them much of anything. Tahn had especially searched for that painted house. And the old woman remembered him, that seemed clear. Lorne knew her reaction to them had pierced Tahn, but Tahn wouldn't talk about it. He'd only said they would try again in the morning. They would keep asking around until they found someone to tell them about that day.

Tahn lay awake long after Lorne slept. The old woman had been afraid. She knew who he was, he had no doubt. And it made him wonder. *Dear God, what did I do to put such fear in an old woman's heart?*

He rolled over, remembering the crowd again. Lady Netta had been horrified when she learned what had happened, as though there were nothing that could possibly justify such treatment of a child. But he'd never been sure. Inside he'd always held a dark shame, an overpowering feeling that it must have been his fault. And the woman's fearful shouts seemed to witness to that.

"My Lord," he prayed, "you've given me so much mercy. I've asked for so much. And you've not failed to forgive. Help me learn the truth here so I can clear my heart before you again. I don't know the woman's name, but give her peace, Lord. Help her to rest well without fear of me in her sleep. I did not come here to be a trouble to anyone."

He knew someone had run up to the old woman when

60

they left. He'd heard the footsteps and a murmur of voices behind him. But they had a right to be left alone.

Sleep came hard that night. And he dreamed hard, for the first time in a long while, of Samis's whip and the cold clank of his locking door. He saw the sword in his own hand drip with blood again and again and the poison of it filling his soul. He saw a man named Karll fall before him, the life draining away. And he knew he would have turned that sword on himself were it not for his terror at the flames that awaited him.

Samis's raging face possessed his dream, and he shook, a little child living in fear. But suddenly someone was holding a lace kerchief over his wound and speaking words of peace. Netta. The dear Lady Trilett. She touched his hair. And he rolled awake.

For a moment the blood of his past overwhelmed him again. But Netta had said that God sees only the blood of his dear Son, washing away the sin forever.

He sat up with a question suddenly in his mind. *Have you forgiven yourself?* Lord Trilett had asked him that once. And he was still never quite sure of the answer.

"You all right, Tahn?" Lorne was suddenly sitting up beside him, looking strangely pale in the darkness.

He sighed. "Yes. Did I wake you?"

Lorne was quiet for a moment before answering. "No. I was dreaming of fighting again. And Samis."

Tahn shook his head. Was it a poison in this place? "Thank God for Jesus," he told his friend.

Lorne nodded. "Does it ever bother you still?"

It wasn't easy to know how to answer. And then it came to him. "I think there are two valleys in my mind, Lorne. In God's, I know all is well. But in the devil's dark valley, the burden is cast at me again, and I would despair of myself. I thank God I am free to live in his valley and not claim the other."

"The devil keeps trying, though, doesn't he?"

"He likes the pain in the world. He wants us to not only feel it but cause more of it."

"He'll never have me again," Lorne declared. "A night like this, when I dream, I'll just use it to thank God all the more."

Tahn smiled. He looked out the tiny window with sudden confidence. "The sun will be up before long. God will guide us today. We will find something before it is gone down again."

That afternoon, Orin Sade had filled himself at his brother's tavern and was on his way home. By then he'd heard about a stranger who had come asking about Sanlin Dorn, though not by name. Orin was one of many who remembered the day they'd hanged Dorn, and he was no more anxious than anyone else to talk about it, especially if the stranger was Sanlin's son. There'd been tales of the boy surviving to become just the deceiver and more of a fighter than his father had been. A man like that could be seeking vengeance, and Alastair would have good cause to fear.

He saw them first as he was crossing Market Street. Just two men and their horses. One he might have seen anywhere and never batted an eye. But the other! No wonder people were nervous. He had the look of Sanlin Dorn about him. The same wavy hair and the same dark eyes. The same strength in the way he moved that made people want to stand clear. It didn't matter that he seemed smaller. It was like being in the presence of a ghost.

Orin could see the old weaver shaking his head and the strangers beginning to move on. But then the dark one looked up, directly into his gaze. He nearly choked. It wasn't just a casual glance. And the stranger was definitely Sanlin's son. He didn't turn away, he didn't even move, as though he were waiting for Orin himself to bridge the distance between them. Orin's heart pounded. What could a mite of a boy remember about that time? He greatly hoped it wasn't much. But he saw the young Dorn say something to his companion, and they both started in Orin's direction. It was more than he could take. He turned and fled.

"Magna!" he shouted as he neared his yard. "You know nothing! You haven't seen me! You hear me?" He ran past her and headed straight for the old horse behind the house.

But she ran after him and caught his arm. "You've been drinkin' again, Orin Sade, and it's makin' you crazy! There's nobody at all behind you!"

"You just haven't seen him yet! He's comin', all right. It's Sanlin's boy come back. Magna, let go of me! There's no tellin' what he'll do!" He jerked away from her and grabbed frantically for the bridle that hung on a post.

He climbed through the rail of the fence and started for the horse, but the mare knew his anxiety and wasn't eager for him in that frame of mind.

"Sable, you blasted horse leather! Stand still!"

"Orin, are you sure?" Magna tried to calm him. "Maybe it was someone else."

"It was him. It was him, you'll see. You tell him whatever you have to. Tell him we didn't live here then."

Magna looked back in the direction her husband had come. There was one rider. A handsome young man with short blond hair.

"Orin—you've been drinkin'. Did he even talk at you?"

He didn't try to answer. He had the rope on the horse's neck and was fighting to set the bridle straight.

"You gonna ride her barebacked?" his wife questioned.

"There's no time," he said. He thought he saw a shadow, something move by the house, and it made him near panic. "Get out of here, Magna," he said. "Go to your cousin in Joram." He tried to mount the horse, but his tension was making her skittish. And suddenly, the dark-haired stranger appeared in full view, ahead of him, beside the grape arbor. Magna Sade screamed.

"Please," the stranger told them. "Don't fear me! I just want to talk to you."

"Leave us!" Magna pleaded. She fell to her knees. "God have mercy."

63

Tahn didn't move. Samis had counted it a pleasure to be feared. But it cut at Tahn, and all the more because he didn't understand. "I won't hurt you," he told them. "God is my witness. Good people, please. Just let me ask you questions." He fought back his own tense emotion and gestured to Lorne not to get too close. It would only make matters worse for them to keep drawing in on the frightened couple.

"You got no reason to be here!" Orin shouted. "Leave us alone!"

Tahn lifted his hands. "I'm not armed. And I've not come to hurt anyone. But you know me—I know you do! Please tell me what you know. I was here as a child. With a man I barely remember. I need to know what happened. I need to know if I have kin."

Magna looked up at her husband. "He was little, Orin. Maybe he truly don't know."

Orin shook his head. "You can't believe him. He aims to see what we'll say. He aims for us to let him get close."

"What's to stop him gettin' close if he chose to, anyhow?" she asked. "He could have rushed at us. He could have had you in the dirt by now." She stood to her feet and looked Tahn over carefully. "What's your name?" she called.

"Magna, shut up!" Orin demanded. "We've got to get away from him."

"I'm Tahn Dorn," Tahn answered the woman. "The man behind you is Lorne Graise. We'll not harm you. Our Lord Christ is witness to the words that we've come only for information. Please help me."

"What if he really don't know?" Magna questioned her husband. "What if he's tellin' us God's truth?"

"What if he's not?"

"What's your pa's name?" Magna called out to him again.

"I don't know, lady."

"Who was your ma, then?"

Tahn could only sigh. "I don't know. I remember a man

64

was hanged, and I believe I had been with him. But I know nothing before that. If you could tell me anything more, I would owe you my gratitude. Please. Do you know who he was?"

Magna stared at him in silence.

"We can't tell you anythin'!" Orin shouted. "We know nothin' of the kind! Go away!"

Tahn bowed his head. People knew what happened. That was obvious. But no one would speak of it. What terrible thing had made this town so afraid? What kind of a monster had the man been? And himself so young. Was he a monster too?

"I will go," he said slowly, "if that is what you want. Please forgive me for frightening you. Forgive me for whatever I may have done. But I want to know of it, sir. Whatever it is, I need to know. If there are people here I've hurt, I want to make it right somehow. Whatever we did, I'm sorry! But tell me! Please help me know where I've come from. I swear to you I'll hurt no one now."

He stood waiting for an answer, feeling broken and small.

"We've got to talk to him," Magna whispered.

"No!" Orin scolded. "Let him go. We don't have to tell him nothin'."

"He's standin' there askin' forgiveness of *you*, Orin! How can you let that be? He was a child!"

"He'll kill me if we tell him the truth."

"He's naming Christ, Orin."

"That don't matter."

The stranger suddenly whistled, and Orin jumped. But nothing happened until a horse came from behind the next house and toward him. Tahn Dorn was unarmed, like he'd said, but there was a sword among the horse's bags, and it made Orin all the more jittery.

Lorne had progressed in a wide circle around them and was nearing his friend. "I don't know what you fear," he said to them. "But we only want to know if Tahn has family. Was the man his kin? Were there any others? We have money. We will pay you."

Neither of the Sades answered.

And Tahn turned toward his horse. "Leave them a silver for their trouble, Lorne. I seem to owe them something."

Magna bit her lip and looked at her husband again. "Wait!"

"Magna, no!" Orin grabbed at his wife, the panic gripping him.

"Let me go, Orin! Don't you owe *him*? Don't you? Can't you remember the skinny little thing running so hard? Can't you remember his screams? Can't you? My God, Orin! Don't you care what you done?"

Tahn fell to his knees, shaking his head. And Lorne jumped from his horse.

"Shut up, Magna!" Orin screamed. "Shut up!" He slapped her hard, and she fell backward. He raised his hand to slap her again, but Lorne was suddenly upon them.

"Don't be hurting the lady," he warned. "We're about nothing but the truth, and I aim to hear it! We'll not harm you, sir. But I won't watch you beat her! Let her go."

Orin released his hold on his wife and faced him, now trembling. "Just go away! It was a long time ago. It wasn't my doing. I can't change anything! Just leave us alone!"

Lorne ignored him and turned to Magna. "Will you please talk to my friend? You have no idea what this means to him." He reached his hand to help her up, and slowly she moved hers to accept it. She rose up with a tiny nod, wiping tears from her eyes.

"Curse you, Magna!" Orin hollered. "You wouldn't leave me. You just always wanted me dead! Ain't it so?" He went back to his horse, grabbed the rope, and pulled the bridle into place.

He rode out of Alastair at a run, and they didn't even turn their heads.

Magna Sade approached Tahn slowly. He was still on his knees, just watching her, looking afraid and suddenly very young.

"He . . . he poured it, didn't he?" Tahn choked the words out with a shudder.

Magna knelt in front of him, her eyes filled with tears. "Yes, lad. I'd been heatin' the pot. But I didn't know . . . he didn't tell me—"

Tahn reached for her hand, and she grasped both of his and squeezed them. He looked down at the ground but then up at her again. "Please . . . tell me why."

"Dear God, help us," she whispered. "Do you remember anything of your mother, lad?"

He shook his head. "I'm not sure. I think I've remembered her touch. But I don't even know her face."

"Her name was Karra Loble. They say your father killed her. It was an awful crime, and it was him who was hung. His name was Dorn too. Sanlin Dorn. You resemble him a great deal."

"Did I help him? Is that why they did it? Did I help him kill my own mother?" He was shaking, unable to picture it, unable to take it in.

And she leaned forward and put her arms around him. "How old were you?"

"Four. Maybe. I've never been completely sure."

"They said you helped him. But can you even imagine it possible for one so small?"

Tahn looked down at the dirt. "I used to think that I was born for nothing but darkness. I can't say what I might have been capable of."

"And you don't remember it at all?"

Tahn shook his head again. "I dream of running down a street, looking for her. I hear a baby's cry, and I follow the sound, but it stops. I get very upset that I can't find her."

Magna nodded. "There were women who could not believe it could be true of you, or any child. I think you had a care for your mother. I think if you did any of it, it was unknowing, or by the force of your father."

"Do you know anything of a baby?"

"Your sister. Half or full, I don't know. There was question whether you were truly her mother's, or she even truly

67

your father's. I think she has the Dorn in her, though. Her hair is so much like yours."

His heart leaped into his throat. "She's alive? Still in Alastair?"

She smiled. "Yes, lad. And she works for my brother-in-law. You're not what they say at all, are you?"

"I'm not sure what they say. I've been much."

"It's a relief to me that you're not minded for revenge. It was an angry mob and no legal justice done."

"My sister. Where can I find her?"

"Vale Sade's tavern by the coppersmith. Her name is Tiarra Loble. She's so much your size. I think you would know her by the looks."

They rode through the early evening streets, paying no attention to eyes turned their way. Tahn's stomach had never churned so dreadfully, not even when first facing Lord Trilett, or Netta's first kiss.

"Lorne," he said suddenly. "She would know about our mother's death, I'm sure. Perhaps she'll not want to see me."

"How could she not?"

"If I had a part, killing her mother—"

"Tahn, you could no more have been responsible for that than I can for being sold."

"How can you know for sure?"

"I know you."

"And you know what I was."

Lorne nodded. "I know how you killed, Tahn. You were too good at it. But it was Samis who put you to it. And he couldn't have done it if he didn't have you bound beyond reason. Lucas told me the state you were in. Not sane in his hands. You thought you'd burn again, endlessly, if you disobeyed him." Lorne looked over at his friend. "Am I right?"

Tahn bowed his head. "Yes."

"But you stopped. You defied him anyway, while still expecting his torture. Right?"

"Yes."

"Then it's not in you. It's not *you*, Tahn. It can't be. If you hurt anyone here, you were forced to it, and just as cruelly."

Vale Sade's tavern was an old square building that looked like it had weathered a lot of traffic. Tahn insisted that Lorne go in alone to find the girl. He didn't want to see the shock—or worse—the fear in her face if he just walked in to her. Let her have a moment for it to sink in and to decide for herself whether she would see him.

There were just a few patrons inside, with one big man tending the liquor. And a thin girl with Tahn's hair wiping at a table. Her back was to Lorne. Her clothes were poor, and she wore no shoes on her dirty feet.

"Excuse me," Lorne said, and she turned around. He hesitated for a moment, struck by her features. She didn't look much like Tahn in her face. There were bruises that brought questions to his mind. But she was truly beautiful anyway, and he found himself catching his breath. "Are you Tiarra Loble?"

"Yes," she answered with some hesitation in her voice.

"My name is Lorne Graise. I'm a friend of your brother's. He stands outside, dear lady, longing to meet you."

She put her hand on a chair and stood straight, hoping he could not see how she quaked inside at his revelation. Her brother really had come to her. What should she do? "Why has he come?" she asked with a quiet voice, glancing over at Vale, whom she knew was watching them.

"To find if he had kin, ma'am. He's anxious to know you. He only found out today that you live."

She wondered at that. Had he thought she'd been killed too? Was that part of the plan back then? "I think he's not welcome in Alastair," she said, still quiet. "We do not favor killers here."

The man called Lorne shook his head. "Please, miss. Don't judge him until you know. He's a good man. He only knows part of the truth of this town, and he is wounded for it. He needs to meet you. Please come and talk to him."

She stared at him. How could it be as he said? "You're his friend. Perhaps you're all the killer and thief he is."

"I am redeemed of God," Lorne replied. "As he is."

The words angered Tiarra. The same God who let street children suffer, killers could claim! "Just go from me!" she cried. "Tell him to go back to his rich life and leave me alone!"

But Lorne would not give up. "It is your own brother. Just look on his face! It will break his heart if you won't. He's no threat to you."

She was quiet. She glanced over at Vale again, but he said nothing and gave her no indication of anything. It would have been easier if he had commanded her to stay at her work. But she knew how her heart would have leaped outside then, wishing for a glimpse of her brother, if only to know close up what her own flesh and blood might look like.

"Please, miss," Lorne begged again. "Speak a word with him."

She glanced toward the heavy door and stepped toward it with an instant decision she hoped she would not regret. Emotions tumbled inside her as she pulled it open. What did he want? What might he do?

Her brother was standing in the street, his horse behind him. She was surprised that he looked scarcely bigger than she. She remembered the long hair from last night at Martica's. But his eyes were so dark and stormy that she could not keep her gaze on them. His clothes were very decent ones, right down to the good boots. And she couldn't help but think of him living high, while she struggled every day with her endless burden. "Do you do anything there at the Trilett estate?" she asked without thinking. "Or just live off the love of your lady?"

The words surprised him, she could tell. But he didn't respond.

"He's the captain of their guard," Lorne answered for him with anger in his voice. "Set to protect the family."

She lowered her head. "Perhaps you should not be so far away from them, then."

70

She could feel Tahn Dorn's eyes still on her, and it made her nervous. Had it been a mistake to come out here? Martica would think so.

"I will go back to them," her brother said slowly. "You are right. But please tell me if it is well with you. You seem hurt. Are you safe? Are you happy?"

His questions took her by surprise. She would never have expected him to care. "Why are you here?"

He took a step toward her but stopped. "I had to come, to find out if I had family. But I never thought you could know more of me than I know of you."

The words shook her. Was this a trick? How could he not know if he had family?

Before she could say anything, more words came tumbling from him. "Please tell me of yourself! Tell me what you know of your mother, if you would. I remember almost nothing. Surely someone has told you. I'm so sorry. A woman told me of my father, why he was hanged. I'm so sorry! I remember looking for her. And you've been in my dreams! After so long, God would have me find you. Please don't be afraid. Whatever I've been to you, please believe that I would never hurt you now!"

She stared at him. He looked so sincere. Even wounded, like his friend had said. But how could he not remember? A boy of twelve, well practiced in the cunning ways of his father? Martica had told her all about it. "You're lying to me," she said. "You knew my mother. But you never gave me the chance."

Tahn just closed his eyes. But Lorne persisted. "How could you think he would remember her well? How could you hold him accountable? He was only four years old!"

She turned to him in shock but slowly shook her head. "You're lying to me! What do you want, to come here deceiving me? We have nothing! Go away!" She turned back to the tavern's old door, thinking of Martica, who took her in, gave her a home, saved her alive when she had no one. With shaking hands, she went back in to her work, leaving them standing alone outside.

"There's something strange about this town, Tahn," Lorne said. "We're not getting the whole story."

But Tahn said nothing, only reached behind him for the reins of his horse.

"She just doesn't understand," his friend assured him. "I don't think she knows what really happened any more than you do. Someone's told her something, but that doesn't mean it was accurate."

Tahn mounted Smoke in silence.

"I don't want to leave," Lorne told him. "Not till we know more. It's not right. This town's holding on to a secret."

"We're not leaving," Tahn said as he turned his mount. But that was all he would say, and they rode together down the darkening street.

8

Just a few minutes after she heard them leaving, more horses arrived, plenty of them. Tiarra had never been scared by the sound before. There were always men descending on this place. But this time it made her shiver inside. She wanted to run away as far as she could and just throw herself down and cry.

It was the rough group of men who had talked about her brother, all six of the ones who had been there the previous night, plus two more. But they were two of the ones who had attacked her! The sight of them set her heart pounding, and it was all she could do not to turn tail and run.

And they had noticed her too. "Will you look there," one of them said. "Toma, it's the wildcat Lucas saved."

The other one was looking her over with his cold eyes. "Yes," he agreed. "I guess we bruised her. But I seem to recall we had unfinished business."

"Sit down," Burle told them gruffly. "This is a decent establishment. If you've got something to settle with the pretty little wench, we'll see to it later." He turned to Tiarra and winked. "Fill us up and keep 'em full, girly, and we'll be especially good to you tonight."

Tiarra was angry, disgusted at these beasts who acted as though they had a right to treat her as they pleased. But she was scared too, like she'd never been before. She knew they would linger. They would be waiting for her when she left, or they would follow her out if they stayed that long. And she could not count on that strange man, Lucas, from St. Thomas's to be there for her this time.

73

She went to Vale with her plea. "Let me go, please. These are the ones who hurt me."

He shook his head. "They'd likely follow you out, girl. You don't want that. Wait it out. Maybe Mikal'll come again. But there ain't much I can do. Just stay here. They'll get tired of waiting around eventually and move on."

But she knew better. She knew by the eyes of the big one and the one named Toma what they had in mind. And they would not be willing to leave without it.

It was a torturous night, serving them drinks and trying to keep out of reach of their filthy hands. They talked and they laughed. They said they should hunt down that Lucas and skin him alive, since he'd become trouble to them in this town.

And they cursed Tahn Dorn and his young friend. They said they were like women to go and work as guardsmen for a noble house. And they laughed about him being in this town again, wondering out loud if he still screamed in his dreams.

It chilled her, making it nearly impossible for her to think of her work. She tripped once. She spilled things three times. But for once, Vale said nothing. He was scared, she knew he was, that they might start something right here in the tavern. He wouldn't be much help—he couldn't be against so many. And if it came to that, he'd far sooner leave with his life than risk losing it for her.

Other customers came and went, but the men at the back table lingered. Tiarra found herself wishing she had a strong poison to top off their drinks and kill them all where they sat.

But finally, Burle rose to his feet. "Any of you who can still ride had better come with me," he told his band. He nodded to Tiarra with a smile and another wink. "Be seein' you again."

They were going out, every one of them, without incident or another hand in her direction. Vale was breathing relief, but Tiarra was not comforted at all. She could hear their horses leaving, but she knew it was not done.

74

She stayed at the tavern longer than she ever had, hoping Vale would let her stay till daylight. But after a while, he called her to him. "You'd better go home," he said. "You stayed past your time already. Martica will be sore wondering at you." He was silent for a moment and then added, "We heard 'em leaving with their horses. They're well gone."

She stepped into the black night, glancing over the rooftops in the direction of St. Thomas's. But the sight of it made her angry somehow in a way she didn't understand. What if those men *were* out here somewhere? What if they killed her? What was there so good to live for anyway? The hungry eyes of children, and a brother who wouldn't even give her the truth?

The only thing so bad about dying might be the letting them get it done. Better that they be accosted themselves, that they might know what it felt like.

She ran down the street like a cat, wary of every shadow. At the head of the second street, she heard horses and turned to go the other way, but it was too late.

"There she is!" someone yelled.

One of them ran from the doorway of a building, another two from behind a fence. The others were still on their horses, and two of them drove their mounts into her path, cutting off her retreat. She screamed and started to fight, knocking away the first one who reached her on foot. But a strong man on a horse grabbed her and was pulling her up to him. They would just carry her off, do what they wanted, and leave her in some ditch somewhere. She tried to wrench her arm from the man's grasp but could not get away.

Suddenly there was the rush of other horses. She barely saw the dark shadow of a man who leaped from his mount at the bandit that held her. She landed in the dirt, and they were right beside her. She knew the long hair of the man on top, and she shivered and jumped to her feet. Tahn Dorn? Her brother? Come to save her?

One of the other bandits rushed in their direction, and she punched at him with a wild scream. Then she saw that the

75

blond man was there too, standing beyond her and holding off another bandit with the point of his sword.

"Brothers!" Tahn shouted with a cry that pierced her. "Leave in peace. You will gain nothing here."

She stood and stared at him as the biggest man stepped from his horse and approached them.

"This is nothing to you, Tahn! Get out!"

"No," Tahn told him. "You're leaving. All of you."

Burle laughed, the drink emboldening him. "You and Lucas are so high and mighty. I don't know what the devil happened to you, but we don't interfere in *your* doings. You've got no business in ours! I told you about a quarrel, Tahn. You're coming very close to getting yourself one."

"You've got two minutes this time," Tahn said with icy intensity.

But Burle just laughed again. "That's not gonna work this time around! We're not afraid of you. Look at how many's with me. You've got nothing but Lorne and that feisty little tavern wench!"

Lorne had pulled Tahn's sword from Smoke's back and tossed it into his hand.

"You've got one minute now," Tahn said.

"He's got the fire in him," one of the bandits said nervously.

But Burle wasn't about to back down. "I can't let you rule me, Tahn. I'm never going to let any man rule me again! This is my town now, and I'll do what I want here, no matter who puts himself in the way. I curse you and Lucas, and Lorne! Why don't you go back where you came from?"

"I already have." Tahn pulled his sword from its sheath with a prayer in his heart. *You know I don't want to do this, Lord! You know I don't want to shed blood. Help me! I can't just let them do what they will!* He looked at his sister, with her fiery eyes and doubled fists. "Stay by my horse," he told her. But she didn't even seem to hear him.

"Get around 'em, men!" Burle shouted. "If they aim to fight, they won't any of 'em escape!"

He and Morrey rushed Tahn, and swords clashed. Morrey

76

fell first, but another man took his place. Lorne was just as occupied, struggling to keep back two. Toma rushed forward, still determined to get his hands on Tiarra, but Tahn slashed his arm from behind. Tiarra kicked her attacker to the ground and ripped the sword from his side. By that time, Lorne had a man down. Then Tahn thrust at Burle, and the big man lost his balance. Tahn was standing so close over him, he tried to come up with a thrust of his own, but Tahn cast his point deep into his shoulder and then spun around to push away the man behind him.

"Give it up, Burle!" Tahn pleaded. "Or I'll have to kill you."

All around them the fighting stopped. There were two men still with the horses. Of the six other bandits, four of them were wounded. Toma backed away from Tiarra, and two of the others retreated toward their horses.

Burle sat and stared at his bloody shoulder, his sword arm now weakened. "The fight's yours tonight," he said, pulling himself up slowly. "But curse you, Tahn! It's not over! I've got more men. I'll not let you do this to me!" His own oozing blood was making him feel faint. He turned and looked at one of the uninjured men. "Get me my horse!" he yelled. Then he turned back to Tahn. "You'd better leave this town! I'll find a way to kill you and that stupid wench, and anybody fool enough to help you. There's more of us. You know there is! And you've got yourself a quarrel now."

"She's my sister," Tahn told him with quiet steel.

As though his words were a fiery sword, all of the men moved to their horses, some of them already riding away. But Tiarra still held a sword in her hand. She hadn't gotten to use it. Quickly, she moved to the injured man who trailed the rest and lifted the weapon high. But Tahn was behind her and caught her by the wrists. The sword fell to the dust, and she turned to him with angry eyes.

"Are you all right?" he asked abruptly. "It doesn't help to fall on their backs. It doesn't make you feel any better."

She stood silent, fuming at him, but knowing just the same that he had saved her life.

77

He turned to his friend. "How bad is it?"

Tiarra spun around in surprise. She hadn't realized that the blond man was hurt. But he was losing blood from his left arm.

"I'll be all right," he said. "God is with us." But he sat down in the street beside an iron hitch post.

Tiarra watched her brother take water and a cloth from his horse. He cut Lorne's sleeve to expose the wound, washed it out, and then held the cloth tightly over it. "You need to go back to Onath," he told his friend.

"There's no way I'm leaving you here alone!"

Tiarra watched them, still uncertain what sort of men they were, grateful as she was. They knew those bandits. Tahn had even called them brothers.

"I'm going home," she told them suddenly.

"Not alone," Tahn told her. "You will wait for us. We'll take you."

He didn't ask her permission. He just said how it would be. But she didn't argue.

"Lucas has been here," he told Lorne. "God be praised for him! If he's here yet, we'll have to find him."

Tiarra glanced toward St. Thomas's. Should she tell him? Was he a true friend to the someday-priest? "Who is Lucas?" she decided to ask.

"Like a brother," Tahn answered. "We were warriors together once, all of us." He turned and saw her uncertain eyes. "I'm sorry for what's happened. We'd best get you home."

He wrapped Lorne's arm carefully and helped him mount. Then he took Smoke's rein and turned to Tiarra. "Is it far?"

"Not bad."

"If you can ride—"

"I don't need to ride."

He held the rein out to her. "You may."

"No." She abruptly turned away from him and started walking. They followed, she knew it, with the blond on his horse and her brother walking, leading his mount. Could he

78

not ride if she chose to walk? It infuriated her. She fought the tears in her eyes and the questions churning inside. How could he seem so good? And why was she being hateful toward him anyway? She should tell him Lucas was at St. Thomas's. She knew she should. It seemed they had a common enemy. But she was unwilling to trust him. Their father had been so clever at seeming good too. Tahn Dorn must be lying about his past in Alastair. He must be. Or Martica was. And that would make no sense.

When they reached Vermeel Street, Tahn knew the house they would go to. He watched his sister quicken her pace toward the home of the old artist, and he wondered all the things that the woman could tell him, if only she would.

But Tiarra wondered how Tahn would react to Martica after she'd screamed them away before. And she was equally concerned for Martica's reaction. It would be better, certainly, not to bring these men inside. She stopped in the street and pointed. "There it is," she said. "Thank you for seeing me here. You should go now."

But Tahn hadn't stopped. "Not yet."

"She's been sick," Tiarra protested. "You shouldn't come in."

He was studying the little old house in the darkness, remembering how it looked in his dream. So much fresher. "Have you lived here always?"

"No," she answered with some venom. "I had a mother once."

Tahn turned and looked at her. That bitterness might always exist between them. But he dared to ask more anyway. "Is the woman kin to us?"

Tiarra didn't want to answer his questions. Still, it didn't seem right to deny him when he'd just rescued her. She would try. Maybe he would go away peacefully then. "She's no kin. A friend of my mother's."

"What has she told you about me?"

"That you are a killer." She knew he would react to that. He would have to.

"In God's grace, people change." He held the horse as Lorne dismounted.

It frightened her that he did not deny it. It frustrated her that they were not leaving, despite her request. What should she do? She couldn't ask them in. Martica wouldn't have it.

She heard coughing inside the house and turned her head.

"Let me in with you to see her," Tahn said. "I have many questions."

"She doesn't want to talk to you. We can't trust you, whether you fight bandits or not."

"For God's sake!" Lorne exclaimed. "You know he won't hurt you! Why can't you talk with him?"

Lorne's earnest eyes constrained her. Could they both carry a deception this completely? Martica would have to understand that they'd helped her.

But the old woman had heard voices and was not happy about it. As their footsteps crossed the first room, she cried out, "Child! What are you thinking to bring strangers into the house?"

"The bandits were at me again," Tiarra said hurriedly. "These men helped me, Martica."

"You needn't bring them home at night!" The old woman looked up as Tiarra entered. And right behind her came Tahn Dorn.

"Get out of my house," she said immediately.

"Please, Martica," Tiarra cried. "He saved my life tonight."

Martica stared at him a long while, puzzling over what to do. She wouldn't have expected such a deed. Why should he help anyone in Alastair? And now, Tiarra was beholden to him. But maybe that was the point. "You say it was bandits, child?"

She nodded, looking from Martica to Tahn quickly. Martica looked angry, despite what she'd just been told. But Tahn looked like he was in pain, as though he'd seen something that grieved him terribly.

"I heard it said that before Onath you were a hired fighter," Martica was saying as she stared hard at Tahn. "And that some such men are become bandits now, robbing all the travelers passing by here. Are they the same men you were with?"

"Some of them."

"Then you know them well?"

"I once did."

"Tiarra, child!" Martica exclaimed. "How can you know what this one is about? He might have set the bandits on you himself, just so he could play the hero for you!"

Lorne started to speak, but Tahn grasped his arm and stopped him. Tiarra was staring at the old woman in shock.

"Martica—"

"No, child. I want you to listen to me. This world is full of deceivers. The devil himself would appear as an angel of light! Did he let all the bandits get away?" She coughed with a straining effort, and Tiarra was stricken at how quickly she could be so sick again.

"They all left," Tiarra said in a tiny voice.

"I could have told you that. What are you about, Tahn Dorn? Why have you come? What do you want with this dear child?"

Tahn was quiet for a moment, just looking at her. When he spoke, he sounded somehow far away, in another time. "Why do you hate me so?"

She coughed and then struggled to get her breath. She was so nearly choked again. Tiarra got her a cloth and water. Martica feared not for her own death, nor even for Tiarra, who was almost in the clutches of her strange brother. She feared now for whatever of her own life remained, that Tiarra would catch her in her lie and leave her alone to suffer. She must try to keep her, somehow.

"You know what happened to your mother, child," the old woman stammered. "You know you can't trust him."

"Tell me what happened," Tahn pressed.

"You're a wonder to come back here!" Martica exclaimed.

81

"The people fear you, or they wouldn't stand for it. I heard what they say, that a killer is in our midst again."

He ignored the harshness of her words and asked, "Was Karra Loble my mother?"

Martica coughed again. "She was your mother, but you were not her son! You were Sanlin's son, traveling with him, stealing people blind."

"Was it he truly who killed her?"

Martica stared at him for a moment and then struggled angrily to sit up. "You're a fiend!" she yelled. "Even I had no idea you could be such a fiend! How could you dare come here and question that? Have you chosen the devil's part so much? He killed her, and none of your lies can change that. She was a good heart, and you took her away from us. Curse you, boy! How dare you claim otherwise!"

Her words stabbed at Tahn, and Tiarra and Lorne both knew it. They looked at each other for a moment. Tiarra did nothing, but Lorne put his hand on his friend's shoulder.

"Tell me what happened," Tahn pleaded of the old woman again, kneeling at the same time.

"I don't want you in my house."

"I understand. But I'll not hurt you. Please, before I go, tell me my part in what was done, that I may take it before God, lady. It is better to have all in the open and ask his mercy."

"Mercy, you say?" Martica shrieked nervously. "You came looking for her! She knew Sanlin was trouble. But you were her son. How could she refuse you? You came looking for her and received her tender embrace. And then you led her away to her death, boy, to where he was waiting! And you used the knife he'd given you, didn't you, child, always ready to work at his side?"

Tahn just looked at her, struck speechless.

"Do you really expect mercy?" she asked him. "Did your mother receive any?"

He couldn't answer her. He was remembering her, angry and afraid, staring out at him from her doorway. "He's the one!" she'd shouted to someone. "He's the one!"

He looked down at her gnarled old hands and thought of her pointing finger. He'd been looking for his mother. There was no way he could deny that. It had followed him in his dreams. And he had led her to her death? Was that the fear he'd felt? He thought of that soft touch and started shaking. She had loved him. She had claimed him, to her own hurt. Tears filled his eyes, and he bowed his head, unable to contain them.

But Lorne was not willing to believe the tale. "Did you see it happen?" he questioned.

"Get out!" Martica demanded. "Get out of my house!"

"Did it ever matter to you that he was a *child*?" Lorne persisted.

Martica stared at him, the simple question cutting to her heart. Of course she knew he'd been a tiny thing, despite what she'd told Tiarra. And seeing him here, she knew he didn't remember. She should feel guilty, seeing him so affected by her words. His meekness was difficult to bear. How could he have grown to manage that? He was still Dorn's son, even trained by Sanlin's murderous kinsman to deceive and destroy. "I told you to get out," she told them coldly. "I have nothing else to say to you! Go away!"

But Tahn's words jumped into her mind again. *It is better to have all in the open. Ask God's mercy.*

She watched the blond man lean over his friend. She watched them slowly rise in front of her. She remembered the past so well. Sanlin's boy coming in and leaving again with his mother. But in the morning, when Martica already knew that Karra was dead, the boy had come back, alone, searching for his mother again with fear in his eyes. He couldn't find her, for all he tried. And when the crowd came at him, he'd looked so confused. He didn't know. He didn't know why they were angry. He didn't know she was dead. He'd looked for her even then, among the faces of that horrible crowd.

The knowing of it choked at her, and she coughed again, worse. It would gnaw at her, she knew it would, what she was doing to him. But she couldn't tell him in front of Tiarra

83

and have her know how she'd lied. She couldn't make him look the victim in front of the girl! How could she ever keep Tiarra from his grasp then? He might have worked his way into noble graces, but Karra would have feared that for her daughter as much as the lawlessness.

They were leaving, because of her words. But Tahn faced her again, his eyes so deep with hurt that she could not look into them. "I gained no mercy from Alastair then," he said. "I had no chance to beg forgiveness. I do so now." He turned and looked at Tiarra. "Of both of you. Please forgive me."

Martica could scarcely bear it. "Just go," she told him, the emotion breaking over her voice. "Go away from us."

She looked up at Tiarra, who stood in stony silence against the wall. The girl would hate her if she knew. She would hate all of Alastair if she knew what no one would dare to say. They'd known. Men of Alastair had known that Karra was going to die. The cunning old baron had told men he could trust who it was that would do the deed and what must be done to make sure he didn't leave their town alive. Even the boy was supposed to die, that's what the baron had ordered. But no one had known of Sanlin's kin. No one knew of the terrible man who would come and snatch the boy away before he could die in his agony.

She coughed, and suddenly she cried in the midst of it, still haunted by Tahn's words. *Have all in the open. Ask God's mercy.*

Openness might never happen. Not in Alastair, a poor city that bowed to the will of a powerful man who held debt against them. Among the mob that was gathered, someone should have tried to help Karra. Someone should have questioned how the baron had known what would happen, and why no one had witnessed the act. But no one questioned. And now the screams of a child always stood in the way. No one wanted to face the awful depth of their shame.

"Are you all right?" Tiarra asked her, knowing her tears. But Martica couldn't bear her sympathy. Perhaps she deserved to die alone and hated. "Please, child," she said. "Leave me alone."

Tiarra obeyed, struggling in her mind over all she'd just seen. Martica had truly loved her mother. That must be why she was moved so. But she could not understand her brother's tears. If anything really mattered to him so much, then how could things have been the way they'd been?

She followed them out, wondering what they would do now. Would they just go back to Onath? Or would he want to stay, hoping to find jewels, as Martica had said before? She shook her head suddenly. Whatever Tahn Dorn was about, it wasn't that. It just didn't fit him. They were by the horses in the moonlight, and Tiarra stood in the shadow of the doorway watching them.

"Remember the valley of God you told me about," Lorne was saying. "The devil would have you in this, friend, but don't listen to his condemnation. Whatever the truth is, you were a child, and God loved you even then."

"I know," Tahn assured him. "He loves me still, and he's known the truth all along. I'm all right, Lorne. Don't be worrying for me."

"So what do we do now? Find a room again?"

Tahn shook his head. "I don't want to leave Tiarra alone. I shouldn't have told Burle she's my sister. Now he'll think he has a way of getting at me and that he has men enough to do it."

Lorne was quiet for a moment.

"They don't want us in their house," Tahn told him. "But they can't stop us from staying within sight."

"No!" Tiarra suddenly burst in. "You can't. Martica would not have it."

"Forgive me," Tahn told her, "but I've just found you. Regardless of the past or what you think of me, I'll not lose you now to Burle's ragings. Have they troubled you before?"

"Yes," she told him. "Three of them, once before."

"Is that how you got the bruises?"

She nodded.

85

"Do they know where you live?"

"I don't think so."

"Stay here, then," Tahn commanded her. "Don't go back to your work until we have this settled."

"But I have to work!"

He shook his head. "You need to stay here, and Lorne will stay in sight of you until I find someone to send with him back to Onath."

"No!" Tiarra protested. "You can't just decide this!"

Lorne had a protest of his own. "Tahn, I don't want to leave you here alone. Burle will be looking for you."

Tahn sighed. Almost he could wish to leave Alastair himself now. It would be so much simpler. But he knew Burle had meant what he'd said. People would be in danger, especially Tiarra. He couldn't walk away from it, no matter what else this town bore for him. "Do you think I'm wanting to fight them again, Lorne?" he asked. "I want no part of it. The sword! The killing!"

He spoke with such intensity that Tiarra stared at him.

"They'll not be slowed by drink the next time. And they've already been a terror on the roads. We know that. They will either kill people in this town, or we will have to kill some of them, unless we have men to patrol these streets. But right now, the only men I know who would do that are in Onath. I will send you to ask for men, so long as we leave the Triletts well guarded there. But you can't go alone. They'll be watching. Burle is a killer true. He won't hesitate if his own blood's not at stake."

Lorne was looking down at the ground, listening. "You would find Lucas, then, to send with me?"

"I would indeed, if I knew where to look for him. I pray God that he crosses our path." Tahn sighed. "I will have to go to Marc Toddin. He promised me his friendship, and he lives near this town. Perhaps he would help us by going with you."

"But we would be leaving you here alone, Tahn."

He didn't answer. He was quiet for a moment before turning to Tiarra. "I will see that you don't lack. Please don't go to market or anywhere else alone yet. If you are seen by them, it will not be well."

"Your friend can't stay here," she protested again.

"He would be of help to you if they come while I am gone. And they will try. I'm sorry, my sister. But Burle has never cared for me. If he can better me in any fashion, it will make him proud. And I could not bear it to be at your expense."

She hung her head, knowing he was right. She hadn't been safe from them before. And it was certainly no better now. But here he was, trying to save her. It made her think of how he had wept at Martica's words, and something shook inside her. "Sir," she said with voice barely audible, "your friend is at St. Thomas's."

He stood stunned by her words. Lucas had loved that grand old church when he was a street orphan, before ever he'd been snatched up by Samis and forced to the sword. It made Tahn happy to think he was back there. "Thank you, Lord," he whispered. "And thank you for telling me, sister."

9

St. Thomas's was one of the grandest churches in the land. Every noble house claimed a different church for its own, and Baron Trent and his family claimed this one. Tahn wondered if they cherished it as much as the House of Trilett did Our Holy Redeemer in Onath.

Stepping through the beautiful doors in the light of morning made him think of Netta and how she loved going to Sunday worship. She'd been so happy the day he finally decided to join them there.

This church was huge inside. He saw no one and didn't hear a sound. There was a gold crucifix at the front that stood several feet taller than he did. He stepped forward and knelt to thank the Lord for his abiding mercy and for the discovery of a sister. But he heard the hushed sound of movement to his right and turned immediately, not willing to let his guard down completely, even in a church.

There was a priest, an extremely short man, at the edge of the room. He just looked at Tahn for a moment and then began to turn away. "Continue with your prayers, stranger," he said. "Don't let me disturb you. God's house is open for this."

"I am finished," Tahn told him. "And I need your help. I'm looking for a man named Lucas Corsat, and I was told I might find him here."

The priest frowned. "Why do you seek him?"

"He's an old friend. I would like to rejoice with him that he has come again to God. But I must also tell him that there are men who seek his hurt."

"The bandits?"

"Yes, sir. They have threatened his life."

"You are the Dorn, aren't you?"

Tahn was surprised. He hadn't expected to be recognized in the church. He had thought this might be a place where his identity wouldn't matter. But it was the baron's church, and he could not know what to expect here. He nodded to the man. "I need to see Lucas. Please tell him I've come."

"He's not here today. But he surely knows you're about. He will seek you if he chooses."

Tahn studied the priest for a moment and then shook his head. "Why do you also fear me? I have come in peace for the sake of a friend. If he knew I was here, he would be seeking me already. If you know him, you know it is so. Why won't you take him my message?"

The priest did not even try to address the question. "Years ago, you were part of a difficult time in this town, Mr. Dorn. Some people believe you have come back seeking revenge, and they fear you."

"If all they sought then was to rid their streets of killers, then they are better left alone about it now."

The priest stepped toward him. "Those are wise words. But is it your heart in truth?"

Tahn sighed. "It is, Father, and I'll be pleased when someone here believes me. I seek no one's hurt. God is my witness."

"Lucas speaks the truth of you, then?"

"Lucas always speaks the truth."

The priest nodded. "He's a good man. But even such a one could be deceived."

"Please tell him I've come."

"He's not here today, as I said. I sent him to Tamask with my business, hoping he would avoid you."

Tahn shook his head in frustration. "Pray God for his life, sir, if the bandits are watching that road! Why would you endanger him, just to keep us apart?"

The priest crossed the distance between them and touched

Tahn's arm. "I didn't know the danger. Except that you might take him from us, and we need him here sorely."

"When did he leave?"

"Yesterday. He will be back tomorrow if all goes well."

"Pray that it does." Tahn was considering. He did not want to leave Lorne and Tiarra long enough to go and seek Lucas, especially since he could not be completely sure of this priest's words. He certainly couldn't send Lorne alone. So he would have to wait, trusting Lucas in God's hands. He would find Marc Toddin instead.

Without another word, he turned from the priest to go out, but the short man reached his hand up to Tahn's shoulder. His sudden touch was cold and it made Tahn uncomfortable, but he allowed it anyway.

"Tell me about the burns, son," the priest asked with solemn voice.

Tahn's stomach knotted. "Why?"

"I am searching in this town too. I was not here then."

"But you've heard."

"Yes, I've heard."

Tahn sighed. "You probably know as much as I do, then. Maybe more."

"Not of how you fared. Lucas said he met you when you were about seven, and you were a tormented child, still struggling with the scars."

"He tells you the truth."

"What do you carry now for your enemies?"

Tahn shook his head. "Nothing." He would have left then, but the priest still held him. "Why do you keep me?"

"I believe you should know that it is better sometimes not to pursue things, not to find all there is to find. You are safer that way."

Tahn spun around. "*I* am safer? Have any of you cared about me? Lorne was right, I think. You hide something, and it is not for my sake."

The little priest nodded. "I think of you, whether you would believe me or not. But I also think of Lucas." The man took a deep breath and looked up at Tahn nervously.

"It's better to leave the past alone and not let your enemies see you searching about, even after so long. It would be a shame, and Lucas would grieve, should this cost your death. I'm not anxious for more trouble here, nor to see your enemies become his."

Tahn stared at him. This couldn't be about the actions of men swept into the fray of an indignant mob. He understood that now. There would be nothing to hide if that were all. Nothing new to find in the search, and no special danger in trying. Suddenly it occurred to him that neither Martica nor Magna Sade had told of any witness to Karra Loble's murder. Perhaps things were not as they seemed. "When you say enemies, good priest, you mean my father's enemies, don't you?"

The man squirmed. "I have said too much."

"No. I need the truth."

"I cannot tell what is confessed to me. Surely you know that."

"Someone wanted us dead."

"I told you I can't say."

"Then tell me who can."

"I can't do that. You're a soldier yourself. You can understand the danger to him if I speak of his confessions. You need only know it's best for you to go back to Onath."

Tahn stood still, tossing about the new questions in his mind. Finally he voiced the most important one to him. "Who killed Karra Loble?"

"People say it was Sanlin Dorn." The priest turned from Tahn's dark and searching eyes. "You should go. I can tell you nothing more. Leave Alastair, and thank God for the new life he's given you. There's nothing you can accomplish here."

Miles from Alastair, Orin Sade rode his old horse toward the walled mansion that was one of four belonging to the House of Trent. He prayed to find the baron at this nearest one. He banged and hollered at the gate, creating all the commotion he could until a guard appeared and demanded to know his business.

"I need to see the young baron!" he pleaded. "Tahn Dorn is seeking my life!"

The young man scoffed. "What is that to my lord, sir?"

"It is for *his* sake! It is for service to the Trent honor that I stand in peril. It is his obligation to help me. Let me in to him!"

The guard gave him a quizzical look. "Wait here. I will ask if he would see you."

Lionell Trent stood surrounded by his tailors when one of his guardsmen called to him.

"What is it?" he snapped. "I am very busy right now." He turned to the man closest to him. "I have to have purple to line my cape. And nothing dull. It has to match the crossed lines in my sash, and I want a roll to walk on of the same color."

"Sir, a man is standing outside, asking to see you."

"I don't have time. There is too much to do preparing for my wedding. Tell him to come back after I'm married. But not too soon after."

"Sir, he says Tahn Dorn seeks his life. And he claims he has a right to expect your help."

"Tahn Dorn, you say?"

"Yes, lord."

Lionell smiled. "What has the man done? Offered himself as another suitor to the fair Lady Trilett?"

"I daresay not, sir. He seems rather too old for that sort of thing."

"Did he tell you what the matter is, then?"

"No, sir. Only that it involves you."

"I have nothing to do with Tahn Dorn. It was my father's folly to try killing him. Not mine."

"Shall I send the old man away, then?"

Lionell was quiet for a moment. And then he abruptly dismissed everyone who had been in the room, except the trusted guard from the gate. "No," he told him. "I have wondered much about the mysterious murderer who now seems to do good. I could scarcely accept that Dorn could be nearly killed by our soldiers, without someday seeking vengeance. I want to know what he is up to. Bring the man in to me."

Orin Sade bowed gratefully to the young Baron Trent, who waved his hand impatiently. "Get up, man! I have business to attend to! Do tell me the Dorn's quarrel with you. Were you one of Samis's men?"

Sade was not sure who he meant. "No, sir. I am from Alastair."

"Were you the tracker, then? Or one of the archers hired to see that he was caught?"

"No," Sade told him, still not understanding. "It was I who burned him, on your father's word."

"Burned him? I hadn't heard about that. But when Father decided to blame him for the Trilett murders, it was guaranteed the wretch would suffer. Surprising that he's waited a year for his revenge, though, eh? I suppose he thought that was long enough."

Orin stared at him, truly perplexed. "It's been seventeen years, sir. But I always knew the day would come."

Lionell frowned. "Seventeen years? Tell me what you're talking about."

"I acted to please your father, sir."

"Yes. You said that. But go on. I was only nine years old then. Was the Dorn any older?"

"No, sir. He was very small. But his father came to kill a woman who had come to our city. And your father charged us not to let them escape."

Lionell leaned back and folded his arms. "Why did the baron take such an interest? Who was the woman?"

"Some say it was Dorn's own mother, sir. Karra Loble. She seemed a decent woman. I saw the body. It was a shame, her to be stabbed such as she was. A gruesome thing that was done."

But Lionell was staring at him, stunned. "What did you say her name was?"

"Karra Loble, sir."

"By God! And you say she was Dorn's mother?"

"Yes, sir. That's what I've heard said."

Lionell raked one hand through his bushy hair and then stood. "Why, then, wasn't he killed years ago?"

"He would have died, sir, but kin of his took him from the place."

"I don't just mean back then, fool! I mean in the interim. What was Father waiting for? Why wait until last year and then make such a production out of it? Gads, he was stupid! Surely he could have found the child and his wretched relative. If Dorn had been killed as a boy, there'd have been no public spectacle from which to spend a year saving face!" He turned to the guard, who stood in the doorway. "Did you know anything of this?"

"No, sir," the man replied. "Seventeen years ago I was a boy of nine, just as yourself."

"Yes, I know," Lionell said impatiently. "But Father might have told you something since then."

"No, sir."

Lionell snorted. "It is times like this that I wish he were still alive that I might kick him for all the trouble he's caused me! I should have been told of this. Karra Loble's son! Good Lord!"

Orin just stared at him, completely at a loss to know what he was talking about but afraid to ask questions.

Lionell turned to him again. "Tell me, old man. Is Dorn in Alastair?"

"He was when I left there. I don't know if he still is. He may be tracking me now. I need your help, sir—"

"Yes. We'll get to that. His father—was he killed?"

"We hanged him, sir. The same day the woman died."

"And you're sure—you're sure Dorn is this woman's son?"

"It's been said, sir," the man answered with confusion.

94

Lionell took a deep breath. "You burned him. But he survived, and now he hunts you?"

"I know he will."

"Then it is just a matter of time before he turns his vengeance on all things Trent."

Orin shook his head. "Perhaps not, sir. His eyes are on Alastair, but no one there will speak of your father. Or any of it. And he couldn't even tell us his mother's name."

Lionell's eyes gleamed. "He doesn't know?"

Orin couldn't be sure what the young baron meant. But he remembered Tahn's questions and was fairly confident of his answer. Magna, after all, knew nothing of the baron's orders. "He knows little, sir, except that it was I—"

Lionell suddenly laughed. "It is important that we kill him, then, before he finds out!" He turned to the guard. "Lagen, get me Saud here! And Korin!"

"But my lord, sir—Saud and Korin are at your estate at Copen taking care of your business—"

"I don't care what they're doing. I want them here! Send word for them to come to me at once."

Orin Sade was stunned. He'd hoped to be heard but would never have expected such a reaction as this. "You will protect me then?" he dared ask.

"What?" Lionell faced him. "Oh. Yes. Yes, good man, I will. So long as you tell me everything you can of the Dorn and what he knows. And whoever else knows about this. I will not have my wealth nor baronship at risk to that wretched, mercenary dog!"

Lionell dismissed Sade to another room and sat wondering if his mother knew anything of this, or any of his seven aunts. Surely not. Surely they would have said something to him by now. And most of his eleven cousins, all of them girls, were younger than he was. Better that they never know.

Karra Loble had left a son. And Lionell knew very well what that could mean.

IO

Tiarra was cooking when she heard Martica's horrible coughing suddenly cease. She rushed to her side, afraid that she might find the old woman struggling for her last breath, but Martica lay still, staring up at the ceiling.

"Are you all right, ma'am?" Tiarra asked her, and Martica slowly turned her head. She was terribly pale, almost gray.

"I'm glad you got rid of Tahn Dorn and his friend," she said.

Tiarra nodded, unable to tell her that the blond man was still outside, and her brother would surely be back as well.

"I was out for a while, yesterday, child," Martica told her.

It hardly seemed possible, by the looks of her. Tiarra knew she was weak again and could not rise now on her own. She took the old woman's hand. "I'm glad you could do it."

"I promised you. I meant to keep my word." She coughed again faintly. "I went to see Mrs. Ovny. I asked her about your mother's necklace. It's a beautiful thing. She still has it. She said she'd let you see it, if you'll not want it in your hands. You should go before she changes her mind. This very afternoon. She does not like a morning caller. That woman can be quite the sort, you know it, child."

The girl's heart pounded. She would see a piece of her mother's own jewelry! "Thank you, Martica! Mother was beautiful with it, wasn't she?"

"She was beautiful, girl, adorned or not. And as good as any lady could be. God love her memory!"

Tiarra smiled. Martica could be so harsh. But not when she spoke of Karra Loble. Tiarra could like the old woman then, and feel liked for a moment in return. "I'll go, just as you said. Are you hungry yet?"

Martica scowled. "No. But I should try to eat, I suppose. I've hardly been able. I am not long for this world, girl. Whatever will you do?"

Tiarra didn't know how to answer. Martica had never spoken of such things, and she hadn't expected that she ever would. "I'll manage, ma'am," she told her. "Don't worry for me."

"Get yourself a man, girl. But be careful of your brother and his friends. They're cutthroat thieves, pure and simple."

"Yes, ma'am." Tears filled her eyes briefly, but Martica wanted nothing of such things.

"Get up and get me my food, child, before it burns over the fire unattended!"

"Yes, ma'am." She jumped to her feet.

"Do carry yourself well in Mrs. Ovny's presence when you go," Martica told her. "You know how she fancies herself. It wouldn't help you to be brash."

"Yes, Martica."

Tiarra fed the ailing old woman and hurried about her other duties, but finally she had done all she could think to do in the house, and Martica slept. They were needing meal again. And other foodstuffs. Surely the blond man would understand that. He and her brother could not keep her restrained to the house. They were not even invited here. But she looked down at the bread on the table. They had helped her. They were still trying to. She didn't know if the young man outside had eaten. Perhaps it would be proper to do him a good deed.

Lorne was leaning against the neighbor's cart when she came out. She brought him the bread and the remnant of the stew she'd made. The gesture obviously surprised him.

97

"Thank you," he told her. "That is more than kind."

"Everything deserves to eat," she said. "Had I a dog, I would surely feed it."

He smiled. "You have a way of putting things. But thank you again."

She watched him bow his head for a moment in prayer and then begin to eat. It was hard to imagine that he could be anything but sincere. He looked so innocent. And scarcely older than herself. "How long have you been with my brother?"

"I first met him when I was eight. But I haven't known his friendship well until the last year, miss. To have Christ makes a difference in everything."

She didn't know how to accept his religious talk, so she ignored it. "How old are you?"

"Seventeen."

"And he is about twenty-nine?"

He looked at her with an odd expression. "Twenty-one, so we think, miss."

"So he says. He looks older than that."

Lorne shook his head. "When I met him, I thought he was older than twelve. Were it not for his small size, nothing could have convinced me. He acted and talked like a man, an old man even, sometimes. The life he had aged him, miss. I doubt he was ever truly a child."

"Did you ever see him kill anyone?"

The young man's sigh was audible. "Better that you give him such a question," he told her. "He'd not be afraid of it, or any other. He won't hide his past. But he's not the same."

"Why do you take up for him so? What has he done for you?"

Lorne smiled again. "The first thing he did, years ago, was to stop the bigger boys from harassing me when I was new in my training. But in the past year he spared me an execution and got me a job. He shared his Savior with me."

"Then you owe him."

"I'm here because I'm his friend."

"Have *you* killed anyone?"

He met her eyes. "Yes, ma'am. And I am not proud of it. I did it as a slave, but it troubles me still."

She looked long at him and then sat down. "A slave?"

"My parents sold me. To feed my brothers and sisters. I don't fault them. They didn't know how hard it would be for me."

"You're not truly a killer, then, if someone made you," she said with a quiet voice. "You'd have to have the anger in you, the bitter fire that makes you want to. I feel it sometimes. I could kill someone. I've wanted to hurt a lot of people. And my brother's just the same, isn't he?"

"Not anymore. And I think it was never really him but the pain at work. Perhaps it's that way with you too, miss."

She suddenly stood. She should not be talking to him this way. Martica had said to be careful. But he made himself so smooth and easy to like. "I need to go. But don't worry yourself. I'll not be long, and I'll watch carefully."

He rose to his feet immediately. "They may be watching too. I'll not risk that, or my word to Tahn."

"We need provision from the market. You can't keep me here."

He met her determined eyes but did not answer. Instead, he turned quickly away and looked over his shoulder. "Do you know that boy?" he asked her.

Tiarra looked but didn't see anything. "Who's watching me today?" she called.

The dirty little face of a street boy no older than six or seven appeared from behind a rain barrel. "Just me, Miss Ti," he answered shyly as two other children peeked out at them.

"Tell them to come," Lorne told her.

She glanced at him in question.

"It's all right. I'm not going to hurt them."

"Jori, Ansley, Rae," she called. "Come closer." And then she turned back to Lorne. "I don't know what you want. But they're timid. They're street children, sir, but as good as the next. Don't you frighten them."

He smiled. "We need your help," he told the children, motioning them closer. He pulled several coins from the bag at his belt and knelt on the children's level. "Miss Tiarra needs certain things from Market Street. Will you fetch them for her?"

One of the children nodded.

"Good," he said and put his coins in the hand of the assenting child. "Whatever she tells you, get two the same. The second part is for you. That will be your pay for helping me. Is that all right?"

All three of them stared at him with wide eyes and then nodded with excitement.

"I can't take your money," Tiarra protested.

"You're not. But we should help in your inconvenience. Don't keep the little ones waiting. They might be hungry. You'd better tell your needs."

Ordinarily, she would have been angry to be told what to do. But it was such a kind thing to do for these children that she couldn't be angry. The way their faces lit up made her almost want to kiss Lorne for having such a thought. She'd been worried for them. But this young man understood what it was like to be hungry. She knew he must from the story he'd told.

"Thank you," she whispered, and named the things she wanted. She watched the children speed away happily and then sat down again. "That was very generous."

He sat a few feet from her. "Well worth it to me. They earn it. And they're good as the next, as you said."

He went back to his unfinished food, and she studied him in silence. She hadn't let herself notice before how very handsome he was. She'd only been seeing her brother's friend, and not trusting him because of it. But now he'd taken on a different light. His was something like her own heart. She couldn't name one other person who would be so quick to befriend the street children.

━━━

Tahn went to the place Marc Toddin had told him about, but there was only a heap of ashes there in the stead of a house. He stood just looking at it for a moment, asking the Lord for guidance. He obeyed his heart in returning to the home of Magna Sade, hoping to ask her more questions, but there was no one there. She would not be back, he knew it somehow, and he yet wondered what had become of Toddin and his family.

He knelt in the Sades' abandoned yard and prayed again for guidance. There would be more trouble with the bandits, he was sure of it. How could he keep both his sister and Lorne out of danger without help?

When he rose to his feet again, he had peace despite the precarious spot he was in. Only one companion, now wounded, stood with him against twelve to fifteen bandits or more. In a town where he couldn't count on the smallest courtesy, let alone any real help.

"We need your help, Lord," he whispered. "And I know you will supply it."

Suddenly he thought of Netta and the upcoming Trent wedding. He was glad they weren't attending. He couldn't consider it safe, though Lionell had done nothing to continue his father's deadly assault on Triletts. Yet their absence would surely be an insult to the baron. He shook his head. It was not his part to worry on that. Benn knew such matters. But something about it burdened him anyway, so he stopped again to pray for the people who held his heart in Onath.

Lucas and Marc Toddin were on his mind when he finally turned to mount his horse. "You know I need them, Lord," he said. "But I don't know where to look. You will have to bring them to me, and I know you can."

Suddenly there was a shout behind him. "Dorn!"

He whirled about, not sure what to expect. There were two men, both of them big, headed his way. The one he was sure he'd never seen before. But the other was Marc Toddin.

II

As the day grew long, Tiarra was in a quandary, thinking of Mrs. Ovny and her mother's necklace. She longed to see it, to beg a price as a daughter and begin work to gain it. Martica had said she must go today. And Mrs. Ovny was difficult. There were no guarantees Tiarra would be welcomed if she waited.

But there was this Lorne still here with her. He could not send the children for this. Would he understand her need? She thought he might, and she considered telling him about it, even allowing him to come along, but Martica's words haunted her. Might Tahn Dorn have an interest in his mother's jewels, regardless of how he portrayed himself? And no matter how Lorne seemed, he could not be expected to keep this from his friend. It would be a betrayal of Martica's trust to let the young man know. But how could she manage to go and not have him follow or prevent her?

The Ovnys were several blocks away, nearer to Sade's tavern than home. There was no way the handsome blond would consider it safe for her to go alone. But he had used the street children. Perhaps she could too.

She waited till the youngsters were back with the food and then took them inside with her, telling Lorne that she would help them cook their share. Martica still slept, and that was a good thing, but it worried her. There was not much time left for her.

Lorne sat on the ground, hoping Tahn was making headway in his absence. It bothered him to think of going back to Onath without him. The Triletts would be dismayed by

102

this turn of events, to say the least. This town was like a bed of thorns to Tahn, even without Burle's threat. Lorne considered that it would make better sense to stay here himself and have Tahn go, but he knew Tahn would never accept that. He would hold the responsibility too close to him.

After a while, the three orphaned children came out of the little house. They left together after thanking him vigorously. They seemed happy and carried with them the food they hadn't eaten. He could imagine that it made them feel very rich, just as he had felt as a child whenever he had opportunity to see food enough for more than one meal. It made him think of the children at the Trilett estate who had once lived by their wits and what they could steal, just as these now surely did. Lorne himself had found the little boy named Briant, curled up among fallen leaves, shivering with the cold. At Samis's orders, he'd taken the boy to their mountain stronghold. But now he thanked God that Briant was well and not under the hand of that cruel master. He would be warm and safe this winter. But what of these?

Suddenly, he was aware of Tiarra's presence and looked up. She was standing in the doorway of the little painted house, just watching him.

"I want you to tell me something plainly," she said. "How old was my brother and where were you when you met him?"

"He was twelve, in Joram. He was with Samis when he bought me. He was the first I met of the other boys. Not the easiest, though."

She frowned. "What do you mean?"

"He would barely talk to me, or anyone else. All of us were scared with Samis, but when it was just the boys and Samis was occupied, the rest of us managed to relax a little, make some mischief, or talk. But not him."

Tiarra was obviously uncomfortable. "Why are you telling me this?"

"You asked."

"I asked about when you met him, not for all of this."

103

"I would have expected your interest."

"Samis was your master?"

"Yes, miss."

"Did you hate him?"

He sighed. "It was hard not to."

"Then there is one other thing my brother did for you, isn't there? He freed you, didn't he, when he killed the man. And you would do anything for him now because of it. You gladly lie for him, and you make it seem so real with the good heart you hide underneath!"

He just looked at her for a moment, unable to fathom how she could still feel so strongly against her brother. "I haven't lied to you. And Tahn did not kill Samis."

"Did you see his death?"

"No, but—"

"Then you don't know!"

Lorne shook his head. "Did you see your mother's death?"

Tiarra's face turned angry. "I was a baby! How could I?"

"Then you don't know. People tell you things. That doesn't make it true."

"I know what happened then!"

"You know what you've been told. But what kind of sense does it make? He was too young to—"

"No! You're lying to me! He put you to it, didn't he? Telling me he was twelve when you met him. That's impossible! He was twelve when he left here."

"Miss Loble—"

"I can't fault you. You owe him too much. But it isn't right. You don't need another master over you."

Lorne stood. "That's enough. I don't know why you won't give Tahn the slightest chance. Who holds you so tightly that you can't think for yourself? He saved your life! He'd endanger himself to do it again. We haven't lied to you. He was *not* twelve! This town left him near dead, and you all act like he has no right to even ask why! What do you think he is, Miss Loble—a demon, that he doesn't deserve the kindness you'd give a dog?"

She was quiet, fighting away the churning tension within her. Lorne had a passion in this. But was it truth? "What do you mean . . ." she began, but then hesitated when his eyes met hers. He had a tender fire in him for her brother. He owed him truly. He couldn't help himself. But the questions wouldn't leave her. "What do you mean, sir, that this town left him near dead?"

Lorne stared at her in disbelief. "You don't know?"

"I know our father's brother came and took Tahn away after the hanging. I have no way of knowing what happened then, except that he became all the more a killer. Under your Samis, right? But does he ever talk about an uncle?"

Lorne leaned against the wall of the house and shook his head. "He had no idea he had any family at all until we heard about you. But the old woman never told you what happened to him?"

"She told me all she knew."

"About his burns?"

"What burns?"

He shook his head again, angrily.

"What?" she pressed. "What are you talking about?"

"She told you he was nearly grown, didn't she? And that he helped kill your mother and then just left with a relative without punishment or regret?"

Her heart pounded as he glanced into the house with his face tight and pale.

"What did he tell you about it?" she asked timidly.

"He was perhaps only four, miss. And a man in the crowd poured a boiling pot over him. It must have been the purest agony! His body has healed well, over time. But God only knows the inside, with what Samis put him through on top of it."

"It can't be," Tiarra said. "Martica would have told me."

"You would think. But she lied. I don't know why."

"No."

He turned from her. "You'll have to find out for yourself, if you won't believe us."

He walked back toward the neighbor's old cart and sat

with his back against a wheel. "God help you, Miss Loble. Tahn wants to add friendship to the common blood. You're the only kin he's ever known."

Tiarra was suddenly feeling numb, trying to make sense of this. "I told you an uncle—our father's brother—took him away."

"It was Samis, the mercenary monster, who took him. He got him a healer's help. He put him in training when he was able. But Tahn was still his captive. He was tortured to obedience, miss. And when he escaped, he took eight children out with him so they would never have to go through what he did under that man."

"Then you believe him."

"In all! I've seen enough of it for myself. Even his scars!"

Tiarra shook her head. "What reason could Martica have to lie to me for all these years?"

"I have no idea."

She turned to face the house, thinking of the dying woman inside it, and how she'd lain in her arms once when she was a child trembling with fever. "My brother might have good reason to lie about Alastair," she stubbornly maintained. "You might, even, if you seek more in this town than you say. Vengeance for our father, perhaps. I know not what else. I don't doubt you're his friend. I think you would do anything in the world for him."

Lorne had bowed his head. "Except wrong. Yes, I would, miss," he said solemnly.

She glanced back at him, and her eyes filled with tears. How could these things be so? Martica said Tahn was a fiend, a deceiver, a villain like their horrible father. But this man seemed none of that.

At that moment she saw the little girl, Rae, obediently on her way back to them down the dusty street. She had the perfect distraction for a young man with a caring heart. But now? Oh, now Tiarra only wanted to run inside and beg Martica for answers! How much of what Lorne had said was true?

"Miss Ti! Help!" the little girl suddenly called. Lorne jumped to his feet.

Rae was running now, and Tiarra glanced at Lorne. He looked like a soldier, standing ready. What could he do but help a pleading child? It made her feel guilty, but she knew she wouldn't stop it now.

"Miss Ti!" Rae screamed. "Please, help! Jori's hurt!"

Tiarra ran out to meet her. "What happened? Where is he?"

"The old house where he likes to go. He was in there, and part of the roof fell in! We heard him holler, but we can't even find him!"

Tiarra was quiet for a moment. But then she turned to Lorne. "These are my friends. I need to try and help. I'm not sure anyone else will."

"All right," he said without hesitation. "We'll go. Let me get my horse."

He had unburdened his animal, and all of his things were on the ground in a neat pile next to Martica's house. Tiarra watched him quickly take up his blanket, the water skin, a rope, and his sword. He turned to the little girl. "How big is the house?"

"Bigger than this one. It's been empty a long time now."

"A lot of roof fell?"

"Almost half."

"C'mon, Freedom," he said to the horse. "Might need your help."

Rae took off running in the direction she'd come, and Lorne was immediate in following her. Tiarra stayed at his side, knowing his earnestness, knowing that she was about to destroy any trust that could have been between them.

Why must you believe us, Lorne Graise? she lamented in her heart. *Why must you be so willing to help? Would you do the same if my brother were here? Or would it be him running down this street to rescue a child you don't even know?*

It didn't take them long to reach the old house, a derelict

107

place with a gaping hole in its top. It almost looked like it could fall in on itself. And it was at least twice as big as Martica's house.

"Where was he?" Lorne asked. "How far in? Which side?"

The boy named Ansley stepped from the structure and wiped his brow. "I still can't find him, Rae," he said. "I'm scared."

"He likes the middle room," the girl said. "Ansley, could you get to the middle?"

"Not very well."

Lorne moved to the doorway. "Jori!" He turned to Tiarra. "I'm going in. You and the children stay here. It's surely not stable."

When Lorne disappeared inside, Ansley could barely contain a chuckle. But Rae looked ashen, almost angry. *She knows it's not right,* Tiarra thought. After he helped them, to trick him this way. But she gave the children a quick hug and whispered her thanks.

"What will we tell him?" Rae asked softly.

"Whatever you must. I'll be back."

<hr>

"Jori!" Lorne called again.

And suddenly he heard a voice in answer. "Here."

He moved through rubble toward the sound, still not seeing the little boy whose voice he'd heard. "Jori? Talk to me."

"Over here."

"Are you hurt? Keep talking. I can't see you yet."

But there was silence for a moment. Finally a timid voice answered, "I think I'm okay."

Lorne continued his search until he found the child, curled up beneath a slab of door. He crawled out of the hiding place on his own.

"It's all right," Lorne told him. "You look pretty good. Were you hit by anything?"

"No, sir," Jori answered, beginning to feel a bit scared. He'd been willing to do Miss Ti a favor, but he hadn't considered whether this stranger might have an angry temper about him over such deceit as this.

"God is good," Lorne told him. "Let's get out of here before we lose more roof. Can you make it?"

"Yes, sir."

Lorne took the boy's hand and led him out the way he'd come in. It occurred to him to wonder how the boy could have managed the collapse unscathed, but not until he got outside did he know that something was amiss. The other two children stood together waiting. But Tiarra was gone.

"Where did the lady go?" Lorne asked immediately.

"She had something she had to do."

"What?"

"She had something she had to do," Rae said again. "But she'll come back."

Lorne stared at them for a moment. Neither of them ran up to their friend Jori or asked if he were all right. They just looked at Lorne rather anxiously, all three of them did, as if waiting for something. "Where is she?" he asked them, his discomfort growing. No one rushed to an accident just to slip out before the outcome was known. She wasn't as callous as that. But she was certainly cunning, to play such a trick as this.

"We don't know where she went. Honestly, sir."

They knew he was angry. They could see it in him. And it was frightening, not knowing what to expect.

"When did that roof fall?" he asked them.

"Two weeks ago," Jori answered with a tiny voice, followed by tears. The young man could beat them. He had a right.

"Do you know why she put you up to this?"

"She had something to do, by herself," Rae said again.

Lorne shook his head. He'd have to find her. Tahn had left him with a charge. "There are men who want to hurt her," he told the children. "I only want to keep her safe. We have to find her before she gets herself in trouble. Will you help me look?"

He looked at Ansley, the oldest, but the boy turned from his eyes and fled down the street.

"What about you?" he asked the younger ones. "Are you going to run too?"

"We didn't mean you no harm," Rae told him.

He sighed. "I can't expect you to help me against her wishes. Just tell her to be careful, if you see her. This is no game. Tell her I'm looking, and we're here because we don't want anything to happen to her."

He mounted his horse.

"He was really trying to help," Jori whispered to Rae.

"I know," the little girl said. "I don't suppose he'll hire us for nothing no more."

Lorne rode through the streets, knowing she hadn't had time to get very far. But there was no sign of her. He was upset with himself for letting this happen. He should never have let her out of his sight, regardless of the circumstance. He'd had his assignment. A good guard doesn't set duty aside for something else. He should have known. He rode closer to the old painted house and saw that there were horses out front. At first he didn't know them, but then he saw Smoke with Tahn.

"Oh God." His stomach knotted; he dreaded seeing Tahn's reaction to this. But he rode swiftly toward them.

"What's wrong?" Tahn asked at once.

"I'm so sorry. She tricked me. She took off alone."

Tahn only nodded. "She feels safer alone than with us, I guess. There's no sign?"

"No. I'm sorry. There were street children. They said she told them she wanted to do something alone and she'd be back."

"She'll have to be," Tahn agreed. "For the sake of the old woman. But she has her free will, Lorne. We can only offer our help. We can't make them want it."

There was sadness in Tahn's eyes, but he spoke no more of it with business at hand. He motioned toward the men with him. "This is Marc Toddin and his brother Lem. They've agreed to help us, thank God."

"Does this change things?" Marc asked.

"No. If she wants away from us, I'll leave her alone. She can come and go as she pleases, but I could still keep her safe if Alastair were policed. And there should be a guard at the church. They'll learn they can find Lucas there, if they don't know that already."

"Are you sure of what they'll do?"

Tahn shook his head. "I can only be sure Burle will do something. He'll let his anger fester over the wound I gave him till he won't be able to manage not avenging himself. He's like that. I stopped him twice. And Lucas did once. He won't be able to let it go. He won't let us challenge his authority that way."

"It will take a while to get men from Onath," Marc said. "Are you sure it will be necessary? There are four of us. Five when we find Mr. Corsat. And we could recruit more."

"Would it could be so simple." Tahn was looking down the long street. "Even to stop the bandits who plague them, Marc, men in this town will not rally to me. And if they knew the cause only and came, they would back away when they learn I am involved."

"I can't fathom this town!" Marc exclaimed. "In Onath, in Joram, in Merinth, you are a hero. People know what you've done for the Triletts."

Tahn sighed. "I must be a clever deceiver then."

"Dorn . . ." Marc shook his head. "I wish we understood. I wish we'd been here then to know the root of all this."

"We'll learn. Eventually. But right now I must not think only of my sister and Lucas. Any traveler who ventures this way is in danger, and any woman the bandits take a fancy to. I can't let that go on, knowing it will just get worse now that Burle is out to prove a point. But I need authority to stop it, and Benn Trilett can give me that."

Lorne knew what he meant but questioned it. "Alastair's such a way from Onath. Are you sure he'll want to stretch his hand so far?"

"And this is Baron Trent's territory," Lem Toddin added.

"Have any of his house been assaulted?" Tahn asked.

"Not to my knowledge," Lem answered.

"Then he'll do nothing. But it might upset him to find me with a Trilett guard set up here."

"Then we're asking for more trouble?"

"He won't oppose Benn Trilett openly. That image could destroy him. He's still trying to prove to the other nobles that he's not like his father. Lorne, go on to Benn Trilett and take the Toddins with you. Explain everything and send back men. Just don't let him leave himself short there."

"I don't like leaving you here alone."

"I don't like it either, Tahn," Marc agreed. "You're the one most vulnerable to trouble here. You go. I'll watch for things."

"I'm not leaving," Tahn insisted. "I can't help but think God led me to this, and I'm not running from it."

Marc shook his head. He'd once seen this man deliberately ride into a trap and pay dearly for it. Tahn's own principles put him in danger. It wasn't the bandits who troubled Marc so much as the undercurrent in this town, the unspoken tension he could see as they rode the streets with the Dorn. "Let me stay with you, then," he suggested. "We have a friend by Batan Falls. I think he could be persuaded to go with Lem and your friend. He's a good man with a strong arm. I wish I could name more I could place confidence in. But after eight years, I'm still a newcomer here."

"There might be trouble on the road," Tahn told them.

"There might be trouble here."

Tahn was quiet for a moment. "All right. We'll do it your way."

Reluctantly, Lorne rode off with Lem Toddin, aware of the little spying eyes that were watching them. He prayed for those children, and for their difficult friend, Tahn's sister. He hated to leave, not knowing what would happen next. The secrets of this town worried him as much as the bandits did.

12

Tiarra stood just inside the Ovnys' door, looking in wonder at the stunning piece of jewelry before her. She'd never seen anything so beautiful. "Can I hold it for a moment?"

"Dear me, no, child!" Mrs. Ovny exclaimed. "This is old now! And you don't know how to handle valuables!"

Tiarra frowned. It wasn't easy to abide this selfish woman. "Did you know my mother?"

"Oh . . ." she hesitated. "Not very well. She seemed due a measure of respect, though, you know. And she had some lovely things. Like this necklace. I've kept it in a case all this time. I never even wear it on account it's such a special piece, worth a lot of money."

Tiarra looked up at her with a sudden fire. "Did you give Martica a lot of money for it, then?"

Mrs. Ovny's face reddened. "I—I gave her what she needed," she stammered. "Exactly what she needed at the time."

"She needed a fair value."

"She was happy with our bargain. How dare you imply I cheated her!"

"Martica had little choice. And I had nothing more of my mother's memory. You could have been fair."

"How dare you! The money I gave her fed you, girl, when Martica couldn't work for all the time it took caring for the sickly thing she was stuck with!"

Tiarra stared at her. "I was sickly?"

"For a time, I suppose, missing your mother's breast. You

113

were trouble soon enough, though! I had a time, purging Mikal of the things he learned from you."

Tiarra thought it better not to address that topic. She could surely enflame Mrs. Ovny by telling tales of her son. "I am sorry," she said politely. "But I'm sure you can understand why this would be important to me. I have nothing of my mother's. I would love to be able to claim it, for her sake. Please, Mrs. Ovny, let me repay you what you require—"

"What!"

"I'd like to pay you for it."

"You have no money."

"Not yet. But I can work. For you, if you wish. Or I'll bring you part of my pay every week, ma'am. I'll be true as gold to my word."

"I have no intention of parting with this. And you're a tavern maid! What need do you have of it? You couldn't possibly take care of it. I heard you were robbed. You would probably lose it in a week!"

"It was my mother's," Tiarra pressed. "What does it mean to you?"

"There's nothing else like it in this town, girl! It shouldn't be cast about the streets!"

"You said my mother seemed worthy of respect."

"Well, yes, child. I thought so."

"As her daughter, aren't I worthy of consideration?"

"That's not the same."

"Why?"

"This is ours now. You have no need of such things. Besides, it's already spoken for. I promised to give it to Mikal's bride."

Tiarra's heart pounded. "Did you tell him that?"

"Of course."

"Does he know it was my mother's? What did he say?"

"He said it would look stunning on Mary Stumping's neck! I suppose you think he should be marrying you so that he could be placing it on yours. Well, I thank God that he's got the good sense to understand you're not right for him. You weren't raised to be any woman of standing,

Tiarra Loble! You had a scoundrel for a father, and that's just the way you are!"

Tears burned Tiarra's cheeks. "But it was *my* mother's! Mary could wear a hundred other things for her wedding! Mikal could buy her whatever he fancied!"

"But this is special," Mrs. Ovny cooed. "And I bought it fairly. Now why don't you go home? You've seen it. Perhaps one day Mary will let you see it again."

But Tiarra stood her ground. "I'll manage any amount you say, if it takes years."

"I said no, girl. Can't you hear me?"

Tiarra stared at her for a moment. Then she wiped her eyes and turned away.

Alastair seemed so quiet. She left the Ovnys behind her, feeling numb. She thought she should go back home and check on Martica. But then she thought of Lorne and what she had done. Would he be angry? Would her brother be angry? They would have some right. They were true in their concern. But she didn't feel like facing their presence, or their displeasure. Would *they* think her worthless and irresponsible too?

She went to the alley behind Market Street, where she knew she would find familiar faces. Some of the street children huddled together there at night, using wooden crates for shelter.

"Miss Ti?" It was Ansley, peeking out from behind a box. "You look sad."

She didn't want to reply to that. "Was the young soldier angry, Ansley?"

"He didn't do nothing to us."

Little Rae suddenly poked her head up. "Aren't you going home?"

"I don't think I can yet."

"But I told him you would."

"I will. Just not now." She fought back the tears that pressed at her. "I'm afraid they'll despise me, like everyone else."

"We don't, Miss Ti!" Rae objected. "He might be mad. But he don't seem to want to hurt nobody."

"Will you go for me, then?" she asked. "Tell him I'm fine. Check on Martica for me. I just need time to think."

Rae looked at her a long time and seemed to be struggling with something. "You could say you're sorry. You could explain what you had to do."

"But I wouldn't get out of his sight again. And Tahn Dorn might be worse still. And I think there's something else I need to do tonight."

Rae looked truly worried. "He said to be careful."

"I know. Tell him I understand. Ansley, go with her. See that Martica has eaten. Tell them I'll be back tomorrow."

She turned away from them with a churning tightness within her and addressed her mother in her mind. *I know you never liked a thief, Mother. Martica has told me, more than once. But I'll be doing this for you. Because I've always wished to be close to you somehow.*

Ansley and Rae obediently made their way to Martica's house. Jori had joined them, as he always did. But they stopped up the street, seeing the two different horses. Marc Toddin was standing near the house.

"He's really big," Ansley said uneasily. "Where's the one we fooled?"

"I don't know," Rae whispered. They snuck closer and saw Tahn step into their view.

"That's the one who was here before," the girl told the others. "He's scary."

"Maybe we should go," Ansley suggested. "The other man's not here."

"We can't," Rae insisted. "Miss Ti told us to check on Martica, remember?"

"But how do we get in? They'll see us!"

"You reckon they'll thrash us good?" Jori asked.

"I don't know," the girl answered. "I don't even know what Martica will say. But Miss Ti told us to. And we owe her plenty."

"Not a beating," Ansley protested.

"Maybe two," Rae reasoned bravely. "We'd have starved by now, I think. Come on."

"But Rae!" Jori exclaimed.

"I'm going," she insisted. "You do what you want."

She stepped from their hiding place toward the house, and Tahn turned his head.

"Please, sir," she begged him. "Let me go in to see about the old woman."

"Do as you wish, miss," he said. "We'll not trouble you."

Relieved beyond words, she smiled and bowed and then darted inside. In a few moments, Tahn could hear Martica shouting angrily.

"What the devil are you doing here? Where's Tiarra?"

"She told me to come," came Rae's reply.

"Go tell her to get herself home! There's men outside my door! Tell her to get rid of them and do it now! I don't need no beggar coming to gawk at me!" She took to a fit of coughing.

Marc looked over at Tahn. "Difficult woman?"

But Tahn didn't interrupt his thoughts to answer. Tiarra knew how sick Martica was. She was worried enough to send someone. But still she didn't come. What could be of such importance to her? He waited in silence until finally the little girl came out.

Rae started to run as soon as she passed the doorway.

"Wait, miss," Tahn called.

"I don't know you," she said. "Miss Ti told me what to tell the blond one, but you're not him."

"He had to leave. I'm his friend, and we have common concerns. Do you know where she is?"

"I know where she was, but I don't know where she went."

"Please tell me her message."

"But you're the one she said would be worse—aren't you?"

He sighed. "I don't know what she said. But I need to know she's safe. Please tell her of my concern."

117

Rae looked at him with wonder. "She's safe. That's what she said to tell the other man. She'll be back tomorrow. That's the message."

"Thank you. Tell her thank you."

Rae wrinkled her little brow. "Why are you here? You're strange. You're scary and people don't like you, but you don't seem so mean up close."

Marc Toddin folded his arms but said nothing. And Tahn smiled. "Come and sit for a moment. Tell your friends to come too."

She looked at him with surprise. "You know I had friends with me?"

"They're still with you." He pointed. "Two of them. Right over there."

She couldn't even see them from here. So how did he know? Had they been that loud?

"Jori! Ansley! Come here!"

The two boys came out of hiding.

"We didn't mean no harm," Jori said right away. "We just wanted to help Miss Ti get alone for a while."

Tahn nodded slowly. "So you helped her trick Lorne, didn't you?"

"Yes, sir."

"I had thought it would take more than one bright mind to distract him."

"He didn't tell on us?" Ansley asked in amazement.

"No. He didn't." He turned his eyes to the little girl. "You're friends of Miss Loble. So I want to tell you why I'm here. Sit down."

All three children obeyed, and little Jori took Rae's hand timidly.

"Do any of you have family?"

They shook their heads.

"I didn't think I did either. I came to find out for sure. And I learned Miss Loble is my sister. We just met. It isn't easy for her, and I understand that. I would go and leave her alone except that there are a lot of men, bandits, who tried to hurt her, and I think they will try again. I don't want them to find her, and I need your help. Are you willing?"

"What would we have to do?" Ansley questioned.

"Watch her. If you know where to find her, just keep your eyes open all around. You don't have to tell me where she is. She has a right to her own life. But watch for young men traveling together, three or any number more. If you see armed men with horses, tell her right away, and then one of you come and tell me."

"Would they kill her?" the bigger boy asked.

"I think they might."

"Why?"

"They didn't want her to escape them. They'd try to prove their mettle by not letting her. There's not much sense in it, boy. She's done nothing to them."

"She wouldn't want us spying for you."

"You're not. You're looking out for your friend. If you have other friends, tell them. If any of you see the men come into town, come and tell me."

"Can we ask her about this?"

"Yes. That would be fine."

Ansley looked at him with skepticism. "You're strange."

"That's what your friend said."

"Are you the one folks talk about, then?"

"That's possible."

"But you kill people."

He looked down at his boots for a moment. "I have. I won't lie to you. But that was a different time, and God has set me free. I will do what I must to protect my sister, but I pray not to kill again. It is a terrible, terrible thing."

"Was you one who disappeared?"

Tahn looked at the boy. He seemed about twelve or thirteen, and he'd obviously heard about the days when street boys simply vanished, only to turn up later bearing arms.

"Yes."

"Oh! What was it like?"

"Terrible. No matter what you've got, boy, you're far better off."

"I got nothing."

"But you're well blessed."

He looked puzzled. "I don't understand."

"It's all right. Have you eaten today?"

"Yes," the boy said. "Because of your friend."

Tahn smiled. That would be Lorne, all right. "Good. And don't be hungry tomorrow. I'll not turn you away."

Rae was stunned. "You'd feed us? Why?"

"I trust you'll help me. And everyone, no matter who they are, has a right to eat regardless."

"He sounds like Miss Ti," Jori whispered.

"He oughta," Rae answered. "He's family."

"Thank you," Tahn told her quietly. It was a good thing to hear.

<hr>

After the children were gone and the night had progressed over them, Tahn lay listening to Martica's pained cough. It only worsened, leaving her gasping for breath. She didn't call for anyone. In Tiarra's absence, she couldn't. But it didn't seem right that she should be struggling alone. Slowly, he rose to his feet.

Toddin was sitting up. "Need help with anything?"

Tahn nodded. "Please pray. The old woman hates me, but I'm going inside."

He took up his skin of water and asked the Lord for wisdom. She would not be pleased to see him. She would throw him out if she had the strength. Still, he felt compelled to offer a gesture of kindness.

As he entered, Martica lay curled beneath a ragged blanket. He knelt beside her with water, but she tried to push him away.

"Please," he said. "Drink. It will help."

She was thirsty, and she knew he was right. Just a sip might ease the awful dryness of her cough a bit. It angered her that he would just walk in this way, though her pail of water was emptied and she hadn't the strength to fill it. But he was determined. So with shaking hands, she made an effort as he lifted her head and shoulders.

"Go away," she said when she was able. "Leave me alone."

"I wanted to thank you first," he began. "For raising my sister. I'm grateful that you opened your home for her."

She looked at him with suspicion. "You've no right—" she began to say but started coughing again before she could finish.

He lifted her head and held it, giving her drink again. Then he noticed a bottle sitting in the corner next to a folded garment. "You have medicine?"

"Not much left."

"Should you be taking it?"

"No. I don't want it anymore."

"Does it help?"

She shook her head. "I said I don't want it! Leave me alone!"

"Let me get the bedding I saw in the other room first, ma'am. I can prop you up a bit with it, and the breaths should come easier." He rose without waiting for an answer and was back almost immediately with Tiarra's meager bedding.

"What have you done with my girl?" she asked.

"I wish she were here as much as you do," Tahn told her. "I wish I knew where she is, but I don't."

"She's run off scared from you!"

"I don't think so. But she'll be back for your sake, and I hope soon."

"Before I die, you mean," Martica answered bitterly.

"Bluntly put." He arranged the bedding carefully and lowered Martica onto it. Her breaths did come easier, but they were still labored. "Do you know the Lord, ma'am?" he asked with quiet voice.

She scowled at him. "Did your father teach you to make use of religious talk, boy?"

"You know there wasn't time for that."

She drew in a breath and stared at him fearfully. Of course she did know. And he must know about her lies. Almost she could expect him to smother her where she lay. It would be

121

an easy enough retribution. But of course it was unnecessary. It would not be long for her now anyway. And instead of Tiarra at her side, here was Tahn Dorn! She shook her head. *Surely I deserve this,* she told herself. *God, what a way you have in your judgment!*

But he spoke again in a soft tone. "Will you allow me to pray for you?"

She started shaking. She couldn't help it. Was he serious? Almost she yelled at him to leave her, but she saw the sadness in his face, the concern in his eyes. "I went to church often when I was about your age," she told him. "But God is not smiling on me anymore."

"That can change in a moment, if you truly give him your heart."

"But you're a Dorn," she said suddenly.

"What does that mean? Please tell me."

"That you're a liar, a swindler—" She coughed again. "A cutthroat."

"Was my father those things?"

"Yes. You can't be preaching at me!"

"I love God's mercy, ma'am. It would please me to see it thrive in you."

"You've a smooth tongue on you, just like him."

He sighed. "Don't let your opinion of me stop you from being assured of God's peace. It wouldn't be worth the cost."

She stared at him, knowing in her heart that he was sincere. "Who taught you his mercy?"

"The first was Netta Trilett."

She was puzzled. How could such a one be willing to hear and accept the walk of Christ? Wasn't he raised to be a terror? "What of your uncle?" she asked. "What did he teach you?"

He looked surprised. "I know nothing of an uncle."

Martica coughed once, then shook her head, unwilling to believe him. "That's not what the baron's man said."

"Baron's man?" He sat beside her, and his intense eyes seemed to look into her soul.

But she turned away, shocked by her own indiscretion. How could she have told him that? It just came out, before she could think.

"Please tell me what you can, ma'am. What had the baron or his men to do with me?"

"Curse you, Tahn Dorn!" she suddenly exclaimed. "You get words out of me that I shouldn't speak!"

"Your heart would stop your tongue if that were so."

She couldn't meet his gaze. He was right, and it pained her. Her heart would be willing to break loose with the truth and be clear of it, as he'd said! But it was not that easy. "No," she told herself more than him. "You have no right to speak to me that way. You can't judge my heart. And I owe you nothing."

He nodded. "I would like to know at least what my mother was like. Please consider that."

"First you tell me what you intend for Tiarra."

"I'm concerned for her poverty," he said. "I want to help, but I'll do nothing beyond her will. I fear trouble with the bandits again. That's why I stay. To protect her."

"You say it. But you were one of those mercenaries. They're your friends."

"We were cast in together. But never truly friends."

Martica scoffed. "Then you admit you took up with your uncle's devilish trade! Did he teach you religious words along with the sword? And deception! Surely after he carried you off, he told you all about your father. But you pretend you don't know."

"It was Samis who carried me off," he protested. "The mercenary leader. He told me nothing of my family, lady. My first days with him are a fog." He was quiet for a moment before continuing more slowly. "I knew nothing but the pain, and then his harsh words. He told me what he wanted me to hear and destroyed everything else I had. I don't know of an uncle. I have little memory that survived that time. That's why I need your help. I was too young and confused to know clearly on my own, lady, you know that."

There it was again. Almost an accusation. *You've lied,*

old woman! But he had no malice in it. "You're a puzzle," she said and coughed again.

"Help me to sort it out, then. Tell me about my parents, and—"

"No." She lay coughing, and he sighed in frustration. He offered her more water, but she shook her head. "You pray, do you?" she asked coolly.

"Yes."

"Are you going to marry that Trilett lady of yours?"

He lowered his head. "The future is God's. I can't tell it."

"Your mother would have liked God in your speech. But your father would have loved the nearness to wealth. You're clever like him, aren't you?"

"I haven't planned my life. Not a piece of it."

Martica looked long at him and sighed. "Not even coming in here to sway my opinion?"

"Not even that. But I would like you to consider a prayer. God is the help in such times."

She coughed. "Are you telling me I'm dying?"

"You need no one to tell you."

Almost she smiled through her weakness. "In that you speak the truth, you beast." The coughing suddenly had worse hold of her again, and it took several moments for her to catch her breath. "I'm near dead already," she said when she could finally speak. "Tiarra knows it. And she cares little anymore. But I do wish to tell her good-bye."

"I expect that she cares more than you think. And God may grant you that wish if you ask him."

"You are persistent."

"It's important."

She coughed again and then squinted at him, her eyes looking gray and sunken. "Why don't you hate me?"

"For what?" Tahn asked. "Helping my sister survive? Or mourning my mother so?"

Abruptly, she turned her head. "Curse you! Why must you make it so hard to despise you? Devil son of Sanlin Dorn, the betrayer of my dear lady! You're supposed to be a villain. More truly, you're supposed to be dead. Years ago! But you can't make it easy for anyone, can you?"

He swallowed hard. "Tell me what you're talking about while you've time."

Martica's gaze was distant. She was thinking deeply, considering the path she'd chosen. "Tiarra doesn't even know," she began. "She would hate me for it." She coughed and then took a deep breath. "Your mother wanted her among the common people, bless her. But your father's way was too perilous. All the family he knew were bandits, scoundrels like himself. And Karra had quickly learned the way of nobility to be just as bad. She would have wanted me to be more careful for her daughter's religion. She would have wanted us to leave Alastair for a town where the church could be trusted, but I have nowhere else! What was I to do? Everyone expected the girl to die back then. And it might have been better if she had!"

Tahn felt an old tension stirring in him. "Who wanted us dead?"

"You don't know who you are, do you, boy? Those burns took from your mind what you had before?"

"Tell me."

"I think it pleased Sanlin, to have a son to train. But he was a devil. He was supposed to kill all three of you. But the baron knew he would keep you at his side instead of cutting your throat the way he should have. That's why he told the town not to let you escape. You weren't supposed to survive."

Her words felt strange, as though cold hands were twisting him inside. "Why would the baron wish us dead? And how could my father be expected to accomplish it?"

"He was paid well enough. And money mattered to him. He was in the baron's employ for years. The old master would have such bad sorts in secret, you know, to accomplish his ends."

"You call him master? You were the baron's servant?"

"Of sorts. He paid me."

"For what?" Tahn could scarcely breathe for the shock of this tale.

"I used to paint for him. But he also paid me for telling him that Karra had come to Alastair. I kept her here so he could find her easily. She trusted me—"

The woman suddenly seemed to choke on the words. With increased effort, she continued. "I know, you would think I should suffer for such a thing. But . . . but I didn't know then what would happen. It seemed fair enough for him to be seeking his kin."

"Baron Trent's kin? My mother?"

Martica coughed. "Yes. And . . . that's why she died. I—I didn't know what was in the baron's heart until it was too late. A wonder he let your sister live. But more, you! A male! Karra knew that would be trouble. The day before she died, she . . . she told me about hiding among the common people, trying to keep you a secret from the baron. But Sanlin betrayed her, letting people know he had a son."

She coughed, and Tahn struggled to comprehend the things she was saying. "Did he truly kill her?"

"I believe it. But he wouldn't kill you. He was too proud, boy. He took you from your mother to ride about with him. It grieved her. But I didn't know the baron's plan! I thought it was only Sanlin to trouble her!"

Martica drew a difficult breath and then continued with considerable effort. "The baron was cunning. To silence Sanlin. A wonder he forgot you children these years. But you didn't know what you were to him."

Tahn could only stare. The words came hard. "What are we to him?"

"Kin. Didn't you hear me?"

"What kind of kin?"

"The baron was your mother's brother. Not full. She . . . she was illegitimate. But the House of Trent acknowledged her. Lionell . . . he is your cousin." She coughed. "No more questions. Do you hear me? I am such a fool."

Tahn looked down at the floor. "I thank you. For talking to me." It was much to fathom. The late Baron Trent.

126

The treacherous noble who had tried to destroy Netta and her family apparently *hadn't* forgotten Tahn Dorn. A year ago, the baron had been determined to kill him, even paying Samis well for the privilege. But why did he wait so many years? Why want to kill them at all?

Martica rolled over and gasped, and for a moment Tahn thought the worst. *Not now,* he prayed. *She should not die now! I need to learn more. She should pray. And my sister needs to be here!*

But Martica still breathed.

"Ma'am—" Tahn began to speak.

"I have said enough."

"But does . . . does my sister know these things?"

"She thinks you . . . chose your father's life." Martica sighed. Her voice was growing weaker. "I didn't want her pulled to that evil world. Nor to the baron. Karra told me of his evil too late. I wish I'd known . . ."

It was hard for Tahn to picture any of this. His mother, with a tie to the Trents and in hiding. How had she met Sanlin Dorn? Had there been any love between them?

Martica called the old baron his uncle. But she'd also said it was an uncle who carried him off so long ago. Was Samis his uncle too? How could it be? They were the worst men he'd ever known, the vilest enemies he could have imagined facing. What would Benn Trilett think if it were true? What would Netta think?

"You still have water?" Martica asked.

"Yes. Yes, let me help you." He leaned forward and held the skin for her, carefully supporting her head.

"You were right," she whispered. "It's cleansing, finally to talk. Tell Tiarra I'm sorry. I only meant to protect her. It was all I could do . . ." She fell back weakly.

"Pray to God, lady."

"Do you know what I did to you?"

"You pointed me out to the crowd." He swallowed hard. "Was I guilty?"

"I—I thought you might be. You always copied your father. But I was afraid. I couldn't take you in my house—they might kill the baby, even me. And there was no hope for you. You were the son. I thought if you died, it would be over. Perhaps he'd leave Karra's daughter alone. You could kill me, boy, for your burns . . ."

"No."

"They left me the baby. They left her alone. I don't know why."

"God wanted her alive."

"I—I hope God forgives me. I've done miserably." She closed her eyes. "It's so cold tonight." Her breath was suddenly shallow.

Tahn's heart sunk. *Tiarra, where are you?*

"I want to tell your sister good-bye."

"Pray, lady. Please."

"I should. And you're . . . you're Karra's son. You can help me."

He prayed. But the old woman only nodded her assent and said no more. She lay very still, and her breaths grew weaker. When he left her, Tahn knew she was unconscious. But he took her water pail to fill it for her anyway, in the hope that she would live long enough to need it, and to see Tiarra face to face one last time.

When he rejoined Marc Toddin, it was with a heavy heart. He could find no words to express his burden. Where had Tiarra gone that could be so important? What would be for her now? Would she be able to hear him if Martica could not tell her the truth? And what of the Trents? What might this mean to the new baron, Lionell?

13

Lionell impatiently watched Captain Saud enter his private chamber followed immediately by Korin, the quiet, graying guard who took care of training most of the younger men. They had been his father's most trusted guards.

He could see on their faces the uncertainty of being summoned. But Saud, the capable and arrogant leader, stood straight before him as always and gave him barely the courtesy of a nod.

"What is the matter with you?" Lionell demanded. "I am your head. How dare you keep vital secrets from me! You must have known what my father knew!"

"What, my lord?" Korin asked, looking stricken.

"My wealth is at stake! My power is at stake! I should have you both killed! Why was I not told that Karra Loble had a son!"

"Ah, yes," Captain Saud answered slowly. "The Dorn."

Lionell fumed. How could the captain so coolly admit to this knowledge? He was about to burst out with a stream of curses when Saud interrupted him.

"You were not told, my lord, because your father didn't want you worrying yourself or trying to handle things on your own."

"Father was a fool!" Lionell lamented. "But more than that, he is dead now. Why didn't you come to me?"

Korin cleared his throat. "My lord, sir—your mother pledged us to the secret."

"Who? Just the two of you?"

"Yes," Korin continued with obvious discomfort. "Because . . . because we were the ones charged to help your father with the problem before."

"Well." Lionell stared long at him. "You failed miserably. When did my mother acquire your pledge?"

"Last year. When your father died."

Lionell scowled. "Didn't it occur to you that with my father gone I had become the baron in his place? Why are you heeding my mother?"

"For your own sake she insisted, my lord," Korin answered. "She was afraid you would do something rash and Benn Trilett would rally the other nobles against you. She was afraid you would get yourself killed."

"This is not my mother's business. And Tahn Dorn is no Trilett. Why should Benn Trilett care?"

"He claims the dog," Saud answered abruptly. "He's made the Dorn captain of his gate."

Lionell turned to face him. "How can you let a woman rule you, Saud? I know it would be your pleasure to kill him."

"I don't let her rule me," Saud replied sourly. "But there's a time for such things, and it's not been yet. Not while Dorn is under Trilett watchcare."

"And when did you think to tell me of this?"

Saud met Lionell's eyes without wavering. "In time, sir. The matter has required patience and secrecy."

"Yes! Of course! But I am your baron, fool! You do not keep secrets from me. Mother be hanged! You do my bidding."

Saud smiled. "And what would you bid us do?"

"I want Tahn Dorn dead! As soon as possible, no more delay. How could Father have waited all these years? What was he thinking? He even knew where Dorn was. Why did he not send men to see the matter finished years ago?"

Saud gave an audible sigh. "He would have liked nothing better. But you forget whose care Dorn was in. Imagine if Samis had discovered what he had. That devil would have destroyed the House of Trent and taken everything to himself

130

in the name of the Dorn! Far better that your father keep Samis ignorantly employed and await his chance."

"But he blundered! You all blundered! Don't you realize that?" Lionell fumed. "Dorn lives. He has returned to Alastair, and he is bound to learn things. This is serious!"

"He is in Alastair?" Saud brightened. "The best of news. He'll not reach Onath again alive."

"I don't want him leaving Alastair! Do you hear me? Or anyone else who knows of this! Do you understand?"

Korin suddenly coughed. "Sir—"

"What is it?" Lionell snapped in his direction.

Korin swallowed down a heavy breath. "Alastair doesn't know for certain the boy was Karra's son. They don't know truly who she was, my lord. And none of the nobles know she bore children at all—"

"Children? There are others?"

"A daughter, sir," Saud said abruptly. "She was a baby. Left in the care of an old woman in Alastair."

Korin frowned. And Lionell groaned. "Why was she left in Alastair?"

"It is a girl, sir." Saud shrugged. "No threat at present. And the old woman knows to keep quiet. "

"Not she only," Korin said quickly. "The townspeople won't speak of what happened. Those who know your father's part are loyal. They'll tell Dorn nothing. You needn't worry for these things—"

"I am not fool enough to stake my future on your opinion," Lionell said sharply. "I must have Dorn's dead body. And I want the girl before she has a chance to bear some peasant scoundrel any sons."

"You will have your desire," Saud told him with a callous smile. "Do you want the girl here?"

"Father had such foolish taste for the cousins!" Lionell scoffed. "But I have girls enough! She's too dangerous. Kill them all."

"Yes, sir." Saud bowed and turned for the doorway.

"Take all the men you need and go at once," Lionell told him.

"Indeed, sir."

Korin shuffled from one foot to the other. "My lord, sir—"

"What is it?" Lionell barked in his direction. "You want to go, is that it? To take your part finishing what you should have accomplished years ago?"

For a moment Korin stood in silence. He seemed paler than the other man. Finally the aging guard replied, "Yes, sir. I would go."

"Very well. Be gone! And don't return to me until the job is done."

<hr>

As he left Lionell's chamber behind him, Saud relished the idea of what lay ahead. Tahn was a hateful annoyance, a continual thorn. It would be a pleasure to kill the arrogant fool.

The old baron in his grave would be pleased to finally have this unfinished business taken care of. Of course, Lionell's mother would not be so pleased. But that was only a woman's fears. Nothing that need get in the way.

Saud wondered why Tahn would dare return to Alastair. But it did not really matter. The Triletts would never know what truly happened. Alastair was the perfect place for the Dorn to die. No one could be surprised if that town were to slay him with a silent vengeance impossible to track down.

<hr>

It was a long night. Tahn could scarcely sleep, and he woke at dawn feeling restless. Something was stirring, he knew. He rose to his feet with new tension and woke Marc Toddin in time for him to hear the first vigorous shouts down the street.

"What is it, Tahn?" Marc asked immediately.

"I don't know." He started in the direction of the sound, pausing only to secure his sword at his waist. Shouting in Alastair! It put a chill in him.

Marc was right behind him, trying to sort out the sounds they were hearing. A banging noise. The shouts of more people now. A scream. "We don't have to get involved," he said.

"You're wrong." Tahn kept going, quickening his pace.

"Dorn—"

But Tahn paid no attention to him. Ahead of him he was beginning to see a crowd gathering, drawn from neighboring houses by continuing calls for punishment of a crime committed. Is this how Alastair dealt always with such things? Noise and an angry assembly? He ran toward the people, afraid of how he would react if forced to witness a hanging again on this street.

Suddenly a child burst from the crowd and almost ran into him.

It was the little girl, Rae. "Mr. Dorn, sir!"

He took her arm with his heart pounding. "What is it? Are you in danger?"

"No." She shook her head, and tears streamed down her face. "It's Miss Ti—"

He didn't wait for an explanation. He shoved his way toward the source of those shouts, tormented inside over what might have happened to his sister and that he hadn't gone looking as soon as he knew of her absence. Martica lay dying. In what shape was Tiarra?

"We all know the due for thieving!" a man was shouting. "Caught in the act! There's no denying it!"

There was a struggle in process, just to his left. Three men were trying to hold their kicking prisoner. Tiarra. Her hands bound and her arms held, she was fighting still, her face an angry red.

"Bring her to the post!" the tall, well-dressed man shouted. "She's got to learn her lesson! We'll not tolerate a thief!"

They would whip her, he realized. Bind her to the post erected for such a purpose and give her whatever lashes the supposed victim might require.

He stepped forward, aware that there were eyes on him now, prepared for whatever trouble he might bring. But most of the people had not yet noticed him, and there were shouts of assent to the first man's judgment.

133

"Stop!" he cried, the pressure like a knot in his heart. Here he was in the midst of this crowd, surrounded by people. "Stop!" he yelled again, and heads turned. Tiarra stared at him, her face suddenly paling. "People!" he cried. "Would you do judgment without hearing the matter?"

The well-dressed man looked at him in anger. "You cannot walk into our town and interfere. You're not part of us. There's nothing more to hear. This woman broke into my home to steal my wife's necklace! We caught her in the act. My neighbors know what justice is! In Alastair we flog a thief!"

"It is rightfully mine!" Tiarra turned her face tearfully to Mr. Ovny. "You know it was my mother's!"

"It was fairly bought," he told the crowd. "It is my wife's. And this girl tried to steal it. Those are the facts, and she cannot deny them." He nodded to the men surrounding Tiarra, and they pulled her forward. A broad-shouldered man followed them with a whip.

"There's nothing you can do, Dorn," Ovny told Tahn with a smile. "You know it is not wisdom to stand against a crowd."

Something shuddered within him, but he kept his steel. "If you speak the truth, I will bear the lash for her."

"What?" Marc Toddin stepped to Tahn's side. "You can't be—"

"I will bear it," he repeated. "Let her go."

The crowd stood in stunned silence. Mr. Ovny looked long at Tahn. And then he nodded. "Someone has to be punished. It is a brother's right."

"No!" Tiarra cried.

Tahn met her eyes with a calm that hid the tempest inside him. "Best to give it to an experienced back, miss, and not mar the fresh."

"No," she said again, shaking her head. "You can't do this! I'm the one responsible! I did what was said! He knew nothing of it!"

"He is older, girl," Mr. Ovny said. "With your father gone, it is his decision."

134

Tahn glanced up at the man. He was a cruel one, to make mention of their father that way and throw Tiarra under the authority of someone who was a near stranger to her. But at least it would work to spare her the blows. Her mother's necklace? That would be something to hold, all right. The theft was wrong, but who could fault her for the longing?

He removed his sword and handed it to Toddin, who shook his head in dismay. "You need your strength, man."

"I have enough."

"Untie the girl," Mr. Ovny was saying.

"You can't do this," Tiarra protested. She turned to Tahn in stormy bewilderment. "Why are you doing this?"

"Go home to Martica," he commanded. "Please hurry. She needs you." He looked at the crowd around him and shook his head, sorry for her. The town would link her forever in their minds with him now, with cutthroats and criminals. Perhaps she had been her own once, but how would she ever escape their harsh opinions after this? And whatever comfort Martica might have been would be gone soon enough.

He walked to the post of his own accord, and Tiarra, as soon as she was untied, ran forward. But Marc Toddin caught her by both arms.

"His mind is made up, Miss Dorn," he said. "We'll not change it, much as we would wish to."

She stared at this stranger, and tears met her cheeks. "I—I am not Miss Dorn," she stammered. But she was. She knew she was Dorn as much as he was. And now he was being a brother to her in a most terrible way.

"Take your shirt off," Ovny was telling Tahn, who obeyed in silence.

Tiarra caught her breath. His back! The scars! He had said he was experienced. And there were stripes, but the skin around them looked strangely taut, almost waxy. The burns? The torture Lorne had told her about? It was too much for her. "No!" she cried again, pulling away from Toddin.

"Keep her back," Ovny commanded. "Or we'll have them both."

"He aims to spare you, miss," Toddin said, grasping her again. "I'm not liking it. But he gives us no choice."

Still Tiarra struggled. "No!"

"He's claimed the family right, girl," Toddin told her, staring at the coldhearted man at the head of the crowd. "We can only hope your accuser has decency enough to respect the mercy that should be in such a case."

She stood shaking her head, wanting to scream. Why was Tahn doing this? Why would he come back . . . and then do this?

"In the face of courage, and sacrifice, it is a time for mercy," Toddin loudly insisted.

But Ovny would not hear him. "Tie his hands at the top," he commanded his men, but Tahn shook his head.

"Fine," the wealthy man smirked. "Fall in the dirt if you want to."

The crowd was restless around them, unwilling to cross Ovny's will or deny the crime. Yet Tahn's gesture had taken them by surprise. It seemed that mercy would indeed be an appropriate response to the courageous gift, even for this fearsome stranger. But Ovny was not so minded.

Tahn gripped the bar at the top of the post and closed his eyes. "God help me," he whispered. "What else could I do?"

He stood straight as the first lash fell, not moving to betray the shock of it. But as the second fell across his back, he could hear Samis's screaming voice, and he started shaking. He couldn't run. He could feel chains now tight at his wrists. There was nothing he could do. Up against a wall in a darkened room, he'd just had to take it.

Somehow he kept his hold on the bar above him. He stayed on his feet, though the dismal room swirled around his mind and Samis kept on, blow after awful blow.

But a shout in the crowd drew him back to Alastair, the place of deadly mobs. Another lash fell across his back, and then another, and he could hear the shouting growing around him. "Killer!" someone shouted. "Hang the killer!" He was a child again, and he shuddered as the memory pressed over his mind. The chase of the crowd. The senseless terror.

Another blow. He wanted to scream. His neck, his back, even his legs were touched by liquid fire. This was Alastair.

He didn't know how long it went on. He stood silent, quivering, his knuckles white around the bar he held.

"Tahn."

Someone touched him, and he shook his head.

"Tahn, let go. It's over." Marc Toddin put his big hands around his friend's and pried them open. In his weakness, Tahn nearly fell, but Marc caught him. "Let me carry you."

"No."

"For God's mercy!" Toddin exclaimed. He pulled Tahn's arm up over his shoulder and supported him as he led him away from the people who stood watching in silence.

It was all so unreal. That there was a friend this time, bearing his weight, seemed nothing short of a miracle. "Where are we going?" he asked.

"We're closer to the church than to that woman's home."

But Tahn shook his head again.

"You're bleeding," Marc explained. "I need to have you down away from these fools to tend to it."

"Let me help you." It was Tiarra's voice, and suddenly she was taking Tahn's other arm over her own shoulder.

He glanced up at her, and their eyes met for a moment before she turned her face away from him.

There was fear in her eyes, he knew. More of it, and of a different nature than she'd had before. He couldn't understand, and he hung his head. "Please go home," he told her again. But she wouldn't leave them.

They laid him down almost as soon as they entered the church doors. But they hadn't been there more than a minute when they heard a rapping at the door behind them. Tiarra answered it and found a bowl of water and a pile of cloth abandoned on the church step.

"See what someone has brought us," she told Marc. "Perhaps they were shamed."

"They should be," he replied. "How are you doing, Tahn?"

"We shouldn't stay here. The old woman is sick."

"We'll move on soon enough. Just try to relax and let us help you. I'll bandage him, miss. Wash him, will you, while I lay out the cloth?"

Tiarra worked with tears in her eyes. She'd brought on this trouble. It was hard, bathing the blood from her strange brother's back, seeing the awful welts and wounds laid out on top of a barrage of old scars. What must he be like on the inside? Maybe he was just as Lorne said. No wonder his eyes were so deep and haunted. But she couldn't talk to him. She was afraid of whatever he might say now, whoever he might really be.

Suddenly there were footsteps behind her, and she whirled around. It was Lucas, the someday-priest, standing there in his black clothes and dangling golden cross. For a moment he didn't move, and then he jumped forward in recognition.

"God above! Tahn!" He knelt at his side, searching their faces. "Why? How could they do this? What happened?"

Toddin glanced up at Tiarra but didn't answer.

"Lucas," Tahn spoke. "Thank God, Lucas."

But Lucas jumped to his feet again. "Let me get you a drink. And a cover." He turned to Toddin. "Will you need more cloth?"

"Don't know yet."

Lucas was gone for only a moment. He left a blanket and cloth at Tiarra's side and took a bottle and knelt at Tahn's head. "Let me help you drink," he said. "This should help you. God knows it's good to see you again, but not like this." He looked up at Tiarra and took a deep breath. "Surely not the bandits—"

"No," she said. "The town. He took it for me. I—I tried to steal."

"Our mother's necklace . . ." Tahn whispered.

And Lucas looked at him in surprise. "This is your sis-

138

ter?" But he didn't wait for a response. "Can you raise up enough for a drink?"

"No," Tahn answered, and Marc and Tiarra both looked at him with concern.

"Pray for me, Lucas," Tahn went on. "I lost myself, I think."

"What do you mean?"

"At the pole. I wasn't there. I was . . . I was in the memory."

Lucas sighed. "Lord give you peace. Tahn, what do you expect? This town? I thought they'd have to drag you in chains to get you to come back here."

"I found a sister."

"Yes." He looked up at Tiarra. "God bless you both. You've had need of each other." He set the bottle down and laid his hands on Tahn's hair. "You asked me for prayer. How did you know you could do that, brother? When I left you—"

"You're in the church now. It must feel like home."

Lucas smiled. "It does. In its strange way." He bowed his head and prayed a short and careful prayer. Tiarra watched him closely.

"You should stay here," Lucas told Tahn. "You need a place to heal for a while."

Tahn shook his head. "Tiarra must go home. The old woman's worse."

"I can take her," Marc offered. "You stay here with your friend."

"Yes," Tahn told them. "Go. But be careful. There'll be trouble soon."

They went out quickly at his urging, leaving Lucas to finish tending to Tahn's wounds. "The old woman cannot last long," Tahn said with quiet voice. "My sister will be left alone. And I think she's never had much."

"You're right." Lucas sighed. "They're very poor. And I saw the old woman bitter and hard with the girl. It can't have been easy, living in her charge."

"Burle is after her. And after you. I tried to find you yesterday."

Lucas shook his head in disgust. "What does he want? That a girl should lie still and let herself be violated? Or that I should hear screams and turn my head? I have a conscience toward these people now, Tahn! Let him come if he will."

"He will." Tahn took a deep breath. "I fought him off. Wounded him. Now he has a blood grudge. He'll come."

Lucas was silent for a moment, considering. "Burle has plenty of men. Fifteen. Maybe more by now. We should bring your sister back here. You should stay in the church. The people would not be pleased to see it desecrated. There'll be no fighting within its doors."

"The Trents claim St. Thomas's," Tahn protested.

"Yes, Tahn. But they're seldom here."

"Their friends? Their soldiers?"

"Sometimes." Lucas nodded his understanding. "I don't trust them either. But the people here have great needs. And they're not all bad, believe me."

"The priest?" Tahn asked.

"I believe he is sincere."

"Did he tell you I met him?"

"No."

Suddenly there was another voice. "Have you need of a balm?"

Lucas turned his head. "Yes, Father. Thank you."

The short priest disappeared as quickly as he'd come, and Lucas put his hand on Tahn's shoulder. "He seeks to help you, friend. He did tell me you were in Alastair. I was about to go searching."

Tahn didn't answer. He only sunk his head into his hands. *Oh, Lucas! Here in the baron's church! And we don't know yet what that might mean.*

Lucas wiped the cool water again across Tahn's bruised back. "Is it pretty bad?"

"I sent Lorne to Onath for men. That's how bad I expect it to be."

"I meant your back, Tahn. The pain."

140

"I'll live with it. You know that."

"You've lived with too much of it, I think."

Tahn tensed. "You live your days, Lucas. What choice is there? It's my lot, it seems. But it won't stop me."

Lucas looked carefully at him. "The Lord is your lot now, my brother. The Triletts. The children. They are all well?"

That was like another world to Tahn now. Netta's love, like a dream, seemed too far away to touch him. In this place, Samis seemed closer. Sanlin Dorn, whom he could scarcely remember, seemed more real. And the hurt threatened to consume him.

"What's wrong with me, Lucas?" he gasped. "I can't see past the pain! The battle that's coming holds my mind. I'm afraid for you, and my sister. And it's not just Burle. It's this town! I don't understand it all. But it will raise up its head and try to destroy us. I thought I had peace. Now I'm not sure I ever will. The things I learn . . . of who I am . . ."

He stopped. How could he explain the war in his heart? Was he really kin to Samis, the sadistic killer and stealer of children? And kin of the baron too, who'd ordered the murder of an entire family as they slept? Both dead men haunted him still. And Samis's legacy in Burle posed a problem. Would Lionell Trent prove a threat as well?

Lucas had bowed his head. "Tahn—about who you are . . . there's something I've needed to tell you." With one hand on his dangling golden cross, he sighed. "I couldn't say it before. I didn't want to trouble you. But I can't keep it from you any longer. Samis talked to me. When we rode to find you. He told me that his father had been a bandit and he'd had a brother he scarcely knew. It was Samis's brother who was hanged here, Tahn. That's when he took you with him—"

"No." Tahn tried to get up, but Lucas took his arm.

"I'm sorry I didn't tell you before."

"Then it's really true. He was my uncle." He closed his eyes, trembling.

"Tahn—"

"Oh, God! He said I was like him. He said the sword

141

was part of me, something I'd never escape. But he never told me this! Did he hate me that much?"

Lucas bowed his head. "I can't say there was much in Samis but hatred for anyone."

"I hated *him*, Lucas! God help me, I don't want this! I don't want him a part of me. But now—"

"Now you're free," Lucas declared. "Do what you must in this town. Help your sister. Then go back to Onath and the ones who love you."

Tahn lay sunken before him. "Samis took pleasure in the things he did to me."

"I know. And I know it was worse for you than the rest of us. But in his mind he was grooming you to take his place. To be the hardened killer who could rule Valhal and all the men after he was gone. He thought he was right, that he could make what he wanted out of you. I thought he would drive you insane. But you have peace in God now. Don't forget that. Your uncle or not, Samis has no more hold on you."

<hr>

Marc and Tiarra moved with quick steps through Alastair's streets. Tiarra was in too much of a hurry to stop, but she wanted answers from this stranger nonetheless. "Were you one of those mercenaries too?"

"No, miss."

"But you're my brother's friend."

"I'm honored he counts me such."

"I was guilty. He knew it." She brushed back tears. "Why did he let them whip him?"

"Everyone in the crowd knew why!" the big man exclaimed. "To save his sister. Why else could there be? He thinks you despise him. And he may not know you yet, but he loves you, girl. I hope you can see that."

"He shouldn't have—"

"I agree."

Tiarra turned and looked at the man's solemn frown. It should have been her; of course he thought that. "How could he do it, then?" she asked with a tremor in her voice.

"I don't think he can bear to watch someone hurt, miss. I tracked him once. I was paid to do it by the men hunting him. They caught a girl he didn't even know, but he walked into their trap and took arrows trying to rescue her. It's the way he is, I guess. Driven at caring for others. Overmuch and to his own expense. Very well he knows he'll need to fight soon. And now he's badly hurting. It's not going to be easy."

"I'm sorry! Is that what you want me to say? I didn't know this would happen!" She thought of the bandits, and the agile strength Tahn had against them before. It frightened her. The man was right. Faced with their swords now, her brother would be vulnerable. He might even be killed.

"But he's a praying man," Marc suddenly added. "God gave him a way to survive the arrows. He'll help him again. Don't worry. It's a good time for you to be thankful and think of the Christ. He does the same thing for you, girl! You're guilty, and he takes the penalty. All of it. And then you're free. It's a wondrous love."

Tiarra looked at him again, but this was too much for her to bear. Christ and Tahn Dorn. Both trying to save her. And how she'd cursed them both! She could picture the Jesus of the crucifix in St. Thomas's, bruised and whipped, shedding blood because of her guilt. She saw Toddin's eyes and knew he could see that she was suddenly shaking. She turned and fled, as fast as she could run, toward Martica's house. The big man's footsteps were close behind her, but at least she wouldn't have to listen to any more of his heart-rending words.

In the church, Tahn sat up with a moan. "I need to be up," he said. "And tend to business." Lucas had spread the priest's oily balm across Tahn's back, and he buttoned his shirt over the bandages that covered it.

"You should rest longer," Lucas protested. "It won't hurt you."

"But it won't help us. I need to go see the man from the street."

143

"Which man?"

"The one with our mother's necklace in his house."

"Tahn, are you sure?"

"It means something to my sister, Lucas. Don't worry. I won't hurt anyone."

"That's not what concerns me. He's the one who chose to whip you, yes?"

"Yes."

Lucas shook his head. "Tahn, he won't want to see you—"

"No one does here. But he'll see me. They all will, at least until I know my sister is treated fairly. The baron wanted us dead. The old woman told me that. But this town did the ugly work. And I won't have its bitter medicine spilled now on Tiarra. She was an innocent babe, Lucas. She deserves more than she's been given." He pulled to his feet and groaned again, leaning against the wall.

"You're not ready, Tahn."

But he pushed away and moved toward the door. "I won't be weak, Lucas. At least not for long."

"Let me come with you then."

"I think that is what your priest feared would happen."

"I'm not bound here. I can't let you go without help."

"You're a good friend. You were always that to me, even when I tormented you."

Lucas moved immediately to the door. "It wasn't your fault. You can't control your dreams."

"Only pity the soul who had to share quarters with me, eh?" He started out.

"Lean on me, Tahn," Lucas urged.

"No. Not as long as I can manage."

"Let me get you a staff, then. You look like you could fall."

"I'll take the staff. But stop worrying."

"I know you're in pain. I wish you'd wait."

"I can't. But I do want you with me—they'll be looking for you or Tiarra, and I don't want you alone."

"What do you expect to do?"

"Ask God's wisdom. Trust his hand."

Lucas went for the staff, and Tahn stood in the church entry, leaning at the doorpost and looking out. A young woman was hurrying past with a baby strapped to her back. She glanced up at him but then turned her face anxiously away.

"God bless you," he said aloud.

And she stopped. "You should go," she told him quickly. "Leave Alastair."

He saw the tears in her eyes as she turned to move on. "Wait!" he called. But she would not.

Lucas came out, and Tahn pointed. "Do you know her?"

"No."

"I forget that Alastair has people like any other town, with needs and conscience." He held the staff and the stone rail and made his way down the steps. "Tell me what drew you back, Lucas."

"What you told me. If I got in trouble, to come to the church. I hated myself. I was going to jump from the cliff by Devil's Falls. But I wanted to see St. Thomas's one more time, and sit in the back pew like I did when I was nobody's child. It wasn't the same priest who came out. But Father Bray told me about Christ, Tahn. He convinced me to give Christ my life. I think you could like Father Bray. I have told him much about us."

Tahn took a deep breath. "But . . . St. Thomas's prospers with Trent money."

"I know."

"Pray God the priest will not have to choose his loyalties."

Tahn and Lucas moved slowly across the churchyard. And behind them at a window, the short priest watched.

Tahn didn't know the name of Tiarra's accuser, so Lucas asked the wheelwright whom it was who had led the crowd at the whipping. Jothniel Ovny.

Lucas knew right where to go. The Ovnys' was a large

house, the finest in Alastair, with a pillared front. It stood so close to some of the poor houses that it seemed built to shame them. Tahn was about to approach the door, sweating and pale, when Lucas stopped him.

"Are you sure you're up to this, brother? It can wait. Better that it does."

"No. He doesn't expect me now." He wiped his brow, took another deep breath, and steeled himself against the brutal ache. Then he rapped boldly, and they waited together.

Mikal Ovny answered the door. "Go away," he told Tahn at first, but then he saw Lucas. "Reverend sir," he stammered. "What can we do for you?"

"We would see your father," Lucas answered simply.

"He did what was right according to our custom," Mikal said nervously, with a wary eye on Tahn.

"Of course," Tahn told him. "Fetch him for us on a matter of business."

"Just a minute." Mikal disappeared behind the closed door. In a moment, his father stood in his place.

"What do you want with me?" Ovny asked Tahn but then turned toward Lucas. "I beg your pardon, Reverend sir. It surprises me to find you in such company."

"I've known the Dorn a long time, Jothniel," Lucas said. "I stand with him the same as a brother."

That made the man nervous. "You can't fault me, sir. It wasn't my sin. His sister—she was the one who did wrong. And he came to the post willing."

"Yes," Tahn affirmed with growing effort behind his words. "We're not here to fault you. I ask to see the thing my sister tried to steal. Give me a chance to view what was my mother's. I bear you no blame for the carriage of justice, sir."

Ovny looked at him a long time and then turned his eyes to Lucas again.

"Family is deserving of that much courtesy," Lucas told him.

The man fidgeted a bit, seeming unsure what to think of

146

the Dorn showing up with a representative of the Church. "Mikal! Bring the Loble jewel!"

"But Father—"

"Quickly, now," Ovny insisted. He smiled at Lucas. "You didn't tell me whether the church had an opinion of what happened today."

"It is written, 'Blessed are the merciful, for they shall obtain mercy,'" Lucas told him with a solemn expression. "You could have forgiven the deed."

"Outright theft?"

"Caused by a poor daughter's longing."

"That doesn't excuse it."

"You're right," Tahn put in. "She should not have done it." He leaned his hand against the door frame. "Did you know your mother, Mr. Ovny?"

"Yes."

"And you have respect for her?"

"Of course."

"My sister and I lost our mother. You know. We have no pleasant memories to share. We seek a piece of her to hold in our hearts. And . . . we need your help. We need you to respect her as surely she deserves, by respecting our need."

Tahn took a deep breath, willing himself strength for the sake of his plea. "Tiarra did not have what you did, sir. No mother's hand, not even the fleeting memory I have. It must be an open sore in her heart, for her to violate your home. I'm sorry for that. But I beg you . . . to consider allowing me to purchase what belonged to Karra Loble. I will pay you whatever you ask. A gift of healing for my sister is worth that to me. Surely you understand."

"But she will have won!" Ovny protested. "Just to have it handed to her now—"

"Blessed are the merciful," Lucas said again.

Mikal brought a box to the door and looked at his father with a frown. "Mary loves this piece, Father."

Ovny looked at him sternly and then opened the box. It held a beautiful golden necklace set with rows of tiny white gems and one large spectacular green stone. Tahn felt weak at the sight of it. It was almost exactly like one Netta Trilett wore and cherished, which had been her grandmother's. Who was this Karra Loble, kin to Naysius Trent? Had she known the Triletts too?

The necklace was a locket. He knew that because of Netta's. But it did not appear to be one. It opened directly behind the large stone, and the setting carefully hid the tiny crack. Netta's locket held a tiny bit of lace from her christening gown, which her mother had placed there when Netta was an infant. Might there be some sentimental treasure in Karra Loble's hidden locket too?

"It's not for sale," Ovny was saying.

"I'll give you three hundred porthets."

Three hundred? Ovny gazed at the man in surprise. He didn't look like he could be possessed of such a sum. He didn't act like it either. Was it true, then, that he was backed by Trilett wealth and power? Here he stood with a churchman, offering this fantastic amount. And he was strangely calm and accepting of what was done to him. Would he stay that way if his offer was refused? Ovny shook his head. He'd never seen anyone carry himself so steadily so soon after a flogging. What more could he be up to?

"We won't sell this!" Mikal exclaimed and tried to shut the box. "You've seen it, same as Tiarra did. Now, please go about your lives! We regret the loss of your mother, but it's not our fault."

Jothniel Ovny looked into Tahn's eyes and shuddered at his son's words. Not their fault? What if this young man with the strength to stand before him should find out how he'd rallied men at the baron's request, ready to hang his father and yet do nothing to protect the mother who was bound to die? They didn't warn her, or shelter her. Nothing. Because it was the baron's bidding. He told them what would happen. And that was just the way it had to be. This very house was the gain for that horrible obedience.

What Mikal doesn't know! Jothniel Ovny had pushed and pulled the other men, gathered them, stirred them, for the baron's sake, for the money's sake. And he had even more influence now because of it. It was not hard to lord it over Tiarra. She could do nothing. But this man, with powerful friends, might be a different story. Jothniel had thought to chase him from town with that flogging. But here the man stood unfazed. "Three hundred, you say?" he spoke nervously. "That's a fair price for a piece of jewelry."

"Father!"

"Mikal, you could buy your love five fine necklaces for that price, and have a plenty left for a pleasant meal."

"You promised Mother."

"That would be my business."

The young man stormed away, and Mr. Ovny made his agreement quickly. "Three hundred porthets and our peace," he said. "No bitter feelings for what has taken place between us."

When they were away from the Ovny house, Tahn leaned against a gate and looked the necklace over carefully. It was so much like Netta's. He turned over the great stone and pried at the tiny crack behind it. Almost to his surprise, it opened. Inside there was only a curled lock of hair, long and fine and black as coal. "Tiarra's, surely," he told Lucas. "It would be like a mother to save a lock from her baby."

But Lucas shook his head. "She wasn't old enough for it to be that long. It would be more like a mother to save a lock from the first cut of her firstborn son."

Tahn touched the soft hairs, and a lump rose in his throat. Could she have treasured him so? Almost he could feel that tender touch again, and it broke his heart. "I wish I'd known her better . . . I wish she'd had more time with us."

Lucas put his arm around his friend, and Tahn suddenly looked up at him. "I'm sorry," Tahn told him. "You had no mother yourself."

"Mine died in childbirth," Lucas said. "My father moved on, not wanting a little one to slow him down. I can't fault you any, your feelings. Your history deserves a second look. Your mother must have known wealth, to have such jewels, but they say she lived poor and had poor friends." He shook his head. "You've been uncommon since I first saw you. And your mother was uncommon. She must have had reasons."

They went together back to Martica's house with the necklace secure in its box. Marc Toddin was sitting outside. He was surprised to see their approach and rose quickly to his feet. Tahn looked terribly pale.

"You shouldn't be up," he said immediately.

But Tahn pressed himself toward the door.

"She's dead, sir," Marc told him. "She was gone when we arrived."

Tahn shut his eyes. It wasn't supposed to be like this. Tiarra should have had her good-bye. "My sister—she is inside?"

"Yes."

He took another faltering step but collapsed into the outside wall. Both of his friends rushed to his side.

"You've got to rest, Tahn," Lucas urged.

He nodded but was clearly trying to pull himself up again. "First I need to see my sister." He took hold of the little box Lucas had carried and rose to his feet with a groan.

Marc started to take his arm, but Tahn waved him back. "Let me be," he told his friend emphatically. They watched him struggle through the doorway.

"Why is he being so stubborn?" Marc asked. "He'll drive himself into the dirt."

Lucas had no words to answer him.

Tahn found Tiarra sitting against the wall in Martica's room, the corpse at her feet. He knelt down painfully and sat beside her. "I'm sorry," he whispered.

"For what?" she cried, her face damp with tears. "For what are you sorry?"

"I wanted you to see her again. You shouldn't have come with me to the church—"

"But it was my fault! How could I not?" She looked up at him and saw his weakness. He was such a mystery. "How did you get back here? Why did you come now?"

150

He didn't try to explain. He only handed her the little box.

She recognized it immediately and was almost breathless, but she shook her head. "Mother's necklace."

"Yes."

Seeing it made her afraid, and all the things Martica had said raced through her mind. "What did you do?" she asked in a hushed voice, not knowing what to expect from him.

"I bought it. For you."

Tears filled her eyes again. "I—I can't take it."

He looked confused. He opened the box for her. "Why not? I want you to have it."

It made her tremble. That he would buy it legitimately. For her. If this were true, he was more than generous, more than fair. "You paid for it, sir. A terrible price for my sake. It's rightly yours now."

But he touched her hand. "I have a little sister. I want her to know that her peace matters to me. You should have . . . what was your mother's. She would have wanted that."

He leaned back against the wall wearily.

"You're not well," she said.

"I'll be fine."

"But you're in pain."

"As you are." He looked over at Martica's body. "Was she good to you?"

"Yes. Of course."

"Always?"

Tiarra looked at him in question. For so long, she hadn't believed that he could really care. Now she knew he must. But she didn't want to tell him how hard the woman had been. "It doesn't matter, now that she's dead. I should have been here." She leaned over and kissed Martica's forehead. "I couldn't bear to cover her. But I suppose I must."

"Would you like me to?"

"No. Don't move, please. You look terrible." She reached and pulled a tattered blanket over the body. "She worried about me," Tiarra said sadly. "I worried about her. Now all that's over."

151

"Will you stay here?" he asked her.

"I have nothing else."

He nodded solemnly. "I'm hard to accept. I know that. But I'll be a brother to you."

At first she didn't know how to answer, but then the words came in a rush. "How can you be this way? You let them whip you—and you've been hurt before, God knows! What do you want?"

He opened his arms to her, and she stared at him, trembling. She'd taken his arm on the way to St. Thomas's. But could she embrace him now?

"I want to be your family," he said, his voice low and sad.

She knew he saw her hesitation. He lowered his arms. *He thinks I still hate him,* she thought. *Even now. He thinks I don't want a brother, or his embrace. After what he's done! Why am I still afraid?*

Slowly he sunk to the hard floor and lay on his side. "My friends will help you with the burying. Just tell them what you need."

It made her ache to see him like this. He had seemed so strong that he was frightening. But now he looked beaten down, painfully weak. "Can I bring you water?"

He'd closed his eyes. "Please."

Soon he was asleep. And Lucas began to help her wrap Martica's body.

It was hard for her to think straight, hard to concentrate on what she was doing with her brother lying so close. He looked younger now, and so vulnerable. It was the flogging that had done it, she knew, and she wondered at herself. What now? Could she trust him, despite Martica's caution? But how could she not?

He rolled in his sleep, lifting his arms to protect his head. And it made her hurt inside. Before the Trilett peace, what kind of life must he have had?

"Lucas, sir," she whispered, motioning to her brother. "What does he fear?"

152

He glanced at Tahn and nodded kindly. "He dreams, surely. He'll be all right."

"But what sort of dream? What threat? Tell me! You know him!"

Lucas couldn't help but smile. "Oh, sister. This dream is mild. He doesn't even cry out. The dreams used to tear him, possess him almost. It was horrible to see."

She remembered what the bandits had said. "He would scream?" With a chill she thought of Lorne's words again, and the scars.

Lucas sighed. "As though it were real, good lady. He dreamed of burning again, of being condemned by God and cast aside to flames. I think now that what happened here—to be punished and not know why—I think it was twisted in his mind." He bowed his head with emotion. But then quickly he lifted his eyes to look at her again. "It would be Samis to make him cover his head, though. He was very hard."

"But Martica told me my brother was a killer," she countered. "Willingly. Not a captive as you and Lorne tell it." *The scars tell it!* her mind screamed. But she couldn't voice those words.

"People call him a killer," Lucas answered patiently. "But he was bound, drowning in that evil. God spared him, and it was the greatest miracle I could imagine. He has a tender heart now, to care for the hurting. I hope you will let yourself know him."

Tiarra stared at Lucas for a moment, still struggling over Martica's words. How could she ask further when she thought she already knew what Lucas would say? How could she be so stubborn? But she had to know for sure. "Was he only four when he was here, Reverend sir?"

"As best we can figure. No one knows the time of his birth."

"And from then he was with Samis? For how long?"

"Sixteen years, lady. And he's been free but one."

He can't be lying, Tiarra thought. Not the someday-priest. But why would Martica lie to her? She was still trying to sort it out in her mind, to find a way that Martica might only have been mistaken. But she couldn't see it. "Has he been back here? Since Samis took him away?"

"Not till now. He wouldn't enter this town. Even when others of us did, he refused."

"He is only twenty-one?"

Lucas nodded. "He'll never lie to you. And he'll never hurt you. I have all confidence in that."

"I hurt him," she said in a quiet voice. "What if he can't fight?"

"God will help us."

"Why would Martica teach me to hate him?"

"I don't know. She must have been afraid somehow."

Tahn moaned softly and rolled again. So many thoughts swirled in Tiarra's mind. She looked down at Martica's body with an aching heart. "She lied."

"Let us lay her to rest prayerfully," Lucas admonished. "She must have had a care for you."

Tiarra could say nothing. She felt empty.

"Would the neighbors gather for her in a procession to the church?"

She nodded. "Some would. They've known her a long while."

Tahn did not stir as the preparations were made. Lucas returned to the church to ask Father Bray for a wagon, and Tiarra hung a long black cloth beside the front door. She cast dust upon her head and sat tensely, wondering what sort of words Lucas or the good priest could find for the burying of a person like Martica. Sharp of tongue and long to avoid the church's shadow. God have mercy on her soul.

There was no one to wait for, no one else to tell. So when Lucas returned, they moved the body, and Tiarra stood outside as Lucas and the young man he'd brought back with him clanged the bells they'd carried from St. Thomas's. Most of the people from the neighboring houses already knew of Martica's passing. They'd seen or heard the goings-on before Tiarra ever hung the black cloth. Not many came at the sound of bells. There were some to just stand by and

154

watch warily the house that had seen so many strangers of late. But some did come, slowly, and among them two wailers gracious enough to stand at Tiarra's side, though she could offer no pay.

She couldn't wail with them. She didn't even want to go and leave her brother lying on the floor in that cold house. But Marc Toddin stayed with him, and there was nothing she could do but be the focus of the procession, be the daughter Martica had never had, and see her to the churchyard with all the dignity due her. Were it not for Martica, she might have died. But all along the march to St. Thomas's, Tiarra thought of Tahn Dorn and Martica's words about him. Lies. Angry, desperate lies she still could not understand. And she thought of his somber question to Martica: "Why do you hate me so?"

Why indeed?

She was glad to come back to the little house with Lucas as the sun sank low. But the sight of Marc Toddin's pacing was no comfort.

"How is he?"

"Resting, at least. Not good, though, I'm thinking."

Fearfully, Tiarra went in to Tahn's side. She didn't know if he'd been awake in her absence. But he lay in the same spot, murmuring something in his sleep. She took water and bathed the perspiration from his face. He seemed so warm. It plagued her that he might take ill from his wounds.

Her touch seemed to startle him. He moved away from her hands. And then he opened his eyes.

She knew his surprise to see her there. Perhaps he would still expect rejection. She thought of him raising his arms in sleep, to ward off punishing blows. And she knew she might have beaten at him herself, in other circumstances. She might have killed him given the chance, for all her terrible anger. Now she felt miserable about it. What could she say to him?

But he'd already noticed the absence of Martica's body. "I'm sorry," he told her. "That I couldn't help . . . forgive me . . ."

She shook her head. "Please stop."

He looked at her with hurt in his eyes. He must have thought she was still pushing him away. She bowed her head. "I—I need to tell you. I hated you. I hated what I thought you had. I just didn't know. I'm sorry."

He quivered a little as he looked up at her.

"Do you need a drink?" she stammered.

"Please."

His eyes followed her as she fetched the water quickly and returned to his side. "Where are Lucas and Marc?" he asked. The words came out slow.

"Just outside, I think." She gave him a ladle of the water. "Are you hungry?"

He was quiet for a moment. "Don't worry yourself tending to me. I need to be up."

"That's not what Mr. Toddin said."

He sighed. "I trouble you all." He tried to rise.

"Please wait. You seemed feverish."

He looked at her with wonder. "Thank you for your concern."

But she lowered her eyes. "Do you remember, sir, anything at all of our mother?"

She knew the question might be painful. He answered in a quiet voice. "Only a moment—the softest touch. I think I've missed that, as you have. I wish you'd had her arms to hold you."

He looked so vulnerable then. He didn't move at all. And she leaned forward and put her arms around him. Tears filled his eyes as they embraced.

"Can I call you by your first name?" she asked.

"Of course."

"Didn't that Samis tell you about our father or mother?"

"No."

"He died a year ago?"

"At Onath. He'd come looking for me."

With tension she remembered the bandit's questions. Tahn might have killed the man. But perhaps it didn't matter if

156

he *had* killed such a cruel fiend. "I'm sorry," she told him. "For what happened to you."

"I don't want you to be alone," he said. "Will you let me help you?"

"I don't know what I want," she answered honestly.

"We can at least protect you from Burle."

"He hasn't come. Maybe he won't."

"He will. I know him. And before long. But Lorne will be to Onath soon. They will send help."

Tiarra wondered that he could be so sure of any noble. "What is your lady like?"

He smiled faintly. "A beautiful spirit. Full of love. I can imagine our mother to have been like that."

"Is she pretty?"

"Indeed."

"I would like to meet her sometime. She must be a special one, to find your heart beneath the pain."

He was quiet, as if those words had taken a moment to settle over his mind. He nodded but then glanced out the tiny window. It was almost nightfall. "Can you ask my friends to come to me, please? I must know we're prepared."

"You expect the bandits in town tonight?"

"Yes. I trust you'll have no other business."

She nodded, understanding his gentle rebuke. "I'll stay here. But I fear I've lost my job forever in being away this long."

"I said I'd help you," he said simply. "You shouldn't be at such work, anyway."

He wiped his brow and sat up straight, but she knew it was only by force of will. She had seen his weakness, hard as he tried to veil it, and she wondered if he could even stand.

14

Lorne drove himself on and the men with him, not allowing for rest. The Trilett's estate was a welcome sight indeed, and he was glad to give his greeting at the gate and send for an immediate audience with Benn Trilett. They must know quickly the struggle Tahn was facing.

He had expected them to be glad for some word, but he had not expected to see Netta Trilett running from the house before the horses were even stabled.

"Lorne! Is he all right? Why didn't he come back with you?" She glanced at Lem Toddin and Jak Thorm with some trepidation but didn't ask who they were.

"He's well, lady," Lorne told her quickly. "But there is some trouble. He sent me to speak with your father—"

"He is waiting. But Lorne—"

"I will tell you together. Come quickly."

⚊⚋⚊

Benn Trilett ushered all three men into his marbled chamber and told them to sit. "You've had a long ride. Can I send for you a refreshment?"

"Not yet, lord. Tahn sent me for your help. I must tell you what he's up against before I can be satisfied to rest."

"He is in danger?"

"Yes. I believe that he could be."

"Then why didn't he come back at your side?"

"Because he wouldn't leave his sister."

Netta stepped forward with her heart pounding. "His sister?"

"Yes. The baby in his dream. She's seventeen. And she

158

knew of him, but she's been taught that he's something to be despised."

Netta looked from Lorne to her father and wrung her hands. "I must hear more of this, but please, tell of the danger. What trouble is there?"

"The bandits. They would have robbed us when first we neared Alastair, but they feared injury because of Tahn's skill. Later, they accosted his sister, and we fought them for her sake. They're angered. Especially Burle, at Tahn's challenge to his authority there. We are sure they will be planning some vengeance."

"Against a doer of justice?"

"Tahn had to cut him to prevent the carrying off of his sister, lady. Burle will not forgive the injury."

"Alastair must be a city of horrors."

"I would not argue. I saw little good there."

Benn sat on the edge of his great oak desk. "What remedy does he ask?"

"That you send men, sir. To police the streets against the bandits. There are more than a dozen, I am sure. We don't know how many. But there is no way for peace or justice in that town without the presence of men."

Netta tensed and seemed to pale in front of them. "He is alone? Against so many?"

"We left him with a friend, and there is another, Lucas, we trust that he shall find."

"I remember the man called Lucas," Benn told him. "You are sure he can be trusted? He was in Samis's sway."

"Tahn is sure, my lord. Samis does not sway us now."

Benn took the time to learn the names of Lorne's companions, and then he sat back with a sigh. "Tahn asks a hard thing. Alastair is in Lionell Trent's domain. He would not take kindly to my interference."

"He does nothing. And it is for the safety of all the people, not Tahn alone."

"But has Lionell been asked?"

"You know the blood of that house," Lorne said patiently. "Tahn would not send me there. We could not trust it. And if

159

any of the people of Alastair have asked for the baron's aid, I can't tell. We could scarcely get a one of them to answer the simplest question."

"You are hurt," Benn said suddenly, noticing for the first time the bandage on Lorne's arm, so nearly hidden by his cloak.

"The bandits. It happened when we fought. It's not bad."

Netta sat down, shaking her head. "Father . . ."

"I will send men, daughter. I don't know the outcome, or what trouble it may cause me among the nobles, but we have little choice. Tell me, Lorne, who taught this girl to despise her brother? Why could they not accompany you back here where they would be safe?"

"His sister would not have come with us. The old woman who raised her has claimed that Tahn was partly responsible for their mother's death. It was their father who was hanged. And they say Tahn helped him in the murder."

"Of his *mother*?" Netta asked in dismay. "It cannot be possible!"

"I hope Tahn believes that. But his sister would not trust us. And there is more to the tale, I'm sure. Few in Alastair will talk about what happened. They hold a secret they are not willing to share."

"What is this sister's name?" Benn Trilett asked.

"Tiarra Loble, my lord."

"Loble?" Netta questioned immediately. "Not Dorn? What were their parents' names? Did you learn them?"

"Sanlin Dorn, the father. Karra Loble, the mother, my lady."

"Karra Loble?" Netta turned her eyes to the Trilett lord. "Oh, Father! Do you remember Karra Loble? Among the Trents?"

Lorne was confused. "Trents?"

Benn spoke softly, looking down at the floor. "We heard that the old baron had a sister, Karra. But she was with them only a short time, and she disappeared years ago. We wondered what became of her."

160

Lorne did not understand. "But she is called Loble?"

"Her mother was a common woman of that family. Her father, Naysius's father, did not acknowledge the girl until she was grown. She could have been called Trent, but the name was not formally given."

Netta nodded. "My mother met her. She was a beautiful woman, raised apart from the Trents. There was some stir when her father decided to claim her as a blood descendent."

"But that would make Tahn a Trent!"

"He is still Dorn," Netta said, suddenly quaking inside. "Father! I think Tahn would not be happy to learn he is kin to the man who sought our lives!"

"If this is true, you are right. He'd not be happy with a tie to the Trents. But more than that, I fear Lionell's reaction to such news. Trent sons are scarce. Karra's father adopted Naysius in order to have a male heir. And that may mean that there is more Trent blood in Tahn than in Lionell."

Lorne stared at the Trilett patriarch. "Might the young baron know this? His father craved Tahn's death, my lord. Can this be why? Could they consider a cousin to be such a threat?"

"There were two boys in the generation of Karra's father," Benn answered with a sigh. "The baron then was an uncle to both. When he grew ill, Karra's father and his cousin fought. And they continued to fight until one was dead and the other was given the baronship. It was not the first time something like that had happened. It has been said among the other nobles that one son is all the Trent family should ever have."

"Father, it is not safe for Tahn in Alastair!" Netta cried. "Should this be known, there is naught to say what Lionell might do. We'll have to fetch Tahn back here."

But Benn Trilett shook his head. "I expect he'll not be fetched until he can be assured of his sister's safety. Let us ready our men and horses for the journey."

15

Captain Saud stopped his troop of soldiers in front of the tall cathedral of St. Thomas. This should be easy. Clergy always heard what was going on in a town. And Alastair's priest was a blesser of Trents. He should be happy to be of service. It would not take long to learn what the Dorn was doing in Alastair, and where he was.

Dismounting from his horse, Saud could not help but smile. He thought of the satisfaction that besting Tahn Dorn would bring him. And how would Lady Netta Trilett react when she heard the news? Perhaps she would swear in her grief to accept no other suitors and leave Benn Trilett without an heir. But no one could blame the House of Trent for any dishonor. Everyone in the land knew how busy Lionell was with his wedding. It was the perfect time for a murder.

Followed by Korin, Saud moved rapidly up the stone steps to St. Thomas's carved doors. To his surprise, he didn't have to open them.

"Ah, friends from the House of Trent," the short priest was saying. "Do you seek prayers? Or a meal, perhaps, in your journeying?"

"No," Saud said quickly. "We are come for information. Do you know of a man named Tahn Dorn arriving in the city?"

Father Bray looked long at him and then turned his eyes to Korin. Slowly he nodded his head and ushered them inside.

"It is important that we find the stranger," Saud told the

priest. "But the baron asks that his business not be told about."

"I'll publish nothing without his leave," the priest said. "But why does he seek the Dorn?" His eyes were on Korin, and the old soldier shifted uncomfortably.

"We have a message for him," Saud said quickly. "Do you know his whereabouts? Or that of his sister, the girl called Tiarra Loble?"

The priest shook his head. "What message requires so many men, and at night?"

"Only a precaution. Dorn can be dangerous. And there are bandits about. Do you know where he is or not?"

Father Bray sighed. What was he to do? He looked again at Korin, surprised to find him in Captain Saud's company. Korin had confessed so much to him, and because of that the priest knew the kind of man Saud was. And he knew that any message from the Trents would be one of death for Tahn Dorn. It was a decree unfulfilled, after so many years.

"I am not sure where they are," Bray said carefully, thinking of Korin. He knew how this matter had long burdened the old soldier, had driven him to repentance time and again. And now, it seemed, the soldiers had been sent again to seek a conclusion. "The old woman died today," he told them. "Tiarra Loble was in the churchyard in mourning for the burial. Her brother was not with her. And when she left here, I do not know which direction she went."

"Then you're little help," Saud growled. "Can you tell us anything about the Dorn?"

Bray thought of the things he'd seen this morning, the poor man's back whipped raw. But he could not tell them that. He had no stomach to see Saud's glee at knowing his opponent was so weakened. Better that he make them think the Dorn was strong. "Perhaps it is good that you brought men," he said. "Truly there are bandits. And they know the Dorn. Did you realize that?"

Korin looked at him in surprise.

"What are you telling us?" Saud demanded. "Would he ride again with the men of Samis?"

For a moment, Father Bray could not answer. He thought of the solemn man who had risen from prayer and talked with him here in the church not so long ago. Tahn Dorn had held no malice, only concern for his friend. It seemed wrong to misrepresent him. But he had Lucas's life to think about as well. Perhaps it would be worth the deception, if he could get the soldiers to leave.

"You'll not be able to deliver the baron's message without his business being known," he told the men. "You are sure to encounter any number of bandits if you seek the Dorn. If the baron values his secrecy, perhaps it would be better for you to go and tell him to seek Dorn at some other time."

Saud bore an odd look on his face. "He has left the Triletts, hasn't he? Their walled fortress has become too tame for him. I should have known. Has he come to claim the following Samis left behind? And Valhal itself, perhaps?"

The priest said nothing.

Saud laughed. "He'll be prince of scoundrels, won't he? King of thieves in Samis's stead?"

The priest looked down uncomfortably. "There is no good fruit in continuing to seek him. You should return to your lord, perhaps—"

But Saud shook his head. "Better to storm Samis's Valhal now and have the matter done. This is perfect! What need do we have of secrecy anymore? The Dorn is fool enough to put himself in my hands! We can kill him openly and be applauded for our war on the bandits. The baron does good service to rid the land of its scourge. Thank you, good priest. You've been a great help."

Father Bray watched in dismay as the baron's captain turned from him with a smile. He felt a sickening weight in his chest, but what could he do? The damage was done. Korin turned to look at him before following his captain, and his eyes were filled with the same sad guilt the priest had seen in them so often. "God go with you," Bray told the man. "The will of the Lord be accomplished."

The door closed behind them with a thud, and Father Bray felt strangely hollow. *God, what have I done?*

Burle pulled himself into the saddle with an angry curse. His right arm was nearly useless, thanks to Tahn.

So the Dorn had a sister! Strange that he would care to come and see about her now, after all this time. But she was a pretty one, Burle considered. She would supply his men several good hours of pleasure before they had their fill of her and slit her throat. Would that Tahn might be easy to kill as well! Surely it would not be too difficult, so long as they could find him. Burle would be riding in full force tonight. No one, not even the Dorn, could stand in the face of nearly twenty armed bandits.

With satisfaction Burle watched his men mounting around him. Tahn was supposed to have been Samis's successor! But of all Samis's men, it was Burle himself who was the most powerful, to ride now with the men under him. Oh, a few had gone their own ways. A few had even gone to Tahn's side. Lorne, the boys Marcus and Vari, and even, he supposed, Lucas after his own fashion. But half of Samis's men rode now with him, freely, because they had chosen him their leader. And well it should be so. There was no one more able.

They rode in the dimness from their camp, leaving only the wounded behind. Except him. He would not miss this. He would watch as his men surrounded Tahn, closed in with their numbers, and finally overwhelmed him. *I will let him beg me for his life,* Burle decided. *And for his sister's life. But I will deny him.*

Lorne he might keep for a while, let him carry water, let him slave under them until they tired of the game. The miserable boy! Burle remembered the day Lorne was brought to the halls of Valhal. Resigned already to his lot, in pitiful obedience to his father, Lorne had obeyed Samis's smallest command, despite the tears in his eyes. Oh, how he had cried at night! Pitiful slave! *I was always stronger,* Burle told himself. *I wanted the life of a soldier.*

He was proud to be one of only a handful actually hired

165

to Samis's service. How infuriating that Tahn, the miserable wretch, had been the master's favorite! Tahn had been scrawny and scarred, possessed by night, not even considered sane by the other men half the time. Why had Samis bothered with him? And how in the world could the Trilett family bear his presence now?

Perhaps the nobleman had given Tahn a house of his own, where he could roam the halls or thrash and scream in the darkness without disturbing anyone else. Almost Burle could envy Tahn for gaining Trilett favor. And probably Trilett money. He wondered if the Triletts would actually mourn Tahn. The young fool Vari would. Lorne would too, if they gave him a chance. If they didn't kill him first, and make Tahn watch.

Burle and his men rode together toward Alastair, as Burle wondered where to begin his search. Tahn was a stranger in town, but one with a history people would surely remember. And his sister was no stranger here. They would not be hard to find. He could ask almost anyone. Chances are, he'd be pointed the way quickly indeed. It would be a pleasant night. And a particularly memorable victory.

16

In her father's meeting room, Netta was growing more and more frustrated. Why couldn't her father see how important this was to her? "I want to go!" she cried in protest. "You've agreed to allow Lorne to return, and he is wounded!"

"He knows where to find Tahn, child. He knows much about those ruffians, and he has trained with our men. I know Vari is displeased that I would not agree for him to go as well, but there is no need to endanger him, or you."

"Vari loves Tahn, Father. And you know I do. We want to be with him."

"There is no question that he would want you to stay home."

"But I could be a comfort to him. Perhaps I could talk to his sister. Imagine how he must feel, faced with such an accusation! And then if he learns he is part Trent. Father, only kinship to Samis could be worse in Tahn's eyes!"

"I know, child. And he must surely miss you as much as you miss him. But he would not want you in harm's way. He sent for our soldiers, Netta. Our armed men. He would think I'd taken leave of my senses to allow you into the middle of a situation like this."

"But what about you? Why would you consider going with them?"

"Because I know that if Lionell Trent should become involved, he'd not dare to break peace to my face. He will not try to harm Tahn if I am there, not unless he wants the other nobles of our land to take to arms against him. They will have no more Trent aggression against us. I have been assured of that many times over."

"But it is still a chance to take. You know what Tahn would say! Should Lionell try to harm *you*, Father, the other nobles would not reach you in time."

Bennamin nodded. "I know how Tahn would caution me. But in truth, Netta, I want to look on the world he sees in Alastair. I want to see the city of torments become harmless in his eyes. Perhaps you do too, but I cannot let you set foot there, not until a great change has taken place."

"But what if Lionell or the church should object to our soldiers—"

"They may. But I will explain the necessity as best I can." Benn smiled. "Perhaps Tahn will think me foolish. But it seems not so strange that I should go. Lionell's wedding is to be in Alastair's magnificent church, after all. In only a month. I could simply say that I have come to the town early to bear a gift personally. How could they fault me to stay and enjoy myself with feasting and entertainment?"

"Father—"

"I might even send messengers to others of the nobility and invite them to join me, to fill Alastair with our men and our merrymaking."

Netta plopped in a chair, very near tears. "Then why would you not let me go with you? I wish I were there already. Imagine Tahn there tonight, perhaps believing that wicked city's wretched tale against him. And with only Mr. Toddin to help! What if the bandits do not wait? What if they assail them tonight before anyone can get to them?"

Benn sighed. "Lorne believes they will likely try. And there is nothing we can do but begin our journey and pray God has upheld them. He would want you to pray, dear child. But that is all you can do."

Netta did not look at her father, or even try to answer. She understood the words. She understood his caution. But she could not be satisfied.

In Tiarra's house, Tahn leaned his shoulder against a mud-ded wall, willing himself to stay upright, to listen to the men before him.

"The neighbors have been aware of our doings this day," Lucas was saying. "There is no way we can truly hide our presence here, even if we conceal your horses. I think it better to return to the church. Father Bray would receive you there, I am certain. He did not turn you out this morning."

Tahn shook his head. "He spoke a caution to me before. Of enemies. My father's enemies, I think he meant, and that has more to do with the baron than the bandits. Going to St. Thomas's is like sitting on the baron's doorstep."

"But the priest—"

"May not be so quick to approve as you think. He does not want you with me. He especially does not want you hurt."

"Neither the baron nor the bandits know me," Toddin said. "It is already dark. But if we are careful, we could leave the midst of the city and wait for your men at my brother's home, where we've been staying since the fire took my house."

"I would not endanger your family, or his," Tahn said softly. He took a long, deep breath, hating to tell the rest. "In truth, friends, I don't think I can travel. To the church or anywhere else. Not tonight."

Across the room, Tiarra paled to hear him speak such words. She sat in silence. Her brother and his friends virtually ignored her in their talk. But as she listened in, she hoped they were wrong about the bandits coming tonight. Maybe they would not find this little house. But she knew Tahn was not wrong about the last part. She could see how he tried to be strong, but he could not hide his pain any longer. He could not hide his weakness.

"You're in no shape to fight, Tahn," Marc Toddin said. "It will be no easy job to defend ourselves here with only two able men and an unarmed girl."

Tahn glanced at his sister and closed his eyes for a moment. "Perhaps—by the grace of God—the girl and I will manage to be more able than you realize."

"Not against so many," Toddin continued his argument. "We can pray they don't find us. But you know the trouble if they do. And I know the shape you're in."

Tahn said nothing at all to them, only leaned his head back wearily and took a deep breath.

"Please lie down," Tiarra begged him. "You have to rest, even if you must talk about this. Let me get you my mat. Please." She did not wait for an answer. She only hurried to bring him her woven mat and a tattered blanket. Maybe she should offer to run and get the healer. Would the man come for Tahn Dorn?

"She's right," Lucas was saying. He had moved to Tahn's side and carefully helped him ease down onto Tiarra's mat, as Toddin went to look cautiously outside.

"You are too warm," Lucas said gravely.

Quickly, Tiarra raised her hand to Tahn's forehead. Warm? The reverend was remarkable at understatement. Tahn was hot. Fiery hot and sweaty. What could they do for him now? It was fever. And that could be adversary enough, even with nothing else to face.

"Can we cover you?" Lucas was asking.

"No. I'm all right."

Tiarra felt like screaming at him. Why must he be this way? He was not all right! Anyone could see that he was not all right! If the bandits came, he might even die because of this weakness. Because of her! And he had not even complained against her about it. Not one word.

"I—I know a healer," she dared to say aloud.

Lucas nodded. "I was thinking the same thing, miss. I can go—"

"Why do you think . . . he would come for me?" Tahn asked them with increased effort. "Alastair would know only relief if I perish."

"They'll know the wrath of God if they are truly so heart-

170

less," Marc Toddin said bitterly as he returned to them. "I can find the healer. I'll get him myself."

"No."

"It looks like you're needing some help."

Tahn shook his head.

"It will not take long," Lucas pressed. "And it is sensible that Marc should go. We'll be all right while he's gone. And the bandits don't know he would have anything to do with Tahn. Even if he were seen, Burle wouldn't know. And I can—"

"No, Lucas," Tahn interrupted. "He should not go . . . you are no fighter."

"I can fight."

"Yes," Tahn answered him weakly. "But you are no fighter."

Tiarra wondered how he could mean such opposite words. Perhaps he didn't completely realize what he was saying. Could the fever have so quickly taken hold? Even upon his mind? She was afraid. Of the sickness for his sake. But also of being without his guidance tonight. She knew that the other two men followed his judgment. It had been the same with Lorne. Tahn was unquestionably the leader.

"I'll go," she told him quickly. "It's not far. And you need help. Surely he'll come if I beg him—if I tell him of the fever. I'll not be gone long."

"You . . . should not be alone . . . should not beg anything for me."

Tiarra stared at him with her heart pounding in her chest. How could he say such a thing? Did he think she owed him nothing? "How can you tell me I should not! You begged yourself a whipping! My whipping! When you could have gotten on your horse and left me to the crowd. You could have gone back to your lady's side and been done with this town! And you tell me I shouldn't get you a healer? You can't stop me! You won't."

"Tiarra—"

"No! I won't hear it! I know fever! I know it can get so much worse!"

171

Marc Toddin stood stiffly against the wall. She knew he was probably agreeing with her, probably hoping she would just go and not really caring if she got hurt or not. But he said nothing. She did not realize at first that Lucas had moved now to the doorway, listening and looking out on the darkened streets. But then he spoke.

"There's someone coming."

Tiarra had to steady herself against the wall. She had so much hoped that her brother was wrong about those bandits, that maybe he'd frightened them enough on their last encounter that they would just stay away. But he was not wrong. She knew that now.

"One man?" Tahn asked Lucas. "Or more?" He tried to get up again. He managed to pull himself to a sit, but he was looking pale and shaky.

He can't fight, Tiarra thought. *He can barely sit upright. He is too sore, and the fever makes things so much worse.*

"One," Lucas was answering the question. "But by the size and the walk, it may be only a boy."

"Miss Ti!" an anxious voice suddenly called to them from the distance. "Miss Ti!"

"That's Ansley," Tiarra told her brother. "One of the street children."

"Bring him in," Tahn told her, his voice sounding somehow different.

With trepidation, Tiarra ran to meet the boy as he approached her doorway. She had seen little of the street children today. Glances of them, as the cart had carried Martica's body to burial, but that was all. She had not fed any of them. And perhaps the food they'd gotten from the young man Lorne was gone now too.

"Miss Ti!" Ansley burst out. "We thought . . . we thought it would be all right since you're back home and . . . and you're together. That man—your brother—he told us to tell if we saw men come."

"Yes, quickly, come inside." Tiarra ushered him in. The boy tried to stop in the first little room, but she hurried him

172

to her brother's side. "Tell us," she urged. "What about the men?"

Ansley looked down at Tahn anxiously. "You—you really done what they say?"

Tahn took a deep breath. "They may say . . . many things. Please answer . . ."

"You took her whipping." Ansley's frightened eyes were studying Tahn. "But it's worse than they think. You look—"

"Please, Ansley," Tiarra interrupted with her heart pounding. "We may not have much time. Did you see the men?"

He nodded. "There's a lot of them—with horses. And they've got swords. Over toward the tavern. I hid from them. They didn't see me."

Toddin moved toward the door to look out.

"How many?" Tahn asked.

"I don't know. More than I can count on two hands."

"Are they stopped at the tavern?" Lucas asked the boy. "Or traveling past it?"

"They're not stopped for long. Two or three went in, to talk to the tavern keeper."

Lucas looked gravely at Tiarra. "They will try to get him to tell where to find you. Does the man have it about him to refuse or mislead them?"

"Not if his life is at forfeit. He would rather lose his barmaid."

"Then we have not much time," Lucas said.

"You should go, boy," Tahn said solemnly. "We thank you."

"I don't understand something," the boy persisted. "Some folks say—they say you're evil. Why would you do what you done for Miss Ti?"

Tahn took a deep breath. "Why did you come? Knowing . . . there might be trouble?"

"'Cause I love Miss Ti. She's good to us."

"I love her too. She's my family."

In her whole life, Tiarra had never heard such words.

"Will the men really try to hurt her?"

"No doubt," Tahn acknowledged. "But you must go."

Ansley hesitated. "I could hide her. She could come with me. I know some good places, not far, where nobody'd think to look."

"No," Tiarra protested. Faced with those awful men again, in other circumstances, she might indeed be tempted to run and hide. But Tahn had endangered himself for her sake. "My brother is hurt," she told the boy. "I can't leave him. Except to get the healer."

But Tahn's dark eyes met hers. "His words are good."

"You cannot tell me to leave you!"

"There is no time to argue. You can hide quickly. Away from this house."

"What about you?" Tiarra protested. "There are too many. You can't hold them off. They'll kill you!"

Ansley looked afraid. "He could . . . he could come."

"How far?" Lucas asked immediately.

But Tahn was shaking his head, trying to pull himself to his feet. "Two of you . . . will be quicker . . . safer alone. Go, while you've time."

"Tahn," Lucas urged, "they will find this house. Even King David fled when there was need. Even David hid."

"I don't know David." Tahn tried to stand but sunk against the wall suddenly, and both Tiarra and Lucas rushed to his side.

Tiarra couldn't say a word. She touched her hand gently against her brother's cheek as Lucas lifted him. She could feel the sweat and far too much warmth. How could the fever have taken hold? How could this happen?

"Marc!" Lucas called. "Do you see anyone else yet?"

"No. Not yet."

"This boy's quick to have gotten ahead of them, but we haven't much time. Better to leave this house while we can. Help me carry Tahn."

"You mean to follow the boy?" Toddin asked, coming toward them.

"I would still like to get to St. Thomas's for the priest's help. We've got to get clear of this house. Even if we hide

174

behind barrels or something on our way there, it will slow them considerably not knowing where to look."

Ansley suddenly stared at Lucas with new worry in his eyes.

"What about the horses?" Marc asked.

"We'll untie them. Let them wander to find grazing. If we try to ride, we'll be too easily seen."

"Sirs . . ." Ansley spoke anxiously.

"What is it, boy?" Marc asked him. "Speak up."

"About St. Thomas's. You should—you should know that Micah said he saw the baron's soldiers there earlier. Are *they* looking for you too?"

"God have mercy," Lucas replied.

Tiarra could barely breathe for the tension building in her chest. Only moments before, Tahn had warned them of the baron's men. What did this mean? Were they truly come because Tahn was here? But there was no time for questions. She took Ansley's hand. "We cannot go to the church. Or stay. Lead us. Help me hide my brother."

Marc nodded. "Let me carry him. He's not big."

"No," Tahn began to protest.

"No time to argue, brother." Toddin lifted him carefully to his shoulder with a grunt. "Go on, boy, lead us." He turned his eyes to Lucas. "I'd thank you to watch the trail behind, Reverend."

Tiarra stood still, shaken by the pain in her brother's face. She knew he did not want to be carried, nor to hide, though she wasn't sure she understood why.

"If you're coming, girl," Toddin called to her, "get your brother's sword."

At the abruptness of his words, Tiarra snapped into action. She grabbed Tahn's sword and held it tight in her hand, but she also hid her mother's locket in her clothes. And when Lucas was quickly untying the horses, she took her brother's bag and tossed it over her shoulder. She had no idea what was inside. But he might lose his horse this night. She would save for him what she could.

"How far?" Lucas was asking Ansley.

"The first place is very close. I've used it before, when a merchant was chasing me."

Ansley ran, and Tiarra stayed beside him, leaving Lucas and the big man to follow. Every noise in the distance was frightening. Tiarra could imagine it was the bandits' horses, too soon breathing down their necks. Ansley had ducked into the narrow space between two mud-brick houses. "Almost there," he whispered.

Near the next street stood the barrel maker's workshop, an old building in poor repair. Tiarra wondered if they would truly hide behind barrels, as Lucas had said. But Ansley ran and crouched to the ground. He pulled a board aside to reveal a dark hole beneath the building. Then he dove in so quickly that he seemed to disappear. "Hurry," he called to her.

But she looked back. Toddin was right behind her. "Go on, girl," he ordered. "Go first and you can help me guide him in."

She followed Ansley into the crawl space, wondering why she hadn't seen Lucas behind them. And strangely she thought of kindhearted Lorne, her brother's other friend. Would he truly bring them help?

The space widened as soon as she was past the rough rock foundation. It was a dark little room under the structure, just high enough to sit up.

"Be careful getting him through," she said. "It is big enough for us, and dry."

Marc Toddin did not have an easy time of it, helping Tahn along with himself through the narrow opening. But he managed, leaving Tahn carefully at Tiarra's side. And to her surprise, he immediately started back out. "Don't move from here," he told her. "Stay quiet."

"Where are you going?"

He did not answer her, but he took the time to replace the board across the opening. And they were suddenly in almost complete darkness. Only a tiny crack of moonlight showed beside the board, with another far dimmer where a crack in the floor above must have looked upward toward a crack in the wall.

For a moment, Tiarra fought for a breath. It was horrendous to be huddled here in the depths, not knowing what was going on outside. "Ansley?"

"Better to be quiet," he whispered from somewhere to her right. "You could sleep. Time'll pass quicker till the daylight."

"I don't know that daylight will be any safer."

Suddenly something warm brushed against her arm. And then her brother rolled full against her with a tiny, choked cry of pain. She wished she had water. Why hadn't she thought of that? He would need water so badly with the fever. She should be making him drink and bathing his forehead.

"Lucas . . ."

Tahn sounded so far away, though he was right beside her. She could not see his face. "He will be here soon," she promised. "Maybe they are keeping watch."

"I want to die, Lucas . . ."

"What?" Tiarra leaned even closer, not certain she'd heard him correctly, yet afraid that she had.

"But I fear . . ."

His voice trailed off. She could not understand the last part of whatever he said. She could scarcely imagine him fearing anything. He sounded so distant. So strangely young. And now he was shivering. She could feel him against her, and she wished she could think of some way to help.

"You need not fear," she whispered. "Nor think of dying."

Ansley crawled nearer. "He's bad off, isn't he? He's not talking like himself."

"No, he's not." Tiarra took Tahn's hand and held it, but she was not sure if he was even aware.

"What if he cries out, Miss Ti?" Ansley asked barely loud enough to be heard.

"I don't know." She squeezed her brother's palm and reached upward to press her other hand against his forehead. "I don't understand this sickness."

177

"Most folks wishin' to die up and do so," Ansley said gravely, the fear plain in his voice.

"Don't speak such things," Tiarra ordered, nearly choking on the words. "He'll not die. Nor does he wish to."

Ansley said nothing more, and Tiarra was glad for it. She did not want to answer him and betray the silent tears she was trying to keep in check. She lay her head down on one arm, so close to Tahn that she could still feel him shivering beside her. What if he did die? What then? It would be her fault. And there would still be the bandits to deal with.

But even with him living, even if he were strong and well in a matter of minutes, what would happen to her? Without Martica, everything was different. If the bandits and the baron's men somehow did not find them, would her brother want to take her away with him to Onath?

What a thought that was! Wild and frightening, grand and horrid, all at the same time. But he had said he loved her. Tahn Dorn had gotten her their mother's necklace. He had called her his family. Not even Martica had done that.

She wiped at her eyes with her sleeve and scorned such thoughts. Here they were, hiding in a hole. They might not live to see the daylight, and if they did, they might still be hunted. She shook her head. Since Tahn Dorn had come to Alastair, there had been nothing but trouble.

He rolled beside her. She wished she could see in this awful darkness. She wished she knew if his eyes were open. None of this was his fault. She'd been the one to bring trouble on him. The bandits would surely have left him alone if he hadn't ventured to rescue her. And Mikal Ovny's father couldn't have laid a hand on him either.

"No . . . Master . . ." he muttered barely loud enough to be heard.

Tiarra clenched both of her hands tightly into fists. She didn't want to hear any more of his fevered words. She didn't think she could take such glimpses inside him, or perhaps pictures of his past. It was too hard. Much too hard.

Why had Martica lied so? Why had the whole town chosen to blame him and hide the truth from her? How could he even have survived?

"I should go," she whispered to Ansley. "I need to bring water."

"No. That big man said you have to stay here."

"He—he could be dead by now. We don't know."

"All the more reason to stay. Don't go, Miss Ti. It's you they're looking for."

"And my brother. Ansley, he needs water."

"I don't think he's awake to drink it."

"We need water to combat the fever, whether he is awake or not."

"Did he ever come here—did he ever come see you before?"

"No."

"Why not?"

"I—I don't know. But I don't blame him. I don't think he could. He says he didn't know about me."

"Do you believe him?"

She swallowed down something bitter in her throat. "Yes. I think I do."

"I'll get the water," Ansley volunteered. "They're not looking for me."

He was gone before she could even answer him, leaving a larger crack than Toddin had when he replaced the board at the entrance. Still, it was strangely unsettling to be alone in this dungeonlike place with her brother. The dimness and the quiet soaked over her. She wished it were lighter here, that she could look at his back again. She was afraid that moving him or his rolling about on this uneven ground might have torn open his wounds. He could be bleeding. But she could not bring herself to check. He might cry out if her touch hurt him. He might not understand that it was her. And she could do nothing to help him now, anyway.

You could pray.

The words jumped into her mind like a command. *He believes in prayer. You could pray.*

Years of protest tore through her mind. Why pray? God

179

knew all about this. He knew everything. And yet he let it all happen. He didn't do anything. He let her mother die. He let Alastair nearly kill Tahn Dorn, and the only deliverance was almost worse than death. To be slave to a killer. To be forced to obey, to kill or face torture.

"No!" She spoke the word out bitterly to the air. "Why should I talk to you? Have you ever shown that you care?"

Tears broke over her, and she wiped them away furiously. God would not hear her. What was the use to even think about it? God would not hear her, because she did not honor him. She did not trust him to be any help at all.

But here lay her brother beside her. *He* did trust. *He* did believe. But how could he? She suddenly wanted to ask him. How could he suffer burns and beatings, whippings even, and then turn his heart and his thanks to God?

He had spoken to her and to Martica so gently, talking of God's mercy, asking their forgiveness. Marc Toddin had told her about Tahn going in the night to pray for Martica. "He believes the old woman found the peace of salvation," Toddin had said, trying to be a comfort. But the words had sounded so empty to her. So meaningless. Because Martica had died alone. And she'd known very little peace in her life.

But Tahn had a strange sort of peace about him. A strange acceptance, perhaps, of whatever would be, and she did not understand it.

"Why do you praise God?" she whispered. "Why do you feel that he loves you?"

She thought of his fever-laden words, only moments before: "I want to die."

She had felt that way. Many times. She had even thought once or twice about ending her own life. But perhaps she was afraid of what would be. The way Tahn had said, "I fear . . ."

What had changed him? What had made him fearless, able to face Alastair's hatred and his own bitter memories? If it was God, she wanted to understand. She wanted to know for herself what that peace might be like.

180

She could be fearless. But her fearlessness was rooted in anger, she knew that very well. And it was apt to desert her at the most inopportune times.

"I don't understand you," she whispered to God. "Do you truly love my brother?"

She could not speak the rest. *Do you love me? Even though I have blamed you and rejected you, are you like Mr. Toddin said, trying to spare me the way my brother has done? And more, would you give me the peace of salvation? I don't even know what that means! But my brother does, doesn't he?*

"Tiarra?"

She was jarred at the sound of his voice. She hadn't expected him to wake.

"Lucas?" he called.

"He will be here soon. I think . . . I think they may be trying to see that the bandits do not come this way." She knew his struggle suddenly beside her. She knew he was trying to get up, at least to his knees.

"We are . . . beneath the barrel maker," he said.

"I didn't know you were awake to realize—"

"I recognize it. I've been here before."

There was something strangely heavy in his voice, but the peace was there too. "I think you should lie down," she told him. "There is no use going anywhere. Not yet."

"They should be with us. I don't like not knowing . . ."

Strange that he was so much himself again, and not thinking of his own weakness. "Why do you care so much for everybody else?" she dared question.

"They are my friends."

"I wasn't. I hated you."

"You were taught it. I can't blame you . . . what you didn't know."

"Do you blame anyone?" she asked. "For the things that happened to you?"

He was quiet for so long that she almost thought he had slipped away into the fever again. But finally he spoke.

181

"Perhaps it is a test of God . . . that you would ask me such a thing in this place."

"What do you mean?"

"Here." He stopped for a moment, and she waited. "It was here. I ran from the street by your Martica's house. They were chasing. There was an open hole. I tried to hide—but they saw me—"

"The crowd caught you here?" she asked, the breath catching in her throat. *God, why? Why have you led us to this place now?*

"Someone grabbed my leg," he continued. "And then . . . that man . . . poured out his pot. I think they all left. I slid down. I stayed . . ."

Tiarra's heart pounded. "Until our uncle found you?"

For a moment Tahn was silent. "Samis. I never called him uncle."

"Was he always horrible?"

"Yes."

"But he saved your life?"

"Yes. And I never understood why." He pulled himself forward a few feet and stopped with a moan. "I should look out."

"No. Stay still. Please. You were taken in fever, just moments ago. You were talking—of some other time, perhaps."

Across the darkness, his words reached her. "I pray I didn't trouble you. Some of my other times . . . were not . . . holy."

She could not quite understand. "Then is this time holy?"

"In its way. God is with us."

But Tiarra tensed inside. "With *you*! Somehow! Maybe *you* are holy! And I cannot understand it. But he is not with me! I am not with him!" She was sorry for the words as soon as she said them. She was sorry to bare her heart in such a way.

"He is with you," Tahn said quietly. "And you could be with him."

182

"The noblewoman—Lady Netta—she taught you this?"

"Yes. And you also need God's peace."

The words were like a sudden stab. That he would put it that way. Just as she might have herself, were she to state her own need. "I—I don't trust him."

"It's hard. At first. When you trust no one."

Tears stung her eyes, and she felt a hand, far too warm, suddenly on her arm.

"Sister, let me pray with you."

The tears overwhelmed her then. She could not hold them back. "I can't! I'm not like you! I don't forgive! You could have come into this town killing people. I would have! I would have sought out every one of those people and gladly lifted my sword."

"No," he said, his voice sounding weaker. "You are a good heart—God has already touched you . . ."

"You can't know that."

"You love . . . more than the people around you . . ."

She shook her head. "I think you are deceived."

"Who else cares for the street children?"

That question quieted her for a moment. "Your friend Lorne. He fed them."

She could feel him sinking down beside her. He was weak. He could not hold himself up any longer. "*You* fed them," he persisted.

"And cursed God at the same time for such need!"

"But you can pray now—he would forgive you gladly."

"And bear my penalty?" she asked, thinking again of Marc Toddin's words.

"Yes. He . . . already . . . has . . ."

Tahn's words dropped away, and Tiarra turned to him in the darkness, suddenly afraid. He'd come up from the fever so quickly, and yet the fever was still with him. Was he sliding away from her again?

She touched his head and felt the heat. "Pray for me, please," she whispered. "Don't leave me alone."

"You'll not be . . . alone," he said, but she could barely hear him.

17

Lucas tensed at the sudden rush of horses to the painted house where Martica had died. He and Toddin crouched at the corner of a nearby home and watched the bandits circle the little dwelling.

"I should have told *you* to carry Tahn's sword," Toddin whispered. "You're not even armed."

"Old habits are hard to break," Lucas confessed. "I still carry two knives."

"Dorn!" one of the horsemen yelled. Lucas knew it was Burle, the headstrong bandit leader, former troublemaker among Samis's men. He wanted to approach him, to confront him now, but he knew it was unwise.

"Dorn!" Burle yelled again. "Come out and face us!"

"Fool," Toddin muttered under his breath.

"There's no one here," one of the other bandits said. "Where are their horses?"

Burle and three of the other men dismounted and burst inside the little house.

"Now what?" Toddin whispered.

"Be ready," Lucas replied. He didn't know what Burle would do when he didn't find anyone. Not give up. That was sure. They would have to be ready to draw the bandits away if they got too close to the place where Tahn was in hiding. They would fight if it came to that.

He started praying in a whisper, that somehow the bandits would be diverted, the baron's men would not find them, and God would intervene to spare Tahn and his sister, as well as Toddin and the street boy. He did not pray for himself.

But the oversight must have been obvious. Toddin turned his face and looked at him strangely.

Sword in hand, Burle came rushing out of Martica's house with a curse. "They're not here. Let's go!"

"Where?" demanded a cocky young rider whom Lucas recognized as Toma.

"The church! That barman said Lucas lives there. He would shelter them! And it wouldn't be the first time Tahn took refuge in a church. You remember Onath."

Behind the neighboring house, Lucas shook his head. How could anyone who remembered Onath seek to do Tahn harm again? He'd been falsely accused, injured, paraded through the streets, caged like an animal. The baron would have hanged him had not Benn Trilett and the priest given him sanctuary at Netta's pleading. Wasn't that enough?

For a moment he forgot his religion and cursed Burle under his breath. But then he prayed. And pulled a knife from his shirt.

But there would be no need to fight. Burle and the other men were soon back on their horses and riding away toward St. Thomas's.

"Well," Toddin whispered. "That priest will be having quite a night, first with the baron's soldiers, and now the bandits."

"I pray they do him no harm."

"Better that you pray again for us. It's the baron's church, and the priest will help the baron, won't he?"

It was a difficult question for Lucas to answer. He did not want to believe that Father Bray would betray him, or any friend of his. Even Tahn Dorn. But in truth, he could not be sure. "He has nothing to tell them. He has no way of knowing where we are now."

"He knew where we were. We have one troop gone, and another likely on its way."

"Perhaps he has sent them in another direction. Surely they would have been here already were they coming this way."

"Perhaps you're too naïve for your own good. Or self-destructive. Like the Dorn."

"What do you mean?"

"You think he cares if he lives or dies?"

Lucas was stunned. "I think he'd fight with all the strength he could muster."

"Indeed. For his sister. Or for you. Maybe even for me."

Without a word in response, Lucas looked up at the big man.

"Twice with my own eyes I've seen him walk willingly into savagery," Toddin continued. "For someone else's sake. It's going to kill him one day. But maybe you're like him."

"You are here as well, Marc. For our friend, you would do the same thing. And it would be honorable."

"I know. But I still care if I make it home."

Lucas pushed away from the wall. "We should go to the others. I think the boy is right that they'll not know where to search."

He headed back in the direction of the barrel maker's shop. Toddin followed him closely.

"He's in bad shape, you know."

"Tahn is strong," Lucas replied without stopping. "I have seen him survive worse."

"Yes. I know. But we can't let him put himself in harm's way again."

Lucas turned. "He has Lady Netta and the children waiting for his return. You don't think that's important to him?"

"Yes," Toddin acknowledged. "But not enough. And I think you understand."

"Maybe I do. But he'll not jeopardize himself if he sees an option! Do you understand that? He has no longing for death any more than I do! We are in God's hands." He turned around again and walked on.

⚊⚊⚊

Blocks away, Ansley had stopped at a well that he knew. The street children came here often at night because it was closer than the stream and there was a pail tied to the post. Careful to be quiet, he lifted water from the dark depths. He would have to untie the pail and take it with him. He hated to. He knew it was unkind to whoever might follow. But he would return it if he had the chance. Miss Ti's request was important to him. Because her brother was important to her.

He still wondered about that. It must be strange to suddenly meet a brother you'd never known before. And such a brother! All the town spoke of him as though he were a vile criminal, a murderer not to be trusted.

But tonight he was very sick. Only once before had Ansley ever heard someone speaking in the delirium of a fever. His grandfather. And the fever had taken him away forever.

He didn't know if Miss Ti's brother would die. He hoped not, for her sake, because he knew how hard it was to be suddenly left alone. But maybe Tiarra felt alone anyhow, without Martica. He wondered if she might be just a little afraid of Tahn Dorn, her brother or not.

Carefully, he struggled to untie the knot that held the pail. It was not easy. But just as he had it loose, just as he thought he could slip away and go back, he heard horses. Too close. Running horses. He took the pail and ran for the nearest cover.

He shouldn't have run.

"Grab him!" some gruff voice was saying.

He left the pail beside a wall and tore down an alley as fast as his legs could carry him. Why were they chasing? Surely they would know he was not one of the ones they were looking for. And they could not be aware that he knew anything of them. But he was tall. Perhaps he didn't look like a boy fleeing them in the night. Perhaps in the darkness with his uncut hair, he might even resemble Tiarra's brother, who was small for a grown man.

He tried to stay ahead of them. He tried to duck away. But they were too close, and it was only a matter of moments before one of the rough men had him by the arm.

Almost he fought, but he knew he'd not escape them now.

The best thing, surely, was to let them see that he was no one to them. Just a scared boy, running like street children do.

"Let me go," he begged, glad that he sounded weak and frightened.

"Just a street kid, Burle," said the man who held him.

"Why did you run from us?" the larger man barked.

"I—I was afraid of the bandits after dark. Most of the town is sleeping."

"The bandits, eh?" Burle laughed. "You do well to be cautious, all right. But why would that concern you? You have anything of value that might interest bandits?"

"N-no, sir."

"What about information? You see everything, hear everything on the streets, don't you?"

"Not everything."

"I thought we were going to the church," one of the men complained. "This is a waste of time."

"Shut up," Burle commanded. "It doesn't hurt to ask questions, in case that priest had the good sense not to let Tahn through his doors. And this boy was in our path. We might as well see what he knows. What about it, boy? Do you know anything of a girl called Tiarra Loble? Or her brother, a stranger named Dorn?"

"N-no."

Burle stepped from his horse. "You mean to tell me you've heard nothing of a man named Dorn coming to your town? The tavern master says there has been much talk. Quite a bit of unrest. The people don't want him here. They even whipped him."

"I—I know nothing."

"Come on, Burle," one of the other men said again. "Leave the fool of a boy and let's get to business."

"No," Burle said more quietly. "Didn't Samis pick you up when you were living on the streets, Jon? Just like most of the rest of you. When did you not make it your business to know where the dangerous sorts took themselves? When did you not pride yourself on knowing enough to buy your way out of trouble if necessary?"

188

"Maybe this kid's an idiot."

"Maybe he's hiding something."

Ansley was in a panic. He tried to pull away, but the man who held him only grasped tighter. Burle stepped forward and took him by the throat. "There is no one to stop me from ridding this town of you, boy," he said. "You have one more chance to tell me what you know."

Ansley's mind raced around all the things he'd heard. He could not betray Miss Ti. He could not endanger her. There must be something he could do to send them elsewhere. And for some reason they were already on their way to the church. Perhaps he could keep their attention there. "Th-that man Dorn has a friend from the church," he stammered. "I—I don't know his name, but he's a friend of the priest. He'll know where Dorn is. But—but be careful—"

"Careful?" Burle scoffed. "Of what?"

"Th-there are other men in town. From the baron. They're here because of the stranger too."

"The baron's men are here?"

"Yes, sir."

"There's no love 'tween the baron and the Dorn, Burle," one of the bandits said. "Maybe they're hunting him too."

But Burle scowled, took hold of Ansley's shoulder, and shook him hard. "Why do you tell us to be careful, boy?"

Ansley knew there was something strange in his tone. This strong, cruel man was uncertain what the presence of the nobleman's soldiers might mean to their lawless quest. And Ansley thought he could use that uncertainty to advantage. "They might not like it, you coming up, so many men with swords. Tahn Dorn's a friend of Lord Trilett, that's what they say. So the baron don't want any more trouble for him in this town."

"Lies!" the man called Jon scoffed. "The baron protecting the Dorn? More likely that the sky fall down around us! We all know how the elder baron wanted to kill him!"

"That was for a scapegoat, to blame for the killing of Triletts," Burle reasoned. "But the younger baron is sworn to peace with Benn Trilett. If he's sent a guard, it's surely because he can't afford to risk trouble between them right now."

"But maybe he only wants to finish what his father started," a thin man suggested.

Burle hesitated. "What about it, boy?" he demanded with another shake. "Tell me the truth! Why are they here? Might the soldiers have come to capture the Dorn?"

Ansley could scarcely believe how well his spark of an idea was working. "I—I heard nothing of that. Only that they'd have no more trouble. Even if they have to police Alastair with swords."

Burle shoved the boy away with a curse.

"What now?" another man asked.

Burle spat on the ground and then stared up at his men. "You say the Dorn is charmed! All of you say it because he does not die when a man should die. And now he has noblemen taking his part. So be it! But the baron and the Triletts be cursed! I'll yet have Tahn's blood!"

Ansley trembled as the big man turned to him again. But the man said nothing more, only kicked at him and took the reins of his horse. Ansley backed away as best he could as the men mounted and rode away from him. For a moment he stood still, struggling to catch his breath. He might have been killed just now. And it took a moment to steady himself. But then he smiled. Because he might have just saved Miss Ti's life.

18

Saud hurried back with his men from their fruitless ride to Valhal on the mountain. No one was there. The place stood abandoned, and Saud was angry. Where would the Dorn take himself instead of Samis's stronghold? He thought of the old places, the places Tahn would remember from his childhood. Especially the painted house where his mother had once stayed, and the barrel maker's shop where Samis had found him. But Saud could think of no reason Tahn would want to revisit them. He was probably encamped somewhere with a troop of outlaws, reveling in the chance to taste the kind of power Samis had known. But what about the sister? Perhaps he should send men to search.

They rode through the dark streets and passed the church, ready for the conflict that was sure to come. He had expected it to be a simple matter to find the Dorn and quietly kill him, with no one the wiser. But apparently Tahn was not what he had seemed in Onath. He must have either turned his back on the Triletts or been cast out by them.

How many bandits might there be? The priest had not said. The killing wouldn't be quiet tonight. Nor hidden. But Lionell would gain in favor for sending his men to battle the bandits. And Tahn falling in the midst of them would only show him for the scoundrel that he was.

"Riders ahead," a young soldier named Hawke told him gravely.

"Good," Saud answered with a scowl. "The sooner we begin, the sooner it is ended." He slowed his men, and those in front formed a line on either side of him. He wasn't

191

surprised to see the approaching horsemen suddenly stop, blocking their path. "Men of blood!" he yelled to them. "In the name of Baron Trent—"

"This is none of his affair!" the brazen bandit in the center interrupted. "Tahn Dorn is not your business! Go home, why don't you? We seek no trouble from you!"

But Saud shook his head. "The moment you chose to name the name Dorn, you brought trouble on yourselves."

He motioned to his old friend Korin and sent him and another man to go and search for the sister. They had enough soldiers to deal with Tahn's bandits. But was he with them?

Burle stared at the line of soldiers blocking his way in the street, scarcely able to believe that Lionell Trent would send these men, or that Tahn could be so important to Benn Trilett that he insist upon it. For a split second, Burle thought of ordering his men to attack them, but the bandits had become more accustomed to preying on the helpless. This fight could cost considerably. "Go," he told his men. "Fall back. They are too many."

He thought their retreat would be the end of it. After all, the street boy had said that the soldiers were in Alastair only to prevent trouble. But these soldiers did not stop when Burle and his men turned. Rather, they gave chase and attacked.

Ansley was almost back to the barrel maker's shop when he heard the horses returning. With a choked cry of panic, he thought the bandits had somehow discovered his deception and come back for him. He pressed himself into the shadows of a doorway, hoping they would not see him.

He could hear the shouts and then, with bewilderment, the clash of swords. Had they discovered that big man, Toddin, and the priest's friend? Peeking out of his hiding place, he saw some roughly dressed bandits fleeing, and others fighting off a band of well-armed soldiers. At first he almost thought he was dreaming. No one had ever dared fight the bandits. Except Miss Ti's strange brother. Could these be the baron's men? Could the words he'd made up actually be true?

No one paid him any attention. With the water pail in his hand, he slipped from the doorway and came to the corner of the barrel maker's shop. "Miss Ti!" he cried at a whisper. But he knew she could not have heard him. So he ran to the board at the entrance and carefully shoved it aside. "Miss Ti! They're fighting! The baron's men have come."

"Lower your voice," a gruff voice answered. "Did they see you?"

Ansley knew the voice belonged to the large man, the Dorn's friend. "No, sir. They're too busy. A block over. Maybe more." He was about to slip into the hiding place with considerable relief when the big man came out to him, followed immediately by Lucas.

"The baron's men are fighting?" Toddin asked him. "Against whom? The bandits?"

"Yes, sir. But some of the bandits have run away."

"Why?" Lucas pressed. "What quirk of heaven has wrought this?"

"I—I told them that the baron's soldiers would not let them cause the Dorn trouble, but—but I didn't know it would be true."

"It can't be true," Lucas insisted, shaking his head. "Something else is afoot."

"You spoke to the bandits?" Toddin questioned.

Quickly Ansley related his encounter.

"This makes no sense," Lucas maintained.

"Whether it does or not, we can thank God for it," Toddin replied. "But we can't be sure of the soldiers. And this hole is no place for fighting. We had better watch what happens. We don't want them drawing too close."

Lucas passed Ansley's pail of water in to Tiarra, and then all three of them went to a better vantage point.

"From what Tahn said, I might have expected the baron's men to join the bandits tonight, not fight them," Toddin whispered.

"Perhaps they're all bewitched," the boy suggested in a quiet voice.

"It is written," Lucas told him, "that God will bring to pass his work, his strange work. And his act, his strange act."

<hr>

Tahn rolled with a groan, hearing noises in the distance. At first he wasn't sure where he was. But then he remembered the hole beneath the barrel maker's shop. And he swallowed hard.

The darkness was suffocating. And haunted, it seemed, with the screams he'd filled this place with so long ago. But past them, beyond his memories, he could discern the continuing sounds of a commotion, and not very far off.

He took a deep breath and tried to see around him in the dark. He knew his sister must still be here, somewhere. "Tiarra?" He thought of her pleading questions about God, and he was ashamed that he must have slipped from consciousness. *God help me!* he cried in his heart. *She needs me to be stronger. She was crying out to you, and I failed her.*

Suddenly he felt her hand. "I'm here. And your friends were here, but they've gone."

"What is happening?"

"I wish I knew. Ansley said something about the baron's men."

"Do you still have my sword?"

"Yes, but—"

"Do they know this place?"

"I don't know."

His head seemed almost in a fog. How could they not know this place? All of Alastair knew this place. Surely they could still hear his lingering screams.

Feeling strangely hot and cold at the same time, he tried to pull himself toward the opening but wasn't sure whether he'd managed to move more than an inch.

"I have water," his sister told him. "Please, sir, let me give you a drink."

He felt a sudden shock of cool water on his forehead and could not stop the shiver that ran through him.

"You're not well," Tiarra was saying. "Please don't try to go out."

"I can't . . . stay here . . . if they need me."

"They only went to look. To see what was happening. I'm sure they'll be back."

The noises outside seemed even farther away now. The baron's men, she said? What of Burle? What of the bandits? "I meant . . . to pray with you," he managed to tell her.

"I know. And I've been trying to pray, for our safety, for a miracle," she said with timid voice. "Do you think it folly for me to ask such a thing?"

"I think it large faith." He tried to move again, toward the entrance, but she was pressing a gourd ladle into his hands.

"Please drink."

He tried. And the cool water was a welcome relief to his dry throat. But strangely he thought of how good it could feel washing over him. How he missed the stream at Onath! How he longed to dip his head again and feel the coolness on his burning back.

"Are you all right?"

He heard the fear in Tiarra's voice. And it pained him that she should be here with him this way, in this uncertainty, hunted through no fault of her own. "Yes," he told her, willing his voice to sound steady. "And God hears your prayers. I can believe that he will send your miracle."

"I know," she said softly. "You can believe."

He found her hand and gave it a soft squeeze. "Sister—he draws you to believe as well."

Suddenly there was a sharp commotion just outside. The board was shoved roughly away, and the moonlight coursed into their hiding place.

"Ansley?" Tiarra called.

"Shh." Tahn squeezed her arm. But it was already too late.

"Hah!" came a rough voice outside. "I'll get her."

"My sword," Tahn whispered to his sister and felt her press the cold handle into his hand. The dimness around him seemed suddenly to be swirling. And the soreness of his back was like a weight holding him down. But he reached with his free hand for the knife at his belt. "Get back," he told his sister. "As far as you can."

There was a scuffle at the door. He could hear a muffled curse, the thud of a blow. And then someone fell. He expected that Lucas or Toddin would show themselves at the entrance after besting the stranger. He prayed so. But the clink of metal scraping the stone foundation told him that it was not so.

"Miss?" a strange voice called in. "Come out to me, miss. I'll not harm you."

Tahn was glad that Tiarra gave no answer. This was not a bandit. He would know their voices, and they would not bother with such words. But the baron's men could be capable of any deception.

"I understand your wariness," the voice continued. "But . . . but I'll not harm you. I knew your mother."

Tahn heard his sister's tiny gasp behind him. He wanted to caution her, but he said nothing. If this stranger thought the girl was alone, let him think it. Tahn knew that if worse came to worse, he would sorely need the advantage of a small surprise.

The man was coming down to them. The metal of his partial armor scraped the stone again. With all the effort he could muster, Tahn pulled himself to one side and crouched in waiting.

"Miss—"

Tahn sprang at the man just as he reached the dark depth beside him. He was large, round. It took Tahn only seconds to secure a blade against his throat. And the man stopped stark still.

"Dorn?"

"Who are you?"

"E-Emil Korin."

Tahn had never heard the name, but he knew armor such

196

as this, and he knew whose men rode these streets. Thoughts of Onath swirled over his mind, with the memory of his own prayer not to shed blood again. But this—this was a world away from Onath, and he had a sister to protect. Unable to stop his shivering, he swallowed hard and pressed the blade even tighter against the man's neck. The words came out hard. "Tell me why I should not kill you now."

"I mean you no harm."

"You ride for the baron."

"It has . . . it has been my life, and not a happy one."

Tahn had no time to question the words. Sudden footsteps were just outside again. And in only a moment, Lucas's voice called out. "Tahn? Are you all right?"

"I have a baron's man."

"Please—" the soldier tried to speak, but Tahn's jerk stopped him. And Lucas wasted no time coming down to them, knife in hand. He took the soldier's weapons immediately and cast them into a darkened corner.

"Did you best the one at the door?" Lucas asked.

Tahn had to lick his lips before he could answer. "I feared that was you fallen."

"Let me take him for you."

"What of the others?" Tahn pressed him. "Are there more?"

"We thought they'd all gone after Burle's men. Toddin and the boy are watching the streets for them. I came back to check on you. We did not realize—"

"I don't want to kill him." Tahn suddenly felt drenched in sweat. He fought a wave of dizziness.

Slowly, Lucas nodded. "I know, Tahn. Let me have him."

Tiarra edged closer out of the shadows. "The other man—at the door—is he dead?"

"Yes," Lucas told her.

"Then who . . ."

"Please," the bulky soldier tried again to speak. "Please, I mean you no harm."

"Let him loose, Tahn," Lucas said. "Let him explain himself. Perhaps he fought his fellow soldier."

"Yes," the man maintained, but Tahn did not loosen his grip, despite his shaking. His breaths came hard now. Here in the darkness, hearing Lucas's voice—it was like Valhal, that darkened room they had once shared, the daily torment, the anguish of those dreams.

Just a glimpse of his friend's eyes in the moonlight sent a chill over Lucas. "Tahn? Are you all right?" He reached forward, pulling the unknown man away from his grasp. With just an incidental brush of Tahn's hand, Lucas knew the fever was still upon him. Tahn dropped the sword but still clutched a knife in his hand.

To Lucas's relief, the soldier made no move to fight at them or escape. He wasn't sure what he would have done if he had. Somehow he wanted to keep his eyes on Tahn, until the wounded look left him again.

"We—we heard the girl," the soldier was saying. "I didn't want Toril to find her."

"Are there more of you, separate from the group?" Lucas asked him. Tahn sat motionless, his dark eyes focused on the stranger.

"No. Saud sent us to search the old woman's house and . . . and anywhere else the Dorn might remember. He thought we might find the sister while they fought your men."

"They're not our men," Lucas answered simply. "Why would you kill one of your own?"

The man turned his eyes toward Tiarra. "Because . . . he gladly would have killed her."

Tahn sunk against a rock support for the floor above them. Lucas saw that he kept the knife tightly in his hand, despite his shaking. *God, we need time to find the healer!* Lucas prayed. *Help us!*

"Why?" Tahn's voice sounded jagged and weak. "Why did you care what he would do?"

"I knew your mother," the soldier said again. "I would not have faulted you to kill me. It was wrong, all that was done."

Was this Tiarra's miracle? Tahn could not remember the name this man had given for himself. But he was a soldier of the baron. And he wished them no harm? It was hard to believe him. It might have been impossible, except for the body lying outside.

"If you tell us the truth," he pressed, "what was your part with our mother? Did you kill her yourself?"

"No. But I was there."

Tahn could almost feel her gentle touch on his cheek again, but the memory was washed away by a sudden wave of confusion and a sea of faces. This man was there? Had he been part of that crowd? Tahn felt almost too weak to sit up any longer. The faces in his memories were swirling about him, mixing with the faces of his dreams.

"You were there?" Tiarra spat out bitterly. "Then you helped our father!"

"No, miss. But truly I should have."

"How dare you!"

Tiarra moved forward, but Lucas stopped her with his outstretched arm. "Why did you call the bandits our men?" he asked the stranger.

"Because the priest warned us. He said the bandits would stand for the Dorn, and if we sought him, we'd have the lot of them to face. It is not so?"

"No," Lucas answered. "It is not. I don't know why the priest chose to claim it. But perhaps it works to our good."

The burly soldier laughed. The strange sound of it floated into Tahn's ears and all through him. He remembered Burle as a boy standing before him, laughing. "You screamed like a girl last night," he'd said. "Or a stuck pig. You're *pitiful*."

The strange soldier was saying something about the priest daring to lie to soldiers. But suddenly the baby's cry assaulted Tahn's ears. She was so near. He knew it—he reached out with a shaking hand, leaning away from the stone support, but he could not hold himself upright. The dark space pitched like a wave of the sea. Faces drew nearer. Too many faces. And then everything grew blacker.

When he fell, Tiarra rushed forward.

"Tahn?" Lucas called, but Tahn could not answer.

Tiarra quickly bathed her brother's head with the cool water from Ansley's bucket, but Lucas could not tell her what could be wrong. He could make no sense of this. Tahn, who had endured so much with such strength of will, now lay swept away by this mysterious fever. Lucas had known men to become sick after floggings before. But not like this. And not Tahn.

But he could not give him or Tiarra his full attention. He was obligated to watch this soldier and stay alert to the possibility of more. It pained him that they had failed Tahn in their watchfulness and allowed this man to get through to him.

"He is sick," the man said simply.

"We know."

"Reverend, pray for him," Tiarra cried with desperation in her voice. "Why is this happening?"

"Reverend?" the strange soldier asked. But no one answered him.

"God knows," Lucas said softly. He began to pray aloud, his eyes on the soldier, his heart with Tiarra and her brother. "Hallowed Father in heaven . . ."

"We should not stay here," the soldier suddenly said.

But Lucas only continued his prayer.

"Listen to me," the soldier insisted. "The priest's ruse was a good one. We believed him. But Saud will discover the truth soon enough. He will come back this way. And if I do not meet him, he will search the places he sent me. He will come here."

Lucas ignored him and continued the prayer, even though he knew the man was right. He wasn't sure why this soldier would choose to warn them. But if Saud had known to send men here, there might be others at any moment.

"I could go," the soldier offered. "I could ride out to meet him and lead him another way. I'll tell him one of the bandits slipped away from the others and killed Toril. He would believe me that I found nothing here."

"You will not go," Lucas told him. "I can't be sure that you wouldn't lead them here. For now you're our prisoner, do you understand that?"

Lucas wondered if the big man might consider how they could possibly back up such a bold statement. Tahn might easily have killed him just moments before. But Tahn could be no help to them now.

"Yes," the man said. "I understand."

"Should we go back to the house?" Tiarra asked fearfully.

"No. The church. If Father Bray would lie for us, surely he would help."

"Saud will go there," the soldier protested. "The priest will have trouble of his own when the lie is discovered."

"We will go to the church," Lucas repeated.

It took little time to explain the matter to Marc Toddin when he and the boy returned. Toddin didn't like the soldier's presence, nor the idea of returning to the church, but his brother's home was much farther, on the outskirts of the city, and now there could be two bands watching for them. There seemed little choice.

"How did the bandits fare?" Lucas asked him.

"Many of them got away, but some are fallen. Two or three were captured. They will tell the baron's captain what they were about. And they may yet join forces."

"Yes," Lucas answered. "But God is for us."

"Words of faith." Toddin sighed. "Considering our circumstance."

"We can be thankful for the quick thinking of the priest and the street boy."

"What we need now are quick horses under Benn Trilett's men."

"However swift the horses," Lucas told him with a shake of his head, "we'll have to survive the rest of this night without them."

19

Netta sat beneath the canopy of her bed, unable to rest. She had watched her father leave with Lorne and the other men. She had tried to tell herself that he was right and she must be content to obey him and stay in Onath. But her heart warred with her about it. She couldn't sleep. To her own surprise, she found herself longing to defy her father.

The more she thought of it, the more she ached for Tahn in Alastair, alone except for the tracker he didn't know well and the sister who apparently despised him. Perhaps that strange man, Lucas, had been found. But she wondered what help he would be. A year ago in Onath, he had seemed far less than reliable. How could he be counted on, even if he was sworn now to Alastair's church?

She prayed about the bandits' threats, knowing that Lorne took them very seriously, and they were certainly not made idly. But Tahn knew how to deal with such sorts. Alastair's gruesome accusations bothered her far more. How could they think he would take part in murdering his own mother?

The threat of the baron crossed her mind repeatedly, but the thought of it, rather than discouraging her from the place, only drew her all the more. She had to get to Alastair. She had to. She didn't know how. She only knew that Tahn needed her.

He would probably deny it. He'd probably not understand what she was feeling because she wasn't even sure she understood it herself. But the danger for Tahn somehow encompassed more than bandits, the baron, and Alastair's ill will. He himself drew her, as if his spirit were calling out.

"Father," she whispered, "you cannot expect me to stop the ears of my heart."

She cried alone in her chamber, until the weight of her feelings became too much to bear. With her heart pounding, she jumped from her bed and raced through the doorway and down the curving stairs. What could she do? She could not expect Jarel or anyone else to understand. But she had to have a horse. And she must tell someone of her plan, lest her family panic at her absence. It would be best, as well, to have someone with her, if that were possible.

Tobas, she immediately thought. Father Anolle's friend. Surely he would help.

She thought she might leave Jarel a note, take a horse, and hurry into Onath to find Tobas. Surely he would go with her. And they need tell no one else. She threw a cloak over her shoulders and hurried toward the door, but someone suddenly grabbed her arm.

"What are you doing?"

She whirled about to find her cousin gazing at her in surprise. Why had she not seen him? She had not even noticed the oil lamp in the corner, bathing the room in its glow. "Jarel! Could you not sleep?"

"No. And apparently I'm not the only one, but it's an odd time for a walk, Netta. Or have you something else in mind?"

Tears betrayed her, and she hated that she couldn't stop them.

"Please don't worry," Jarel told her softly. "I'm sure they'll all be all right." He tried to put his arm around her, but she pulled away.

"I can't stay here, Jarel!" she burst out. "I can't! Father was wrong. Tahn needs me."

"You're not talking sense," he said immediately. "You know he wouldn't want you there. It's far too dangerous."

"Is it? For me? Or only for him? And how can I do nothing?"

"Our men are on their way."

"Yes," she stammered. "I'm glad of that, but—"

"They would appreciate your prayers. That is all they need from us."

"I have prayed, Jarel. I will pray more. But that is not all. I have to go to him."

"No. Think about this. There's nothing you could do there."

"I *have* thought about it. I can reach no other conclusion! And you can't stop me."

"I can," he said firmly. "Your father left me in charge."

"Of our home!" she cried in frustration. "Not of me! You can't stop me! You won't! Send a man for Tobas, or I will go to him myself. I am sure he would go with me."

Jarel tried to reach for her hand. "Sit down, cousin. Tell me what's gotten you in such a panic. Don't you realize what you're saying? What would you do when you got there? You don't even know where to find him."

Netta didn't sit. She stared at her cousin, knowing the sense he thought he was making. She must look very foolish to him. Panicked, as he said. "I can't explain myself to you," she told him more calmly. "But you know Tahn is not like anyone we know. And the love we have could only have been wrought by God himself."

"Yes. But he would want you thinking sensibly about this."

"I know. He would agree with you. And with Father. That's like him, not to want me in harm's way. But this is different. I can't explain it. I tried to sleep, but it was as if his spirit cried out to me and God himself would not give me rest. Perhaps he's forgotten all the good God has given him here. I don't know. But I have to go."

"Maybe it's the priest you need to talk to more than Tobas."

"Maybe it is. But I can scarcely bear to take the time, Jarel. I have never felt such urgency."

Jarel shook his head. "Do you know what your father would do if I let you leave here?"

"No."

"Nor do I. And I don't want to find out."

"Oh, Jarel! Send Josef with me. Or Marcus. As many as you wish. But I swear you'll not stop me. I'll go alone if I have to. Or sneak away. Anything. But I have to go."

Jarel stood staring at her, still shaking his head. "God have mercy, Netta. I don't know what to think. The truth be told, I slept, but it seemed only a moment. Tahn was in my dream. He was crying like a child."

"You see?" she pressed him. "God stirs us. There is more we must do."

He bowed his head. "Oh, sister."

"Please, Jarel. Help me go to him."

He said nothing for a moment, only stared down at his slippered feet on the woven rug.

"I'm not saying I understand," she pleaded. "I only feel that if I don't go, I'll lose him. And I can't bear that."

"But if anything happened to you—"

Jarel didn't finish. There was a noise. Someone stirring outside. Jarel moved toward the door. "Who is there?"

"Master Jarel? It is I."

They both knew the voice of their trusted guardsman and friend, Josef. Jarel stared at Netta for a moment and then opened the door to him.

"So sorry to disturb you," Josef said. "I was only bedding down a guest on the porch for the remainder of the night."

"Guest? On the porch?"

Tobas, the priest's friend, stepped forward from the darkness behind him. "Forgive me the intrusion," he said quickly. "I told him not to rouse you. The porch is fine till morning. It was troubling me about Benn and Tahn both being gone. I know you have men enough, but I just felt I should be here in case you might need something."

"Yes—" Netta began.

"No," Jarel said immediately. "No, Netta. Don't seize this—"

"Jarel, please! What could this be but God speaking to you and leading Tobas?"

"Heaven help us."

"Yes," Netta affirmed, feeling a newfound strength. "If God be for us, who can be against us? The gates of hell shall not prevail—"

But Jarel was shaking his head. "After the baron's rampage, there are three of us left, cousin. Three! And Benn is already on his way to the devil's lair."

"God is there, just as much as God is here."

"Then God is with Tahn," he insisted. "And you don't have to go."

"But what if it is God who drives me to him?"

"What if it isn't?"

Netta was quiet for a moment. But the words welled up in her, and she would not be stopped. "I will not wait here and ignore my heart. I can't set aside the strongest urging I have ever felt. Though I walk through the valley of the shadow of death, I will fear no evil—"

"Enough! Maybe you're right and I can't stop you. But I can't agree to this. Maybe you can ignore your father's wishes, but I can't."

"I'll tell him, Jarel. When the time comes, I'll tell him you tried to stop me."

"Precious little good it's doing."

"I'll be careful."

"If it came to a choice, Netta, I'd rather see you in mourning than lose you altogether."

"Will you lock me in my room then?" she asked him. "And post a guard at my door and window? Because that's what it will take. You'll not change my mind. This presses upon me, do you understand that? I understand every caution you give me, but I still have to do this."

"Why?"

"I don't know. God knows. By his grace I'll find out."

Jarel did not even answer her. He turned away, staring at the wall where portraits of their ancestors hung. Tobas and the guard stood in silence, unwilling to interfere. Finally, after long, quiet moments, Jarel shook his head again. "I can't lock you in your room, Netta. God help me, maybe I should."

She said nothing, only stepped forward and took his hand, her eyes filling with tears. Jarel looked long at her and then turned his face away, but not before she could see that he had tears of his own. "I would think you were crazy," he told her, "if he didn't love you every bit as much. I've seen it in his eyes, Netta. There's nothing he wouldn't do for your sake."

He breathed a heavy sigh and turned toward the doorway, where the men still waited. "Tobas, Josef—it grieves me. My cousin may make foolish choices. Terribly foolish choices. But she's a free woman, and I can't say otherwise."

"Yes, sir," Josef answered him.

"Whatever she does, don't let her out of your sight."

20

A strange sensation of movement stirred Tahn toward wakefulness. Where was he now? He could hear the creak of wooden wheels and a low murmur of voices. Everything was dark. He was so weak, and the awful thirst was difficult to bear. He could remember being this way before, only a year ago. Why was it happening again?

A rope was waiting. The baron's twisted justice. He could feel the chains at his wrists and hear the taunting of the crowd. But couldn't they see his weakness? What good was hurling stones at a man barely able to turn enough to look at them? The heavy, creaking cage-wagon hit a bump, and Tahn moaned. He thought he heard someone say his name. But there were soldiers on every side. *There is nothing but death for me now,* he thought. *Lord, receive me.*

He licked at his dry lips and thought of the river of God Lucas had once told him about. What a relief it would be. Of the thirst, and of every remnant of pain.

God, I give myself to you. Please. Take my hand.

Someone touched him, and the hand was strangely cool and warm at the same time. He realized that he was shivering. He tried to see who it was with him, but there was nothing but fog before his eyes. And the voices of the crowd filled his ears.

"Hang him! Hang the killer of Triletts! He is not worthy of life!"

A shock of cool wetness suddenly washed across his brow. The strange hand was bathing his face and now lifting his head and touching the blessed water to his lips. Who? An angel? It could be no less. Chained in this wagon, no friend could reach him. And heaven help them if they tried.

"Tahn? We're almost there."

The voice was strange. He could not place it in his mind. But he was afraid, and he couldn't quite understand. Someone should not be here. Someone was placing herself at risk, just being close to him. "No," he tried to warn whoever it was. "Please. Go."

Looking upward through the fog, he thought he saw the tall spires of a church. *It's too late,* in his mind he was telling her. *It's too late. Save yourself.*

The wagon slowed to a stop, but no one loosed the chains. He could feel himself being lifted, carried like a child. The movement hurt him, hurt terribly, but he couldn't cry out. Helpless, he could do nothing but sink in the arms of whoever held him and trust his fate in the hands of God.

<hr />

"He's not conscious, is he?" Lucas asked, the knowing already like bitter gall in his stomach.

"No," Marc Toddin told him. "But at least he can't argue getting a healer this time."

Lucas nodded. It didn't seem to be a time for more words. Except in prayer. He knew Marc still doubted that the priest would help them. He knew there was as much danger for Tahn now from this sickness as there was from the baron or the bandits. But God had allowed them to get here without being seen. They'd all known it was a risk, taking the neighbor's cart and moving Tahn openly through the streets. But God worked small miracles on their behalf. The fog. And the wonderful confusion that had pitted soldiers and bandits temporarily against one another.

Lucas did not rap at the door as some men might have done. And he didn't wait for the priest once they were inside. Instead, he led Toddin and Tiarra and their soldier-prisoner toward the back rooms of the cathedral. Ansley had gone to the other street children. They would be watching for the men's return. Lucas glanced at Tiarra as they walked, remembering her telling him that she would return to the church only when God showed some change in her world. What might she be thinking now?

The tall soldier was considerably older than either he or Toddin. He followed along with them as though he had no more thought of leaving. Still, Lucas could not quite trust him.

"I heard of Martica's death," the soldier said, his eyes on Tiarra. "I am sorry, miss."

Tiarra stared at him for a moment, but she said nothing.

"This way," Lucas told the group, directing them toward a back room. He could hear the priest near them now, but he did not stop.

"Lucas. What are you doing?" Father Bray's voice sounded shaken, as though he'd already met with enough trouble.

But Lucas didn't hesitate. "I am providing refuge." Toddin stood beside him with Tahn limp in his arms.

It isn't right, Father, Lucas prayed in his heart. *Tahn has only had one year. Of safety. Of peace. One year of what life could be like. Barely time enough to learn how to begin.*

"You endanger the house of God," the priest spoke gravely. "We war against the baron's will."

"Yes," Lucas replied. "We. If this house is in jeopardy, good Father, it is you who first brought cause for wrath, with your bold lie."

The small priest came closer. "Forgive me. It was a sin. It plagues me that I might have caused your friend more trouble. There could be hardship from the people should they hear that the bandits do him service."

Lucas shook his head. "By God's grace. You pronounced curse with the blessing."

"I was hoping to thwart the soldiers' intentions, at least for tonight. The baron's captain spoke cordially, but I know murder in a man's eyes when I see it."

"Then we thank you for the effort."

"You cannot keep him safe here. He shall have to leave Alastair."

"You can see for yourself, Father. He's not able. I feared losing him, just moving him again to come this far."

"What has happened?"

"Nothing else. I don't know the sickness. Give us a room, Father. Help us."

"Please," Tiarra spoke softly.

The priest stared at her and then turned his eyes to the big soldier who stood with them.

"Help us purge ourselves, Father," the soldier suddenly added. "He is surely sent here to give Alastair another opportunity. Who is to say what wrath of God there may be if we shut our ears and turn our backs again?"

Lucas looked at the man in surprise. But the priest was slowly nodding his head. "Yes, Emil. I know you are right. These innocents haunt our city." He turned to Lucas. "I cannot refuse you. But Saud will come back. You can't stay in here. Come."

Quickly, he led them through the church and out the back gate. A row of cottages stood behind the church burial grounds on a shadowy street. A sliver of moon peered between clouds at them. The fog was lifting.

"Hurry."

At the second cottage, the short priest rapped three times on the door and pushed it open. A woman in bedclothes rushed forward with a baby in her arms. The priest motioned them all in and closed the door.

"Dominic—" the woman started, and Lucas looked from her to the priest, stricken by the unexpected use of the priest's first name.

Another woman, older, stepped from the doorway of another room.

"Catrin, Anain," the priest said. "These people need your help."

The younger woman looked very afraid. But the older one simply nodded. "Come. In here."

Toddin carried Tahn to the second room, to a bed made of limbs, ropes, and a mattress of straw.

"What ails him?" the old woman asked.

211

"Besides the stripes, we don't know." Lucas knew he'd seen these women before, in the church. But why did the priest trust them above others, that he should lead Tahn here?

He looked back to the room behind them and saw Father Bray give his hand to the younger woman and her child. "Catrin," he was telling her, "we must trust God. To right an injustice, we do his work."

The woman nodded apprehensively, and Father Bray smoothed a tear from her cheek with the gentle caress of his hand. The baby chuckled and pulled playfully at the priest's golden cross. And Lucas turned his head abruptly from the strangeness of the scene.

The old woman lit a row of candles. This room was larger than the first. Herbs of all kinds hung from the exposed rafters, giving the place an odd mixture of smells.

"Help me remove his shirt."

Lucas stepped forward, but Tiarra was there before him. "Don't cry, child," the woman was telling her. "I will do what I can."

"Are you a healer?" Marc asked her. "I knew only of a man on the coppersmith's street."

"Some come to me. I was taught it by my father," the woman answered. "Good that you brought him. He is very sick." She glanced at Lucas. "He looks like his father. Were it not for that curse, he might have come into this town unknown."

Carefully, Tiarra helped the healer ease away Tahn's shirt to reveal the bandages beneath. They were soiled and stained and pulled out of place, and Tiarra could see that they now did him little good. The healer woman began gently to remove them.

"How long since he's been awake?" the woman asked her.

"Not long. But he's been with us and gone several times. He . . . he was whipped last morning. And then the fever came on . . . I think it was beginning by the afternoon."

"Yes. He is warmer than a hearthstone."

"Will he die?"

The woman looked up into her eyes. "Daughter, no one but God knows the time for any of us."

Tiarra felt no comfort in her words. No one but God? So much rested upon a mystery she could not see. Though she'd tried to pray in their dark hiding place, still she felt uncertain. The love of God was no guarantee against hardship. Or death. Where was the peace in that?

"I must go back," the priest was saying. He motioned to the big soldier. "Emil, come."

"No," Lucas protested immediately. "I can't be sure of him."

"Are you sure of me?" the priest asked.

"I don't know right now," Lucas answered honestly.

Father Bray met his questioning gaze. "Know at least that beyond bringing you here, I will do nothing to endanger the people of this house. I would sooner give my life than direct the baron's men here."

"Yes," Lucas answered him. "I think I see that."

"Perhaps you lose respect for me," the priest told him. "But I know this soldier's conscience in the matter, and he will do you no harm. He can help me when the baron's men return. And you will have to trust us."

"I'll go with them," Toddin said. "I can keep watch."

Slowly Lucas nodded. "May God watch over us."

The healer woman reached a handful of herb from a bundle suspended from the ceiling and crushed it into a bowl. Without a word, she moved to the small stone fireplace, hung a pot, and added a chunk of wood to the fire.

Tahn rolled to one side but did not open his eyes. *He would not like this*, Tiarra thought. *He would not like the risk of trusting these people, or even the priest. And Lucas knows that. But what else can we do?*

Solemnly Tiarra rose and pulled away the cloth enough to peer out the room's one small window. The baby began to fuss a little, and Catrin, its mother, sat apart from them and put the child to her breast.

By the moon's light outside, she could see the short priest

213

and the large soldier making their way back to the church. Were they friends or enemies? The soldier had said that he should have helped Sanlin Dorn. At first she'd thought he must be a wicked man, to conceive of such an idea. But what if Martica had lied as much about her father as she had about Tahn? What if there had been love between her parents? She wanted to know. She suddenly wanted to rush outside and make that man tell her the things he'd seen.

Tears filled her eyes, and she let the simple curtain drop back as she bowed her head. What was real? It seemed so plain now about Tahn. He'd done nothing but try to help her, and paid so largely for it. Had their father been somehow like that too?

Lucas stood near her. "Little sister," he asked softly. "How can we help you?"

"You can't," she said, finding it suddenly hard to keep the tears at bay. "I just don't understand. All my life I've been taught that we came from wicked seed." She looked up at Lucas but somehow couldn't voice the questions about her father. She sighed. "The priest said we are innocents. If my brother is an innocent, why does this town still judge him? Why is he in danger from our own kin?"

The healer woman turned her eyes toward them as she washed Tahn's back. She said nothing but continued to listen.

"There is more to the story than they tell," Lucas was saying. "Perhaps it is easier for Alastair to blame Tahn than to accept blame for their own cruelty. And the baron—I can't pretend to know what works in his mind. But he must feel threatened in some way, I'm not sure why."

"I shouldn't have believed Martica," Tiarra told him.

"How could you have known any different?"

"I don't know. Perhaps I couldn't have. But if I hadn't hated so much—if I hadn't distrusted my brother—I might have told him about the necklace. I know I'm at fault in that. If I hadn't wanted it for myself so badly, he would not be hurt like this. And now he could die."

"I understand that he didn't have to do what he did."

214

"That makes it no easier."

"He loves you," Lucas said softly. "It was a gift."

Tiarra trembled. "Like Christ's. I know. Mr. Toddin tried to tell me."

"Have you trusted God? Do you pray to him?"

"I tried to pray—today. I don't know if I trust him. I don't know if he hears me at all."

"He does," Lucas assured her. "Every word. Even when it isn't spoken."

She stared up at him. "How can I know? How can I believe he cares for us?"

The someday-priest took her arm and helped her to a nearby stool. "By faith we believe our Lord loves us so completely that he walked willingly to torment and the cross. Perhaps he let Tahn be a picture of that for you, going to the whipping post."

"It's a hard picture," Tiarra told him, struggling with the words.

"Yes. But a large mercy. Christ died that all of your sins, in this and in everything else, may be forgiven."

She shook her head. "I don't deserve that."

"No. Neither did I."

She looked up at him in question. She would never have expected a representative of the church to be so candid about his own failings.

"You simply accept that it is so," he continued. "Accept the gift that frees you from guilt and hell."

"I—I don't want another to suffer for my sake. It isn't right."

"It may not seem right. But thank God for his love. It is already done."

She glanced over at Tahn and thought of the crucifix they had passed in the church. As always, it had made her so uncomfortable that she'd turned her eyes away. "My brother found peace, didn't he? Because of Christ?"

"Indeed. And he had thought there was no way for him. But God's love knows no bounds."

"He has really killed?"

"Many times."

"It seems unlike him now."

Lucas nodded. "As far as the east is from the west. With his forgiveness, God brings change."

She bowed her head. "He wanted to pray with me."

Lucas smiled. "That is not a surprise."

"But I'm not sure I can believe the way he believes! How can I accept the Lord's death for me? My brother in his strength is not able to bear the weight of one crime! Look at him! How can I claim that Christ should have carried so much more for my sake?"

Lucas was quiet for a moment. "Sister, whether you claim it or not, it is finished already. Now you have only to accept or reject what is done for you by Christ's love."

"How could I accept it?"

"Tell him you believe. Tell him you gladly receive his sacrifice and his forgiveness."

Tiarra took a deep breath. "Why would he love me?"

"Because that is what God is."

She bowed her head, considering. Lucas had said that God brings change. Perhaps that was what she needed, to wash the bitter anger away. "Do you think it would be right?" she asked. "If I try?"

"You mean to pray? Of course. God welcomes you."

"But . . . now? Before my brother wakes? I mean, if I were to pray with you?"

"The heavens will rejoice. And believe me, your brother will too."

Tiarra bowed her head with the someday-priest as he led her in a brief prayer she had never heard before. And she felt somehow lighter, as though a load of hurts had been taken off her shoulders. But she turned her eyes to the bed again and saw the old woman, Anain, watching as she spread a strange sort of balm over the open wounds on Tahn's back.

Tiarra took a deep breath, willing herself to believe he would be all right. She rose to the bedside. "How is he?"

"Good that you pray, child," the old woman said sim-

216

ply. She took a cool cloth and bathed Tahn's face, then his arms.

"Is there nothing you can tell me?"

The woman shook her head. "His back is not so sore infected as I thought it might be when first I felt the fever. But he should take some notice of me, at least to pull back when I touch him with the cold water. It is not a good thing, that he is so far away from us in the sickness."

"Can you help him?" Tiarra pressed.

The healer frowned. "Until he wakes enough to drink medicine, there is little I can do."

"Mother?" Catrin asked from the next room. "Do you need my help?"

"No. Not now. Get Gabriell to sleep again. I am doing what I can."

Tiarra sat beside her brother and put her hand on his arm. He felt warmer, if that could be possible. The fever had already been so hot in him before.

"You truly care for your brother, then?" the old woman asked.

Tiarra turned to her in surprise. "How could I not? How could anyone in this town doubt that after seeing what he has done for me?"

The woman nodded. "It was a brave thing. But there are many sides even to a brave man."

"Maybe so," Tiarra answered, feeling a remnant of anger stirring inside her. "But why do you ask me that? Do you think he is a villain? This city claims it, but how can anyone be so hard and blind? How can they face what they've done to him?"

To Tiarra's surprise, the old woman nodded. "It is good that you don't blame him for what happened here. I have always felt that the sin was not a child's."

Those words were like balm to Tiarra's spirit. "Thank you. For understanding. I don't like it that people hate him. I wish I had known sooner the spot he was in."

"Do you truly believe he has given his heart to the Savior?"

217

"Yes."

"If that is true, child, take comfort that you need not worry for his soul."

"I know." Tiarra sighed. "And I have heard that heaven is a prize to gain. But I pray he recovers quickly anyway. He need not gain it soon."

The old woman glanced her way. "I have heard he is a strong one. Surely he can fight this."

Tiarra nodded. The healer woman turned her attention for a moment to the fire and the small pot that hung above it. In the next room, the baby Gabriell began to cry, and Catrin soothed the child gently with her quiet song.

21

The baby's cries reached Tahn's ears as he watched himself running breathless toward the painted house again. What was wrong?

His sister, that tiny, squirmy baby with the funny hair and indigo-blue eyes, was the most fascinating thing he'd ever seen. It bothered him to hear her cry. She must be hungry. Where could their mother be?

As he neared the house, apprehension welled inside him. Somehow he remembered the old woman coming out with her pointing accusation, and he did not want it to be real.

"Mother?" he called.

A warm hand touched his hand. The baby's cry was gone. Instead he could hear a gentle voice singing a reassuring lullaby.

It was just a dream, he thought. *Mother is here. Everything is all right.*

It was good to feel her soft touch again, and her kiss upon his brow. There were no demons here, no hateful, shouting faces making him want to run. Strangely, he wondered about their father. Why was he not here as well? Where had he gone?

"Mother, I want Father to be happy like us."

"He tries, son," the soft voice answered him. "But there is a battle in his soul."

Such strange words. He didn't understand them. How could a battle be waged on the inside? Where would be the horses, the soldiers, the swords?

"Just know that he loves you," the gentle voice continued. "He will always love you."

"And baby?"

"Yes. Baby too."

"And you?" he persisted, needing to hear the answer.

"Yes," his mother spoke softly. "And I love him too. No matter what shall come."

The words hung in the silence for a moment, and then faintly Tahn could hear the baby begin to cry again. Strangely, he could not run to it now. He couldn't respond at all. He could see himself standing and staring down the dismal street, and he wasn't sure if he was dreaming or if he'd just wakened. But everything was not all right.

"Mother?"

His stomach felt so cold and hard that he could scarcely breathe. He knew all the things that would happen now. He knew that the old woman would point her long finger at him, and the crowd would run him down. But the worst thing of all was that his mother could not answer his cry. He would never hear her gentle voice again.

⚊⚊⚊

Tiarra was sitting beside Tahn, hoping to help the healer woman, when Tahn suddenly started shaking. She didn't know what was happening. She tried to take his hand, to wake him from his dream or at least calm him in his sleep. But she could tell that he didn't know she was there. He curled on his side. He wept like a child, the tears coursing down suddenly from tightly shut eyes. "What's wrong with him?" she cried.

The old woman's brow furrowed with concern. "God knows, child."

Lucas came close to them. His steady voice spoke words of prayer as he clasped hold of Tahn's hand. At first Tahn tried to pull away from his touch, but finally he calmed. Tiarra prayed that he would wake. But he did not.

A rooster crowed in the distance. Over and over, the healer woman bathed Tahn with cool water, but the fever only seemed to worsen. Catrin laid her sleeping baby down and rose to offer their guests bread. But neither Lucas nor Tiarra felt like eating.

They heard horses, many of them, well before dawn, stopping at the church. Tiarra rose to look, but Lucas pulled her away from the window. The baron's men must have come back, just as the priest had warned. Lucas paced the floor in tense silence, but no one came to the small cottage.

Tahn trusts you, God, Tiarra prayed. *But he is so sick. And we are at the mercy of the priest and the soldier. They could yet send the baron's men this way to slaughter us. At least we would know heaven. But help us if you will. My brother believes you can. And I want to believe it too.*

22

At the crowing of another rooster, Tahn began to wake. For some reason, he couldn't open his eyes. He couldn't seem to move. He felt as though a strange fog had encircled him and held him in. But he could hear pieces of a conversation around him.

"The soldiers have gone," Marc Toddin's voice told someone. "And that priest is a devil of a liar."

Tahn knew his sister was near him. He heard her voice speaking something softly and felt her hand on his arm. And there was someone else, an old woman's voice. Martica?

No, he remembered that could not be.

But he heard a baby again, and he was confused. Where was he? What had happened to make him so weak?

"He told them about Tahn coming to the church," Marc's voice was saying.

"That was no lie," Lucas replied.

Marc continued, "But the priest claimed the misunderstanding was not his own fault, that Tahn told him the bandits now rode under his hand."

Tahn could hear a strange rustling of wings. It was hard for him to concentrate on the words floating around him. He wanted to hear what Lucas and Marc were saying. He wanted to respond to them, but the fog still held him. It was hard to tell how much of what he heard was real. He knew the pictures in his mind were somewhere separate from the voices he heard. Martica was spooning something from a pot. Tiarra was just a baby behind her, waving her little arms the way babies do. But she was also beside him with the voices, all grown, and suddenly sounding angry.

"Has he done this on purpose? If the townspeople believe Tahn to be chief of the bandits, they'll be all the more against him! They could gather a mob. Who can tell what they might do?"

Marc Toddin's voice was quieter. "I believe he meant only to slow the soldiers, to convince them that Tahn is not alone nor helpless. And Korin claimed that one of the bandits killed his companion. He and the priest stood for one another and got themselves believed. So the soldiers don't know if the bandits have lied to them, or if Tahn has other men, other bandits, with him in hiding."

Through the gray swirling fog, Lucas spoke. Tahn knew his voice, but it seemed now as though the words were stretching toward him across some great distance. How could this be?

"Father Bray's is a strange plan. I hope it will be to our good. Do you know where the soldiers were going?"

"No. But they'll be searching. For you, as well as Tahn. They intend to offer a generous sum to any man who can tell Tahn's whereabouts."

"Why do they search for Lucas?" Tiarra questioned.

"Because the bandits told of him," Marc said. "And the priest admitted Tahn was looking for him. He got them to let Mr. Korin stay at the church to question Lucas, when he returns."

Tiarra's voice was glazed with anger. "The priest has hemmed us in! Even the reverend will not be safe in the streets."

"Please don't think the good father would mean you harm," another voice spoke. It was a soft, feminine voice, and quiet. "He has respect, especially for you, Lucas. And a conscience toward the injustice of the past. He'll not endanger you or your friend."

Tahn wished he could see the woman, whoever she was, through the fog. But there was nothing but a gray, dusky light. And then a man walked slowly forward to stand beside him tall and straight, with hair as dark as his own. Beyond him the voices began to fade.

"Perhaps he wouldn't endanger Lucas," Tiarra was saying. "But who is to say what he would do with my brother and me?"

The unknown old woman answered her, but Tahn could barely hear the voice. "Before the dawn, child, you trusted God. Trust him still."

Then the man with the dark hair reached and took Tahn's hand, and suddenly they were walking in a gray haze, away from the bed and the voices around it.

"I have to send you far away," the man said. "Your mother and your sister too. You can't stay here."

Tahn looked up at the face in front of him. It was strange to be a little boy again, and to see those tired, haunted eyes. "Will you come too?" Tahn asked, suddenly feeling pinched inside, aching for an affirmative answer.

The long silence was difficult, but he knew better than to be impatient. His father was looking somewhere distant. It almost seemed he was listening for something in the wind. "No," he finally answered. "There's something I have to do. To make sure you are safe. But I will know where you are. I will come if I can."

"What do you have to do?"

His father turned to him. Sanlin Dorn was tall, long of face, older. But still it was like looking in a mirror. *This is who I am,* Tahn thought. *This is part of me.*

His father sighed, and the sound was heavy with burden. "I have to kill a man. He is bad. If I don't, he will send men to follow you, and we'll never be free of him. Do you understand what I'm saying?"

Tahn felt a fearful tension spread in him like fire. "I can help you. I can fight the bad man."

"No, son. I only want you to remember, in case I don't come. A man will fight for those he loves, regardless of cost."

For a moment, Tahn thought he heard someone else talking again, behind them. Warm hands were spreading

224

something cool across one of his wounds. It was dizzying to realize that he was still on a bed. But even as he lay there, he could feel his father's hand. His father stood before him, just as real as whoever it was at his bedside, and he could not tell which was the dream.

"I will remember," he said, suddenly afraid. He should not know two worlds like this. And he wasn't sure if either of them were real. What was wrong with him?

"Father," he asked timidly. "The bad man you told me about—can he make me think strange things?"

There should have been an answer, but his father was gone. He couldn't understand why he was suddenly alone. For a moment he was dazed. But then he could see himself running through crowded streets, looking for his mother. With happy relief, he found her at the painted house and hugged her tightly, confused by what he was feeling.

"Where is your father?" she asked him. A pain he didn't understand made her voice sound strangely different.

"He—he sent me to you."

"Was he alone?"

"Yes." With wonder he studied his mother's smooth face, so lovely, so pale, and yet strong. She turned her eyes to an old woman stirring something in a pot across the room.

"Martica, we are going out."

"You're not going to look for him, are you?" the sharp voice replied. "Karra Dorn, you can't be sure of him! They told me—"

"I know. That he deceived me. That he married me to gain what he could of Trent wealth. I'll not argue it with you."

"And now he wants the jewels, my lady."

Karra actually smiled. "Yes, indeed he does."

Despite the old woman's protests and her own words, Karra grabbed for her shawl. "Come," she told Tahn simply, reaching for his hand.

The baby Tiarra lay sleeping behind them in a basket crib. But Tahn could also hear her at his bedside again, saying something with worry in her voice. He couldn't make out her words or find any way to answer her. So with his hand clasped tightly in his mother's, he went out with her to the street.

"People change," Karra Dorn was telling him softly. "People become new, when they learn to love."

He stared up at her as she continued.

"Don't let anyone tell you that your father is a scoundrel. He was once. I know that now. But he fell in love. And that changed everything. He wants the jewels to pay for our passage."

They walked down the darkened street, farther and farther from Martica's house. They walked through the market, and it was strangely quiet now that most of the people had gone home. *We will be leaving here together,* Tahn thought. *That's what mother wants. To tell my father not to stay behind, not to kill the bad man. We'll all leave together at the morning light.*

Tahn did not doubt that his mother would know how to find Sanlin Dorn. She said he would be with someone who used to be his friend, trying to purchase a weapon he thought he needed. They were passing by the rug maker's booth, but the rug maker was gone. There were only his tables and a few old rugs left in a pile and scraps on the ground in a heap. Tahn thought they would keep right on going, but abruptly his mother stopped, suddenly squeezing his hand so tightly that it hurt. He knew by her voice that she was afraid, and it made him afraid too.

"Quickly. Hide beneath a rug. Lie still and don't move."

She placed something in his hand. Two long necklaces. One was like diamonds sparkling in the moonlight. The stones of the other were rounded like little balls, white as teeth all in a line.

"Tuck them in your clothes and hide. Hurry."

Tahn knew the bed was beneath him. He knew he was shivering with the chill of fever. But he could feel the weight of a coarse rug over his head, could smell the odor of dust in it, along with something else he could not name. For a moment he heard voices—his mother was talking to someone

226

who sounded strangely familiar. He knew he'd heard that gruff voice somewhere far away, in another time or another world, outside the gate at Onath.

He didn't look out, not even when the voices were still. He stayed right there as he'd been told. He waited, knowing his mother would come for him, knowing that this terrible game would soon be done and they would get the baby and Father, and join the caravan toward the sea and the boat that would take them away.

Lucas was talking to him, but he didn't know how that could be. Lucas was part of a different darkness. A locked room in Samis's Valhal. Another time. He curled as small as he could beneath the old rug, waiting. He closed his eyes tight, wishing the time would go faster. His mother would tell him he was a good boy when she came back. She would tell him he'd been quiet and good just like she wanted. He lay very still.

Soon he thought he was imagining his baby sister crying and other voices all around him in some unknown room. New smells reached him, and it didn't seem so dark. He thought he might peek out. But then suddenly, someone gave the rug a swift kick. Stunned, afraid, he jumped to his feet.

"Get out of here, boy! I don't want street trash cluttering up my booth! Go away! Don't come back here!"

He stood, blinking at the sunlight, utterly confused. Where was his mother? For a moment he couldn't move, until the rug maker yelled at him again. The jewels were forgotten. He started running, on legs that felt stiff as boards, for the painted house. Had he done something wrong? Why hadn't she come back for him? He was almost there. Confusing sounds were all around him now. A crowd was gathering. He looked and saw his father in the midst of the angry faces.

Sanlin Dorn had anguish in his eyes more terrible than anything Tahn had ever seen before. He knew he should run.

But he couldn't. He was still shaking, sore, weak from

the fever that held him. He tried to raise his head on the bed but realized that someone was holding him.

"Tahn? It's all right."

Lucas. He tried to say the name, but nothing would come out of his parched lips. *Lucas, what are you doing here?*

Someone tried to give him water. How could it be real? There was nothing for him now except a strange man and the blinding pain. All of this was a dream. It had to be.

There was suddenly a knock at the door. Tahn struggled to open his eyes enough to see Lucas, and his sister, and Marc Toddin. A woman rose to the door and asked with a timid voice who was there. Tahn tried to lift his head, tried to see the woman clearly. She held a baby in her arms. Was it his mother? The hair—it wasn't quite right.

"I need the herb for my joints," a woman's voice was saying. "I brung you eggs again for payment."

The woman with the baby nodded her head, but the voice outside continued. "Someone come to you in the night? Someone sick? I thought I heard somebody cryin' out . . ."

"Yes," the young mother answered quickly. "We have someone very sick. You can't come in. I'll get the herbs. Wait here." She closed the door carefully and turned to the others with worry in her eyes. "Mother . . ."

The old woman pulled half of an herb bundle down from the rafter above and placed it in her daughter's hand. "We cannot have more visitors, Catrin. Take the red sash and hang it outside the door."

"The red sash? Smallpox?"

"Yes. Everyone in their senses will stay away. Hurry now."

Catrin gave the baby to her mother and hurried to the door with the herb and the sash.

Smallpox? Tahn lay on the bed, trying to take in everything around him. Was the baby sick? Was that why she cried?

"Pox!" the woman outside exclaimed. "Why didn't you

228

tell me? Who is it? Who's got the pox? Not the baby, is it? Somebody I know?"

"No, Ula," Catrin said quietly. "The baby is well. Go now. Tell everyone they must not come here."

There was silence for a moment until the young woman latched the door and returned to them. Tahn watched her approach the bedside. She was slender, not very tall. Not unlike his mother. And yet, it was not her.

"We should have thought of that sooner," she said quietly as she took the baby from her mother's arms. "She might have seen in. She might have suspected something."

"Yes. Yes, I know. But it is done now."

"We thank you," Lucas told them. "For keeping us hidden."

"I do little so far," the old woman replied. "Let us hope the soldiers are as shy of the pox as Ula is."

Tahn opened his mouth, struggling to get the words out. "Is my sister sick?"

Immediately every face turned to him. Tiarra took hold of his hand, and the touch was like their mother's, so soft and warm.

"No," she said. "I'm fine. Do you feel better?"

He couldn't answer that. Her eyes were so clear, shining. "You look like her," he said, not quite sure if he'd said the words out loud.

"Like our mother?" she asked him.

But the room spun. He wondered how it could be so cold. Wearily, he closed his eyes. But when he did, he could see their mother again, singing a gentle song, holding him tenderly in her arms.

"Tahn?"

"I don't think he's all with us," the old woman was saying. She pushed a cup to his lips, trying to get him to drink. He tried, and the warm liquid was soothing. But he could scarcely swallow. He knew he needed it, he knew every drop was like rain to the parched ground, but he could barely manage it. Perhaps he jostled the cup too much. He could feel warm drops spilling onto his clothes.

229

"Trouble is coming," he tried to tell them. "Help us."

The old woman answered him softly. "We'll do everything we can."

But he knew she didn't understand all of what he meant. "Not me," he tried to tell her. "My mother. Please."

"Your mother's gone, lad."

The words soaked over him and through him, and he trembled.

"He's remembering, isn't he?" Tiarra's voice was asking. She sounded afraid.

Yes, he tried to answer her, but this time he knew he hadn't managed to get the sound out. *Yes*, he tried again, but the words were only inside him, and she did not hear. *I remember our father now. He . . . he didn't kill her . . . he couldn't have . . .*

"That should be all the proof anyone would ever need," Marc Toddin's steady voice was saying. "If he's begging for his mother's sake, he couldn't have had part in hurting her."

He felt the cup pressed to his lips again and reached to touch the hand that held it. The fingers were bony, wrinkled. And he thought of Martica's long fingers pointing at him in the street. In dreams, God had pointed that way. Angels had looked at him with the faces of an angry crowd. With horror. Repulsion. Hatred and disgust. He was not worthy of life.

He could hear the crowd at Onath now shouting, "Killer! Killer!" He could feel himself shaking. No. He didn't want the sword that was suddenly thrust into his hand.

"I see the killer's eye in you, boy," Samis was telling him. "You were born for this."

He rode a smoke-gray horse behind the master's huge stallion. They were on their way to a house he didn't know. His hands were shaking as he held the reins. He wept in the saddle, wanting to flee. But his horse was tied by a length of rope to the master's. And the opium he'd been given had his head in circles.

"You'll come to enjoy this, no doubt. It will be a great

230

night for you. We will set the place on fire," Samis's voice rang in his ears. "And when they run, we will cut them down with our swords like they are nothing. It will be a game."

"No . . ."

His protest was like the breeze fluttering past them. It could gain no hold.

"It is your purpose. You cannot escape it. You'll die, Tahn. You'll burn again. With flames this time, endlessly, if you defy me. I will see to it."

With tears in his eyes he watched the flames growing, spreading over the unknown dwelling. He heard the screams. They mixed in his ears with the memory of his own screams in Alastair, and the flames in front of him infected him with the terror of his dark dreams.

"No," he said, but the word was weak and powerless. People were running from the horror of the fire. Someone ran past him screaming.

"Cut them down!" Samis yelled. "Or I swear you'll burn!"

In his mind he could feel the touch of the flames on his back and his arms. He could see the awful demonic faces around him. And he couldn't bear it. He slashed with the sword. He struck out in all directions. He had to get out of here. He had to live, to do anything he must to survive, or he would be stranded forever in those flames, in his screams and the endless pain. He saw his own sword rip at a man. Tears streaming from him, he swung again. Samis was right. He had a killer's eye. He could not deny it now, as the man fell, covered in blood.

"No," he said, trying to shake away the scene. That was the first time he'd killed, the night of that awful fire and the nameless man at his feet. But there'd been so many nights. So many men. And between them all, the vials of opium. The locked doors. The whip. And Samis's cruel threats.

Where was the bed in that simple room? Where was Lucas? At least Lucas would understand. At least part of this.

But he didn't call for him. He knew Lucas would be

231

afraid to come to him at night when the dreams were so near. He was possessed by them. Just like the night of that fire, when he felt the torment upon him, he couldn't help but lash out.

"Stay away," he warned his sister. "Please."

"Tahn, it's all right."

He couldn't answer. He couldn't even see her. The darkness had closed in. He lay as still as he could, watching the demonic faces drawing nearer. There was nothing he could do. No way to stop them.

God! You washed away the blood! Every hurt! Every stain! God help me!

He didn't know where the voice had come from, though he knew it was his own. *God! Receive me! Deliver me!*

He felt the cool water as he dunked his head in the Snake River east of Merinth. He let his soaked hair drip down his back, soothing the fire both inside and out. Someone had told him that God is merciful and extends his hand to any who will take it, to deliver them from torment, from flames. Christ on the cross prayed for his own murderers and the mockers who hated him so.

"Father, forgive them. They know not what they do."

Tahn shook with the thought of those words. He had known what he did. Countless times he had seen the bloody sword and yet lifted it again to fulfill Samis's orders. Because it was all he knew, and the thought of hellflames was enough to drive him past his senses. The fear bred the blood, which led to guilt, more fear, more blood. It was an endless cycle, with Samis and his opium spinning the wheel like grim-faced demons.

"The sword fits you, Tahn. You're the best killer I ever trained."

"I hate you!" he screamed at him. "I will kill you one day!"

Samis's retribution for those words, and for his one failure, was horrible. Something different had happened on a rooftop garden, late at night. A man named Karll fell after fighting so bravely. Tahn could remember the screams of the woman with him. And an angel, strong and bright, had stood in front of her. An angel had protected her. From Tahn. From the fury of his sword. And he could not harm her.

Night after night that woman haunted him. He had so often seen the disdain of angels in his dreams. He had seen them turn their backs. But here was someone the angels loved, whom God loved. He could scarcely fathom it. He could not stop thinking about it.

God! To touch your mercy! Your grace! To see your eyes looking upon me untainted by wrath! Help me! I am trapped in the darkness, the blood! But I want you to love me. Can it be?

He heard the baby crying, and the fog descended over him again. He wasn't sure what was real. He wasn't sure where he was. But he knew the woman from the rooftop was far away, much too far for him ever to touch.

23

The fever burned hotter in Tahn, and there was nothing they could do. Marc Toddin came and went twice, each time giving a report of the soldiers searching another part of the city. From the window, Lucas saw Ansley once too, but he didn't enter the little cottage. He was with other street children watching, listening, trying to learn whatever they could.

All the while, Tiarra sat sullenly, sometimes looking at her brother, sometimes gazing at the barren walls.

Lucas prayed for a miracle for her sake. *Show her, God. Show her how much you care.*

The healer woman had tried to get medicine in Tahn, but he had not wakened again for her to give him more. She bathed his forehead and leaned over him, her head bowed. And then she gave Lucas chilling news.

"I think this no natural sickness, Reverend sir. This is a war. Good and evil fighting inside him."

Lucas did not acknowledge the words. Perhaps he'd already known. *Tahn! Once a dark angel, you are no stranger to evil things. But God lifted you. He gave you light and washed the dreams away. Alastair haunts you. That is what it is. But God is with you still. Hear him. Listen for his voice.*

Lucas took Tiarra's hand and prayed with her. And then he rose silently to the window again, listening for any sound from the church. Father Bray would not betray him. Even more, he would not betray this family he seemed to care about. But what was to stop the baron's men from returning with a wrath born of frustration? What was to stop them from searching here?

About midday, he heard the searchers. Down the street he saw them enter a house and then come out angrily and go to the next one. He knew what would come then, and he prayed for God's favor, for the red sash outside to do its job, for the men to hurry away from the dreaded sickness these women had claimed.

The rap was loud at the door. Impatient.

"We cannot open to you," Anain hollered. "We have the pox within! Can you not see the sash of warning?"

"Who is it sick, old woman?" the gruff voice demanded. "Tell us!"

"Sshh! You frighten the baby! 'Tis an old man and woman from Merinth! They came so far, but I fear they may journey no more. They're both stricken. Pray that my daughter and I and her child not be overcome as well."

"That is nothing to me! Know you anything of the children of Sanlin Dorn?"

Tiarra stood at the mention of the name, but Lucas motioned her to stay still, stay quiet.

"All this town has heard that name," Anain answered the unseen soldier. "His children seemed born under a curse. The daughter works at a tavern, I have heard. The boy, I could not say."

Anain turned her eyes upon Tahn on the bed, and then on Lucas.

"What are the names of your sick folk?" the voice outside demanded.

"Petra and Arn Balin," Anain answered without a moment's hesitation. "But they can tell me no more now. Both of them worsen, God help us. Do not come near."

Only silence answered, and then the sound of footsteps moving away.

Thank you, Father, Lucas prayed. *Keep us by your grace.*

"Lucas . . ."

It was Tahn's voice, sounding so weak. Lucas hurried

to the bedside and leaned close, reaching out one hand to touch the heat of his friend's forehead. "I'm here, Tahn. How can I help you?"

Tahn's hands fumbled forward, and Lucas took both of them in his.

"Lucas . . . I can't go on . . ."

The words hit with a weight of stone. "Yes. Tahn, you can, brother."

Tiarra came up close beside them, looking very pale.

"I should . . . give myself . . . the blade I have given so many," Tahn said, his voice low and weary. "Why do I wait . . . when I am only fueling the fires?"

Lucas stared down at him. He remembered those words, the exact words, the day Tahn had come so close to killing himself. Lucas had found him with his dagger drawn, ready to pierce his own heart.

"Tahn," he said quickly. "What good is it to die? You have more to live for. The Triletts, Tahn. Netta Trilett. They still need you."

Only Netta's name had drawn Tahn's attention from destruction that day. Only the message Lucas had carried, that Samis had orders against the Triletts once again. Tahn had found a will to live for Netta. For the hope of saving the mysterious woman who was loved by the angels of God.

"Netta loves you, Tahn. Because God loves you. We didn't always know it. But there can be no doubt now. The angels are here. For you, brother. Because God loves you."

Tahn breathed in difficult gasps. "God loves . . ."

"Yes. He loves you. He saved you from hell, Tahn. He saved you from the wrath of Samis and from all the pain you carried. Do you remember the joy you told me about? Having the children's love? And God's love? Like being alive from the dead, you said. It made me hungry to know the same thing."

"He . . . he loves you . . ." Tahn stammered, suddenly trembling.

And Lucas could not help a small smile. "Yes. I know. God is good. We must never forget that."

"My sister . . . needs him . . ."

"She has him. She prayed with me. She's having a difficult time with this, but she knows him, brother. She's learning."

"She's crying . . . so far away . . ."

He tried to tell Tahn that Tiarra sat beside them. That she was fine and God had hidden them, and everything would be all right. But Tahn didn't respond. The moment's consciousness was gone.

Tiarra sat with silent tears brimming in her eyes. "He almost seems to be leaving us."

"No," Lucas answered her. "I'll not accept that."

Catrin's baby wailed, and it took longer this time to quiet him. She stirred a pot on the hearth when she finally had him settled, and then brought down dishes from a shelf. "You must eat," she told them. "Do not worry so much for your friend that you don't keep up your own strength."

She set stew before them and before her mother. Tiarra tried to eat a little, but Lucas could not. It was a war inside Tahn, Anain had said. Good against evil. The smell of the stew was strong and good, but he couldn't bring himself to taste it. He would stand with Tahn in that battle somehow, though he couldn't even begin to understand it.

In the afternoon, Father Bray returned to the cottage, bringing bread and his prayers. Tiarra watched the baby Gabriell react immediately, stretching his little arms toward the priest. Bray hesitated for a moment and then swept him up and held him.

"He's comfortable with you," Lucas said, his eyes looking sad and thoughtful.

"Yes. It is mutual."

There were no more words between them, and the priest turned toward Tahn on the bed. "Is it a contagion to be feared, Anain?"

"I thought it might be at first. But now I don't believe it. No one else has taken sick. And whatever it is holds his mind as firmly as his body."

Those words troubled Tiarra deeply. When would he be all right?

Father Bray sighed. "Lord be with him."

"Do you mean that?" Tiarra questioned him. "Truly?"

The priest seemed stunned by her doubt. "Yes, daughter, or I would not say it."

His words only stirred the old bitterness inside her, and she could not hold it back. "I'm not your daughter. And you have shown little care for the truth in regards to my brother so far."

"Yes," he acknowledged. "I'm sorry. I only meant for the soldiers to think there would be many eyes on what they did. I had hoped that if Captain Saud couldn't fulfill his quest in secret, he would give it up. I never meant to supply them cause to continue openly."

She stared at him, skeptical.

"It plagues me," the priest continued. "Because your brother's heart was not the way I presented him. He had no ambition at all except to save you and Lucas from the bandits."

"But the people already hate him! They will hate him all the more now! Even if the soldiers have gone, when we step out of this cottage—"

"You'll have to leave the city by night," he said. "When he is able to travel."

"Why?" She pressed at him. "Why should we slip away and hide? You called us innocents. Why don't you announce it to the people of the town? Why don't you tell *that* openly and demand to know why my brother has been blamed and despised all these years? When will someone speak the truth of what happened? Alastair should be begging forgiveness. They have no right to harm him—"

The priest solemnly nodded. "You are right. It is time the truth was known. I've been talking to Emil about that. And he wants to talk to you when he gets the chance."

She felt a chill of doubt. Would it be right to listen to him? "I didn't know if he spoke the truth," she admitted.

"He does. And you need to know that it is not for any

238

guilt of the past that your brother is sought after now. It is because of the kinship. Lionell will not have his wealth and power in jeopardy."

The old woman looked over at them but said not a word.

"Why does he think he is threatened?" Tiarra asked. "Tahn may never even seek to meet him."

"I know. But perhaps Lionell sees all men as greedy. He believes a cousin may try to grasp the baronship for himself."

"Then do they always war against cousins?" Tiarra asked in disbelief.

"Not far from the truth. Male cousins, at least. But daughters cannot become barons. Or claim any more of the riches than what they are given. And that would be why you were left alone so long."

"Why would Tahn want whatever power Lionell has?" she scoffed. "Martica told me about their world. And my brother has enough. Lady Trilett cares for him."

"Yes. I would think that would be enough for any man."

"Then can you tell them their fears are absurd?"

"It would do no good, child," the priest told her. "They only believe what they choose to believe."

Tiarra sighed in frustration. Was there nothing they could do then, to end this senseless nightmare? "I would like to meet this Lionell Trent one day," she said angrily. "I would spit in his face and tell him what a fool he is. Some people have families who gather happily and bless one another. We might have been such to him."

"Indeed," Father Bray agreed. "Were he and his father other-minded, it might have been."

"We might have had our mother with us," Tiarra said more softly.

"And your father," the priest added.

She said nothing in reply to that, only shook her head sadly.

The afternoon was long, and Tahn seemed to be slipping away from them. He didn't speak again, didn't open his eyes. Lucas watched the healer woman moisten his lips with water or a bit of her medicine. But he was not awake. She could not get him to drink.

With prayers circling in his mind, Lucas sat in silence. It should not end like this for a man as brave as Tahn who'd survived so much. He should marry his lady and live to see strong sons. But Lucas knew that death drew near to them. He knew it when he touched Tahn's skin and realized that the heat was still there but not a drop of sweat. It was as though the fever had baked him dry.

Anain kept bathing him on and on until Catrin relieved her at it. And then Tiarra in her turn. But that was not the answer, Lucas's restless mind was telling him. It was deeper. In the battle itself.

Father, we have asked so much. Protection from the baron and the bandits. Healing and strength. Grant your patience as I ask for your wisdom. Show us what to do.

Several times they could hear commotion in the streets. Perhaps it was the baron's men still searching, or restless townsmen hoping for reward. Lucas knew the sun would soon be fading. With the darkness came uncertainty. The bandits might be back. They might be in league with the soldiers by this time. And if they found no sign of Tahn elsewhere, they might become suspicious and demand to see Anain's afflicted patients for themselves.

He wondered if Lord Trilett would truly send men. And if he did, would they be enough against the numbers already here? Lorne had known only to warn them of bandits. Would they be prepared to face the baron's armed soldiers?

He remembered the beautiful Netta, the way she had looked at Tahn, and her gentle care of the knife wound Samis had put in his back. Lucas had not felt that he belonged at Onath. But he had prayed for them and prayed for them often. Tahn was a miracle wrought of God, that salvation could work in him. And Netta Trilett was a miracle to love him, even before the wounds were healed and all of the darkness had died away.

Don't let it end, Lord, Lucas prayed. *Bring them together again. And what of this girl, this sister? She has no one else in the world.*

Tiarra looked at him as if she had understood his silent prayer. And Anain spoke the words neither of them wanted to hear.

"The fever has taken too much out of him. If he cannot wake, he'll not live the night."

Lucas might have expected a burst of tears from Tiarra. But she said nothing. Her face did not change. She rose and solemnly peered out the window and then slowly sank to the floor and leaned her head against the wall. He thought he should comfort her, but he knew she would not welcome it. There was nothing he could do to help.

"Will you eat?" Catrin asked him. "Please. You need to keep your strength up. Even without him, you'll have to escape the city—"

Lucas stopped her. "*Without* him? I do not want to hear such words. You might as well speak of my own death."

"He is that much to you?"

"He gave God back to me, when I thought it folly to think the Lord would ever hear me again."

"If he knows God," Catrin said softly, "there is comfort. He will go to bliss."

"He is not ready for bliss. This world still needs him."

Anain set aside the bowl she was holding. "Why, Lucas, son of St. Thomas? I have heard many things. I know he was treated unfairly here. But I also know his sword was the death of many. He rode with the mercenary of the mountain, the wicked Samis, stealer of children."

Lucas bowed his head. "Perhaps Father Bray never told you that I rode with them too. Perhaps he never explained that Tahn stole away the children Samis held and gave them a new life with the Trilett lord at Onath."

241

"There is much he never said," Anain answered him slowly. "He never told us that you were a man of blood."

Lucas sighed. "There is only the blood that washed away all guilt. Don't you see it? It covers me, and Tahn too, as he lies here on the bed. God brought us here. God has opened the portals of heaven and poured forth his own blood upon men."

Anain and Catrin both stared at him. He knew his words were strange, but they were past him some way, and he did not try to stop them.

"I don't know what God will do. But Tahn lies somewhere between heaven and earth right now. I can't be with him where he is, but I stand with him where I am. And we are all brought together for a reason. This is my family. It's my sister, despairing along with me at my brother's side. I don't know what you are to the priest, some kind of family too, and I'll not ask for any explanation. Only be a mother to us. Be a sister. Let the blood of God hold us together and fill this house. He will feel it. I think he will know."

Anain turned away in silence.

"You speak strange words," Catrin said boldly.

"You do what you are doing for the love of the priest," Lucas answered her. "Let it be for love of God. Please. Give us strength in our battle."

Anain nodded. "If the priest had not brought you, I would have turned you away. I would not have endangered my daughter and grandson."

"But even the child sleeps under the blood of God," Lucas told her. "Do you understand that? This house, with its red sash outside, is covered by the crimson river. The strength of God, and the mercy of God, is here."

Tiarra leaned her head slowly down onto her knees, her eyes glistening with tears. The other women still stared at him, as if he were somehow touched in his mind. But he couldn't help it. None of Anain's medicines could cure Tahn now. Only their faith, his faith, could break through whatever held him. Nothing mattered now except the touch of God.

24

Tahn felt himself floating on a mist, black and silver-gray, thick as curtains and cold as the snow in winter. *Father, where am I? Help me. Help me see.*

Light spread across the corner of his mind, and he saw Alastair beneath him, the city of secrets. Captain Saud rode at the head of a group of men. They were on Vermeel Street, coming toward the painted house. Someone was waiting for them there.

Beyond them, he could see a ghostly crowd in the streets, not real at all, except in his memory. His father's face was among them, warning him away in anguish as they tied his hands and pulled him toward a waiting rope.

God, why couldn't you save him?

Samis was laughing. Saud was laughing. Somewhere a baron he had never seen was laughing too. The cage-wagon rolled to a stop. The silver-black mist closed in more deeply. Strong hands, unseen hands, pulled him toward a rope. Demons. Would this, then, be the end? Not in Alastair's own gloomy streets but in this wretched corner, this sunless piece of a memory that had snared him?

"God, are you not here with me?" he called out. "Even here? Help me. They will steal me away, till I have nothing left."

He could hear the baby crying in the distance and was surprised to understand that it was not Tiarra this time. She was grown into a beautiful woman with a golden heart buried beneath layers of anger and dismay. *Help her. Help her reach her hands to you.*

He felt the rope as they slipped it over his head. He felt them tighten it harshly against his throat. He could not fight. He had no fight left. Even unbound, he could not lift his arms. The eyes around him were hard, hateful, like the faces in his long-ago dream. He had mistaken them for angels and God himself rejecting him, casting him away to torment. But he knew now that the dream was a lie. God did not hate. And these were no angels that held him.

Above their heads, in a swirling mass of clouds, was a tiny light like a star beckoning to him. He looked upward. He fixed his eyes on it, even as the rope grew tighter.

You drew me from darkness. Now I will live or die yours, God. Hold my hand.

Blackness rolled around him, but still he could see that tiny beacon of light. Flames licked over his back with the burn of scalding water and the whip's awful scourge. He tried so hard to keep his eyes upon that light, but the blackness closed in. He was falling.

The panic, the terror, seethed inside him like a living beast, and he lashed out the only way he could. He killed Darin, he killed Britt, he killed nameless others. And a valiant, honorable man named Karll. Screams surrounded him from the night of his first killing and so many other nights that followed. Even his own screams in the locked room at Valhal. And he could see Lucas huddled in the corner, afraid to move lest Tahn lash out again in the pain of his dream.

God, why? Why do the demons hold me here? Help me. Help me!

He tried to reach upward. He tried to find the light. But the weight of the sword in his hand held him down. Even when he cast it away, it lingered with him. It was part of him, Samis had said. Part of the man he'd become.

He struggled in the blackness. The hard hands had become chains dragging him down. Karll's blood dripped over him. Blood flowed all around him, and he was sinking in it, drowning in it. The rope pressed him tighter. He couldn't breathe. He heard Tiarra's tears in the room somewhere above him, but he couldn't reach her. He couldn't see the light. Everything was lost.

The night's darkness crept quickly over the little cottage, and Lucas prayed. Tahn was limp now, pale as winter clouds, and far beyond their reach. His breaths were far too shallow, strained, as though it hurt him to breathe them.

For some time they had heard nothing but silence. Lucas prayed that there was no plan of the devil afoot, that the bandits would stay away and the soldiers would go back to the baron, shaking their heads and telling him that Tahn would not be found. But when he heard a trumpet in the distance, he knew there was trouble. He knew that Saud was alerting his men and there was war in the streets. Had Lord Trilett come? Would the baron's men dare to fight him?

Moments later, Marc Toddin came rushing to the cottage. "Lucas, one of the street boys tells me that Lorne is back with a troop of men. Lord Trilett himself is with them. The bandits tried to stop them, and now Saud is rallying his men. I'm going to go and stand with them should Saud attack. With God's help, we'll back them all down. And I'll bring them—Lorne and Master Trilett. I'll bring them when I can."

Lucas turned his eyes toward Tahn. He knew him well enough to know that upon such a word, had he heard it, nothing could have stopped him from going to his friends.

Tahn's sword was leaning in the corner beside a stool draped with sewing. It had been a year since Lucas had buried his own sword with Samis's body at Onath, and he'd not felt a sword in his hand since then. "The blood covers us and there is nothing more I can do here," he told Marc. "I will come with you."

Tahn's sword hilt felt strange in his hand, almost hot with the anticipation of battle. Lucas understood such things to be only in his mind, but it seemed almost real nonetheless. He would stand in Tahn's stead. He would fight for him in every way he knew how.

"Live," he whispered to his friend as he left the cottage

behind him. "God grant that you're here to greet us when we come back."

The battle drew Tahn to its midst. Soldiers of Samis and soldiers of the baron were lifting their hands in murderous fury against Triletts. In the distance he could see a dozen lonely graves in a meadow near Onath, testament to the lives that were lost to Trent hatred and ambition. *God, let me help the Triletts. Let me serve them as I serve you.*

But then he saw Karll fallen before him, the groom of a Trilett bride. And the guilt that should have been washed away tore at his mind. That was why the darkness held him. Because he was part of it. Part of the murder and the blood.

Help me! Oh, God, how can I help them?

From in him and all around him, he heard the answer, strong and solemn and final.

"You cannot be their help. You can do no more until you have forgiven."

Tahn's own words returned to him, from the night Samis had sought him out at Onath, challenging him to the fight of death. "I want to forgive you. I want to go on with the life God has given."

He had turned his back then, only to receive Samis's knife blade. But still he'd let him go. He'd bowed himself under forgiveness, lain aside the years of anger and hatred that made him want to tear the man to shreds.

God! You know! You know I have forgiven him! I won't let him snare me! I won't let him steal my life now!

But Alastair's angry faces encircled him, and he could hear Tiarra telling him that he could have come back here lifting his sword. The woman who had told him of his sister—she and her husband had expected his vengeance. The whole town expected it. And he could have chased after the man who burned him so badly. He could have chased him down and put the sword through his heart. But he hadn't. By God's grace, he couldn't.

Oh, Father, what more? I want to forgive them. This

town. Samis. The baron. All of them. I thought I had. What more do I lack?

Suddenly he felt himself pulled downward. The sea of blood choked him, and he struggled to pull his head up again, into the swirling black mass of sky.

Far away he could see fighting. He could see the baron's Captain Saud searching for Triletts with his sword in hand. Tahn thought of him as a demon suddenly, sent by the devil to take away what was important to him. But then in the mist he thought he saw a rider coming, hidden by a cloak. Whoever it was had come to claim him, to wipe away his struggle, until he sank down helpless and let the blood have its way.

He felt a touch, soft and warm, on his cheek.

"Mother! I don't want to die. Please. Is there no other way?"

Martica stood before him, accusing him. And he remembered the weight that he'd carried for so long in his own heart. *It must have been my fault somehow. I must have been a monster even then.*

"Who told you you were a monster?"

The question was strong, sudden, and it made him afraid.

"I—I needed no one to tell me. I knew. I have always known."

He looked down and saw the blood on his hands. Karll's blood. And the blood of countless, nameless others. There was so much of it, dripping from him, filling all the space he knew.

"Am I yours, God?" he cried into the blackness. "Are you here with me?"

"Son. Look at where you are."

He looked. But his eyes were veiled, and it was hard to see anything. He seemed to be in a valley, vast and dark, swirling with black clouds.

"Why do you stay here?" the voice asked him. "Do you know who you are?"

"Your saved child! Father, please receive me! I want to be yours. Nothing but yours!"

Again he heard the awful words. "You can do no more until you have forgiven."

He started shaking. He could feel the rope tightening around his neck, and his breath was caught and held in the blackness. *No, God. I don't deserve it. I'm not worthy of you. Alastair knows it. Alastair knows what a monster I am.*

Through the blackness he heard someone bursting through the door and rushing toward him. He knew they had come quickly. But it was still too late. Lucas said something, but Tahn couldn't discern the words. Lucas had someone with him, someone who should not be here. Not for him.

He heard her screams again in the rooftop garden. Karll lay before him on the marbled tiles, his lifeblood draining hopelessly away. "I am nothing," he told the woman. "Look what I have done."

He could hear his sister crying, but he couldn't help her. He had nothing to give. The blood still surrounded him, but he could see himself on a wooden gallows, hanging beside his father. There was nothing else. And no reason it should not be like this.

"Tahn?"

The voice was soft and distant, shrouded by fear.

"It's too late," he tried to tell her. "The darkness pulls me away."

He felt her touch, tender and hesitant, cool as a flowing stream. "Tahn?"

There was heartbreak in the voice, always heartbreak. "Do you see, Lord?" he cried to the skies. "Do you see what I have done? And now there is nothing more I can do."

"Until you have forgiven."

For the third time those words soaked over him, and he wept.

But I have forgiven! Samis. The baron. The man with the scalding pot. All of Alastair! Even my father, God, and

248

I don't even know if he did wrong. There is no one left! I have forgiven them all! Help me!

His sword dripped with blood again. He knew it was there in the room, against the wall. And there were so many people here. But he could never be like them. He could not be one of them. He was dead, hanging in the darkness beyond their reach, with a river of blood rolling under his feet.

He knew it was over. He knew he had no more strength to fight the rope, the blackness, or the weight of shame on his chest. Not even for one more breath.

"Tahn! Please—why are you punishing yourself?"

The words cut through searing pain, and he felt her touch again. She'd asked him the question almost a year ago, but still it hung in the air unanswered.

"I love you," she said, and he knew she was speaking to him now, whispering those words through tears.

No, he wanted to tell her. *Don't love me. I'm not worthy of you. Don't you see? Don't you realize what I am?*

He felt her hand on his face, and he heard her words coming to him again across time. "Jesus counted you worthy of eternal life. Of his love! How could you not be worthy of mine?"

Oh, Netta.

He knew he had not spoken aloud, and yet he had dared to open his heart to say her name. He felt his own tears striking against the blackness, and for a moment he thought he saw the tiny shimmering light.

Father, forgive me! I have killed! I am a man of blood.

And the voice spoke again from all around him. "I have forgiven you. The moment you asked. When you were beside the stream, despairing of life, I spoke into your heart and you received me. I washed you clean from that moment on. I cannot see the blood that plagues you now. But I cannot free you, I cannot give you more, until you have forgiven yourself."

He felt Netta so tenderly beside him, whispering something in his ear. The swirling grayness tried to brush the sound away, but still he heard it. "He loves you dearly. The only blood he sees now is that of his own Son, and it gives you all the favor of heaven."

The blood dripped from his hands; the sword fell away. The cold, hard hands that had held him began to fade. Even the rope was loosening. With a gasp of effort, he strained for another breath. It did not come easy.

The river of blood beneath him seemed to rise, and the rope was slipping away. With horror he realized that without the rope, the chains, and the cruel hands that held him, he would fall into that river and be washed away.

Why? Oh, God, I thought you had given me life.

He looked up into the shimmering light. The blackness was fading, and he saw another valley, peaceful and bright. But the river filled it, and he was afraid. As the rope slipped away, he reached out for it. Grasping at it, he could barely keep his head above the rising waves. Blood. Washing over him. Through him.

"I am yours," he whispered toward the sky. "I am your child."

"It's all right, Tahn," he heard Netta's voice telling him. "Breathe. God give you peace."

"Trust me," the all-encompassing voice spoke to his heart. "I have made you clean."

With his eyes on the light, Tahn finally understood. *I have asked you to receive me. But Lord, it is done. Now help me to receive.*

He felt the river washing over him, the blood rising higher, filling the valley as far as the eye could see. "I will trust you," he whispered and then let go of the rope that held his head above. He could feel himself floating, falling. He remembered his mother's kiss, his sister's embrace. And God's hand that had reached to him in the midst of torment.

"Breathe," Netta had said. "God give you peace."

He breathed in the blood of the river, and it was clear and clean and light as air. "God—God, thank you. I am clean."

He felt the coolness, the wetness on his tongue, and suddenly realized that someone held him again. Someone was giving him drink, and it felt like the rushing river, quenching the fires inside him. He tried to open his eyes and wasn't sure whether he'd succeeded.

Netta was there. It must be a dream. Lucas held him. Tiarra stood nearby with pain in her eyes.

"No, sister," he tried to tell her. "Don't weep. God's river holds me."

Netta leaned and kissed him. He felt her tears brush his face. She could not be here. It was only a dream. But he could see the simple room around him, the dangling herbs, the woman and her baby standing near. And Tobas, friend of the Triletts, was here too. He was the one who had ridden on the horse of his priest through the misguided crowd at Onath, to the cage-wagon to bring a word of hope.

"The Lord look down on us this day," he had said. *"The Lord have mercy on his soul."*

Tahn closed his eyes, soaking in the strange coolness that he felt.

"Can you drink more, Tahn?" Lucas asked. "Please. Try."

He opened his eyes again and looked around him at the faces. No one was shouting. No one was laughing. And the only tears were small and silent, springing from eyes of hope.

"Netta . . ."

He tried to lift his hand to her but couldn't for the weakness. Instead, she leaned and kissed him again. Marc Toddin burst through the door behind her, and Tahn realized they were all in Alastair. This was no dream. Netta had come here to be at his side.

He might have protested in fear for her. But God's words still rested on his heart. "Trust me."

"Yes," he said in answer, and received what more he could from the cup in Lucas's hand. "Thank you," he whispered, but he wasn't sure if anyone could hear him. A peaceful weariness washed over him, and he closed his eyes, letting the river carry him away.

25

He was gone, lady," the healer woman spoke softly with a shake of her head. "His breath was gone. I thought it was done."

Netta did not answer. The heaviness was just now lifting. The shock of seeing Tahn this way had taken her breath as soon as she stepped through the door. *Thank God,* she repeated over and over in her heart. *Thank God he's alive.*

A few feet away, a young woman was staring at her. With Tahn's hair and haunted eyes, she was his sister, there could be no doubt. Netta wanted to say something of peace, to make some gesture between them, but she couldn't find the words. So she only reached out and took the girl's hand in her own.

"It was God's providence that you've come," the man called Lucas told her.

She turned her eyes again to Tahn on the bed. He lay so still, but she was not afraid for him now. His breaths were good. His color was already better.

"Tell me," she said to no one in particular. "Everything."

The hand in hers shook and pulled away. "It's my fault," the girl cried.

Netta quickly spoke words of comfort. "It's all right now. He'll be all right."

She didn't know what had happened to turn this girl's heart to favor her brother, but Netta knew that it was so. She'd known it as soon as she came in, that the fear in those eyes was for him. And it made Netta love the girl, no matter what she had been taught about him or what she may have done. She reached forward and took Tiarra in her arms. The girl shook and sunk away in sobs.

"It's all right," Netta told her again.

"He was dead."

"But he breathes. Peace. He'll be all right."

Slowly, Tiarra nodded. "You don't know what I did to him."

"Little sister," Lucas said quickly. "All is forgiven. He walked to the post willing. And it was not by your hand."

The post? Netta tensed inside. "A whipping post?" Her eyes filled with tears. *Oh, not more stripes, torn across the old!*

Lucas nodded. "The fever came on him after," he explained. "He seemed strong until then."

Oh, Alastair! Netta lamented. *City of horrors! May God judge you!*

"I'm so sorry," Tiarra was telling her. "I know you love him. I can see that you do. And I didn't mean for him to be hurt—"

"Did they do this . . . because of your mother?" Netta saw the weight of uncertainty in the young woman's eyes.

"They did it because of me," she answered. "Because I tried to steal my mother's necklace." She reached beneath folds of fabric to the pocket of her ragged skirt and pulled out a box. "He went and bought it back for me. But I think it should be his. And yours."

She put the box in Netta's hands. But Netta only looked at this dark-eyed girl who seemed to have such an aching heart. "It was your mother's. If Tahn wants you to have it, who am I to say otherwise?"

"Look at it," Lucas prompted.

She glanced at him in surprise and then obediently opened the box. The beautiful emerald shone up at her even in the dim light. Set in gold and trimmed with diamonds, it was a rich piece, and no one else in this room could possibly have known its significance as well as Netta did. It was the Trent jewel, symbol of their title and position, passed down through generations and worn with pride by the wives of barons and the wives of sons destined to become barons.

She knew because she had one like it, passed down through her own noble house and given to her only because she had no living brother. If this was Karra Loble's, it was not such a surprise that she'd been murdered. Naysius Trent himself may have longed to kill her. Because unless she had stolen it, it could only mean that for some reason their father had chosen to exclude the adopted son and pass his inheritance along to his daughter and her descendants.

She looked over at Tahn, suddenly shaking. She had loved him as a common man. He had won her heart as an ex-mercenary, an ex-killer to whom the mercy of God meant everything. She knew he would not want what this necklace represented. He wouldn't want it to matter. She almost pushed it away, but then she remembered the opening it would surely have in back. Each new generation could place a new treasure within. Carefully, she lifted the jewel in her hand and opened the locket. Curls of hair were all it held. Baby's hair, black as midnight.

"She must have loved her children," Lucas said softly.

Netta nodded. "Yes. I'm sure she did." She replaced the necklace carefully and closed the box. "I can't accept it," she told Tiarra. "I have one of my own. It is yours."

Tiarra only stared at the lady in front of her. Netta Trilett. She couldn't take her eyes away. The woman was beautiful and wore the most beautiful clothes she had ever seen in her life. Only a thin gold chain decorated her neck now, but Tiarra could imagine her to have many lovely necklaces at her rich home in Onath. This one surely meant nothing at all to someone born so extraordinarily privileged.

She couldn't help it. Her eyes studied every inch of the lady's dark blue riding gown. And she had never seen a lady's boot before. Slender and shined. She wondered how her own feet would feel in something like that.

But even more, she wondered what favor of God her brother had won that someone like this would love him so greatly. When the lady first came through the door with

Lucas and her guardsman, when she first saw Tahn, she had looked so scared, so overwhelmingly stricken, as though her heart would fall away into a million pieces. Mikal Ovny had never cared so much about Tiarra. What she saw in his eyes had never been anything like what she was seeing now as Netta Trilett looked at Tahn.

Why had he left her side? Why was Alastair so important to him that he would ever leave a prize like this? She couldn't imagine. Alastair was nothing but a wicked town of evil memories. Why had he come?

"Your father is writing his warning to be sent to the baron," Marc Toddin was telling the lady. "He has a way with words. I daresay Trent soldiers will not trouble us again."

"At least not now," Netta said with a sigh. "What of the bandits? Do you know?"

"This is too much for them. They like to bully unarmed travelers and use their numbers to advantage. They've gone. They will still be trouble on the roads, I expect, but not to us here so long as your father's men stand at watch."

"Where is my father?"

"He and Lorne and others of his men were with the priest when I left them. They will seal and send the message by the hand of Lionell Trent's captain. They will be here shortly."

"Does he know yet that I'm here?"

Toddin looked surprised. "I didn't think to tell him. When Lucas and I saw you arrive, we assumed he knew you followed him."

Netta nodded and glanced from him to Lucas. "I thank you. Both of you, for standing by your friend. You've shown the depth of your hearts."

Lucas said nothing, only returned Tahn's sword to its place against the wall. But Toddin answered her with solemn expression. "I'd stand with him again. And it wouldn't much matter what we faced. But my hope is you'll keep him at Onath so occupied at peace that he'll forget the world outside. Maybe he can live a long time if you do."

255

"I hope to see him grow old with me," Netta agreed. "But it seems there is more meaning than that to your words."

Toddin sighed. "I mean he can't see a soul burned but that he put himself in the fire to push them out. It's more than he ought to bear. But maybe you'll touch his heart concerning that. It could save his life."

"Thank you," Netta said softly. "I will remember your words."

Toddin was ready to find his brother among Benn Trilett's men and return to their families. It was with some sadness that Netta bid him farewell, thinking that Tahn might have wanted to speak to him again were he awake. Lucas went out with him, but he would return, he said, with Lorne and Lord Trilett.

Tahn stirred enough to sip from Anain's cup again, but he was not awake long enough to speak to them. Netta watched the healer woman dab his forehead with a damp cloth. He rolled toward his stomach, and the old woman lifted the bedcovers to check the wounds on his back. Netta's stomach tightened to see the sore welts and broken skin. She could tell that Tiarra was just as troubled, and she reached to touch the young woman's hand again.

Anain glanced her way. "We are honored to have you in our house, Lady Trilett. And your father, when he comes. You grace us."

"You have had the higher honor to care for this man," Netta told her. "We are deeply grateful and will happily repay you."

"Strange, your opinion of him," Anain remarked. "It is beyond my heart to understand."

"There is more to my brother than what Alastair has taught," Tiarra told her abruptly. But the old woman did not answer, only turned away solemnly.

Netta wanted to ask the girl about the accusations, about their mother and what had happened so long ago. She wasn't sure she should speak of it now. She wasn't sure of the response she might get. But to her surprise, Tiarra spoke of it first.

256

"I wish I were old enough to remember my mother's last day. Tahn says her touch was kind. I don't think he would think of that if he had hurt her."

"You're surely right," Netta said softly, not wanting to interfere too much in Tiarra's thoughts.

"I would like to know if she suffered much," the girl went on. "And if she at least had some happy moments in her life. But mostly I wish I understood about her and my father." She glanced up at Netta. "No one ever told me if they married. But if there was no love, how did they have even one child, let alone two? And if they did love, then how could he have killed her?"

Netta thought of the days when she had feared Tahn, when he had seemed so fierce, even capable of horrors. But he'd been trapped in a world beyond his control. Had his father somehow been the same?

It was too much for her to understand. Tahn had softened, had learned what it was like to love and be loved. Could someone really grow in the other direction—could they love first, and then turn to darkness and blood?

"There may be no answers to such questions," the old healer woman was saying. And even though Netta knew she was addressing Tiarra, she nodded as well.

26

With a Trilett message in his hands, Saud turned away from the churchyard careful not to show the depth of his anger. Lionell would be furious. Lionell would blame him for this failure, though none of it had been his fault.

Tahn was in hiding. No one had disclosed where. But Saud felt certain he had not left the town. He'd never have left if Benn Trilett and his men had not come.

Why had Tahn come alone to Alastair, followed so soon afterward by the Trilett lord himself? What plan had they determined? He knew it would be a worry to Lionell. Benn Trilett had as much cause for vengeance as the Dorn did. And plenty enough means besides.

Saud mounted his horse and motioned to his men to follow him. They could do nothing else, now that they were watched by Trilett guardsmen. Such scrutiny was a humiliation Lionell did not need right now, when he wanted the other noble families to forget the past and join him in the celebration of his marriage. Saud could imagine his fits of rage. But more than that, fear. What had Benn Trilett planned? Some retribution? Even though he had spent a year talking peace?

At least Benn Trilett's message still spoke peace. Though the warning could not be mistaken: *"I will consider any further aggression against one of my men as an attack upon myself."*

Saud glanced back to see the Trilett lord still watching, standing with a circle of his guardsmen. And Saud bowed his head to them just slightly, thinking such a gesture might lend credence to the things he'd told them. That it was all a mistake. That they had only come to fight the bandits that plagued Alastair. How could they be faulted if Tahn chose to arrive at such a time and make himself a plague as well?

They rode out swiftly, and Saud puzzled for a moment over Korin. He had chosen not to return with them. Something was afoot, something Korin knew about but was not telling.

"Sir!" the young soldier nearest Saud called. "What will Lionell do with this news? Will he punish us?"

"Shut up!" Saud ordered him. "There is no fault of ours here. And there'll be no punishment, except of the Dorn when he is found."

"How can we seek him now?"

"There will be a way!" Saud roared. "Or do you prefer to let him laugh that he has bested us?"

The soldier said no more. And Saud shook his head. Tahn Dorn was a man of narrow escapes and clever hiding places. He'd once hidden Lady Trilett. And he'd hidden himself so well that Samis had to hire a tracker and then lay a trap with archers to snare him. He'd hidden eight children in the wilderness and then somehow managed to convince Benn Trilett to adopt the lot of them. Some of the ex-mercenaries were afraid of Tahn. A few spoke of him as though he held a special magic, like an angel or a son of the devil who could not be killed by mortal means.

Such talk was ridiculous, of course. But now it only fueled Saud's wish to see him dead. Even as a child, Tahn had escaped him. Saud had searched all of one long night with the baron's orders to kill the boy when he was found. But only the morning's tumult had revealed him, and by that time, Saud had grown frustrated and angry enough to order the steaming pot.

Still Dorn lived, mocking Saud's skill as well as the baron's orders. Benn Trilett be cursed! Saud knew he'd not rest until he found some way to settle this matter. For Lionell, certainly, because the pay was good. But even more now for himself.

He saw two or three bandits in the night's darkness as they drew farther from the town. Cursed bandits! They had said they would join him against the Dorn, but they had been no help at all. He was about to pass them on the road, but then a sudden thought made him stop. Bandits will do what bandits do best. And there could be no fault to the House of Trent for that.

He would speak to them. There might yet be a way to catch the Dorn.

27

Netta heard voices outside the cottage before anyone reached the door. Lucas was saying that Tahn had wakened briefly and they believed he would be all right. And then her father gave answer. She wondered if he knew yet that she sat at Tahn's side. He would not be happy with her, but surely he would be able to understand.

She took Tahn's hand in her own and held it as the door slowly opened. Benn Trilett entered first, followed by Lucas and Lorne. Netta saw her father's eyes so full of concern, and then the look in them suddenly changed when he saw her. Despite the certainty she had felt, her heart pounded.

"Netta!"

"I had to come, Father. I needed to be here." She could not keep the mist of tears from filling her eyes.

Her father only looked at her soberly and then turned his eyes to Tahn again. "We will speak of it later. How does he fare?"

"Better. Oh, Father—we nearly lost him. But he's stronger."

The nobleman Trilett stepped forward to the bedside, and the old woman moved to give him space. "Perhaps I should have forbidden him to come here when he asked me."

"No," Netta told him. "I wish we might have spared him the pain, but he would not have found his sister had he stayed."

Benn Trilett looked toward Tiarra, and the girl bowed her eyes from his gaze. "I hope there is peace between them," he said gently.

261

Tiarra didn't answer.

"There is peace," Netta spoke for her.

"I look forward to learning more about you," Benn continued, still looking at Tahn's sister. "But I expect I should tell you first that the baron's captain says there has been no war tonight. Simply a misunderstanding. He says he was only trying to apprehend a ruffian all of Alastair considers a menace."

"Oh, Father!" Netta exclaimed.

"Tahn did nothing wrong here," Tiarra protested. "And they would have killed him. Tahn warned us about them."

"I don't doubt he was right," Benn answered. "There's more to this than what Saud tells. But nothing can be done about them now. At least they've gone and the baron knows better than to trouble me here."

Tahn stirred awake at the sound of new voices. He opened his eyes slowly and looked around him. Benn Trilett stood before him in riding clothes. His face seemed clouded with cares.

"Well, son . . ." the Trilett lord was saying. But Tahn could not decipher the rest of his words. He studied the faces looking his way. Lucas and Lorne, Tiarra, Benn, Tobas, and the old healer woman. But on Netta he let his eyes rest. It was her voice that had called to him in the darkness.

"I love you," he said, trying to put strength enough behind the words that she might hear them.

"I love you too."

Her eyes were so clear, so beautiful, like the emerald stone of Tiarra's necklace. She had taught him God's love. And God wanted him to receive, to believe that in Christ's sacrifice he was made worthy. Suddenly he felt he must trust enough to speak the words of his heart before any thoughts of doubt could get in the way. He opened his mouth again, and the words were strangely bold. "Marry me, Netta."

He'd scarcely allowed himself to think of such things before, even though he knew that others around him thought of it often. He might never have asked her. But now he felt bidden of

God to accept the things he'd been told. He was not unworthy, not in Christ. "Marry me," he said again. "Please."

For a moment she sat stunned. And then she laughed, just a little. She turned and looked at her father, and then she leaned and put her hands on Tahn's cheeks and kissed him so softly. "Oh, Tahn. Such a moment you have for this! Yes, I would marry you! With my father's blessing."

That brought a tightness to Tahn's heart. He'd forgotten he was supposed to go about this in the proper manner. He should have spoken to Benn Trilett first. He hoped the nobleman wasn't angry. "My lord . . ." he struggled to say. "May I ask for your daughter's hand?"

Benn shook his head. "What will I do with the two of you?"

"Make an announcement for them," Tobas said with a laugh. "Start making plans."

"Oh, Father!" Netta exclaimed. "Answer him! You already told me how you felt."

"I never expected to find such folly in you, daughter, to run off against my wishes. And it is not like Tahn to be so bold in such matters as this. Perhaps the fever talks."

"Please give your blessing," Tahn begged him.

For a moment, Benn was quiet. "I would not have thought you to tell your intentions before all these people, Tahn. Sometimes it has seemed hard enough for you to express your feelings to one person alone."

"God . . . touched me."

Benn stood quietly looking at him. "Rest," he said finally. "We will speak of this when you are stronger."

"Father—" Netta began.

"Do not argue, child. You can see the shape he is in. Give him time."

Tahn closed his eyes. He wasn't sure if Benn Trilett's words were meant to be kind or hard. He took a deep breath, feeling the peace of the river on him still. "My sister is here," he struggled to tell them. "She has no one else."

"Don't worry for her," Benn answered him. "I will see to her needs."

263

Tahn nodded, too strangely weary to speak again. But he was happy. He had declared his love openly, regardless of the outcome. And he felt it was what God had meant for him to do.

<hr>

As the sun rose, Tiarra lay against the covers the old woman had given her, watching her brother sleeping peacefully on the bed. The priest had come and taken the Trilett lord and some of his men to the church, where there would be more room to rest. But Tiarra had refused to go, and so had Netta Trilett. The rest of the Trilett guardsmen were outside. And Lorne was in the cottage with them, leaning his head against the wall beneath the window, probably asleep.

Tiarra had tried to sleep too, because the healer had told her to. But she had only lain a long time, thinking of all the things that had happened. Her brother had so easily gotten a promise from Benn Trilett concerning her, to see to her needs. But what would that mean?

Her eyes turned toward Lorne. He was tired. And she had known how upset he was to see what had happened in his absence. She hoped he didn't blame himself at all, even for losing sight of her when first she'd gone to see the necklace. It certainly wasn't his fault that he had cared enough for a little boy's life to take his attention off her for a moment. He was a good man. A kind man to the street children, which was a rare thing as far as she had ever known.

Suddenly his steel blue eyes opened, and he turned toward her. Much to her surprise, she found his gaze more than a little unnerving.

"I—I hope you'll forgive me for deceiving you," she stammered.

"You're a cruel sneak," he said. Despite the words, he smiled at her. "But I'm glad you've changed your mind about Tahn."

"It's not hard now to see that you were right about him."

"I heard about Martica. I'm sorry."

"It's all right, sir. A long time I've known it was coming. Nothing could be done."

"Will you go with us? Back to Onath when Tahn is ready?"

"I—I don't know."

"You know you'd be welcome, don't you?"

"Perhaps. But perhaps no one knows what else to do with me. I have a house—Martica's house. There's no one else to claim it."

"Why would you want to stay here?"

"I don't know what I want."

Lorne sighed. "Well. It doesn't have to be decided now."

She studied him in the increasing light of morning, remembering the things he'd told her about himself. His life had been hard too, though perhaps not like her brother's. "Were you ever whipped?" she questioned softly.

Something changed in his eyes. But she wasn't sorry she'd asked. She wanted to see whatever it was that worked in his thoughts. She wanted to know all she could about him.

"Only once," he answered. "It was different for me. My father had already told me what my lot had become. He made me swear obedience."

"To a killer?"

"He didn't know what Samis was."

"But he made you a slave."

"He knew no choice."

"But why were you whipped?"

He looked at her soberly, and his words were low. "It was an accident. I lost a crate of his favorite wine on the rocks outside Valhal. I wish to God it had been for something bolder."

"Were you always afraid?"

"Anyone who was there and says he wasn't is a liar."

"Have you seen your family again?"

He sighed. "Yes. Recently. And things are better. Except that my father's lameness has only gotten worse."

"Do you love him?"

"Yes." He shook his head. "Why are you so full of questions?"

"I . . . I want to know more about my brother's friends.

265

I was thinking that perhaps . . . perhaps they could become mine."

He smiled. "Well, what would you like to know about Lucas, then? Or Marc Toddin? Or the Triletts, maybe?"

She returned his smile. She couldn't help herself. "Whatever you want to tell me. I don't care."

"You're very lovely," he said suddenly.

She stared for a moment, taken aback at the bluntness of his words. She'd been told that before, and never for a good purpose. Her smile faded.

"I'm sorry," he told her, ducking his head. "I shouldn't have said—"

"It's all right. Only it makes me think of the worst of the tavern drinkers. And Mikal Ovny, the son of the man who whipped my brother."

"Miss Loble—"

"Don't apologize again. I can see that you're not like them."

"But I should restrain my tongue," Lorne said with a sigh.

"Maybe not," Tiarra said softly. "Maybe I should dare to tell you that I think you're lovely too."

Lorne looked at her in surprise.

"I've never seen anyone else offer to feed the street children. It meant so much to them. And I would like to be your friend."

He closed his eyes for a second. "I want to talk to Lord Trilett about the children. I'd like to help them more."

His words stirred inside her. Here was a man with good thoughts, good plans. He should be blessed. He should have good things. "Do you work for him always?"

"Yes, I suppose. If you mean steadily."

"But you are free now. Aren't you?" Sudden tears clouded her eyes.

"Yes," he assured her. "The Triletts hire many. But they have no slaves."

For a moment she couldn't answer. A tear dropped to her cheek before she could stop it.

266

"Why are you crying?"

"I don't know! God has changed so much. For you. And my brother. Even for me."

He leaned forward. He edged toward her and took her into his arms. And she wept, not even sure why. It was hope, perhaps. For herself, and for the street children. She had never expected good to come. But now, any number of things seemed possible.

Lorne held her tight, and she tried to stop the tears. But she couldn't. His warmth, his arms, were so different than Mikal's. But suddenly he pulled away from her.

"You're all right?" he asked.

"Yes," she managed to tell him, afraid to look in his eyes.

"I'm glad we found you. I'm glad things could change for you. You won't have to fear anymore."

"Thank you," she whispered, leaning again toward the soft covers the old woman had given her. "You're a good friend."

Once again he smiled as he pulled the corner of a blanket over her shoulder and then slid back toward the window. "Sleep if you can, miss. It's been a very long couple of days."

28

Benn Trilett protects him? Even in Alastair!" Lionell spun around so swiftly that he knocked a vase from its pedestal stand. The crimson pottery crashed at his feet, but he didn't seem to notice. "God Almighty! He must know who Tahn is! Do you understand what that means?"

Saud shook his head with a laborious sigh. "It may mean only that his guard captain has become valuable to him. Especially considering the relationship between Dorn and his daughter."

"I should have known!" Lionell wailed. "Why would he let a piece of street rabble court a Trilett, no matter what they think that man has done for them! He must have known all along that his daughter's suitor is a noble son!"

"It surprises me to hear you speak of the scoundrel so generously," Saud growled. "Dorn is nothing but a worthless villain."

"Did you see him?" Lionell asked, breathing fast. "Was he at Lord Trilett's side?"

"We saw no sign of him the entire time we were there, my lord. We heard that the town whipped him before Benn Trilett arrived. Surely for that and for fear of us he kept himself hidden."

"Whipped?" Lionell stared at him. "Perhaps he's in bad shape. Pray God that he dies. It would be a perfect solution."

"But not likely," Saud told him. "He's strong."

Lionell turned away and sank into an embroidered chair.

"What can we do? Just when I had things going well again, with Lord Fontler's daughter as my bride! And now this!"

Saud only stared at him. He had expected railing anger. At least that would have shown some strength. But a morose Lionell, devoid of the fire needed to complete his own plans? "My lord, return a message to Benn Trilett saying you had no idea the affairs of Alastair were so important to him. We were simply attempting to make the city a safer place. He has no way to prove otherwise. He can't use this against you."

"Fool!" Lionell responded. "He doesn't need to find cause, or to convince anyone that I've done anything. Don't you understand that? All he needs is the right moment to announce Karra Loble's son!"

"Benn Trilett is no schemer. And it will not matter. I have no intention of letting the Dorn make it back to Onath or trouble us any further."

"What will you do? Attack the Triletts on the trail? Fool! The other nobles will have my head on a platter!"

"Not so, my lord. You can't help it if we weren't finished with the cutthroat terrors of Alastair's roads. Nor if they take their vengeance upon the first noble party passing by."

Lionell turned, his eyes suddenly bright again. "You've hired the bandits."

"More than that. I have left men among them to be sure of the job. In common dress, you can be certain. And they will be ready as soon as the Dorn leaves Alastair."

"Well," Lionell replied, slowly standing. "I'm learning why my father thought so much of you."

"He knew my capabilities."

"Prove them to me," Lionell said with a smile. "And let me know promptly if there are Trilett losses. You know I shall want to properly grieve."

In the little cottage, Tahn woke again. The room was quiet. Netta was at the side of his bed, her head on a cushion near him. At first he didn't see anyone else. He could imagine that he must have slept, and dreamed, a very long time. It was like waking from a fog to find the world now changed. How much time had passed? Why had Netta come?

Her father had been here. And he thought he saw Lorne now, over by the window. At the other side of the cottage, the young mother sat in a chair, her baby clutched close to her breast. The sight of her made him think of his own mother again, and he sighed. There was no way to know if the things he'd seen in his strange dreams had been real. But because of the dreams, or whatever they'd been, he felt sure that his parents had loved their children and each other. He might never have proof. But he believed it just the same.

He reached his hand to Netta's soft hair, hoping not to wake her, but she stirred at his touch.

"Tahn?"

"I'm sorry . . ."

"No, don't apologize. I'm glad you're awake."

"Netta, please . . . why did you come?"

"I had to be with you. I'm not sure how else to explain."

"Is it safe now?"

She smiled. "Yes. We have plenty of guards. And your enemies have gone. You look so much better. Are you in pain?"

"Sore. Some." He met her eyes. "I—I think I proposed."

She smiled again. "You did. I'm glad you remember."

"Have I offended your father?"

"He wouldn't tell me last night. But I'm sure it's all right."

"Will he give his blessing?"

"After he talks to you again, I don't doubt that he will."

He took a deep breath, trying to muster strength. He needed to talk to her further, despite his weakness. "Is Lucas still here? Has he told you much?"

"He went with Father and the priest to the church. He told us what happened to you."

Her beautiful eyes so clearly pictured her concern for him. Her love. He tensed inside. "But did he tell you who I am?"

270

Tenderly she took his hand. "I know about your mother, Tahn, that she was sister to Naysius Trent. But it doesn't matter—"

"How can it not? He . . . he was a coward and a beast."

"I know. And I knew you wouldn't be pleased. But his deeds speak nothing of your mother. Or of you."

"That's not all, Netta," he said softly. "There's also Samis."

Her brow furrowed just slightly. "What about him?"

"He was kin to my father, lady." He struggled with the words. "They were brothers."

"Oh . . ." Her hand tightened in his. "No one said . . ."

"Lady . . . naught but the devil himself could have been more evil." A shudder ran through him, and he lowered his eyes.

"Tahn, look at me." She gently lifted his face to meet hers again. "That's not who you are."

"I know. But I had to tell you. And you must tell your father. You have a right . . . to consider . . ."

"I consider what a gift God has given us. I don't care what your family was! Out of horror God has brought good."

She leaned and kissed his forehead. And before he could think about it, he caught her head with one hand, pulling her toward him. She smiled, and they kissed. But when their lips parted, he had to catch his breath.

"You're still warm," she told him. "You need to rest."

"I need to tell you something more. Netta . . . I think my parents were good."

"It need not be such a surprise," she said gently. "But your father too? Despite what they say about him?"

"I don't think he killed our mother," Tahn said softly. "I don't think he could have."

Netta lifted his hand toward her cheek, but before she could say anything in reply, the healer woman was suddenly approaching them. "Fever's down enough for you to be talking, I see. A good relief to your friends, all right. Let me bring you a cup and check your back."

"He's still warm," Netta told her.

The woman's bony hand reached to Tahn's forehead. "So much better. He was hot as the devil's fire yesterday."

When the old woman looked down, Tahn saw something strange in her eyes. He didn't know her name, but it seemed to him that she was like Martica in a way he didn't understand. He might have been uncomfortable with that thought, except that her cottage had been a safe refuge. His friends had brought him here. He could trust them.

"Strange to think that Sanlin Dorn's children could be kin to the Trents," the woman said. "I can't help overhearing all of you, since you came here. Such a surprise. No one knew where Karra Loble came from, though I once heard a traveler say there were Lobles near Tamask."

"The same family, I think," Netta answered her. "But I don't know if they are still there."

"If Karra Loble were a legitimate child, she would have borne the Trent name," the healer pointed out almost accusingly.

"Her father claimed her openly before he died," Netta answered her. "But that is past. It doesn't matter."

The old woman turned away with a frown. She poured something generously from a small jar into a gourd cup and mixed it with herb water from her pot. She looked toward Tahn. "Everyone knows that Sanlin Dorn came from trouble," she said. "He was a horrid man. And his father and brother were like him."

"There is more . . . more than people know," Tahn told her. "He was misjudged."

"How can you be sure?" the old woman pressed.

Tahn took a deep breath and shook his head. He was still weary, but he had to answer her. "Did anyone search for truth? No one asked questions . . . or sought evidence. Alastair did the baron's will. That is all."

"I'm not surprised that you see this town as an enemy."

She lifted his head and put the cup to his lips. The liquid was odd, but he drank it in. He hadn't realized his thirst. "Thank you," he whispered, looking up at her.

But she pressed the cup to his lips again. "The fever has left you dry. Drink it all."

As he sipped the cup he looked into her eyes again, and he saw the angry, accusing faces of his horrible dream. The medicine drink was suddenly bitter on his tongue. He pushed the cup away.

"Finish it, lad," the healer woman insisted. "You need all the liquid you can—"

"No." He couldn't reconcile what he was thinking. He knew his friends must have trusted this woman. But what he saw in her now, he couldn't ignore. "No."

"Tahn, she's trying to help."

"No, Netta . . ." The black mist was suddenly upon his mind. He tried to shake it away. This couldn't be happening. He'd already won that battle. The darkness was bested because of God's light. Lorne was suddenly beside him, but the room would not stay still.

The old woman was looking down at Tahn. She smiled, just a little. "It seems the sickness still clouds his mind a bit," she said. "Do not worry over it. But he must drink."

Again, she pressed the cup to Tahn's lips. And he was thirsty. His friends had trusted her. He had known her helping hands in his sickness. Was it only cruel imagination now making him doubt? His heart was suddenly racing. The faces seemed to stare at him out of her eyes. *"He is not worthy of life,"* they taunted. *"Kin of the baron, kin of Sanlin Dorn—"*

"No." He knocked the cup away

"Tahn." Netta took his hand, and he saw the surprise and the worry in her eyes. He knew he had splashed her. He knew most of the medicine drink was soaked over the bedding and into his clothes.

"What's wrong?" Netta asked him. "You're safe here. And she's right. The fever was hard on you. You must drink."

"No," he said, but even the one word did not come easy now. The room was gray and in motion. But he could see the old woman mixing another cup. Death. It was black, swirling death as sure as was the valley of demons in his

273

dream. "No, Netta," he stammered, feeling as though he were being pulled helplessly away from her. "Please."

"Tahn, what's wrong?"

He knew she was frightened, and Lorne with her. He wanted to explain. But he couldn't find the words in the gray mist around him. He couldn't find the strength. His eyes were deceiving him. The light of day was gone. And the room was suddenly slipping away.

"He is confused," the healer woman told them with a shake of her head. "The sickness still has its hold. But he is strong. If he has drink in him, he can get past it."

Netta glanced up at her but quickly turned her eyes to Tahn again. He had seemed past the sickness just moments ago. He hadn't been confused at all. And now—now he had fallen away so quickly, pleading with her, as though there were something she had to understand. She reached her hand to Tahn's forehead and was surprised to find him cooler. The fever had broken. It wasn't claiming him now.

The old woman turned to Lorne. "Help me. We can get a little more down him carefully if we try. He needs the medicine at work—"

"No," Netta said quickly, her hand clutching the blanket Tahn had soaked when he knocked the cup away. "No. Whatever your potion is, he said he'll have no more of it."

"He doesn't know what he's saying—"

"But he plainly said no," Lorne agreed.

"Don't be foolish," the woman argued with them. "You can see that he worsens. He could die without more drink in him."

"Lorne," Netta said quickly, "please go outside and ask Josef to bring fresh water."

"We have water here," the woman offered.

"I'll not take it from your hand."

"Dear lady!" the healer exclaimed. "For what cause do you not trust me?"

"I trust Tahn," Netta answered her. "And he does not trust you."

274

The woman scoffed. "Does he trust anyone? Such a man as he?"

Lorne suddenly stepped toward her. "I will go to the door and send the guard for water. But you will move away from my friend and not touch him again."

"Where is Lucas? Where is Father Bray?" the old woman cried. "They know what I've done for him! They brought him here half dead already, and I nursed him—"

"You'll not touch him again," Lorne repeated. "And I will indeed send one of the men for Lucas."

The healer's daughter came nearer, fear plain in her voice and on her face. "Mother, what's wrong?"

"I don't know," she answered abruptly. "These people seem to think that after I spend hours saving a man's life, that I would . . . that I would . . ."

She stopped. She turned from them abruptly and moved into the smaller room. Without another word, she sat in a chair near the door with her head bowed.

"Mother?"

"I have nothing to say. Let them get their water. Let them do what they will."

The younger woman looked at Netta with confusion plain in her eyes. Tiarra rose to her feet and came to the bedside. Lorne went to the door to speak to the guards outside but was almost immediately back in.

Tahn lay still except for a tiny tremor in one hand, his eyes now closed.

"What did you give him?" Lorne demanded of the woman.

"I told you I have nothing more to say."

Catrin moved to her mother's side. "Mother, it cannot hurt to explain the herbs you've used. Perhaps it will put their minds at ease."

"No, girl."

"Mother? Was it sweet balm? Yarrow? Perhaps borage?"

But the old woman said no more. Netta watched the daughter turn with confusion to the little table that was nearly covered with bottles and jars, including the gourd

275

cup newly filled. She only looked for a moment, until her eyes rested on one small jar. It sat out of line from the other containers, and its lid was askew. "Oh . . ."

Without another word, Catrin lifted the cup, her face suddenly ashen. She sniffed just a bit and then sniffed at the jar. "Oh, Mother."

With tears suddenly in her eyes, she flung the cup into the fireplace, and the brown liquid washed over flame with a hiss. She fled to the door. Almost Lorne stopped her, but she pushed at him, almost choking on her words. "I—I'll get the priest."

"What's happened?" Tiarra pleaded.

Netta leaned toward Tahn on the bed, taking his hand and lifting it to her cheek. His breathing seemed different. Irregular. "I think . . . I think he's been poisoned."

The old woman rose to her feet. Without a word, she moved toward the little table. She had her hand on the jar before any of them could stop her. With the lid off quickly, she lifted the jar toward her lips. But before she could drink, Lorne was at her side and knocked the stuff away. The jar broke, and the dark concoction seeped through the cracks of the floor.

"If you will die over this, let it be later!" Lorne yelled at her. "What is the stuff? Tell us! What can be done?"

"Nothing," the woman said bitterly. "Nothing."

"Why?" Netta cried. "Why would you hurt him? We trusted you!"

Tiarra stood quietly. Before anyone could notice, she moved to the corner and took Tahn's sword in her hand. "I thought the trouble was done," she said in a low voice. "I thought we would have peace—"

"Put down the sword," Lorne told her softly.

Tiarra glanced his way. "She told me she was glad I didn't blame him, that he was done wrong. I thought she rejoiced with us that he would live. What evil is this?"

Lorne stepped between her and the healer. "Your vengeance cannot help him."

"She is Dorn," the old woman said coldly. "It is in her blood to seek blood."

"How is it better to betray trust and poison the helpless?" Netta demanded. "She is far more honorable to face you openly for the sake of her brother! God judge you!"

"One day you will understand, dear lady—"

"No! I pray that *you* understand! You don't know him. He would harm no one, now that his life is his own and the Lord's. Why can't you see that? If there is any way to help him—"

The woman shook her head. "There's nothing to be done."

"Then what you gave him . . ." Netta said with a tremor in her voice. "It is death?"

"I cannot say if he will live or die now. I couldn't get the full cup down him. It may not be poison enough."

"Why?" Tiarra screamed at her. "Why would you do this?"

"Oh, girl." The old woman looked at her sadly. "You only see him. And yourself."

Josef hurried through the door with water. Tiarra stood tensely, but Lorne gently pulled the sword from her hand and put a protective arm around her shoulder. The old woman turned from them and solemnly returned to her chair.

With her heart pounding, Netta bathed Tahn's forehead and tried to wet his lips with the cool water. "Father God," she murmured.

Josef went back outside, and in a moment Lucas burst in. He took one look at Tahn on the bed and turned his attention to the old woman.

"Anain! What did you give him?"

"Scarlet berry and the devil weed, sir. There is nothing you can do but pray."

He grasped both of her arms and pulled her from the chair. Netta could see the anger in him, fierce and horrible. He shoved her toward the door and almost out it. But Catrin and the priest came in, followed promptly by Netta's father.

"Lucas," Father Bray called sternly.

277

"What do you want?" Lucas yelled in answer. "You brought us here! You told me we could trust you! And your friends—whoever they are to you!"

From a nearby bed, the baby started crying.

"What will you do, Lucas?" the priest pressed.

"Throw her outside. Out of this town. I don't know."

Benn Trilett moved away from them, toward the bed, and put his arms around Netta. "Is there anything we can do?"

Netta was near tears. "I don't know, Father. She says not, but I don't know that we can believe her in that, or anything."

Catrin hurried to the bed, not even stopping to answer her baby's cry. She looked from Netta to Tiarra to Lord Trilett, her hands shaking. "I am so sorry. So sorry. I don't understand—"

"Can you help?" Netta begged her.

She shook her head. "I don't know how. I don't know what to do. It was a potion she used so seldom. For the fits. And only one drop. Just one drop in a spoonful. She told me once how dangerous—" She stopped, glancing toward her mother and the priest. "I don't understand. I'm so sorry."

Father Bray pulled at Lucas's arms, but he would not let go of the old woman.

"Let me talk to her," the priest insisted.

Lucas stared at him, his eyes blazing fury, but he let go, forcefully, shoving her away.

The priest caught the old woman before she could fall and, with a glance at Lucas, helped her to a chair. "Anain? You are my friend. Tell me they are wrong."

But she said nothing.

"Anain, please. Have you done what they say?"

"Yes, Father," the old woman answered with a quiet voice. "Forgive me."

For a moment the priest could do nothing but stare at her in shock. "It was God's hand to help him!" he finally exclaimed. "I told you! Why would you do evil when I brought him here for good?"

278

"I think of this city, Father. All of the people."

The priest shook his head. "You know Alastair's stain as well as I do! We prayed that it might be made right! How can you add to the injustice? Don't you understand?"

"I understand very well!" the woman answered him back. "I am sorry what the lad has gone through and sorry what his life has been! But you must understand that it is better for him to die than so many more to suffer! Can't you see that?"

"How could more suffer?" Lucas demanded. "How could his death help anyone?"

Anain lifted her head to meet his hard eyes. "Don't you know that the baron owns this town? Our lands are his!"

"Yes," Lucas answered bitterly. "That curse has been part of the problem all along."

"The baron holds our livelihoods!" the old woman continued. "Don't you understand? This man Dorn is no stranger to killing. When he is strong enough, what is to stop him from winning a terrible vengeance for what has happened?"

"Why would he?" Lucas questioned her. "He has no desire—"

"He has blood in his soul! But to know he is also Trent! He is a stronger sort than Lionell. He'll take for himself all that belongs to the baron. And then he will own us, don't you see that? I think of my neighbors, the people of Alastair. You know they are not all guilty! But we would be at his mercy, and we have given him no cause to be kind. At least the baron Lionell has other things on his mind. At least he allows our lives to go on as if he were no cloud over us—"

"Then you would kill him," Netta said quietly. "Just as Lionell would, to keep him from Trent power."

"I thought he would die on his own, but he wouldn't. Now if he lives, lady, you will soon enough understand. Of course he did nothing to us before. How could he? But now he is clever enough even to use Trilett means—"

"Stop!" Netta cried. "How can you see him so? He is no monster plotting destruction! He threatens no one. God is my witness, he is a lamb!" She shook, and tears blurred her vision.

"Love blinds you, lady."

"And what blinds you?" Netta could not help her tears. She turned from the old woman and could not accept her father's outstretched arm. She fell on her knees beside the bed and laid her head against Tahn's chest. "Oh, Father. He is so faint."

"I will hang the woman if he dies," Lord Trilett pronounced. And Catrin burst into tears. She picked up her baby, who reached his tiny hands to the priest with a squeal.

"It is God's judgment and not the Dorn's that I feared for Alastair," Father Bray said gravely. "Now I fear all the more."

The old woman turned her eyes away as Tahn moaned and rolled to his side, drawing shaking arms toward his stomach. Netta spoke his name, but he did not respond.

"It might go easier for you, Anain," the priest told her, "if you tell us a remedy."

"There is none."

"I would not trust anything from her hand now," Lucas said bitterly. "Nor the daughter's, nor yours."

"You think this was done at my word?" the priest questioned.

"You brought us here," Lucas answered with a shake of his head. "I don't know what I think. You should go. All of you."

"This is my daughter's home," the old woman argued. "Surely you would not make her leave."

"Do you think I would move my brother?" Lucas demanded of her. "Look at him."

Tahn had grown as pale as the bedding around him, and the shaking was worse. The sickness had left him with nothing to vomit, but the poison worked heaves in him anyway. And a trickle of blood flowed from his back, where renewed movement had reopened the unhealed stripes. Tiarra took a damp cloth in her hand and bathed his forehead. But the look in her eye was raw with pain.

280

"Oh, Father," Netta whispered.

Benn Trilett slowly shook his head. "Daughter, please take his sister outside. You should not see this. Neither of you."

"No!" Tiarra roared. "We can be his help! But if he is to die, we should be beside him. If he can know we are here, let it be comfort! I'll not go!"

"Surely he'll not die," Netta said carefully, reaching for Tiarra's hand.

With tears in her eyes, Tiarra accepted the gesture and turned her eyes to the Trilett lord.

"You are right," he sighed. "God be our help. But Lucas is also right. We cannot move him nor trust those who have dwelt here. Father Bray, I would thank you to remove the women to a room in your church. I will set a guard there for the elder."

"Yes, sir," the priest said solemnly. "I will do as you wish. Will you allow my prayers?"

"I covet every prayer," Benn told him. "But speak them in the church with my gratitude after you have removed this family. Their cottage is forfeited to us so long as we have need of it. They may take with them what they will."

29

Tiarra stood staring at Tahn. She felt numb. Empty. Like the whole world and everything in it was senseless. *Why, God?* she asked in her heart. *It is all so wrong.*

Almost it seemed as if none of what had happened over the last few days could be real. Perhaps she might wake up and hear Martica's coughing in the next room. And then go to her horrid work and hear news of her brother so far away. She wiped her eyes. He should be far away. He never should have come.

Benn Trilett stepped closer to her, watching her. "I want you to know," he said in a gentle voice, "I will not forget the promise I made him. I will see to your needs, whatever happens."

"I don't care about that!" she burst out at him. "Don't you understand? I don't care!"

Lady Netta was immediately at her side. It was strange. So strange that the Triletts would think of her feelings. But the lady was enfolding her in her arms. For a moment, Tiarra shook, almost pulling away. But then she let herself return the embrace and wept on the lady's shoulder. Lucas and Lorne had knelt beside one another. And to Tiarra's surprise, Bennamin Trilett knelt with them.

"He can't die," Tiarra whispered. "Or there is no justice under heaven."

"Sometimes this world seems void of good," Netta answered. "But there is justice beyond it. Of that I have no doubt."

"That woman should burn in hell."

"Judgment belongs to God alone," Netta said softly. "I pray she realizes what she has done and begs God's forgiveness."

Tiarra had no answer. It wasn't only the old woman for whom she felt such things. There were the bandits and Lionell Trent who were just as guilty.

Tahn moaned softly, and she and Netta both knelt close beside him.

"What if he dies?" Tiarra asked with pain in her voice.

"I can't answer that," Netta said. "Except that you are my sister. That will not change."

Tiarra glanced at her but could say nothing. She pulled away the damp bedclothes and got another blanket from the bed that had been Catrin and her child's.

"He will not die," Netta told her as she spread the blanket carefully over Tahn. "He has too much to live for."

Tiarra nodded, willing to reach for such a hope. She knelt again, but behind them there was a sudden soft tap at the door.

Lucas answered. He stood for a moment in the open doorway, looking at the tall soldier who stood outside.

"Please," Emil Korin said. "Will you let me talk to the girl? I am so sorry for what has happened."

"Why now?" Lucas asked, his voice raw with emotion. "We don't need you here right now."

"The priest sent me. He said Miss Tiarra might be comforted to know the truth, painful as it is. He said she should not linger in doubt of her father along with everything else."

"We linger with hope for her brother now," Lucas answered. "Surely it can wait."

"Let him in," Benn Trilett told him. "God knows our hope. But perhaps he would have us hear the matter."

Lucas shook his head and stepped aside from the doorway. The old soldier stepped in and turned his eyes immediately to Tahn and then to Tiarra. But she turned her face away. Could she trust his words? She didn't want to hear more lies. And if it were truth, Tahn should hear it perhaps even more than she should.

"Miss," the soldier said, "I know it is a hard time. Would God I knew a way to help! Might I speak with you? Please?"

She closed her eyes and saw Martica in her mind. But she shook the image away angrily. Things could have been so much better if Martica had only spoken the truth. Slowly, Tiarra rose to her feet. "I will hear you," she said. "But God curse you if you lie."

"God curses no man," Benn Trilett said softly. "But a lie is followed by its own curse."

The soldier nodded. "I am tired of the lies. I'm tired of carrying the guilt for my part of what happened. I have confessed to the priest, over the years. But it is not enough. Forgive me, please."

Tiarra stood tensely, staring at the man. Only one question filled her mind. "Who killed my mother?"

"It was the man who rode at our head last night, seeking your brother's life. The baron's captain. His name is Saud."

"And you helped him?" Tiarra asked, a bitter taste rising in her mouth.

"He didn't need help. He is strong. Ruthless, at times. The worst of my plague is that I didn't help her. Nor your father. I raised no hand as they were slaughtered. I held the horses. I helped to spread the lie against Sanlin Dorn. He would have tried to protect her. I learned that was why they risked coming to Alastair. He was arranging travel to the sea and then passage aboard a ship. He had planned to send Karra away, and you children too, to spare your lives."

"Then he loved her?" She could scarcely see through the mist in her eyes. Sanlin Dorn had been innocent.

"And she loved him," Korin affirmed. "He was the son of a bandit. He'd never known another life. But the baron hired him to trouble a family that opposed him, and he met Karra one day by accident in the courtyard. It wasn't long before she found a way to run away with him."

Tiarra moved to a nearby stool and slowly sat. "Why was that so terrible?" she asked. "Why didn't the baron just leave them alone?"

"Because of the baronship. He was afraid of your mother, miss. He'd kept her in the court like a prisoner. Not many people knew. But Naysius trusted Saud and me. We were his friends. He told us much." The soldier stopped and sighed.

"Go on," Benn prompted. "Why did he fear his sister?"

The soldier turned his eyes to the Trilett lord. "Naysius had a weakness for ladies, sir. Even those of the household. His father found him one day with the new baroness, his own stepmother. The old baron was so enraged that he disowned him and swore to give Karra the inheritance." He lowered his head. "Naysius killed the old man that night as he slept. He claimed the baronship before the matter could be widely known."

"But it should belong to Karra's son," Bennamin said slowly, turning his eyes toward Tahn.

"That is why they had to die, sir. That is why, in Lionell's mind, they still have to die."

"The Dorn has no interest in such position," Lord Trilett said. "I know it of him. But I can tell Lionell that I will publish the matter to the other nobles if he ever lifts his hand again."

Tiarra sat in silence, thinking of the things the soldier had said of her parents. Karra Loble might have seen Sanlin Dorn as a deliverer. A hope. "You watched them both die?" she asked, her heart feeling heavy.

"Yes," he admitted again with bowed head. "And it has grieved me these many years. Forgive me."

"Tell me more of it. Please."

"No, miss," the old soldier protested. "What more could you want to hear?"

"Everything," she said, knowing he did not understand why she would ask for details. Tears filled her eyes, but she still wanted to hear every bit he could possibly tell her, as if the knowledge of their deaths could somehow bring her closer to them. "She was stabbed?"

"Yes, miss," the soldier answered gravely. "She tried to fight. But Saud thrust his knife in her many times. We didn't find the boy that night, or he might have died the same way."

"And my father?"

"The news of her death reeled him almost off his feet. He claimed his innocence, but no one would believe him. His last words were a plea for his children."

Tiarra fell into sobs that shook her nearly from the chair. Lorne knelt suddenly at her side, steadying her.

"I'm so sorry, miss. May God forgive us and spare your brother's life again."

She could not answer him.

"I had longed for a way to make things right," the soldier said sadly. "But I know now that there is no way."

"At least you have borne the truth," Benn Trilett told him.

The man nodded. "I should not stay here any longer."

Lord Trilett looked at him carefully. "Will you go back to the Trents' service?"

"I don't think I can. I have family here in the town. I only want to be with them right now."

Benn nodded.

"I thank God that these children have your protection, my lord."

"The Dorn has been protection to me," Benn told him. "It is small, what I can do for him in return."

The soldier rose to his feet. Benn Trilett saw him out the door and then joined Netta alongside Tahn's bed. Tiarra continued to weep, and Netta thought that perhaps they all needed her to give voice to the weight of sadness upon them in this place.

Tahn was still curled on his side, his arms trembling ever so slightly. It was hard for Netta not to burst into sobs of her own.

"I thought there could be such an explanation," her father spoke softly.

"The Trents are not all of his kin," Netta said solemnly. "Father, Tahn wanted me to tell you that his father was a brother to Samis."

Benn shook his head. "That must have seemed to him a curse as bad as the baron's."

"I know it troubles him. But he said we had to know. Because we have a right to consider."

"Consider what, child?"

"Him. And all the past he carries. To stand at my side. To become my husband." Her voice broke as she spoke the words.

"Oh, daughter. We don't know if he'll live the day."

"He will! Father, he must!"

He took her carefully in his arms. "Netta, I pray he lives, and I would gladly give you to him. I'd not deny you, regardless of his family."

She hugged him. And then she eased beside Tahn on the bed and held his head in her arms. Leaning back, she stroked his long hair and sang a song she remembered that he liked, a hymn he had once heard Jarel sing at Onath.

Hours later, they were still at their vigil. Lucas was on his knees. Tobas had brought bread from the Trilett guards' provisions, but no one felt much like eating it. Netta asked if some broth might be prepared for when Tahn woke, and Tobas had been quick to bring that as well, but it sat untouched beside the healer woman's fire. Lorne had kept the fire burning and brought Tiarra water and bread, though she scarcely wanted either.

Netta's father had gone to talk to the priest. It troubled Netta for Catrin's sake that he might truly hang the healer woman for her treachery. But she knew she would not argue with him about it.

Netta had not moved from the bed. For a time, Tahn's tremors had been horrible, and she was glad she was there to hold him. But he was much calmer now, breathing shallow breaths and murmuring something occasionally that

287

she could not discern. "I love you," she whispered in his ear, hoping that he was able to hear her.

Tiarra came to the bedside and knelt down again. "I almost wish he hadn't come here," she said. "Though I'm glad I could meet him."

Netta nodded, but Tiarra only bowed her head sadly. "Do you think things will ever be different? So long as we have living kin, perhaps he'll never be safe."

"It will have to end," Netta told her. "Lionell cannot continue to threaten. My father will make sure of that."

"But what of some other soul with foolish fears, like that old woman?"

Netta sighed. "Perhaps Mr. Toddin was right that Tahn belongs in Onath. And you too. No one fears the baron there."

"We shouldn't have to run," Tiarra maintained. "Or hide."

"I agree. But you needn't see it as such. We're just going home."

Tahn rolled slightly, and Netta gently brushed a strand of hair from his face. But she did not expect his sudden reaction. He cried out and knocked her hand away. With his other hand he swung out wildly, striking Tiarra on the shoulder.

"Get back," Lucas warned, rushing to the bedside. Tiarra obeyed him with frightened eyes, but Netta didn't move.

"He'll not hurt me."

"He doesn't know it's you." Lucas reached quickly to take hold of Tahn's arms before he could swing out again. "Tahn! It's friends."

"Peace," Netta whispered, remembering the time in the cave depths when Tahn sprang at her after she'd tried waking him from a horrible dream. Surely those days were past.

"Wake up to us," Lucas was pleading. "Tahn, open your eyes."

Carefully, Netta reached her hand out again. "We love you," she whispered with a tender touch of his hair. Tahn shook but he didn't struggle. "It's all right," she said. "You're safe."

Slowly his eyes opened.

"Are you all right, brother?" Lucas asked. "Can we get you water?"

Tahn lay very still, looking up at him. He closed his eyes for just a moment but then managed a weak nod.

Lorne was quick to bring a ladle of water, and Netta held Tahn's head and helped him drink. Lucas loosed his hold with a sigh of relief and sat down beside them. "Thank God, Tahn. Thank God you're alive."

"Lucas . . ."

"Yes, brother?"

"What . . . have I done?"

"What do you mean?"

"You held me. Did I hurt you?"

"No." Lucas shook his head. "No, Tahn. I'm so sorry. I was just being cautious, for the women you love."

He turned his eyes for a moment to Netta, and then to Tiarra standing behind Lucas. "You're all . . . all right?"

"Yes," Netta answered immediately. "And so glad you're alive."

Tahn looked around them, his dark eyes taking in what he could of the room. "Where is the old woman?"

"In a locked room in the church," Lorne answered. "We know what she did to you. It was poison. Thank God you knew. Before she managed to get it all inside you."

"Why?" Tahn asked them, struggling for a breath. "Did she say why?" He moved his arms toward his stomach. Netta tensed, knowing he was in pain.

"She was afraid you'd take vengeance," she said softly. "On all of Alastair."

"Did no one notice," Tahn gasped, "that I came in peace?"

Netta knew that the injustice was like a weight on him. *God! Is there no good here? It breaks his heart!*

"This town wears a shroud of fear," Lucas answered. "It seems they can't judge anything aright."

"God help them," Tahn said slowly, closing his eyes.

And Netta was immediately concerned that he might be sinking from them again. "Tahn?"

"I want to go home," he said with quiet voice. "But not . . . without my sister."

"We'll go," Netta promised. "As soon as we can."

She helped him sip the water again, and then he lay on his side with his eyes closed. He was pale and warm to the touch. That worried Netta, but she prayed that the worst was past. She leaned and kissed his forehead. "Rest now. God give you peace."

Lorne left the cottage to tell Benn Trilett that Tahn had waked.

"Will he be all right now?" Tiarra asked timidly.

"I believe it," Netta told her.

"God has touched him," Lucas added. He went to the fireplace, added a chunk of wood, and moved the pot of broth closer. "He'll be gaining strength soon enough."

Netta could see the uncertainty in Tiarra. How hard this must be for her, to be here with strangers, not knowing what tomorrow might hold. "He'll be all right," she assured her again. "But you heard that he's concerned for you. You will come with us to Onath, won't you?"

"I'm not sure what else I could do," she said solemnly. "I don't think I belong here. I could cook for you. Or clean, or whatever you want."

Netta smiled. "I think I want a sister." Her eyes turned suddenly to Lucas beside the fire. His dangling gold cross twinkled with the fire's reflection. "What about *you*, sir?" she asked. "Tahn has so often been concerned for you too. He would have liked you to stay at Onath before. I'm sure he'll feel the same way again."

Lucas glanced over at her. "Somehow that's not much of a surprise."

"Please, will you consider coming with us? I know he will ask you."

Lucas turned his eyes back to the fire. "If he asks, I'll consider. But I can't promise. I am needed here."

"And surrounded by enemies," Netta prompted.

"They are Tahn's enemies more than mine."

"But you're his friend. And they surely know it by now."

Lucas threw the last few sticks on the fire and moved the pot closer. "We need more firewood. Let me check outside." He glanced at Tahn and moved quickly to the door.

Netta watched him go, wondering what sort of thoughts were churning in him. She knew that his had not been an easy life. Tiarra seemed to understand that as well.

"Even my hard world seems light compared to theirs," the young woman said softly.

Netta nodded. "Lorne was the same. And Marcus and Vari back home. They were all captive boys. May God heal their hearts. It makes me want to pray for the bandits all the more."

"But *they're* not the same!" Tiarra protested. "They are wicked and hurtful!"

"Because of their dreadful choices. Perhaps by the grace of God, they could yet choose more wisely."

Tiarra stared at her. "You taught my brother mercy."

But Netta shook her head. "I think sometimes that he taught me."

When Tahn woke again, Benn Trilett was sitting beside him. The room was hazy and gray. Tahn hoped that meant it was night and his eyes played no tricks on him.

"Well, son," Benn said. "You slept a long time."

"I'm sorry . . . to beg for help here."

"I'm glad to give it. I wish now I would have sent far more men to begin with."

"Thank you for them."

"Are you feeling better?"

Tahn did not try to answer. "You and Netta . . . you should not have come."

"I knew you would feel that way. So did she. But I suppose we were drawn, as you were, to learn the things we learned here."

"I am hated, lord."

"You were persecuted for what you can't help."

Tahn was quiet, taking in those words. It was true, he knew it now. He bore no guilt against his mother, against this town. There was nothing he'd done wrong, nothing he could have changed. He took a deep breath, trying to ignore his soreness and especially the pain in his gut. Strange gray spots floated in the air between him and the Trilett lord. Whatever was the old woman's poison, it did its job. He was cold, and one of his hands was shaking.

"Tahn, it troubles me the things you've gone through here. I spoke to the priest about it. I want the people of this town to know that there will be no more. Father Bray will gather whoever will come and tell them the truth of what took place. And I am considering what to do with the old woman. I'll have no more of it. She tried to kill you, and I can't just turn my head."

Tahn's heart suddenly raced. He knew that her poison hadn't left him, that it was still working what it would work. The pain was so deep he could not have described it. But there was something wrong in Benn Trilett's words, and he had to make him see. "My, lord—"

Netta's father put a hand carefully on his shoulder. "Are you all right?"

Tahn nodded stiffly. "Sir, what would you do? With the woman . . ."

"I'll tell you honestly that I consider hanging her, Tahn, though you live. We cannot leave Alastair thinking they may do what they will to you. It's abhorrent."

"What . . . what of the man who whipped me?"

"I don't know. I've considered that."

"And the man . . . who burned . . ."

"Tahn, I don't know who he is."

"How many . . ." Tahn struggled with the words. "How many men of this town will you gather and hang? Will you . . . also hang Lionell? And his men? Is the crime of one worse than the others?"

"Tahn, what are you telling me?"

292

"They fear."

"Yes. And it's foolishness. It's evil what they've done."

"I can't . . . can't take vengeance. It's what they expect. Please, prove them wrong."

"You don't want me to do anything?" Benn Trilett asked in amazement. "You want me to let her go?"

"Please."

"Oh, son. Would God that they understood you."

Tahn could not answer. A sudden fiery pain spread across his abdomen. He closed his eyes, willing himself not to cry out.

"What do you want then? That we should just leave?"

Tahn shook his head. "I want to go home. But . . . I can't yet."

"Why, son?"

"Either I die here or I recover enough to leave with strength."

Slowly, Benn nodded. "You'll not die. But I think I understand. You want to give a different message. That you're no threat. That in God's mercy you give them peace."

Tahn nodded. "Please, lord, lay the fears to rest."

Benn sighed. "It is hard for me not to do justice for you. But I understand. And you're wise, Tahn. God has given you uncommon wisdom."

Netta approached them carefully with a steaming cup. "Can I help you, Tahn? Do you think you could drink a bit of broth?"

He shook his head.

"Water, then?" she pressed, sounding anxious. "Can you try?"

He wasn't sure he could hold it down. But he knew he needed it, and he didn't want to frighten her. "Yes. Please."

He could not hide his shaking hands as Netta held the cup for him. He was glad for her to lay him down again and to cover him with a soft blanket. "Thank you," he whispered, hoping she'd heard. But he turned his attention to her father again. There was more he needed to say. "My lord, when you let her go . . . ask her . . . ask her to come and see me."

Benn shook his head. "Tahn—you're still weak. I don't think she should be here."

"Not alone."

He thought for a moment. "All right, son. Not alone."

Tahn closed his eyes. He could hear Benn Trilett's voice speaking something else, but the words went past him. He thought of the stream at Onath. He pictured it wide as a river. And then he was floating in it. The water washed warm over him, and it was gentle as the hand of God.

He woke again when he heard the old woman's voice in the cottage. He saw the fear alive in her eyes when he looked at her. But Lorne was behind her, and she did not try to leave.

"Peace," Tahn told her first. "Tell your neighbors not to fear."

"But how can we know what tomorrow shall bring?" she asked him. "Or even why you choose to stay Benn Trilett's hand?"

He closed his eyes and held his stomach as the pain spread over him again. "Because there's no stopping what went before," he struggled to tell her. "And I want no more . . ."

The old woman's voice was suddenly slow and grave. "You haven't told them, have you? What you feel?"

Tahn shook his head.

"I had thought you must be well recovered. But I can see it, lad. I made the mixture strong."

"I know."

"Then why do you not wish me dead?"

"How could it help?" He opened his eyes to look at her. "Who could it serve? I understand. All men . . . even I . . . thought I was born to evil. Only God gives better things."

She seemed to pale in front of him.

"I forgive you," he told her. "Tell your town the same. Please."

She bowed her head. "Lad, how bad is the pain?"

He only shook his head.

"You don't know if you'll survive this, do you? And you tell me these things?"

He closed his eyes again.

"Why?" she pressed.

"God . . . is the only answer I have." He was suddenly cramping so badly it brought tears to his eyes, but he kept them tightly shut.

"Tahn?" Lorne called out fearfully.

But then the woman spoke again, and he could hear the brokenness in her voice. "I'm sorry, lad. If you mean us no evil, if you'll not lord over us what we've done, I'm sorry. God be with you."

"But he could still die?" Lorne asked bitterly.

Tahn shook his head. "Lorne, don't speak it."

"But Tahn—"

"I'll live. In God's hand. Don't worry them."

"But is there anything we can do?"

"Have confidence." He looked up into Lorne's eyes. "All right?"

Lorne nodded. But then he bowed his head. "Can I see the woman out? If you must let her go, can I send her on her way?"

"Yes. Let her go."

"Tahn, how can we help you?"

"Where is my sister?"

"With Netta. In front of the church."

"Be her friend, Lorne." That was all he could say. The awful cramping worked its way over him again, and he pleaded with God in his mind for the river he'd felt, to wash away the pain. He thought he heard the door. But he wasn't sure if Lorne had gone out or if someone else had come in.

Help me, God. I am yours.

Coolness like a breeze touched his face, he didn't know how. The pain subsided for a moment, but he was suddenly exhausted. He struggled for a deep breath. But just when he thought the pain was gone, it came back again like a sweeping wave. He kept his eyes closed, but he could hear someone moving quietly in the room. He didn't try to talk. He didn't look to see if it was Lorne still there. After a while he heard the door again, and the voices were like music. Netta and Tiarra. Lorne. Lucas now, and Benn Trilett. He knew their voices, but he didn't speak to them. He didn't open his eyes.

Netta's gentle hand touched him, and she whispered words of peace. She thought he was sleeping again, and he knew he should tell her otherwise. But he was afraid that if he opened his eyes right now, if he tried to speak, he would betray the pain that had rushed back so vigorously. Lorne had seen it, and Tahn didn't want to frighten anyone else.

He didn't know how much time passed. He was awake and then not, hurting terribly, and then some better, in cycles he didn't understand. He was given sips of water and Netta's warm broth, never sure if he could hold them down. But he did. It must have been God's grace at work.

Finally, he thought he could talk to them again. He could try, because the pain had lessened. He opened his eyes and saw Netta, her auburn hair all down on her shoulders. Morning light peeked at him through the window.

"Tahn, how are you feeling?"

"Better," he told her. "I hope I don't worry you."

"I'm glad you could sleep the night. You needed the rest. I only hope we didn't bother you, insisting that you drink."

"I love you, Netta . . . Angel."

"I love you too." She leaned close and kissed his cheek. "Your sister will be glad you've waked, but I'll not disturb her yet. She's had far too little sleep."

"How long have we been here?"

"In this cottage? Or in Alastair?"

"The cottage."

"We are just past the third night. Perhaps your fourth."

"Netta . . . has your father given his blessing?"

"Oh, Tahn. He waits to speak to you again. But he will, I know it."

"Tell him . . . tell him I would speak to him."

"Now?"

296

"If it's all right. Please."

"Yes. All right, Tahn." She kissed him again. "I'll get him. But please, rest on. Can I get you water?"

He nodded, and she brought him a dripping dipper. He took it in his hands, but she held his head. "Lorne says the sleep gives you strength."

"Yes," he told her. "He is right."

"I'm glad," she said with a peaceful smile. "I'll go on and get my father, if you wish."

"Yes, lady."

He watched her go, knowing she would be back as quickly as she could. He remembered when he had first met Lord Trilett, after being rescued from a waiting noose. Stretched out on blankets in Netta's church, with two arrow tips just cut out of him, he'd been too weak to get up. But it would be good if he could do so now.

He pushed the covers aside, willing strength into his limbs. He fought a wave of nausea and the fierce soreness to pull himself upright and move toward the bed's edge.

But suddenly Tiarra was approaching. "Can I help you?"

He smiled for her and shook his head. "Thank you for your care for me. But it is time I got myself out of this bed."

"Are you sure you're ready?"

"The sooner I am moving, the sooner we can go home." It was hard, just sliding over to sit at the side of the bed. He had wanted to stand, or at least move to a chair. But the pain was enough that he had to stop. He bent with his arms across his lap and waited for the pain to lessen again. Tiarra stayed by him, but she said nothing. He wondered what she would think of the Triletts' grand home. But he suddenly remembered he hadn't spoken of it to her. He hadn't asked her to come with them. No wonder she was so quiet.

He looked up and saw the uncertainty in her eyes. What must she think? That he would leave her? "Tiarra—forgive me—I didn't tell you I want you to come to Onath with me. They're my family. They'll be yours, if you'll have it."

297

He took her hand, trying his best to sound strong again. "I have a room in the guardhouse. It's yours if you want it . . . but Benn may ask you to stay in the big house with his family."

"Are you sure?" she asked.

"He'll likely call you daughter, the way he calls me son."

"Then why don't *you* have a room in the big house?"

He bowed his head for a moment and then met her eyes again. "I wouldn't. It didn't seem right."

"Why?"

He took a deep breath. "Have you ever killed anyone?"

She seemed surprised at the question. "No."

"Nor have you dared fall in love with Lord Trilett's child. It was hard enough to reconcile both in my own mind. I didn't think I could manage it under his roof."

She nodded. "You're a good man. And I never would have thought."

Their eyes met again, and he smiled. "I like you. You don't hide yourself." He knew it was a strange thing to say, but she smiled too.

"Are you sure you can sit up like this?" she asked him.

"I'm going to ask Benn for his daughter's hand. I don't want to be lying down for that."

She nodded. And she stayed by him until Benn Trilett came in the door. And then quietly she left them alone.

If Benn was surprised to find Tahn sitting up, he didn't say so. He only came forward quickly and sat beside him. "Are you really all right?" he asked.

"I will be," Tahn told him. "It is better."

"I'm much relieved. But you asked to see me."

"My lord." Tahn had to stop and take a breath to steady himself. "I need to ask you for Netta's hand."

"Well." Benn smiled. "I guess it wasn't just the fever talking."

"I would understand, sir, in my circumstances, if you must refuse."

Benn shook his head. "Perhaps. But Netta wouldn't. We've known all along that you were no typical suitor. Nothing of your background dissuades us."

"But she lost one husband . . . because . . . because he had enemies. I would understand if . . . if you don't want to take such a chance."

Benn sighed. "I intend to make sure that it never happens again. But you've seen to most of that yourself, the way you keep us secure."

"I love her."

"I know, son. I've known since the first I saw you, though I must admit it was a bit frightening then."

"You didn't act frightened."

"You were hurt. And you soon convinced me of your sincerity."

Tahn closed his eyes for a moment, willing himself past the weariness and pain that made him want to lie down again. He felt so strange right now. Like he'd been emptied.

"You have my blessing," Benn told him. "I would be pleased to give you my daughter in marriage."

"Thank you." Tears filled Tahn's eyes. He didn't open them, lest Netta's father see their wetness. "May I ask you something else?"

"Of course."

"I asked my sister to come to Onath. I was sure you would approve."

"Yes, of course I do. I don't see another option. We certainly can't leave her here."

"But she has friends, lord—among the street children. I couldn't tell her anything until I talked to you, but I . . . I feel it wrong to leave them destitute."

"Lorne was talking to me about that. We mentioned it to your friend Lucas and the priest. There can be a way made for them. They are willing to help."

Tahn looked up at Netta's father, thinking about his next words. Benn Trilett could be very generous, but was he asking too much of him? "I thought we could bring those closest to her with us. I thought I would offer them, and her, my room. But even for that I would need your permission."

Benn didn't answer right away. He was quiet a moment, thinking. And when he finally spoke, the words were not what Tahn had expected to hear. "Son, do you feel you have nothing your own?"

"I know I have nothing. It's been hard—to accept so much from you. But I'm grateful."

Benn was frowning. "It wasn't meant to be so."

"What do you mean?" Tahn asked, his head suddenly throbbing.

"Do you understand what you are to the Trents?"

His stomach tightened at this change of subject. "Surely a vexation."

"Tahn, I know that you want no vengeance. I think I know what you would tell me of this as well. But you are the rightful heir to everything Trent. According to one of the baron's own men, Naysius had been disinherited. Your mother was the heir as surely as Netta is mine."

Tahn shook his head. "There is yet Lionell."

"But he has no blood link. He holds what your grandfather intended to be yours."

"I know no grandfather."

"I know. But nonetheless, Tahn, he made a choice for your mother and her seed after her. Lionell bears a title he has no right to, if the thing were known. What he has is yours."

Tahn shook his head again in incredulity at such words. "The Benn Trilett I know speaks peace. Not war against Lionell Trent."

"Tahn, you know I don't favor war of any kind. But I would help you for the justice of it, if you wanted. Lionell may not be the murderer his father was, but he showed his intentions here against you, and as far as I am concerned, that is almost the same."

Tahn felt his head swimming. It had been strange enough to learn that he was Trent kin by some means. But the heir? It could only create more conflict. "Please, lord. I want no part of it."

"I expected you to tell me that. I understand. But still it saddens me, what might have been. If Naysius Trent had not killed your mother's father and taken the baronship when he did, you might have been born in the Trent house. You would have owned everything. And you might have turned their deeds for good, with your father at your side."

Tahn didn't know how to accept Benn speaking such things. They were foreign thoughts, and he couldn't get his mind around them. "My lord, I would not have you quarrel over anything Trent, no matter what might have been. God has brought us to this day. And I want no more than what he gives."

Benn smiled. "I should write down your words and send them to Lionell, that he might know his cousin is more honorable than he."

Tahn shook his head.

"Forgive me if such talk troubles you," Benn told him. "But I had to be sure of your feelings."

"I'm sorry I have nothing to offer your daughter."

"That's not why I spoke of it, son," Benn assured him. "My thoughts were of justice for you. But I'm willing to leave it in God's hands. You are right that we should."

Tahn wasn't sure what he should say, so he said nothing.

"I'll not object if you and your sister bring some of the street children to Onath. But you have more to give than your room. I will build you a house if you wish. Perhaps two. I had planned one as a gift for you and Netta anyway. All I have is yours, Tahn. You know I claim you to my family."

Tahn never knew how to respond to such words from Netta's father. Benn loved him. It wasn't hard to see, even though it was still difficult to understand. "Thank you."

He shifted a little. It was getting harder to sit without anything to lean on. His back ached, his stomach and head hurt. One of his arms shook just a little, but he stilled it against his knee.

"Are you sure you should be up for so long?" Benn asked.

Tahn took a deep breath. "I want to walk to the church

. . . in the daylight . . . and lay this town and all it's been to me on the altar. And then walk out again and let them see me leave them in peace."

"That can wait. You look like you could use a rest. Are you hungry?"

"No."

"Let me help you lie back down."

He wanted to protest. He wanted to get up and do the things he'd said. But he knew the weakness he felt would not allow it. Instead, he reached for the blanket that had been over him and scrunched it against the wall at the head of the bed to lean on. It was hard to maneuver himself just that much, but he felt some better with the wall to hold him up.

"You're sure you don't want to lie back down?" Benn asked.

"I'm sure," Tahn answered, but the words came out stiffly.

"I should call Netta and the others back in to you."

Tahn nodded.

"We have double cause for celebration. That you recover. And that there shall be a wedding."

"God is good," Tahn agreed. "He's given me more than I ever dreamed. Even a sister."

"I look forward to a dinner in your honor," Benn said. "When we are home again, and you are stronger."

Tahn said nothing. He hated the idea of gathering a crowd. Even the wedding ceremony, he knew, would be fiercely difficult for him. But Netta was worth that and much more. Being with her would mean accepting Benn Trilett's ways as his own, at least for such occasions. Because God was in it. God had turned all things for good.

"Let a celebration be for my sister," he suggested. "To welcome her."

"A very good idea, Tahn. Very good."

And Tahn closed his eyes, wondering if Tiarra would welcome such a thought. Perhaps a crowd would not bother her as much as it did him. Surely a circle of faces meant nothing more than good company to most people.

30

Burle sat restless in the bandit camp with his shirt off and a steaming rag on his wounded shoulder.

"When do you think they'll leave?" Jonas asked him.

"How should I know? It doesn't matter, so long as we are ready for the moment."

"Do you really think it wise?" the young man persisted. "We had to back away from Tahn when he first came to Alastair—"

"We didn't *have* to! We chose to because we had no reason to trouble him then!"

"Must we now? Can't we just let it go? He'll have the Trilett men—"

"Coward! It is worth gold to us if we fight! And we don't ride to them in the open. We have the perfect place for an ambush. Anyway, we need only stay long enough to strike the Dorn down. Then we may flee to the winds for all the baron cares. The money will still be ours. And victory over Tahn, which shall be sweet after what he has caused us."

"I don't know about this," the young man said.

"You don't know anything. But you don't need to. Just do what you're told."

"Do you think he's in the church?"

"Saud searched the church. But why should I care where he is? He will leave by the road like everyone else."

Jonas hung his head. "The church at Onath took him in."

"Shut up! I know all about that!"

303

"But what if it's true that he's charmed? What if God's with him like Lucas told us once?"

"Have you taken leave of your senses, man? He was whipped again! He's cursed. God strikes him down everywhere he goes! And you're a fool."

Jonas did not answer him. He stood for a moment and then turned quietly away. His horse stood with others beneath a tall evergreen.

"Where are you going?" Burle demanded.

"I need a drink. And we run low of the liquor in camp. I'll go to the tavern."

"Take two with you and watch for signs of the Dorn," Burle ordered. "And bring me back a bottle."

Jonas nodded. Toma and Dann rose to go with him, but he didn't speak to them. He only mounted his horse in silence and rode for Alastair with them behind him.

"The fool," Burle muttered to the nearest man. "Quaking in his boots over a pathetic creature like Tahn, a bug God could crush under his boot. Look at all that's happened to him! If God takes any notice of this world, it's plain he doesn't care for the Dorn."

Jonas rode slowly to the city, ignoring the men at his sides. He was itching for a stout draught, but his thoughts wouldn't leave him alone. The church at Onath had taken Tahn in. The priest in Alastair had somehow sent the soldiers against them. Had he lied on purpose? Or had God himself worked on Tahn's behalf?

He knew most of the men would laugh at him and call him a coward, as Burle had done. But there was a weight pressed on his gut over this. He'd watched in Onath as Tahn was dragged from the cage-wagon to be hanged. But church bells—church bells!—had interrupted the baron's plan. And everyone knew how insane Tahn used to be, hauntingly strange, and especially fearsome at night. But now he spoke of an honorable path, and not dying unmourned. Some of the men had even heard him praying after the arrows had gotten him. Could he be favored of God? Is that how he'd managed to live this long?

"It would be nice if the Dorn's sister were giving drinks again," Toma was saying. "She's a pretty one. I'd still like to get my hands about her."

Jonas looked at him in disgust. "Do you think of nothing but girls? Every time we stop a wagon, you have to search to see if there are any girls."

"And why not? Why shouldn't I enjoy life? Answer me that."

"Wouldn't you rather find a miss someday willing to enjoy you enough to be your bride? Then settle down maybe, and be a normal man for a change?"

Toma shook his head. "I think one woman would bore me."

"What about you?" Dann asked him. "Do you want to be a peasant and leave us behind?"

Jonas looked to the houses and shops they were approaching. "I'd like to know what it's like. I'm tired of being a thief and a cutthroat." He shook his head. "I'd like children someday. And perhaps to learn something useful. Like coppersmithing. It looks so hard."

Toma laughed. "You're quite the bandit, Jonas! Why don't you just go now and ask the coppersmith if he needs an apprentice? And while you're there, find out for me if he has any daughters!"

"Shut up," Jonas answered angrily.

"Well, why not?" Toma continued. "Do you think we would miss you?"

"No." Jonas shook his head. "I would not be fool enough to believe that."

"Well," Dann told him, "maybe you're right that we'll all want another life someday. When we're older. But Toma is right too. Why not enjoy a little when we can? While we're young enough, that's the time to do just what we're doing, don't you think? I wouldn't want to be tied to the same old chores every day."

Jonas said no more. There was no use to it. They passed

by a couple of shops and then tethered their horses at the wooden rail outside the tavern. It didn't take long for Jonas to quench his need for a couple of stiff drinks, and then he was ready to leave. "Take Burle a bottle when you go," he told his companions, plunking several coins down on the table.

"Where are you headed?" Dann asked.

"To talk to the coppersmith."

"Are you serious?" Toma questioned with a snort.

"Yes. Go on without me."

Toma laughed, but Dann said nothing at all as Jonas went outside alone.

He did indeed go to the coppersmith, but only so the man could say he'd been there if anyone asked. But the coppersmith needed no apprentice and Jonas turned quickly away toward Alastair's church. It shouldn't be hard to find the priest. Or perhaps Benn Trilett's men. He'd had enough of being party to Samis's madness first, and now Burle's. Charmed or not, Tahn deserved to be left alone. And for that to happen, Tahn's friends would need a warning.

***

Netta and Tiarra sat with Tahn and told him all the things that Emil Korin had said. It was sad and yet heartening to know that he'd been right about his father. Sanlin Dorn was murdered, as surely as their mother was, by the baron's obsession.

"Do you think you could eat?" Netta asked him gently.

"Not yet."

"But how long since you had something solid?"

"It must have been sometime before the whipping, days ago," Tiarra answered for him.

"Tahn, don't you think you should try? Or at least a bit more broth?"

He didn't. And he was just thinking how to tell her so when Lorne came in from outside.

"There's quite a stir in the streets. The healer woman has been telling her neighbors what happened here."

Tahn nodded. "Good. Perhaps there'll be no stones thrown as I leave them."

Netta put her arm around his shoulders. "Have you always expected such things?"

"Of Alastair, yes. Or any crowd, most times."

"But now those days are done." She gave him a careful hug and then rose to get him broth again.

"Help me, Lorne," he said then. "It's time I got up."

"Tahn," Netta protested, "we needn't hurry things. You should gain your strength back."

"I'll not gain any if I keep lying about." He smiled kindly in her direction. "Forgive me, my lady. I can't let you be too good to me, at least not here."

"You're sure about this?" Lorne questioned.

"Yes. Help me up."

It was a struggle. Tahn felt as though his stamina had been poured out on the rocks somewhere, and he couldn't gather it back in. He had to lean on Lorne, especially at first, just to gain his feet.

"Outside," Tahn said, trying to shake off the weakness.

"Let me help too," Tiarra said quickly, moving to his other side.

Netta stood and stared at them. "Tahn, you expect too much of yourself. But God bless you." She went with them to the door, and they moved slowly, with Lorne and Tiarra supporting Tahn at every step. But at the doorway, he stopped to catch his breath and told them he wanted to walk of his own power outside.

"Stay with me," he said. "But I need to walk on my own."

"The healer has a cane," Netta suggested. "It's there in the corner where that cloak is hanging."

"All right," Tahn told her. "I used a staff already in this town. I can use a cane."

"Where are you going?" Tiarra asked.

"The church."

"Why?"

"I'm going to the altar," he said. "I'm leaving every burden there. No more concerns for this place. Or any place. I'm in God's hands."

Tiarra stared at him, confused. "You must go to the church for that?"

Tahn shook his head. "I want to."

"And then what?" Netta asked him as she placed the long wooden cane in his hand. "You'll have to rest."

"I'll sit. I'll rest. And then perhaps we can go home."

Watching him was not easy for Netta. It was too much like before, when the arrow wounds and horrible bruises had made him have to fight just to get up again. She stood outside the cottage as Tahn took his determined steps with Lorne and Tiarra keeping pace. Lucas ran to meet them. But Netta couldn't seem to move. Almost she couldn't see him through the tears. He'd fought all his life just to live, to recover, and then to have to fight again. How many times had he made himself get back up when it would have been easier just to give up trying?

She shook. She tried to pray. But she could not take her eyes off him, though her vision was blurred.

"You're all right, lady?" It was Tobas suddenly beside her.

She nodded, unable to keep the tears from cascading down her cheeks.

"He's showing you he'll be all right," Tobas told her. "If he can get up, then he can go on from here."

"Oh, Tobas, do you know he's felt unworthy of me? Do you realize that? But he's wrong! I'm the one not worthy of him!"

"Lady Netta—"

"Don't you think? Look at him. All the struggles. All the trials. But he's strong. Even when he's weak, he's strong!"

"He would tell you it's God's strength. Before he had God, he was a desperate man. You know that very well."

"He was sad, Tobas. Terrified. But he was still strong."

"He told me he nearly killed himself. Twice."

"I know. I saw him hopeless. And I've never wanted to rescue someone so badly in my life."

"You did, lady. He credits you for much."

She wiped at her cheeks. "I don't deserve that. He was rescuing me before I had a thought to his well-being. And rescuing the children. It was a touch of God already on him, making him hungry to do right."

"But he was still hopeless until your words touched him with God's mercy."

She was quiet for a moment. "Tobas, I think he's never had the mercy of men."

"Perhaps that is why God has given him what seems like an imponderable amount."

Netta turned to look at him.

"He shares it," Tobas continued. "In large measure."

She nodded.

"Are you going in the church with him?" he asked.

"I will. I'll join him. But Tobas, I've been thinking about what Mr. Toddin said. He's right to say that Tahn puts himself in danger to help others. But much as I might wish to, I can't stop him. Rather, I think it would be pleasing to God if I thought less of my own comforts and were willing to do the same."

"Lady, you were not meant for perils."

"Then was he? More than I? We're all born into a perilous world. If we have privilege and blessing, they must surely be for tools to help us save the perishing."

Tobas nodded. "You have eight orphans at home in Onath and former dark warriors turned to the light. I am sure that in God's eyes you are doing well."

"Not if I rest in that. Tahn grows in sharing large mercies, as you've said, and he never seems to realize how amazing that is. He makes me feel selfish and proud and weak."

"And generous, lady. Selfless. Loving. He draws it out of you as much as you draw it from him."

She smiled and dried her eyes. "We're a good match? You really think so?"

"Don't you?"

"Yes! In God's grace, yes."

"Then maybe you'd better stop talking to me and join him. They're almost to the church doors."

Tahn stopped at the stairs to lean on the stone rail. Every fiber of his being wanted to sink down on the step beneath, to let the weariness and the soreness win. But he'd seen someone across the churchyard. A woman and a boy watching. And then a man passing near the church also stopped to look. And he couldn't sink down, he couldn't, in front of their eyes. He had to make it inside. They had to see him strong, that they would know it was God and not weakness that made his heart harmless to them.

He pushed himself from the rail and stood as straight as he could.

"Tahn, are you sure you're ready for the stairs?" Lorne asked. "There's no harm in resting a minute."

He shook his head.

"Let us help you," Lucas told him.

But Tahn pulled himself up one step and then another, holding only the stone rail and the slender cane in his hand to steady himself. The gray spots returned, and his legs felt like butter, but he pressed on.

Lord, he prayed in his mind, *I would expect to be sore. That is a small thing. But you can take the weakness of the fever and the poison, Father. Give me strength.*

Netta joined him as he reached the top of the stairs. She said nothing, but he could see in her eyes that she knew his struggle.

"Pray with me," he told her. "At the altar, my lady. It is a good way . . . to begin a life together."

"Yes," she said. And there on the top step, in front of every onlooker, she kissed him full and warm. And then she slipped her arm around him, and he felt her gesture lending strength to him.

The priest stepped out. He bowed to them and held the door. And then it was like a dream stepping into the church with Netta beside him. Light shimmering through stained glass windows filled the sanctuary with otherworldly brightness. Lorne and Tiarra stopped near the back, but Lucas stayed beside Tahn until he reached the altar, and then he left him and Netta alone.

Tahn prayed long, in his heart, because he couldn't voice all the things he was feeling out loud. Netta held his hand. She prayed too, quietly, for his healing and for peace. And then he took her in his arms. Only later did he think to wonder if he should have asked first, if such a thing were really proper in the house of God.

But the priest bore no complaint. He came toward them and knelt with them when they were finished. "Thank you," he said quietly. "For favoring this house with your presence. It is a gracious gesture."

Tahn wasn't sure what he meant by that. They were strange words, and he didn't address them.

"Tell me what you want the people of this town to know," the priest said. "Already, some are heart-pricked over what they have found in themselves. But others still believe that you are a villain, or a chief of bandits."

"If I ever come back here," Tahn said slowly, "it will be with the same peace I take with me. The weight of their hearts is before God alone. I will not hold anything against them."

"God favor you for the gift," the priest answered solemnly. "And may God's mercy touch our hearts."

Tahn nodded. He wanted to get up strong, to be done with the weakness and walk away almost as though nothing had happened. But he stumbled as he tried to rise, and Netta and the priest caught him and helped him to sit.

"It is too much too soon," Netta told him softly. "Rest a little longer."

She put her arms around him, and they stayed a long while beside the altar before Tahn was ready to go on. Lucas brought water, and the cool draught seemed to bring strength to him. "I'm blessed with friends," he said. "You're all very good to me."

He truly felt better on the way outside. Steadier. Without the pain of the poison or the swirling weakness. The remaining soreness was something he understood and could deal with well enough.

But still he tired easily. He could see Benn Trilett's soldiers camped about the little cottage beyond the churchyard. He was halfway there when he stopped to lean for just a moment against an iron fence and noticed for the first time the graveyard nearby.

"This is where you buried Martica?"

"Yes, son." It was the priest's voice, though Tahn had not realized the priest had followed them outside.

"Where is my mother buried? Do you know?"

"Yes. She is here. Do you want to see it?"

The unexpected opportunity almost made him tremble. "Yes. I would. Please."

Netta squeezed his hand, but he looked behind her to where Tiarra and Lorne were standing. "Sister, have you been to our mother's grave?"

"When I was much smaller," she said in a voice like a child's. "Martica brought me. But I was never at ease here to come back as I should have."

Tahn let go of the cane he held and reached his free hand to her. With Netta on one side and Tiarra on the other, he followed the priest through an iron gate and into the rows of stone. Vaguely he was aware of others watching him again. Trilett soldiers and more people besides, in the churchyard or nearby. But it didn't matter. He was about to visit some piece of his mother's memory, and he could think of little more than that.

Her stone stood by itself, smooth cut and weathered white. It bore her name, the year of her death, and the single word *murdered*, as though it had been chosen to do nothing but remind the town of their shame. Tahn was tense just looking at it. And there was something very much missing.

"What about my father? Do you know?"

The priest bowed his head for a moment. "Yes. I have looked into such things. There is a section, down the hill—we can't see it well from here—where the homeless and the . . . the criminals were buried."

Tahn took a deep breath. "Take me there."

Tiarra's hand tightened in his. He knew the tears in her eyes. But she didn't speak. And he knew that she'd never gone there. That Martica would never have dreamed to take her.

It was not an easy walk, down the hill to the far corner of the cemetery where a dead tree had crashed upon the stones and the weeds rose high.

"Here," the priest finally said. "I think it is this one."

Almost hidden by a thorny briar, there was a grave marked only by a small uncarved stone. A simple rock that anyone might have passed over in a field and never realized it could bear any significance. He was nothing, that's what this meant. To Alastair, Sanlin Dorn was nothing.

Tahn felt the tears well up and then break upon him like a sudden storm. He couldn't stop. He held tight to Netta and Tiarra as the tears shook him. *It's not right. It's just not right.*

"Tahn," Netta said softly, but he couldn't answer her.

Tiarra fell to her knees. She reached out her hand toward the little ugly rock that was choked by weeds but couldn't bring herself to touch it.

Netta put her arm around Tahn, lending her support. He saw a reflection of his own pain in her eyes. "They should be together," he told her when he had recovered himself enough to speak.

The priest turned and gave them a solemn nod. "They can be moved, if you wish it."

For a moment Tahn couldn't answer. Was it right, to disturb the remains? Karra Loble should not lie here in this forsaken spot. But would there be a place that seemed proper for Sanlin Dorn, in this town that had so long disdained him? "Netta," he ventured the painful words, "do you think your father would let me take them to Onath?"

Her answer, so unhesitating, was almost like a balm. "I am sure he would. Oh, Tahn, I know it. They would rest together. And nearer you."

313

He nodded to her. But it was Tiarra whom he leaned toward and took into his arms.

"I hated him," Tiarra cried. "Even more than I hated you."

"You only hated the lie," he tried to tell her. "You never had a chance to know the truth."

"Oh, God," she said, weeping. "What must they have felt, in their last moments?"

"I pray God that they called on him," Tahn said gently. "I pray that we see them one day."

"M-mother . . . Mother was godly," Tiarra said. "Martica told me."

"And our father loved her." He turned his eyes toward Netta. "She loved him. She would not have failed to tell him of God's grace."

Netta nodded, and the gesture heartened Tahn enough to smile up at her. "We will move them. But we have reason to hope that they are holding hands in heaven."

<hr>

It was a long while before Tiarra could rise to her feet and leave her father's grave behind her. Tahn wiped at her tears and then held her hand as they walked back up the hill toward the other graves and the churchyard. He was surprised to see so many people standing as though they waited for him.

"Have you yet addressed the town?" he asked the priest, not knowing what to expect.

"Not a large group. But I have told the truth to all I could. Some resist it. But I think most have known in their hearts already. No one who heard has ever been able to forget your screams, son."

Tahn stood stark still and looked over the faces. No one laughed, or shouted, or glared at him with snarling accusation. He should go toward them. He should say "peace be with you" and then join Benn Trilett's men where he belonged. But he couldn't get his legs to move.

The priest must have realized his discomfort. "Do you want me to send them away?"

314

"Why are they here?" Tiarra asked. "Are we such gazing-stocks?"

No one answered her. And Tahn did not answer the priest. Slowly, he coaxed his legs to obey him. He let go of Netta's hand and Tiarra's and stepped forward, just a few steps at first, but he willed himself to keep on. He knew Netta followed, and his sister and the priest. And Lucas and Lorne stood nearby. Trilett guards watched the scene, and yet he felt alone.

He neared the faces one difficult step at a time. No one moved. They all seemed like statues except one little boy with wavy black hair and a dirty, smudgy face. That child peeked at him between iron fence rails, first beside one rail and then another. He stretched up as high as his little legs could take him and then scrunched down again and looked at him sideways. Tahn turned his eyes from the other faces and watched that boy. So alive and full of his own world. He couldn't have been more than five years old.

As Tahn reached the fence, the boy bounced on one leg and stared at him. A nervous mother tried to pull the child away, but he would not be pulled. Instead he leaned into the fence rails, squeezing himself almost between them, and reached his hand in Tahn's direction. A strange murmur rose as Tahn lowered himself to a squat and put out his hand to touch the child's.

"What is your name, boy?" Tahn asked as the child's mother leaned down and tried again to pull him away. Tahn lifted his eyes to meet hers, and she stopped.

"Lucas," the little boy answered.

"I have a very dear friend by that name."

"But I never see'd you before," the boy replied.

"There must always be a first time," Tahn told him, "for friends to meet."

"Do you live here?"

"I used to. For a short time."

"What's your name?" the boy asked him.

"Tahn Dorn."

"That's a funny name."

315

"Well. It seems to fit me." He stood and turned his eyes for a moment to the other faces.

An old man started toward him. There was something familiar about him that Tahn could not place. There was no malice in his eyes, but Tahn turned away toward the Trilett men.

"Wait, sir," the old man called.

Tahn closed his eyes for a moment and stood very still. When he opened them, Lucas and Lorne had both come nearer. And the priest was beside the fence rail. Tahn turned himself again to look upon that old man and all the rest of the faces. He didn't know what he could say. He didn't know what they wanted. "Peace be with you," he managed to speak, and to his surprise the words were echoed by at least two voices in the crowd.

"Anain told us what she did," the old man said. "And that Benn Trilett would have hanged her but you wouldn't let him. Tell us why, boy! Let us hear it from your own lips."

He bowed his head. "Is it so hard for you to think of forgiveness? That I might simply want the pain to end?"

He turned away, feeling overcome. He reached toward Netta, and she hurried to his arms.

"I have something that's yours," the old man said. "I should have given it to your sister long ago. But my wife feared people would call me a thief, or even say I killed your mother for it. I think she knew all along that it wasn't Sanlin Dorn." He reached into a large pocket and drew out a necklace of pearls, shimmering white.

Like teeth all in a line, Tahn thought. This was one of the necklaces his mother had given him just before he hid beneath the dusty old rug. His dreams had been real. And this was the rug maker.

"I didn't know who you were at first," the man said. "I didn't find this till after you'd gone."

"There was another," Tahn said softly.

"I found no other," the man said quickly, fearfully. "I would have told you if I had."

"It's all right," Tahn told him. "I might have dropped it anywhere."

"Please take it," the old man said, holding out the necklace.

Tahn let it rest in his hands. "Why didn't you sell it?"

"I was afraid. Of being blamed. Not everyone believed what we were told. But it troubled me, when I heard what happened. You'd just been at my shop . . ."

Tahn nodded. "Thank you. For returning this."

But the old man wasn't finished. "I didn't know about the Ovnys' necklace. I didn't know what they did to you until afterward. I might have saved all that trouble if I returned this to your sister sooner."

"Never mind that," Tahn told him. "It's done." He thought of his mother's gentle hands, her urgent voice as she gave these pearls into his care. They were to pay for passage somewhere, for some new life they were never to know.

One of the Trilett men approached Lorne hurriedly. "Do you know a man named Jonas?"

"He rode with the bandits against us," Lorne answered. "Is he in town?"

"He's come with a warning. I left him waiting with our men. He asks to talk to you."

"Not more trouble," Netta sighed and held to Tahn's hand tightly as Lorne went with the man.

"Until we're away from here, my lady," Tahn told her, "I would have to expect it from them."

A tall young man spoke out from the crowd. "If you have peace for us, I will help you go in peace."

Tahn turned his head. "Who are you?"

"Tine Wyatt. My father hanged your father."

Tahn knew there was challenge in his words. The deed had been done by a crowd, and at the baron's bidding. But this young man offered no excuses, no explanations. He wanted a reaction, plain and simple. "What manner of help?"

"You don't seek justice?"

"The baron who set all in motion is dead. And judgment belongs to God."

"My father is also dead."

Tahn almost turned away. "I am sorry for your loss."

"Mother sent me to find out," the young man told him. "She wanted to know which of the things we hear of you are true."

"Tell her I want peace."

The young man nodded. "Sir, if that is so, my friends and I, and any we gather, could ride with your men. We will see you safely away from our countryside. It would be just a small token."

"Go and tell the Trilett soldiers," Tahn told him. "We would appreciate a token of peace."

Tahn did not return to the little cottage. He would let the women and the babe have it back. Instead, he laid himself down on a bedroll among the Trilett guards he'd come to know. He would rest just a while, as Benn and his men decided their best course. Then they would all rise to return to Onath. Lucas came and sat beside him.

"Do you need to sleep, brother?"

"No. I don't want sleep."

"Jonas brought word of a plot between Burle and the baron's captain. They lie in wait for us on the road to the south."

"Did he say why he tells us this?"

Lucas shrugged. "He is tired of being a bandit. Of attacking people. Especially you."

"Well," Tahn answered quickly, "may such thoughts infect the rest of them."

"Indeed," Lucas agreed. "Your world changes. And not for the worse."

Tahn looked long at him. "Friend, are you coming with us?"

Lucas shook his head. "You don't think I'm needed here?"

"I don't think you're safe here. Despite the turn of some hearts. Burle is too near, and he hates you."

"Burle has always hated me," Lucas admitted. "And I have always survived."

"But what holds you here?"

"The church. The people who understand so little of God's heart. The street children, Tahn. You can't take them all with you."

He sighed. "Then almost I would stay."

Lucas looked stricken. "Why?"

"Because you were my first friend."

Benn watched Tahn and his friend talking as he considered the options before them. They could ride into a fight and expect that their numbers would serve them well. Or they could go another way, swiftly, before the bandits had time to put themselves in the path. But there might be some watching every way out of Alastair. There was no surety they wouldn't encounter bandits in any direction.

But if it were only bandits, there wouldn't have been the worry. What bothered Benn was that the baron's soldiers swelled the ranks and added to their resolve. There could even be archers among them, which he had no way to safely combat.

He could send Lionell another message. He could even stay right here until Alastair was full of noble guests for Lionell's wedding. Tahn was anxious to go home. They all were. But any message out was a risk to the messenger, and any attempt to leave was sure to meet with conflict and blood, regardless of the outcome. He didn't want anyone else injured. Peace practically bid them to stay, hard as that seemed. There would not be such worries with the other nobles present. He had but to mention his concern and they would ride out together in a circle of noble parties. Lionell would not dare to interfere.

He had no easy task telling his daughter such plans. Netta seemed more anxious than the rest of them to get Tahn out of Alastair. He explained things the best he could, but she was not happy. And he expected that Tahn would not be either.

But Tahn took the news better than Benn expected. And that very night, they had evidence of the city's change of heart toward Tahn, when a group of women came bringing food "for the Dorn children."

Benn began to wonder why Tiarra had been called Loble after her mother, instead of Dorn. No one seemed to question that she was Sanlin's child. Perhaps they'd never married. Perhaps Karra Loble had never used the name Dorn. So why wasn't Tahn called Loble too?

Eventually he asked the priest, who found no record of a marriage in Alastair. But he did find an old woman, Martica's neighbor, who said the marriage had been in Tamask and Karra had been using Sanlin's name. But Martica told the townspeople the name Loble for her headstone, and after that no one in Alastair would call Karra or Tiarra after the name of the man they'd presumed to be a killer. It hadn't seemed just.

"As if they'd cared for justice!" was Tiarra's immediate reaction. But she sat and cried when she learned that she should have been called Dorn.

Tiarra gave Martica's house to Lucas to use as shelter for the street children. Tahn gave him all of the money that remained in the saddlebag Tiarra had saved for him. Benn had not minded that. It was, after all, money he had given to Tahn to use as he saw fit.

But then Tahn gave his sword to the priest. Benn thought he understood why Tahn would do it. The sword was given by Samis and represented a life Tahn had never wanted. But still, Benn did not like the idea of Tahn being unarmed, so he gave him a sword of his own. He accepted the gift, but he didn't wear it.

"Not yet," he said. "Not here."

Father Bray hung Tahn's sword, hilt up like a cross, on a wall inside the church. He knew some might protest. "But let it remind us," he said, "of how great is the mercy of God."

Benn thought it an appropriate sign of the mercy God had extended—to Tahn, to pull him out of Samis's darkness, and also to this town, for its part in tragedy.

The priest hired men to carefully exhume the bodies of

Sanlin and Karra Dorn and to wrap the delicate bones for travel. Such goings-on in the graveyard attracted a group of observers curious about what was being done. Tahn was only solemn about it, but Tiarra was angered that people would watch. She even told them loudly to go home to their own affairs, and most obeyed her, but it wasn't long before more onlookers stopped to see what was taking place. It would be a strange thing, Benn thought, carrying bones with them to Onath. But he agreed that it would be right.

In the days that followed, Tahn mended well. He walked daily through the streets, though never alone, because Benn would not allow it. He still could not trust Alastair completely. Most of the people shied from Tahn, but there were always some watching, and a few ventured forward to greet him, to apologize, or to share a gift from their own tables. Alastair didn't seem such a city of horrors anymore. It was just a town. With people like any other. Benn wanted no chances taken, nonetheless.

Missing the children at Onath was what seemed to bother Tahn most about not leaving. He talked to Benn at length about their options and finally agreed that the best way to make sure nobody else got hurt was to wait.

Benn wondered what the bandits were thinking and what Lionell Trent was thinking. He formulated in his mind the things he could say to him when they met face to face. One night as Tobas entertained the group with songs around a fire, Benn thought about how Lionell might react if he dared bring Tahn with him to the wedding. Picturing his horrified face made Benn chuckle out loud, and Netta and several others turned to look at him. But he offered no explanation. How fitting it would be if Lionell should have to meet his cousin in his own church! On his wedding day, surrounded by nobles who would all expect him to live up to his promised peace.

But Benn knew Tahn wouldn't agree to such a thing. Tahn would never care if the other nobles knew of his claim. He would certainly never want their attention. Benn began to wonder about his daughter's wedding. How would Tahn manage it? How would Lionell react?

Watching Tahn now, surrounded by friends and seeming finally at ease, he believed it might be easy to forget all the struggles. Tahn was sitting with his arm around Netta and had relaxed enough to join in the singing. But Benn wondered what the future would bring. Tahn's cautions about the risk of Netta losing another husband to violence were wise. Perhaps he understood that Lionell would never be content to let the matter rest. But it wasn't Tahn alone who could be a target. In his scheming, Lionell might also try to strike at Netta before she could bear Tahn a child, or even Tiarra before she could have a family of her own. Maybe none of them would be safe so long as Lionell lived, unless he had the kind of change of heart that could only happen if he gave his will over to God.

The burden was a difficult one. There remained only Netta and Jarel with him now of the Trilett line. He could adopt all the children Tahn cared to bring him, but he didn't want to lose any more of the Trilett blood. Yet he couldn't refuse Netta's heart. He would let her marry her guardsman-warrior, even if that man had a price on his head and a thousand enemies on every side.

31

What are they doing?" Lionell lamented, pacing his bedchamber in a long robe. A bundle of garlic swung against his chest, but its fumes did nothing to cure his raging headache. "What the devil are they doing?"

"Nothing," Saud answered coolly. "At least nothing apparent. They camp. They walk about."

"Has Benn Trilett gone mad? How dare he stay here! Why would he want to?"

"You could send men to ask him, lord. It is certainly within your rights. But there is another matter immediately pressing."

"What? What are you talking about?"

"My men tell me it is noised about that I killed Karra Loble and put the blame on Dorn's father."

Lionell spun around so fast he nearly fell. "Did you?"

"Of course. But my point is that we have a traitor who must be silenced before he can cause us more trouble. I should have known better than to leave him in Alastair."

"Who are you talking about?"

"Korin, sir."

"Korin? Are you sure?"

"He was the only one who was there. And we told no one but your father how the deed was done."

Lionell's eyes narrowed. "Korin's talking? Gads, man! He knows everything!"

"I'll have to kill him."

"Yes! Yes, of course. Be quick about it! Do you know where he is?"

"We are fairly certain he stays with his relatives. After the last report, I was about to go there myself, but you called for me."

"Go! Go! Before the whole world learns the story!"

Saud bowed out quickly, and Lionell slumped breathlessly against his divan. It was probably already too late. Benn Trilett surely knew what he had in his hands. He was probably plotting the best way to use the Dorn for his own advantage. He might think it sweet revenge for the loss of his family members to destroy what he could of the House of Trent and give whatever was left to his wretched captain.

A gentle tap at the chamber door interrupted his thoughts. He tried to ignore it, but the sound persisted until the carved door swung open and a white-haired woman in flowing robes strode in.

"Mother," Lionell growled. "I am in no mood for your conversation."

"But are you feeling better, dear? I was very concerned when you barely touched your pie."

"Concerned? Mother—you're a giant's share of the problem! Why didn't you tell me about Karra Loble's son? Why did you dare stop the soldiers' mouths from telling me? I might have found some way to end this sooner!"

"Don't be foolish. Benn Trilett and the other nobles have watched you closely. Too much aggression will give them cause to destroy us! Your father's plans were grandly intentioned, but they have set us back markedly—"

"My father was an addle-brained buffoon!" Lionell shouted. "And you're like him to think that hiding things from me could possibly work for good!"

"Son—"

"Don't even talk to me! You've made me too angry."

She folded her arms. "I may have saved your life in this."

"Get out. Leave me alone."

"You can't pursue this, Lionell. We learned that already. You can't fight Benn Trilett. The other nobles have warned us."

Lionell fumbled with the belt of his robe and then threw the thing down in frustration. "If I do nothing, all we have is taken away! I can't let that happen. You're right that I can't fight him openly. But there are ways, Mother. To put the blame on bandits, or somebody else."

"Lionell, you must leave the Triletts alone. Do you hear me?"

"It's not about Triletts! Don't you see that? It's about self-preservation now. All I need is a dead cousin."

"Your father is dead. That is what this has already cost us."

"He deserved to die," Lionell spoke bitterly. "He was ignorant."

"How dare you!"

"Go away, Mother."

He turned his back and sat staring at the tapestry on the wall.

"Lionell, listen to me."

But he sat still, refusing to reply.

"Lionell!"

"You can't stop what has to be done, Mother. One day, you'll thank me. When I put a grandson on your lap with no threat to what is his, you'll look back and bless the day I wouldn't listen."

"I pray God you give me a grandson," she replied gravely. "I pray you live to see him."

Lionell stared straight ahead and didn't answer her. And after a moment he heard the click of the door behind her. She had finally left him alone.

Saud went that night to the home of Korin's family in Alastair. He couldn't knock on the door, of course. He hid himself in the shadows, hoping for some indication that Korin was still there. He waited through the night, thinking that Korin was foolish to take such chances, to stay in Alastair so near the baron's wrath. But by the morning's light, he soon saw that Korin did not intend to stay. Two young men and a girl began loading a wagon with belongings from the house. Still he watched them, waiting. Perhaps he might just follow the family when they left the town and call his men to slaughter them all.

When the wagon was nearly full, Saud found the chance he had watched for. Korin came out alone to the horses. Quietly, Saud crept forward as Korin harnessed one animal to lead to the wagon. He knew Korin hadn't seen him. He seemed at home here, casually preparing for an ordinary journey.

Saud was upon him quickly. He didn't care that it was daylight. He didn't even care if he were seen. He was confident no one would know him in a poor farmer's clothes, nor dare to lay a hand on him before he slipped away. He needed only to catch the neck of Korin's cloak and jerk him back enough for one clean slice across his throat. The horse jumped away from them, and Korin sunk to the ground.

Saud stood for a moment and stared down at the man who had been his friend for so many years, so many secrets. "If only the Dorn could be so easy," he said and then turned away to disappear down the street.

At first, all kinds of tales circled around the town about the killing. Some people said that the Dorn or Benn Trilett's men had done it, though no one knew for sure why they would. Netta was especially troubled because no one had seen it happen.

"Father, we have to go home."

"I know, child. But I can't have you in the middle of a conflict with bandits on the road."

"Are you sure they'd trouble us? An armed group?"

"I am very sure they'd try."

Netta looked around her in frustration. "They may try it here."

"That would be harder to accomplish or explain away."

"Why doesn't Lionell just come and talk to Tahn? You'd think he'd want to know if his fears have any foundation."

"You'd think. Perhaps I could persuade him. He might be here tomorrow. Mr. Korin had long and faithful service to the Trents and was close to some of the family. The priest tells me they may be well represented at the burial."

Netta's heart pounded furiously. "Father! They may have ordered the murder. Because of what he told us. You know that!"

"I have little doubt. And I told the priest my concerns for his safety now. He and Korin have done much to turn this town's blame away from Sanlin Dorn. Lionell and his captain cannot be happy about that."

"What if he brings a troop of men? What if he attacks us right here?"

Benn shook his head. "Far too many witnesses. And we're too strong for them. They know they could not stop us all."

"Then why don't we leave? We would be strong on the road too."

"Netta, I'll avoid a fight as long as I can, because people will get hurt. Maybe I would feel differently if you weren't with us, as well as Tiarra and the children she hopes to bring along. Even Tahn. I'm not sure how strong he is yet. I don't want to carry anyone home wounded, or worse."

"Oh, Father." Netta shook her head. "I hate this."

"I know. But don't worry. I would think it good for Lionell to come. It would give me opportunity to speak to him."

"I don't need to tell you how Tahn would feel about that," she said in dismay.

"Oh yes. I know. He doesn't want me anywhere near Trents or their men. But it's too late for that now that I've come to Alastair."

Netta did her best trying to help a few of the men prepare the midday meal as her father sat apart talking with Lucas, Tahn, Josef, and Tobas. But she was clumsy and distracted, and Lorne finally bade her to sit down and let them finish. They were gracious to serve her first, but she couldn't eat with her stomach pressed tight.

She was afraid. She hated to admit it, even to herself, but

327

she was feeling the same dread weight as the night Tahn had kidnapped her. She'd expected to be tormented and killed. And now she expected that her father's efforts to avoid bloodshed could all be in vain. *Don't be so faithless!* she scolded herself. *Who would have thought that Tahn had come as a rescuer then? And who can tell now what God will do?*

The thought of Lionell and his men so close stirred a cold tension inside her. Her father's men camped within sight of the graveyard, practically at the church's back door! And the baron's men could be cunning devils. Like Emil Korin's murder, things could happen so quickly.

But Netta knew her father was confident that he was doing right. She watched him talking to the four men he'd drawn aside and wished she knew what was being said. She could imagine that Josef might feel like her, willing to trust God's grace and their strength on the road. But maybe Tobas would favor a large presence at tomorrow's burial because he wasn't a man easily backed down.

She didn't really know what Lucas would think, or why her father had included him, except that he knew the church and Tahn trusted him so well. She watched Tahn bow his head and wondered what his word might be. He was cautious for them almost to extreme, and yet he would fearlessly step into the most heated of fights if need be. *Lord, give them a plan,* Netta prayed. *Guide us. Protect us.*

It wasn't long before the other men rose and left Tahn and Benn alone. Josef and Tobas took three other men and went in the direction of the markets. Lucas came to the fire and ate with Lorne but did not say a word.

Netta couldn't bear the waiting. Welcome or not, she set her food aside and rose to join her father and Tahn, who was solemnly shaking his head.

"It can't help," Tahn was saying as she sat down. "It makes no difference what I say. He'll believe as he chooses."

"He could at least look on you."

"That is like asking a wolf to care about what he devours."

"There'll be no devouring," Benn said sourly.

"You know what I mean," Tahn persisted. "It could even cause you trouble, sir. If I presume to meet him, he might think I make myself his equal."

Benn gave a frustrated sigh. "Why must you be so humble? Tahn, you *are* his equal! You're his better."

"And such words are exactly what he fears."

"Well, what would you have me to do with you, then? Hide you? Or treat you like my servant in his presence?"

"I *am* your servant, my lord."

"No. You're not." Benn rose to his feet. "Netta, he's impossible. I can't for a moment make him see that he has a right to lift his head before Lionell Trent."

She shook her head, aghast. "There's too much risk! By all that's holy, Father, why would you want him anywhere near the man?"

"Because it is just. And I will not fear Lionell. We will be at the burial tomorrow because we have a right to be. And this camp will stay right where it is, despite their arrival. I intend to put myself directly in his path."

"Father!"

"What do you think, Netta? That I can back down from him? If he comes here, he gives me no choice but to stand my ground. We've no safer option. The more I turn this around in my mind, the more I understand that if he wants a fight, I have to give him one, whether I like it or not."

He turned toward the church. "Let me speak a word to the priest a moment. Tahn, before the men leave, I'd like a word with them as well."

Tahn nodded, and Netta stood and stared after her father as he walked away. "He was just telling me he didn't want to risk us on the road," she said. "But he—he puts himself in danger right here! And you! Perhaps you could speak to him again."

Tahn answered her in a quiet voice. "If I do, my lady, I would have to tell him he is right."

"What?"

"God would not have us fear." He reached out and took

329

hold of her hand. "Would you like to go with me and see where my sister was raised?"

"Now? Today? Before this is settled?"

"I think it's already settled. Your father is going to the burial of a Trent soldier tomorrow because the soldier had the heart to be honest. Of course, men will accompany him. And I'll set the rest in their orders. We'll not fail to be watchful."

"But Tahn—"

"Lucas is going to stock Martica's house with a staple of foods and begin to feed the needy there. Tonight, I think. But we need to look about the place and furnish it more carefully. It would sleep more if we could build stacked beds. Have you seen those? Donas and Morrey built a pair once at Valhal, but most of us slept on the floor."

She could only stare at him for a moment. It was the first memory of Valhal she had ever heard that was not laced with horror. But not only that, Tahn had turned his mind so easily to this new project. What had happened to him? He had so often seemed obsessed with the details of their safety, even in the peace at Onath.

"I also want to talk with the street children." He rose to his feet and took her in his arms. "Some will want to come with us. And I think I need your help. How many can we accept? I don't want your father to be troubled for his generosity."

She reached to touch an old scar on his cheek. "I scarcely know how to answer you."

"I know. It's a hard thing. Many may choose to stay, now that they'll have a home, but I'd hate to take some and refuse others."

"No," she told him, "I meant that you don't seem troubled at all. You dismiss tomorrow from your mind."

"Right now there's no more I can do for tomorrow."

"Yes, but—"

"We might as well be useful with our time." He smiled.

She was still stunned, but she couldn't help but return his smile. "All right. God love you, I'll go."

330

Tiarra and Lorne were coming too. Netta was surprised to see that the tenderness Lorne had shown toward Tiarra when coaxing the sword from her hand was growing. The way he looked at her was unmistakable. Netta wondered if Tahn was aware.

Lucas led them eagerly, with two familiar guards following behind.

"In Onath, do your men go with you everywhere?" Tiarra asked.

"Not within the estate," Netta answered. "But without, your brother insists on it, though there's scarcely a need there."

"I don't know that I'd ever get used to it."

"You'll have to," Lorne told her. "At least so long as Lionell lives."

"But he's always ignored me."

"Because your heritage was hidden. Who's to say what he'll do now?" Lorne spoke with heaviness, and Netta understood that he was as worried as she was.

It was strange to see the house where Tiarra had grown up. It was no bigger than the healer's little cottage and in far worse repair. Crumbled bits of mud plaster with flecks of scarlet and blue were on both sides of the door. Faded eyes and faces, among other designs practiced long ago by an artist's hand, gave the place an eeriness that made Netta uncomfortable. No wonder Tahn would remember it, even if only in his dreams.

The place was worse on the inside. Cracks in the walls, sagging fireplace, dirt floor. And no furniture at all except a rickety old table.

"It's perfect," Lucas pronounced. "But we'll want a few chairs and shelves for supplies. Lots of food. Plenty of bedding."

Perfect? Netta was speechless. But Lucas had been a street orphan himself. Anything with a roof might seem good to him. She looked up and was perplexed to notice at least one visible gap in the slats and thatching. "Is it leaky?"

"Yes, ma'am," Tiarra answered her. "We used to catch

331

the rain in the pail and the pot. Then we could use the water."

Netta looked at her a moment. The pail and the pot? She turned toward the hearth and saw that there was indeed only one cooking pot in sight, next to a flat stone and a pottery jar with a bare handful of utensils. A small pail for carrying water sat to one side with what looked like a nearly empty meal sack beside it. Two bowls were on the mantle shelf beside an oil lamp, a worn basket, and a cloth. That was all. There was nothing else to see except the bare opening to another room in back.

With a glance at Tahn, Netta went to the doorway of the next room. But she could only stand and look for a moment. There was a thin woven sleeping mat on the floor. A ragged blanket or two in a heap beside it. And a folded garment in the corner with a cup and what looked like a bottle of medicine. Except for a half-spent candle, that was all.

It made her cold inside that Tiarra's childhood here was far better than Tahn's. And that the street children, even if they were crowded in with nothing added to the place, would find the house a genuine blessing. There was so much need in the world. It was horrid to think that such dwellings as this were common and not the worst to be had.

She felt like crying but didn't want their questions, so she steadied herself completely before turning around. But thoughts of her own grand home filled her mind. With its winding staircase and spacious rooms of furniture, it was not filled even after taking in eight children. And that place had only been secondary. The other estate house, even grander, had been destroyed by the flames set by Samis's men sent by the baron for destruction. The Triletts even owned a third property sitting empty in the forest south of Onath, something of a retreat cottage, but far better and larger than this.

"Well," she said solemnly, "I can think of a thousand things this place needs. We'll not have it all done in one day, but we can make a good start. First, of course, we must find someone in the marketplace with materials for repair of the roof. And the walls need to be plastered afresh in and out. Already the nights grow colder."

Tahn smiled. "I knew we'd need your help."

Strangely, his innocent comment made it all the harder for her to hold back the tears. "It's none of your faults," she told them, "that you're ill-acquainted with such details."

Netta herself had no idea how to go about the work, but she had little trouble finding someone in the marketplace who could supply materials. As a stout merchant bundled things together for them, the man's small son peeked around a table at Tahn and then suddenly reached his tiny wooden mallet to him.

"Here you go, sir," he said. "You might need this. And I've got it worn to the hand for you."

"Thank you," Tahn replied with all seriousness. "But a good worker such as yourself shouldn't be without his tools."

The little boy giggled. "It's just a toy. Didn't you know I was only playing?"

"I thought perhaps you'd built this stand, where your father displays his things. Nice work for a small lad."

Netta smiled at Tahn's response, and the boy and his father both laughed.

"Look, Papa," the boy said. "Isn't he the man who gave his sword to God? He thinks I made this place."

"I think he's playin' as much as you." The father nodded to Tahn. "Thank you for your trade with us."

Netta wasn't sure Tahn would answer. It seemed to take him a moment to find his words. "You're very welcome, sir," he finally said. Netta took his hand. They walked on a little ways, and she was glad that the looks they drew did not seem to be malicious ones. Everyone seemed to know him. Everyone watched. It was a bit unnerving. She shuddered to think what it had been like for Tahn when he first entered the town.

"Where has Tobas gone?" she asked in order to draw her thoughts elsewhere. "He could not only repair the house but

333

probably also build your stacked beds. And hang shelves. He's handy at all sorts of things."

"We'll probably find him if we pass by anyone with clothes to trade," Tahn answered her.

"Clothes?" She couldn't imagine why Tobas would be in need of any, but it wasn't long before she spotted him and the men he was with. They were indeed buying clothes, old work garments off someone's drying line. They'd also acquired a handcart full of basketry, and a mule. But no one offered any explanation.

Tobas stayed with them while the other men returned to see Netta's father. Soon they had borrowed a rope-and-pole ladder, and Tobas had Lorne with him on the roof.

They'd barely started when a dirty little face peered at them from behind a neighbor's house. Netta smiled at the child, but he only ducked his head until Tiarra called, "Jori, come here! Don't be afraid."

The little boy slowly stepped into view, followed immediately by a girl barely taller. "Come here," Tiarra told them again. "Let us tell you what we're going to do."

"That blond man who was mad at us is tearing pieces off your roof," the girl reported soberly.

Tiarra laughed. "He's not mad. And they're fixing it, Rae. For anyone who needs a place to stay."

The girl stared at her, not comprehending. "You're going to trade away your house, Miss Ti? Where will you live? With your brother?"

"I'm going to Onath with him, yes. This house belongs to Mr. Corsat now, the aide to the priest from St. Thomas's. He's going to feed people here, and give them a place to sleep. But"—she glanced at Tahn—"if you want to come with me, you can."

The girl couldn't seem to make any answer to that, but the little boy beside her turned his eyes to Tahn. "Why?"

"You're her friend, aren't you?" he asked. "I thought she'd miss you."

"More than that," Tiarra said with a shake of her head. "He's going to see that we have a place to stay at the Trilett estate. And this house will be for those who want to stay here, so you won't go hungry. Or be in the winter's cold."

The girl seemed to find her voice then. "How many is there work for at Onath? What will we do?"

Tiarra didn't answer right away. Instead, she turned her eyes to Netta, who for the first time realized the level of Tiarra's blind trust. Tiarra didn't know what to expect any more than these children did.

"Well," Netta answered quickly, "I rather favor children to learn their letters and a bit of sums. That's hard enough work. Hildy and Ham take care of most things about the house, though it'll be time to pick the apples soon, and Hildy always asks someone else to climb in the trees for her."

The children only stared. Tahn gave Netta a smile and knelt to one knee. "What she means is, they're not looking for servants. Benn Trilett has already given a home to eight orphans. He has room for more."

Still, neither child answered. Little Rae's eyes widened, and she seemed to be trembling.

"I would especially like for the two of you to join us," Tahn told them. "And the boy called Ansley, because you've been so close to my sister. I know she fed you. And no one here will be left hungry. That's why in her absence, this will still be a place to come for your needs. Will you help us? Can you go and tell the other homeless children? Any that you know."

Jori's little head pumped up and down, though he never stopped his staring. And Rae suddenly burst forward and hugged at Tiarra's waist. "Do you really want to take us with you?"

"Yes. I think it will be fun."

The little girl was in tears. "I used to pray all the time, Miss Ti. I used to pray for you to be my sister and us to move to a house so grand you could dance about and not bump into nobody or nothing."

"You should see our home," Netta told her with a smile. "I think you'll like it."

Rae wiped at her eyes a bit and then jumped to give Netta a sudden hug. "Thank you!"

But then she turned to Tahn, and she stood very still. "I think . . . I think folks who called you a devil was wrong. You and your friends, and Miss Ti—I think maybe you're part angel instead. I never heard of this before. Not ever."

"Will you tell the others?" Tahn asked her again.

And she nodded. "Come on, Jori! Let's go and tell!"

The little girl went running out, and Netta wondered why she hadn't given Tahn a hug as well. But the boy gave him a bold handshake and a nod of his head before hurrying to follow her.

They spent the rest of the daylight at Martica's house or going to the market. Netta picked out cookpots, dishes, wash basins, bedding, chairs, and a sturdier table. Tahn took the time to pick out a pair of shoes for his sister, and Tiarra was speechless with surprise. Then they brought all the food they could carry and cloth for a curtain at the window of the little house. Street children began to appear, at first two others, and then more. Netta or Tiarra explained to each one of them their plans while Tahn helped Lucas try to reconstruct the "stacked beds" they'd seen. Eventually, Tobas had to help them.

"You think it's time we learned a trade?" Lucas asked him good-naturedly.

"I wouldn't shake a stick at God's work, sir," Tobas answered him. "Nor the protection of Triletts neither. You may as well stay where you're called."

Tahn looked out the window. "It's time we went back."

His voice was solemn, with a trace of the old worry, and Netta looked at him in surprise. Her mind had been so occupied that she'd forgotten Lionell Trent, nor had she paid any attention to how much of the day was past.

"I'm going to stay here tonight," Lucas told him. "Because there are children. But I'll be back in the morning to your camp in case you need me."

Tahn nodded. "Lorne, stay with Lucas. Tobas and Tiarra, come with me."

336

Netta noticed the fleeting look on Tiarra's face when she knew they would be leaving Lorne behind. But no one argued. No one said a word. They only started off toward the churchyard again as the streets became dusky and the sky grew pink.

At midday Tahn had said there was nothing he could do about tomorrow, but now in the evening's dim light, he spoke by twos and threes to every guard in the camp. Netta's father sat a while with Tobas and Josef. Netta looked about for the three men who had gone to market with them, but they and their cart and mule were nowhere to be found.

Tiarra approached her slowly, rubbing her arms against the increasing chill. "I don't think I'll sleep tonight," she said. "Tomorrow is important to us. I feel it in my bones."

Netta nodded. "It is too bad for the man who died. It truly seemed he had turned his heart aright."

"Do you think the man called Saud will come with his baron?" Tiarra asked, and Netta realized she hadn't even considered that.

"I don't know. I hope not."

"I hope he does," Tiarra countered. "My brother knows his face. We could catch my mother's killer."

"No," Netta said immediately. "We don't want to apprehend anyone now, or fight with them! Please, we need only to leave in peace."

Tiarra looked up at the stars. "I know," she said with a sigh. "I just get swept up wishing there could be justice. It doesn't seem right to leave her killer walking freely about."

"I agree. But it isn't our job to deal with him. At least not now. I hope you understand."

Tiarra nodded. "The man who ordered it is dead, anyway. At least that's something."

"Much more than that," Netta maintained. "God has brought good. For a lot of children. It may seem hard, but if there had been justice sooner, we would not be here today to accomplish that."

"If we had known justice as children," Tiarra said, "you

would be in Onath. And I might be in a Trent palace, wondering why my brother doesn't go and court the Trilett daughter he favored at a snooty noble party."

Netta stared at her. Tiarra was a dreamer. But, indeed, what might their lives have been like if Karra Loble had been able to raise Tiarra and Tahn as Trents? She couldn't imagine. Tahn as a noble son? With pretty clothes and pampered ways, too much wealth and not enough work? She thought of all the noble families she knew. Every one of them produced men spoiled by plenty, who thought themselves better than the commoners. She thought Jarel and her father were different. But that was because of Christ, and especially in Jarel's case, because tragedy had made them turn their hearts from ordinary things.

She couldn't picture Tahn as a noble. And not even the realization that he *was* a noble, by right of the inheritance that should have been his, could change her mind about that. To her, he would always be the man who risked his life for the captive children, who had wept with surprise at the favor of God, and was just as comfortable on the ground as on a bed or a chair.

"It's strange," Tiarra said suddenly, "that you aren't courted by the rich son of a lord. Don't you like them?"

"No," Netta answered. "I guess I don't." Of course, she had married a noble once. All of the other nobles paled in comparison. But Tahn was something different. His need had drawn her, and his strength had held her. "Your brother is special," she said softly. "Our love is special."

"I've seen that." Tiarra grew very quiet. "Do you think his friends are like him? Are they special too?"

Netta smiled. "Do you mean Lorne?"

"Lucas the someday-priest is a wonderful man," Tiarra said quickly. "I have much to thank him for. But . . . yes. I mean Lorne."

"He's always been very quiet. He's humble, like your brother. They seem to understand each other. We weren't sure when Lorne first came, because he'd been with Samis.

338

But Tahn never had doubt of him. And now we trust him with our lives."

Tiarra nodded. "I rather like him."

"I know."

"Do you think my brother would mind?"

"Not if you'll be in no hurry."

Netta watched her father rise and return to the church with Josef and another man at his side. And then Tobas came walking in their direction. "Get some sleep while you can," he said. "There'll be early rising tomorrow."

"What is my father doing?" Netta questioned. "And Tahn?"

"We were deciding who would go to the burial and who would not. Most will not. They didn't know the man, though he seemed to deserve our respect."

"Tobas, are you telling me there is no plan?"

"Only to defend ourselves if necessary. Tahn has set men to posts for that."

"But where have the three gone with the mule?"

He smiled. "A long way. And that, too, is for our defense."

Netta thought perhaps Lionell would not come. Emil Korin was no family member, after all, and if Lionell knew the things Mr. Korin had told them, he wouldn't mourn his passing even if he wasn't responsible. But before the morning sun climbed high, she heard a long, low trumpet in the distance. The mourner's horn. It was a noble tradition in the north parts of their land. She hadn't heard it in a very long time. But it meant Lionell had decided to give Mr. Korin the customary respect due his faithful years of service. Or else he wanted it to appear so, that he might draw closer without suspicion.

Lucas had joined the priest at Korin's home, readying the body for procession. The body would be carried on a wagon through the streets, she knew, and whoever had come from the Trents would join them as near to the procession's starting point as possible. Others who knew Korin would join in as the line passed near them. Netta knew her father

339

would wait till the last, till the procession drew close to their camp and the graveyard.

As they drew nearer through Alastair's solemn streets, Netta expected Tahn to strap on the sword her father had given him, but he didn't. He sat on the stone rail by the church steps, watching. He must have assigned Tobas and Lorne to Netta and Tiarra's safety. They stayed with the women even as the other men moved to places appointed to them.

When the procession grew near enough, Netta saw Lionell. He had a large group of soldiers with him, their horses draped in black. Most of the soldiers were very young men, and for that reason, Netta thought Korin had perhaps been charged with their training. In front of them, behind the handbell ringer and the wailers, was a woman with two young men and a girl. With them were an older man and his wife. Korin's relatives.

They stopped at the church. Two family members, with Lionell and three of his soldiers, went inside with the priest as the others waited. Only a few from the town seemed to know the deceased well enough to join the procession, but others began to gather near the graveyard's iron fence.

Sudden ringing of the church bells struck at Netta's heart. She thought of her mother, now so long dead. And of Karll and all those who had died the night Samis's men unleashed their violence upon her family. And then she wondered if Alastair had given Tahn's mother bells. Certainly his father had no mourners.

When the group came back outside, the priest spread another cloth over the body as Trent soldiers stood in salute. The family took their places again behind the waiting wagon, while Lionell spoke a word to the priest. Father Bray returned to his place with Lucas, one at each side of the horse that drew the wagon, as Lionell mounted his own horse to rejoin the procession.

The bell ringer in a black robe resumed his ringing, never lifting his eyes from the ground. There were six wailers behind him, probably because Trent money had provided for more than two. Behind them the family huddled together and moved very slowly. The woman nearly fell twice and had to be supported by a young man who was almost surely her son. Lionell followed them, with his men around and behind him. Townspeople and acquaintances were at the back, and Netta saw her father, with Josef and four other men, move to join them.

Her heart pounded as she turned her eyes to see where Tahn had gone. But he hadn't moved from the side entrance of the church. It was almost sure that Lionell could not have seen him yet, but from where Tahn sat he had an open view of the graveyard.

She clenched her hands tight together and paced but two steps and back again.

"Come," Tobas told her suddenly. "It is time to gain the sanctuary's shelter, now that Lionell is finished with it. Let us pray for the family of the deceased."

"Tobas," she exclaimed. "If my father ordered you to have me out of view of what he does, you could tell me plainly."

"All right, my lady." He nodded. "That too. But it is a proper moment to pray."

He took her by the arm as Lorne escorted Tiarra. They went past Tahn on the church steps, and he nodded, but he did not turn his eyes from the scene around him to look their way.

32

Lionell glanced around him for a full view of Benn Trilett's men. He had known they would still be here. That was, after all, why he'd chosen to proceed with this ridiculous show. Saud was right that proper mourning tended to turn blame away from oneself. Of course, to be seen with Saud after the rumors of late would have worked the opposite, so the captain had stayed with men on the road just outside of town.

In other circumstances, Lionell wouldn't have cared who knew that he'd had one of his chief men killed. But he was still under some scrutiny from the other houses. And Benn was here. So he would show the proper respect, even though he considered Korin's burial nothing but a handy excuse to come to Alastair, where he could question Benn Trilett's intentions. He'd had no idea Benn would join the funerary procession. The implications of that were troubling. Had the two men met?

There could be little doubt that Benn at least knew of Korin, and therefore of the things he'd claimed. That Saud was a killer? If it were only that, Lionell could have Saud executed and leave the blame with him. But Alastair well knew the baron's connection. If they believed Korin's words, they would know the blame was given to Sanlin Dorn by design and Saud was only an agent of the baron's will.

It seemed an impossible situation to get out of. Benn Trilett probably knew by now about Tahn Dorn. What would he do with the knowledge? When would he act upon it? And hang it all, why hadn't he left already, Lionell wondered, so the bandits could do their jobs?

It occurred to him that the Trilett lord might simply be waiting here until the wedding. And then, when representatives of all the nobles had gathered, he could present to them his daughter's suitor with the shocking revelation that he'd found the Trent heir proper! What recourse could he have then? To fight Benn Trilett openly was suicidal. To do nothing would be practically the same.

Ahead of them, the wailers were wailing as they were paid to do, but the endless sound grated at him, and he wished he could order it stopped. Likewise, the droning handbell was an annoyance. He didn't care that the tears of Korin's family were heartfelt. He would only be glad when they got the body in the ground and this part was done. Then perhaps he could learn his fate in Benn Trilett's eyes and begin a counterplan to save the status that he would rather die than lose.

At the graveside, most of the soldiers and townspeople stayed back in a circle. But Benn Trilett made no effort to keep himself back with them. He approached the weeping woman and the rest of Korin's family boldly with his men to express his condolences. The widow seemed more than a little surprised that another noble would take an interest in her husband's burial, but to her credit, she accepted his comfort graciously and asked no questions.

The priest spoke at some length, and as soon as he was done, Lord Trilett began to move away. But that action enraged Lionell as much as anything. Of course Benn Trilett had made himself part of this, not for any genuine condolence but because he was wishing Lionell to see his boldness! He wanted a confrontation, curse him! How dare he step back now, to make an empty show of respect to the dead and the grieving family before issuing his inevitable threats!

"Master Trilett," Lionell called sullenly. "Let us not make haste to part before we have accomplished so much as a greeting."

"I will greet you, Lionell," Benn answered. "But let us speak at a good distance. Come with me to the churchyard proper."

For the first time Lionell began to consider that this circumstance might be meant for a trap. If Benn had surmised that Lionell would be here, he and his men may also have chosen assassination as the easiest way toward their ends. Lionell scanned the churchyard, taking note again of the positions of Benn's men. Could they really be so foolish? And then he saw a solitary shape upon the church steps. A lean, dark-haired man, watching him. The Dorn. He knew it, as surely as he was born.

"Do you take me for a fool?" he raged. "You would walk me to within yards of a killer? I think not."

"I know no killers here. But very well," Benn agreed with a sigh, "if you are uncomfortable near the rest of my men, let us walk a bit among the stones." He stepped ahead, escorted by two of his men. "I'm pleased to have this opportunity to speak with you."

"It is mutual," Lionell said curtly, almost forgetting his customary pleasantries as he motioned his own men to follow. "It has been a long while. I trust I find you in health?"

To his surprise, Benn Trilett laughed. "In health? Yes, Lionell. God is good. And yourself?"

Lionell sighed. "It is with growing anticipation that I look forward to my upcoming marriage. For which ceremony, of course, I would be honored to have your company."

"Yes," Benn answered with what seemed like a note of impatience. "And now that we've been formally civil, Lionell, I ask you to tell me what you expect to gain by setting your men on the road in wait for me."

Lionell had to swallow down a sudden lump of bile. "My men? In wait for you? Most certainly not! There are bandits, quite a scourge in this area, but I assure you they are not in my employ."

"Really? Then I can be assured you'll make no trouble for me should I wish to depart for Onath this afternoon?"

"Of course not, good sir. I have no reason to trouble you. We are at peace, for which I am truly grateful after the breach my father created. May his memory not come between us."

Benn turned and looked at him skeptically. "It is not his memory that does that."

"What do you mean?"

"There's no reason to toy with one another, sir," Benn said. "You know that the captain of my guardsmen has come to this city. And I know that you tried to kill him. Your father didn't provide that tension. Even if you build upon his foundation, these new stones are yours."

Lionell's heart was pounding heavily. "Master Trilett, I don't know what you're talking about."

But Benn would not back down. "We both know that you do."

Seeing Benn's stony gaze, Lionell's temper almost got away from him. "Your guardsman? Why here? Did you send him to test me? To murder me? Or is this a trap you've set to win your vengeance just as surely, by giving the other houses cause for my destruction?"

Benn suddenly stopped walking. "By now you should know that I seek no vengeance for your father's deeds. All of that lies in the hands of God. I came here because Tahn Dorn asked my help. And I find that it is you laying the trap for him. And for me, perhaps, because of him."

Now they'd come to it, and Lionell trembled inside. It was all about the Dorn, and Benn Trilett knew it. But he still called him his guardsman and nothing more. "My apologies," Lionell said quickly. "I thought my captain explained to you that the trouble here was a misunderstanding. We were simply trying to contain the ruffians—"

"Don't toy with me, Lionell," Benn warned. "You are not a good enough liar."

"Nor are you!" Lionell fumed. What use pretending ignorance of these things now? Benn knew far too much. "You speak peace. But you don't admit to all that is in your mind. You have found the perfect way to destroy me."

"I could," Benn told him quietly. "There are those who might think that I should. But your cousin is not one of them. He has urged me to keep peace with you, and he wants nothing that is yours. You have no cause against him."

"Why should I believe you? Tahn Dorn is a murderer."

"He is sincere. He's shown that to me beyond doubt. And he's done nothing against you. You have no reason to wish his death."

For a moment Lionell considered denying such a desire. But he and Benn Trilett had come down to the straws between them. Denial would do no good. "You know very well," Lionell answered bitterly, "that he is the greatest threat I shall ever face. Do you expect me to ignore that?"

Benn took a deep breath. "God touch you, Lionell. All we want is your peace."

"And my title. And my riches."

"No. I'd not fight you for such things. I've never warred against you, or your father. And I swear to you by the God who made us that Tahn Dorn wants no part of what you have."

Lionell shook his head. "Those are easy words to say now. But what if the nobles were standing about, willing to hear your word over mine?"

"You have my pledge to peace. I wish to God you would hear it."

"But you're not the root of this trouble! Why should you let the Dorn be your business? And how can I be faulted if I simply protect myself from reasonable danger?"

Benn folded his arms. The set of his face was hard, immovable. "There is nothing reasonable to this. You've hunted a man without cause."

"Why is it something to you? There must be a thousand better suitors for your daughter. And you have plenty of guards. What do you want with him?"

Lionell's blood ran cold at Benn's answer. "The Dorn is my friend. He is soon to be my daughter's husband. You will leave him alone and let him live his life, or I will see that you lose everything you have."

"Then you do threaten me?"

"If you give me no choice. I would rather you keep the peace you have promised."

"I didn't promise it to a usurping mercenary scoundrel!"

"What will you do, Lionell?" Benn asked wearily. "Fight me for your cousin?"

Lionell shook his head. "The bandits are fierce these days. One can never guarantee safety on the road, but that is not my fault. A shame, if they cause me another funeral."

"I sent messengers," Benn said soberly, "before I left Onath, to tell the other nobles I would be here for the sake of a friend. I sent more yesterday, that they might know I can't be sure if you'll give us passage to leave or try to slaughter me without cause. If anything happens to my party, Lionell, they will know that you are responsible, bandits or not. And they will come against you for it."

"You lie! There have been no messengers sent. Especially not from here!"

"I knew you would have men watching. Do you think I'd send them in a group with Trilett insignia so they could be recognized? They are long gone by now, and they may have been robbed, but they weren't suspected or you would not be so surprised."

"Curse you!" Lionell shouted. "You tie my hands against you!"

"What can you expect?" Benn demanded. "For God's mercy, man, should I stand aside and let you kill who you please?"

Lionell turned away. "There is nothing more to be said. If you want to go, then go. You don't belong on my land. I should bring cause against you for sitting here. Go back to Onath. Go! Curse Tahn Dorn and you with him!"

"May the Lord persuade you," Benn said solemnly. "And may our future dealings be on better terms."

Lionell turned abruptly away from such maddening talk, only to see Tahn Dorn and the rest of Benn's men still watching. A thousand blights to the lot of them! He didn't know if Benn told the truth about messengers or not. But how could he take such a chance? How could he find himself a solution now?

33

Tahn was glad when Lionell walked away. The tension of seeing Benn so close to him had been difficult to take. He hated the risk, hated Benn being here when he should be back in Onath in his marble-floored meeting room. He motioned to his men to keep their watch on Lionell's soldiers, then jumped from the stone rail and moved to Lord Trilett's side. At a distance he could see that Lionell was watching him.

"You were right," Benn told him sadly when he drew near. "He'll hear no plea on your behalf. Only fear of the nobles backs him down from us. Tobas was also right to send the men, though I hated to endanger them."

"They were willing, lord. And he selected men the soldiers and the bandits have had no opportunity to meet."

"I pray they got through unhurt."

"I pray it too."

Much to Tahn's surprise, Benn leaned forward to embrace him quickly. Tahn couldn't help but consider what Lionell might think of such a sight. The young baron was in a circle of his soldiers. Near them, the priest stood alone with Korin's family. He told them something, and they both looked up toward Tahn and Benn.

"We must go. Soon," Benn said soberly. "I think the consequences will hold Lionell from trying to stop us now, but you can't consider yourself safe. He'll try again if he gets an opportunity. Netta is right that we must get you to Onath. If we linger, he'll devise some treachery as he did against his own soldier."

"His treachery might just as likely be against you," Tahn answered.

"You don't stop thinking of others first, do you?"

"It's my job."

"How deep is the bandits' quarrel?" Benn asked him. "Lionell cannot sanction their attack now. But can he hold them if they're determined against you?"

Knowing Burle and the ways of his men, Tahn could be confident in his answer. "Without the baron behind them, they'll not risk face to face with our numbers, my lord, much as they might like to."

"Good. I'll be glad to be away from here. It worries me to see Netta so fearful."

Tahn glanced toward the church. "Forgive me for saying that you should not have brought her."

"I didn't. She followed, against my order."

Lionell spoke something to the grieving family and then turned with his men to their horses. The priest embraced the widow, and then with a nod he began to lead Korin's family toward the church.

The woman barely looked up as she came near them. Her grief was such that walking was difficult. But one young man did not take his eyes off Tahn, even as he supported her. "I'm sorry for your loss," Tahn told them as they passed by. The woman gave barely a nod in recognition, and her son made no acknowledgment at all.

"Do you think it will be safe for them here?" Tahn asked Benn.

"We can pray for their safety. They don't want to leave with us. Father Bray has already asked them. He will watch for them, at least."

The church doors opened, and Netta stepped out, anxiously looking in their direction. Tahn was glad to see that Lionell Trent was mounted with his men and beginning to ride away.

"A relief to have him gone," Benn commented. "Relax, son."

Tahn nodded.

In an hour's time, they were ready to leave Alastair. Benn had purchased two wagons. One for the five street children who had chosen to accompany them, and one to carry the remains of Sanlin and Karra Dorn. It was hard for Tahn to say good-bye to Lucas again, especially to leave him behind in Alastair. He embraced his friend, who returned the gesture carefully.

"How is your back, Tahn?"

"Better." Already Tahn had asked him more than once to change his mind and come with them. But he wouldn't. So they'd already discussed Benn's plan to leave two men with him in Alastair until they knew that the baron and the bandits would not trouble him. There was nothing else to be said.

Tahn rode on a horse of Benn's not so familiar to him as Smoke had been, but it couldn't be helped. Nothing had been seen of Tahn's horse since the night the baron's men first came against them. A crowd of people gathered to watch them leaving Alastair, some sullen and quiet, some more cheerful and even waving. Tahn recognized the son of Jothniel Ovny standing apart from the others, watching Tiarra intently. But Tiarra only looked away.

A woman stepped from the crowd to offer Tahn a riding cloak made of the finest linen. He almost didn't accept the gift, but the woman urged him. "We owe you restitution," she said. "Please accept this token."

One of the merchants followed her with a small purse of coins. "Please, sir. Accept this gift in the stead of your father's belongings."

Tahn hardly knew how to respond to the words. He didn't ask questions. It would do him no good now to understand better what belongings the man meant, or why he felt he had to pay for them. Tahn only accepted the purse with a nod and continued on.

Children peeked at them from the windows of houses. Men and women stood in doorways. "It looks like you will not be forgotten," Benn told Tahn.

"Perhaps they're looking at you," Tahn answered him.

"Or claiming another look at your daughter and my sister while they can."

Benn only smiled at the suggestion.

They stopped at the city's edge long enough to greet Marc and Lem Toddin once more and thank them for their help.

"Have you seen your horse?" Tahn asked Marc.

"No. I expect the bandits found her wandering and took her for easy gain. But it's all right. I have another."

"Let us give you the price of her with my apology for your trouble," Tahn suggested.

"It wasn't your fault, friend. It couldn't be helped."

"Then call it a reward for your valor," Benn told him. "Please. With my thanks."

Reluctantly, Marc agreed. "Stay at Onath," he told Tahn then. "Don't come back to this place."

"Things change," Tahn answered.

"Not enough. Not so long as the baron Trent and that bandit leader still live."

"Come and tell us if there is trouble, Marc," Tahn told him. "And remember you are welcome in Onath."

They, too, parted with an embrace. And then it was good to move into the open woodland toward home. Tahn was glad to leave the city behind. The street children seemed glad too.

"This is the first time I ever rode in a wagon," the little boy Jori announced. "I wish I could ride a horse too."

"Wait till we are past the creek south of Merinth," Tahn told him, "and you can ride this one."

"Really?" Jori asked in excitement.

"Why then?" Ansley asked with more reservation in his voice.

"It is flat, open ground," Tahn answered simply, without telling them that the rocky, woody area they traveled now was favorite territory of the bandits. He would not have the boy on his horse until he got past here, and past the confrontation that he expected.

But for a long while the ride was quiet. Tahn let his mind

351

dwell for a moment on what it would be like to marry Netta. Of course, there would be a grand ceremony at the church in Onath, with nobles in attendance for the sake of Benn Trilett and his daughter. He himself would invite Lucas and the Toddins. He didn't have anyone else who wouldn't be with the Triletts already.

He couldn't quite picture what the ceremony would be like. He'd never been to a wedding. But he knew he would be glad to go home afterward, to begin his life with Netta, as strange as it all still seemed.

He might have to join her in the big house, until a home of their own was built. She'd never been in his room at the guardhouse. She probably never would be. He turned and looked at her sitting in the wagon with the street children. She looked radiant in the green and brown dress he loved, even though she didn't consider it grand enough to be kept for special occasions. She was learning a finger game invented by one of the boys and keeping them happy with her attention. She loved children, that was very clear. How long might it be before they had a child of their own?

Benn Trilett would be happy with grandchildren, the sooner the better. And he should have them, plenty of them, to carry on his good deeds and conscience. But it was still a new thought to Tahn because he'd never expected to live long enough to leave his own seed on the earth.

His thoughts continued on such happy paths, even considering the fondness he thought he'd seen between his sister and Lorne. God had done richly, abundantly, at giving him family and friends, when he'd once thought that he was unworthy of either and despised by heaven.

I thank you, God, he cried in his heart. *Your goodness has amazed me! Let your blessing be with us on our homeward journey.*

No sooner had he prayed it than he heard a muffled sound to the right ahead of them. He signaled to Lorne and Josef immediately, and the entire group closed tight together around the wagons behind him. He glanced back at Netta just as she looked at him. When their eyes met, he knew she was still more worried for him than anything else. Even though he'd assured her the bandits would fear to fight them, she was still afraid that they would try to hurt him somehow.

"There's the Dorn running back home with the Triletts!" a voice taunted from the trees. "Guess Alastair was too much for him. Couldn't make it on his own."

Netta watched her father and Tobas ride up beside Tahn as they neared whomever it was who called out so unkindly. Tahn didn't answer. He rode straight in his saddle, his eyes already on one spot in the trees, though she could see nothing.

"Poor boy got whipped again!" the voice shouted out and then laughed. "At least it wasn't a scalding pot this time. Eh, Tahn? That why you're leaving? Too many pots going on the fire back there?"

How dare they? Netta bristled with anger. *They must know that we want no fight, especially with women and children along.* But to throw such things in Tahn's face when he'd been nothing but honorable—it was wickedness! She seethed inside.

"Show yourself!" she demanded, shouting so loudly that she surprised even herself. "If you would be so cruel, at least have the courage to show your face!"

"Netta . . ." her father cautioned. But it was too late. Movement ahead of them revealed three mounted men emerging from the trees, followed closely by two others. The large man in the middle had one arm bandaged to his side, but his mouth was quick and cutting.

"Got you a fiery one there, don't you, Tahn? She had to come all this way to save you again? What would you be without your Trilett nursemaids? Eh, Tahn? Think you'll ever dare go anywhere without them?"

No one answered. Netta thought that man was the ugliest she'd ever seen. Trained by Samis, no doubt, who also had a way with words designed to tear at Tahn's spirit.

"Poor little boy!" the man continued. "Hurry and take him home where he won't get hurt again!"

The men around him laughed. Netta wondered that her father didn't say anything, but perhaps he understood it would do no good. They could only ride past these men and watch to make sure they did no misdeed. It would not help to speak again in Tahn's defense. Perhaps it would even fuel them.

"If it weren't for your nursemaids, I'd cut you down to size, Dorn boy," the man continued in his bold voice. "Pathetic little whelp. Do they cage you at night? What a pet you'd make."

"Shut up!" Tiarra screamed at them.

"No, Tiarra," Tahn told her immediately.

And she was still, but Netta could see that neither she nor the men, particularly Lorne, could well abide the senseless harassment. But Tahn stayed calm, only watching the men as he kept riding forward with no response.

Two more horsemen joined the bandits' ranks from the right. Netta thought they were going to get past them with no more trouble, but suddenly Tahn stopped. Her heart pounded. Of course it would be difficult for anyone to take such words. But what would Tahn do?

"Toma," Tahn said suddenly in a low voice. "You've got my horse."

"Tahn," Benn said quickly, but Tahn held up his hand and quieted him.

"He doesn't like you," Tahn continued. "Look at his ears."

"I don't like him either," the young man answered. "Had to beat him to get him here. But who says he's yours? I found him in town."

"You know my horse," Tahn told him.

"I know you should have trained the beast! He's not worth a copper he's so stubborn."

"I'll pay you far more," Tahn said. He held out the purse the merchant had given him. "Get yourself a mount that suits you."

"Maybe it suits me to keep yours," Toma said and then laughed. "What are you going to do? We heard you're hurt.

And your master there doesn't like a fight. How do you think you'd ever get this horse away from me?"

Several of the men chuckled. But Tahn said nothing more to them. "We might as well go on," he told Benn. "I'll not waste your time." He turned his mount to the road again, and they all started moving.

"Ah!" the first man shouted a mocking lament after them. "He had to give up his horse! His only friend! Poor Smoke. Stubborn beast. Maybe we'll try horsemeat at the fire tonight."

Tahn whistled. Quick and low. Smoke broke from the group of bandits with Toma on his back and trotted forward to follow Tahn. Lorne and the other men laughed at the young bandit's efforts to stop his mount. Smoke would not be stopped. He fell in line directly behind Tahn's mount despite his protesting rider, and Netta smiled. Smoke would follow Tahn anywhere. She'd never seen a relationship between man and horse quite like theirs.

"Will you take the money?" Tahn was asking Toma.

"No!"

"You'll be coming with us to Onath, then." He rode on without looking back, and Smoke continued to follow.

"Tahn!"

Tobas was close enough to reach across for Smoke's reins. "I'll hold him long enough for you to climb down if he'll be held," he told the bandit. "Can't say you've earned his price, though. Get out of here before Benn Trilett decides to teach you a lesson for bothering us."

Toma sat for a moment more, and then with a disdainful look across at Lorne, he slid from Smoke's back. "This horse isn't worth the trouble."

Tahn kept right on going. Happy to be riderless, Smoke ran up beside him, and Tahn reached out one hand to pat his nose. Toma only stood watching as they rode away. And none of the bandits, not even the big one who'd been so cruel, said another word after them.

34

Onath was a joy to behold. The peaceful city nestled in green hills stirred feelings in Tahn he hadn't expected. Netta was right. It was home. The first man to see them was a farmer raking in a field outside of town. His immediate shout of greeting was a happy one, echoed quickly by another man just down the road.

Netta had been singing with the children, and she kept it up even now as they rode into the town. Everyone knew it was Benn Trilett coming home. People waved on Market Street and from the doorways of their houses.

Tahn was riding Smoke now, at a walk, with Tiarra on the other horse beside him. She looked around her with eyes touched by tears. "They love you," she told him softly. "And they're staring at me."

"They love the Triletts," he told her barely above a whisper. "They're just curious about you."

"It isn't only Triletts," she answered. "This place is like morning after Alastair's night."

He smiled. To think of Onath as the pleasant morning after a lifetime of bad dreams seemed appropriate, and he appreciated the thought from her. "We're almost home," he said.

"And you seem different," she told him. "Like you left a weight behind."

"I gained a blessing."

Benn Trilett was stopping at the church, but he didn't have to go inside before being greeted by Father Anolle coming out to them with a smile. "Welcome. Welcome," the priest

356

declared. "Master Jarel petitioned our prayers, and they have been with you gladly."

"They are answered, Father," Benn replied. "We are not only home safe, but with blessings. Come and meet those God has added to my household."

Tiarra stopped and stared when she heard his words. Tahn knew that she hadn't quite understood the entirety of Benn Trilett's acceptance, any more than he had at first. He took her hand as Father Anolle greeted the children in the wagon.

"This is Ansley, whose bravery spared much trouble," Benn told the priest. "And these others are Rae and Jori and Micah and Jeramathe, who were all careful eyes on my son's behalf I am told." Father Anolle touched each head in turn, and then Benn turned his eyes toward Tahn. "Do you wish to tell your own blessed news, son?"

Tiarra was watching Tahn with her eyes wide. Son. Benn Trilett had called him that so many times before. But there seemed to be a new joy in it, a new sureness.

Tahn knew Benn spoke of the engagement just as much as of Tiarra, and he debated which happy news Benn would have him tell first. But he glanced at his sister and squeezed her hand. "Father, may I introduce to you my own sister? Miss Tiarra Dorn."

The priest approached them with quiet seriousness. "Child," he said as he extended his hand, "may the Lord bless you. God be praised."

Tahn knew Tiarra didn't quite know what to do. She nodded her head and thanked the priest, but he didn't turn his eyes away. "You are an answer to prayer," he told her. "I have known your brother, that there was a bareness in his spirit not to be cured except by something or someone of his past. Do you understand?"

She nodded timidly. And Tahn thought he understood too, even though he'd never heard the priest mention such a thing before.

"God be praised," Father Anolle said again. "This is happy news indeed."

Tahn glanced over at Netta and cleared his throat. *There is more*, he wanted to say, but he couldn't quite get the words out. He had thought Netta might help him. This was, after all, the priest she'd known since she was a child. He was almost a grandfather to her, and Tahn would've thought her to be bursting to tell of her engagement. But she said nothing, only sat quietly with her glowing smile.

"Father . . ." he stammered. "Father . . . Netta and I . . . we would like to request your services. I have asked . . . we've agreed . . . to wed, sir."

The priest's smile only broadened. "Splendid! This is news to be spread about!"

"Not yet," Benn told him. "Not until Jarel knows. And of course Vari and the children at home."

"Of course," the priest agreed. "Godspeed on your way, then. They're anxious for you. Don't make them wait."

Tiarra didn't know what to expect as they left the church behind them. She knew it couldn't be much farther before they saw the Trilett estate. Netta had told her of her home, but Tiarra still couldn't picture it in her mind. She'd never seen the baron's estate. She'd never seen any home richer than the Ovnys'.

It was the wall she saw first, as Tahn had told her. It seemed to go on an unreasonably long length before turning to claim land in yet another direction. But not till they approached the gate could she see the grounds and the grand home within. And she sat speechless for a moment, though the street children were affected in an entirely different way.

"We're going to live there?" Jori shouted. "It's big as heaven!"

"I'll bet it has stairs," little Jeramathe announced. "Lots of stairs. Like mountains. I've heard about stairs."

"Do you think we'll have our own beds?" Rae was asking someone.

Ansley answered her. "We might have anything we want. There's room enough for the moon to bed down here."

"And look," Micah said in awe. "There's a garden on the roof!"

Tiarra watched her brother break away from the group. Netta's eyes turned to him for a fleeting moment of renewed concern. Tiarra wondered if there might be some secret between them that only such a homecoming might call to mind. But Netta said nothing. Tahn only rode ahead of them to the gate. And Netta's eyes brightened when she heard him announce their arrival with a happy voice.

The gate swung wide. They were not all through it before children ran at them from the yard, and more children came dashing from the house, followed by a tall young man and a plump older woman with a generously sized apron.

Ansley jumped from the wagon before it stopped moving, and Micah followed him. To Tiarra's surprise, her brother jumped from his horse to greet the first running child with an embrace that lifted the little girl clear off her feet.

"Temas!" he exclaimed. "It's good to be home."

"We missed you," the little girl said. And then she was joined by the crowd of other children gathering around. Tahn embraced them all. Except the biggest, who stood apart from the rest, waiting. When Tahn stood again, the big boy still held back, looking at him far more seriously than the others had.

"Are you all right, Tahn?" the boy asked. "I can see the pain in your stance."

"It's nothing, Vari."

But Vari seemed not so sure, until Tahn hugged him anyway and told him that the worries were past. The big boy finally smiled and turned his attention quickly to helping Netta from the wagon, though the lady scarcely waited for help.

Tiarra smiled to see her just as eager to hug at these children as Tahn had been. And she was quick to introduce Ansley and the others. But then the tall young man from the house took her arm.

"Netta," he said almost severely, "it is a relief to see you return home safely."

"I'll have a word to speak with you about letting her go, Jarel," Benn told him immediately, though his voice was kind.

"It was not by my choice," Jarel answered him. "You've raised a hardheaded daughter. Whatever will you do with her?"

"Confine her to Onath for her own safety, I suppose," Benn answered with a smile. "Until the wedding. And then let her husband figure it out."

Jarel's eyes went wide. "Wedding?" He laughed. "Netta! You get what you want, don't you?"

"You're getting married!" the boy Vari exclaimed. "You asked her? Oh Tahn! You really did?"

All sorts of commotion followed, but Tiarra noticed only part of it as Lorne came to her side and helped her gently down from the horse. "Welcome home," he said simply. His eyes seemed the color of the sky.

Vari was looking at her, and Tahn introduced her to him in a way she couldn't have expected.

"This is the baby from my dream."

"She looks like you," the little girl called Temas observed.

"Only prettier," added a little boy with a scar on his face and an endearing giggle.

"Well! Quite a crew we make!" the old woman with the apron exclaimed. "Just when I think I know everybody, there comes some more. Well, the more the merrier, Benn Trilett! I've got food aplenty. Come on, now. I'll learn your names later. Let me feed you."

But she dished out a hug to Netta first, and then a nod in Tahn's direction with a gently teasing smile. "Are you coming to the dining room with your guests today, sir? Or will I be sending food to you out here beneath a tree?"

Tahn returned the smile almost shyly. His reluctance to join the Trilett table had vexed Hildy for some time. "I'll come to the dining room, Hildy. With my family."

"Where you belong," Netta added softly. And they all crossed the wide yard to enter the grand house together.

That evening in a grassy meadow, Tahn carefully laid to rest the remains of his parents in the plot Benn Trilett had given him not far from his own loved ones. Tobas had offered to do the digging and the burying, but this was a task Tahn felt he must do with his own hands. These bones had held the life that gave him life, and even this small connection to them was somehow sacred.

Tiarra knelt beside the grave as he filled it, silent tears streaming down her cheeks. "We should plant flowers here in the spring," she said. "Do you think they would have liked flowers?"

"I'm sure," he answered quickly, but it was hard to get the words out, hard to say anything at all right now.

"How can you love someone you've never known?" Tiarra asked him. "I feel as if they're close to me. As if they're with us today."

He couldn't answer. He glanced toward the wagon in the distance, where Netta waited with Lorne, Tobas, and Vari, giving him and his sister this time alone. Perhaps one of them might have answers for her later. But he could provide nothing now. Solemnly, as the sun sank low, he leveled the grave and marked it with the two wooden crosses Tobas had given him until a stone could be made. *Sanlin and Karra Dorn,* it would say. *May they rest in eternal peace.*

Tahn laid down his shovel and knelt at his sister's side. Somehow the dream that had driven him to Alastair swirled over his mind again. She was crying now. But the search was over. There were no pointing fingers or shouting faces. Tenderly, he reached to hold Tiarra, and she cried against his shoulder as the sun set and purple shadows spread across the sky.

As darkness fell, Netta came and touched his shoulder softly. Vari and Lorne stood beside her, ready to help them to the wagon for the short ride home. He stood to his feet and helped Tiarra with him.

But Vari stood so still, so solemn.

361

"It's all right, friend," Tahn told him. "Everything's finally all right now." He put his arm around the young man for a moment, as Lorne extended a hand to Tiarra.

A stiff breeze rustled the trees to their west. "If we don't go soon, brother," Vari said in a quiet voice, "we'll all get caught in the rain."

Tahn smiled. "You like rain."

"And the world suits my dreams," Vari recalled the words. "I know. But what about you? Do you dream happy now?"

Tahn glanced again at his sister and Lorne. He thought of all the children at the house, and even of Lucas bravely giving himself to God's work in Alastair. But then he turned his eyes to Netta as she reached for his hand. "More than that," he answered. "It's not just a dream."

Softly Netta kissed him as the first raindrops fell.

"We're in for a soaking," she whispered. And he lifted her into his arms and ran to join the others as they hurried to the wagon.

Vari climbed to the wagon seat with Tobas. Lorne helped Tiarra into the back and climbed up beside her.

But Tahn set Netta down and only held her in his arms for a moment. "The rain isn't cold," he said. "Not yet. Do you mind if we walk?"

She smiled. "My father would think I've taken leave of my senses."

"Then you want to ride?"

In answer to that, Netta turned and waved Tobas on. "Go without us," she told him. "We'll be all right."

"Are you sure, lady? Out here alone?"

"We're on Trilett lands," she answered. "Close to home. And God is with us."

Tobas nodded. "We'd be within a shout." He gave the reins a flick, and the wagon began its slow move away from them.

Netta turned her eyes to Tahn, and he could see that the concern she always carried for him was still there. "Do you need to talk?" she asked. "Are you really all right?"

362

He put his arms around her and held her close. "I love you, Netta. Don't worry for me anymore."

And then he leaned and kissed her as he'd longed to do. She moved her hand across his cheek to his hair, and her touch felt so good.

"I love you too," she whispered.

"I think I could not have asked for so much," he told her. "Not in a thousand years."

"You have no idea the gift you are." She took his hand, and they began to follow the wagon. Rain soaked over them, and Tahn knew they'd be greeting Benn Trilett at the house with their hair and their clothes dripping. But Netta had no thought for it. She stopped him suddenly and with her hands in his kissed him again. And then her smile was bright as sunshine. "Welcome home."

L. A. Kelly is a busy Illinois writer who is active in the ministries of her church. She works at home and enjoys spending time with her husband and two beautiful children.